to be a FAE GUARDIAN

to be a FAE GUARDIAN

TRICIA COPELAND

to be a FAE GUARDIAN

by Tricia Copeland

Edited by Jo Michaels
Proofread by Karen Robinson
Interior Formatting by Jo Michaels
all of Indie Books Gone Wild

Cover by Shower of Schmidt Designs
Published by True Bird Publishing LLC, Superior, CO

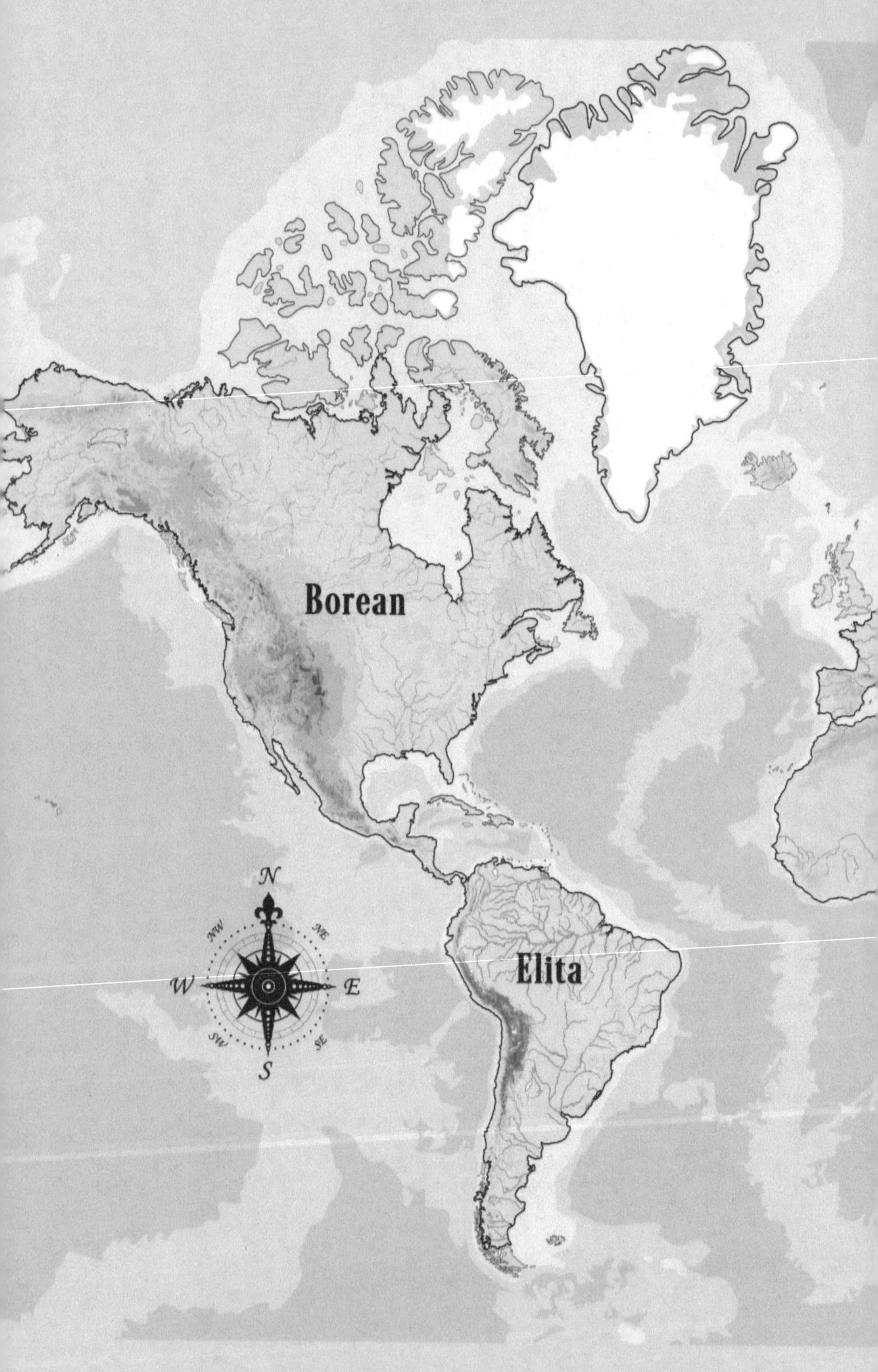

Borean
Elita
N
NW
NE
W
E
SW
SE
S

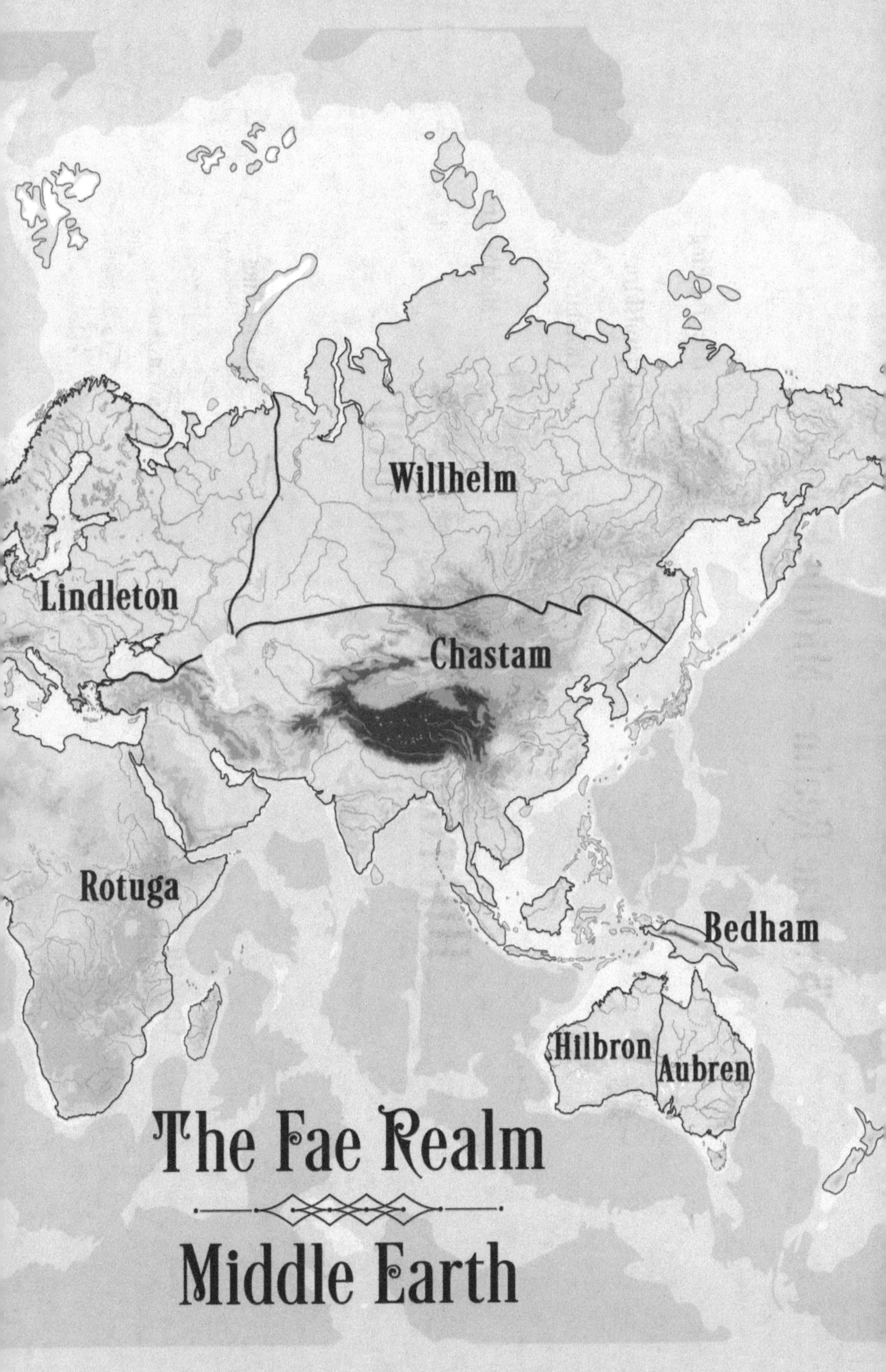

Willhelm
Lindleton
Chastam
Rotuga
Bedham
Hilbron
Aubren
The Fae Realm
Middle Earth

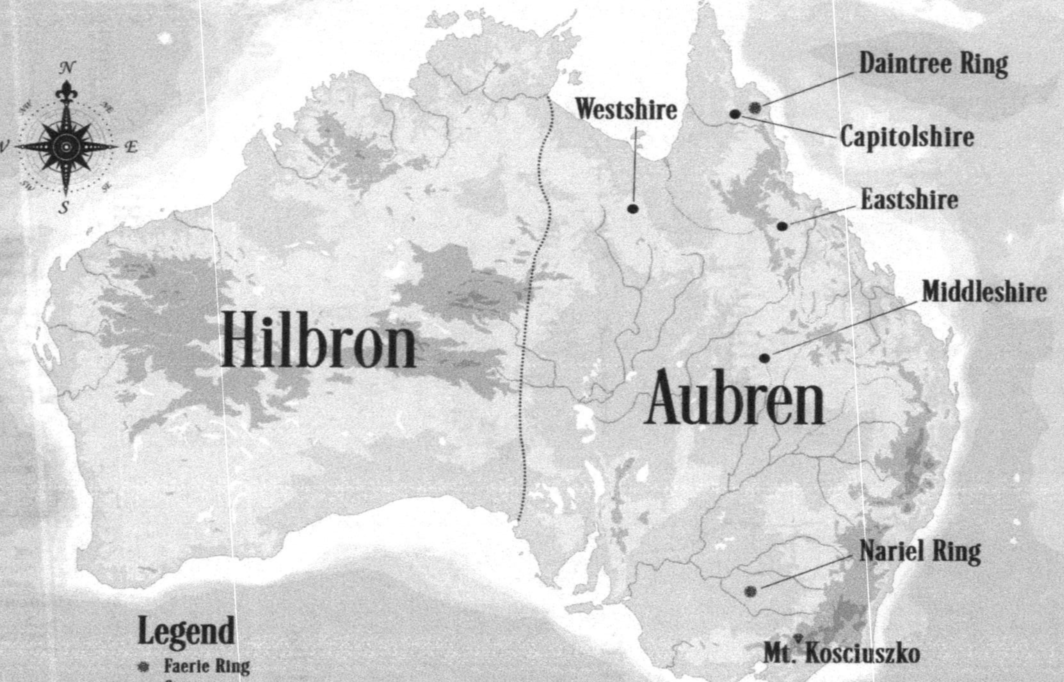

The Fae Realm ~ Middle Earth
Daintree Ring
Capitolshire
Westshire
Eastshire
Middleshire
Hilbron
Aubren
Nariel Ring
Mt. Kosciuszko
N
NW
NE
W
E
SW
SE
S
Legend
Faerie Ring
City
Border

Heaven
Upper Earth
Faerie Ring
Passage Between Realms
The Fae Realm ~ Middle Earth
Lower Earth - Sheol

Chapter 1

BLACK, DARK, VOID. FALLING, HURLING, head over heels through the nothingness, my body flails about as I try to right myself. BAM. I slam into a hard surface, and the air swooshes from my lungs.

Arms searing, I push up on my hands. White vapor appears from nowhere, and it writhes and swirls in front of me then freezes into the form of a face. A woman. Sonia? Reconfiguring, another visage forms. Abaddon.

A thin smile spreads, and the image morphs into that of Lucifer. "You will not succeed. Darkness always prevails."

Sucking in a breath, I open my eyes to see faint shadows of the crystals hanging above. Alive. Awake. In my bed. In my castle. In my kingdom. In my realm. I exhale. Sweat hangs on my brow, and I toss my covers and cross to the water bowl. Dousing my face, I lay my palms on the soft wood of the bureau and inhale. Exhale. *Just a dream.*

Neither Lucifer, Abaddon, nor Sonia possess powers in my realm. They cannot hurt me or any fae here. I lured their mutant kobold army who attempted to invade us into the deep, dark abyss of Lower Earth, ending the hideous beasts. Yes, Lucifer or whatever evil spirit I encountered thought it could trap me in that realm, but the goddesses granted me power to escape.

Inch by inch, I stretch my aching wings to full span.

Perhaps the trinity of witches, Alena, Camille, and Hunter, curtailed the power of the evil spirits inhabiting Lower Earth. I pray they did after we risked much aiding them, opening our rings enabling them to pass into the dark realm. Maybe Sonia, as well as her son Thanatos, and grandson Theron, have been dealt with.

My mind spins with the quandary.

How does one curtail the power of a spirit? Good or evil, souls remain eternal. There is no way to end one. At least Sonia, Thanatos, and Theron cannot pass through our rings. Only souls of the Creator can override our ring magic. Bumps form on my skin, and a chill crawls down my back.

Yes, Lucifer and Abaddon posses the power to enter this realm. No histories describe them doing so, I assure myself. *And again, they hold no power here.*

Still, I have no idea what the witches hoped to, or did, accomplish in Lower Earth. An image of Hunter's pale, slack form crosses my mind. I hope he lives.

I fold my wings on my back and spin to face the window, the faintest glow of light slipping around the curtains. I cannot tarry on this issue. There stands no use while the High Council controls my rings and therefore my access to Upper Earth and the trinity witches. This challenge brings me to a bigger problem, Aleem's trial. The High Council charges him with treason for allowing the witches—more particularly the female Alena, being a vampire-witch hybrid—to cross our realm.

Lifting my eyes to my crystals, I say a silent prayer to the goddesses. My mind jumps to another problem: The speed of charges brought against Aleem, resulting vote for a trial, and descent of the High Council guards gave me no time to replace the set of ring crystals I had lost in Lower Earth. Without them, I have no access to Lower or Upper Earth. And the High Council has Aleem guarded day and night. I doubt I can contact him without being discovered. *Does he possess an additional set of crystals? Has he instructed one of his judges to secure them for me, or should I ask someone else? Who could I trust with such a task?*

Taking a deep, centering breath, I savor the feel of the cool rock on my feet. I draw back the curtains and look out over the meadow. The first light of day graces the sky, forming a yellow hue. I lift my wings and arms, stretching them towards the ceiling. Letting my wings fold behind me, I spin.

There is much to do before those called to be witnesses in the trial depart. Flitting to my closet, I pull on my riding pants and slide into a blouse and vest.

I exit the bedchamber and, nodding to my guards, enter my study. Papers litter the desk, and I sort them into piles. Plans for the summer solstice celebration kept me and my two most trusted counselors, Holden, my Fae at Arms, and Quinn, my cousin and heir presumptive, up well into the night. My early morning will not help me in sorting details of that event either. Even as I try to focus on the guest lists, seating charts, menus, and entertainment options on the pages, my mind wanders.

Who could replace Aleem if the council finds him guilty? His first judge is but fifteen, not yet ready to rise to the Keeper's post. That counts another fact in our favor: Father sides with us as well. Surely, as a hallowed elder, and a prior king, his testimony would also benefit our point of view. Holden can testify to the safety measures enacted even if the council disagrees with my course of action. They cannot persist in turning a blind eye to the growing threat from below.

They *must* allow me to utilize the rings again. We need to know what happened in Lower Earth that day. I wonder if Sonia, Thanatos, and Theron joined Abaddon and Lucifer. *Because if that be the case...* I cannot entertain the thought. *The goddesses be with us all.*

The only way to gain this knowledge is through communication with the witches above. What we do not know of these evil beings *can* hurt us. The council must be swayed to let us work with the trinity. I will go to the trial. That should be my course. I start to the door. It swings open before I reach it.

Alfreda—I cannot call her my handmaid because she serves as so much more, a mother figure, confidant, and friend—stands wide-eyed in front of me. "They said you rose early. Did you have another dream? Is something wrong?"

"Nothing a visit to the High Council will not solve. Ready my trunk to travel with the others to the trial."

She catches my hand as I brush past her. "Not all can be solved with brute force. You need to show you respect their authority. At least appear to be repentant."

"But they are wrong. This is about much more than they realize. If they only knew the evil that I experienced."

Her eyes narrow. "Are you sure flaunting your crystal-adorned brow is wise?"

"The rumors of my appearance exaggerate reality, I am sure."

"The chance that they may learn your secret is not the only problem. You may be a royal, and a monarch, but you know the High Council supplants your authority when it comes to the rings."

"But the mission of the fae aligns with that of the trinity, to guard Upper Earth from the evil spirits of Lower Earth. And Alena forms one of the trinity, her witch heritage allowing her soul to persist."

"She still is half vampire. See it from their point of view. Law forbids interaction with them. Aleem engendered the whole realm."

"Is that what you think? That I put our fae in harm's way?" Tears threaten to form in my eyes. To risk my people would be the last thing I would do.

Alfreda rests her hands on my shoulders "I think you are young and determined."

"I cannot lose Aleem as Ring Keeper." I bite my lip, for I cannot say my other thoughts aloud. *I worry they may do worse, take his wings.* My stomach clenches. In giving me a set of ring crystals, he enabled me to defeat the kobold. But for this alone he could be removed from his post. They could banish him to the cold tundra of Willhelm for a deed I pushed for.

"I fear your presence may make things worse for Aleem."

I grip Alfreda's arms. "I hate feeling—"

"Powerless? Out of control?" Her eyebrows rise.

Lifting her hands from my shoulders, I stand upright. As one of the eldest, Aleem holds a revered position among the Keepers. I must believe they will see his wisdom in aiding me.

"I guess I must have faith the council will see Aleem's wisdom in this."

A smile spreads on her face. "You have a celebration to plan, and you should revel in your victory and the peace that graces our land because of it. Worry not when there is no need."

"You are correct. All will be well." I put on a brave face as my innards scream at me, kiss her cheek, and skip around her.

Exiting my study, I glance down the hall. With no one about, I jump to the windowsill and into the air. I soar high above the castle. Below, the green meadow calls to me. Light bounces off the dewdrops, causing the blades to sparkle as if topped with tiny diamonds. I coast down in wide circles, breathing in the sweet honeysuckle and lavender. The cool air washes across my body. *All will be well. How can everything not be perfect with such beauty?*

Alighting in the empty courtyard, I flit to the table and pluck a grape from the bunch. I wind around and take my seat. Motion catches my eye, and I look up to see Holden, golden wings spread wide, gliding towards me. *Holden.*

My feelings for him grow every day. *How could I not have seen what could be between us for so many months?*

Landing, he lowers his wings and approaches. Blue irises and a perfect smile greet me. Golden hair falls over his brow as he glances around then leans over and kisses my lips.

"Good morning." My smile spreads across my face. How can everything not be perfect when I have his affection?

Jumping the table and sliding into the chair beside mine, he runs his finger down my nose. "How was your sleep, my beautiful queen?"

"Fitful. And not long enough." I rest my chin on my hand and lean towards him, unable to rein in the smile spreading across my face. I take in his fair eyes and light hair, today pulled back into a tight bun on his neck, in preparation for sparring with his soldiers, I imagine. *How is it that just the sight of him elicits such joy?*

He grips my hand. "Have you figured out how to rid the universe of all evil yet?"

"We shall never defeat the darkness as long as beings harbor sins of their own."

"And what iniquities would they cast stones at you for?"

I smile. "Pride and greed."

"I believe one who risks her very life to save her kingdom may deserve a bit of boasting. But what avarice are you guilty of?"

Biting my lip, I wonder if I should speak the words. He declares his feelings for me with ease. *Why should I not?* "I wish to look upon your face every day."

"Then I am just as covetous as you. For I desire that as well."

"To look upon your own face? I should say you are quite proud, too." I laugh.

"You know what I mean." He lobs a grape at me.

I chuck a handful back at him.

Catching one, he tosses it my way again. "And I am definitely not a good role model."

"Yes, how so?"

"Leaving my country to serve a traitorous queen?"

I pelt him with another grape. "I have not been charged with such. But it was I who kept us up into the wee hours of the morning. That will not serve us well today."

He grabs my wrist as I reach for more fruit. "Yes, if you were not so detailed about the celebration, we would have been in bed sooner."

"I want it to be perfect. It is the first celebration when all can truly relax and enjoy a kobold-free realm. If *someone* would not bring wine to planning sessions, I believe—"

"They would be a lot less fun." Picking up an apple, he eyes me with a sideways glance.

"Are you two arguing already?" Landing opposite us, Quinn lowers his green wings and slides into a seat.

"Good morning, cousin." My side catches with grief as I take in his face. The square chin and dark hair so much like my eldest brother. Staving off the passing emotion, I offer him a plate of biscuits. "Prince Holden was complaining about my organization style. He thinks me too detail oriented."

"You do tend to be preoccupied with particulars." Quinn lifts a pastry from the tray.

Holden motions to Quinn. "I like you more today."

I look at Quinn, wondering why he sided with Holden. The two have been on opposite sides of every discussion for the past week. Perhaps Quinn has decided to set aside his jealousy or opposition, whatever the ill feelings are, or maybe he loathes planning festivals as much as Holden. *I need female friends.* But I require Holden and Quinn to help me list the games of skill for the festival. Looking between the men, I vow to demand of Quinn the root of his animosity before they travel to the High Council gathering. I have put the discussion off too long as it is.

"I can finish the plans for the parties while you are attending the trial." I look back to the meadow, thinking of the journals that should be completed as well.

If honest, I dread the task. I do not want to be reminded of what passed the day I entered Lower Earth. The beings haunt my every dream, but it must be done. Each fact needs be preserved in the texts for future generations. My experience could aid fae, as the histories did us, in ways we could not even ponder. Speak with Quinn before he leaves, plan for the celebration, record my victory in the journals, I tick through the items in my list.

Holden lays his hand on my arm. "Someone is way too serious for a supposed day of rest."

"Someone does not know the meaning of responsibility." Quinn points at Holden.

And he returns to mocking Holden. I fight rolling my eyes and think back to the day we first met. They seemed so alike—both soldiers, royals. *Except* Holden bears the title of prince of our neighboring kingdom of Hilbron, and Quinn serves as only my heir presumptive, a tentative title indeed. Perhaps therein lies the root of his angst. But he accepted the position, has said he wanted it, is happy here. *Before.* Before Holden sided with me to aid the witches of the trinity.

Another rabbit hole. As seems to be their pattern, the trinity of witches have disappeared without a trace. If the trinity is still a trinity. If the one they call Hunter still lives and their powers are intact. I hope they persist for I believe we, as well as they, may benefit from an alliance. If he perished, the witches may have lost their advantage in the battle against evil, and I can place no blame with the other two for taking time to mourn and regroup. Tears form in my eyes as I think how the witches' hearts must be broken, especially Alena's.

"Are you thinking of the witches again?" Quinn's voice brings me back to my reality. "I do not see why you are so preoccupied with them. We should shoot in the meadow. Let us plan for the solstice while we practice our aim."

Holden snatches a pastry from the tray. "Oh, Quinn, ever so sensitive. What if it were Titania that died? I hope you would at least shed a tear before taking over her reign. And why do you not see that we share the same goal as the witches? This trinity seems to be willing to do whatever it takes to safeguard their realm from evil."

"Yes, *their* realm, Upper Earth. I did not see them volunteering to fight the kobold."

Perhaps I have misplaced favor on Quinn. *How can he not see our mutual purpose?* Maybe he should not be sitting at this table. Laying my napkin on my plate, I stand.

"Nor did we ask their help. Please, do not argue. We fight the same enemies as this trinity. There is nothing to be gained by this debate."

"I am sure the High Council will have much to say, cousin." Quinn holds my stare.

Does he challenge me? Threaten me? Hold your enemies close. "Yes, cousin. Let us not converse on this further. We should take to the meadow for some archery. I will meet you there in an hour."

Bowing, Quinn jumps into the air. I watch him fly away, wondering if I can trust him with my kingdom. *Differing opinions promote well-thought-out solutions,* I remind myself. *You harbor radical ideas. Quinn's views represent more traditional lines of thinking. You cannot discount him for that. He did not take the issue to the council, Regin did.*

"I do not understand why you keep him here." Holden matches my step as I cross the courtyard.

"He is my cousin, and I have no heir. He stabilizes my reign."

"And what will become of him when you do have an heir?" Holden whispers in my ear.

As his warm breath crosses my neck, I shiver. I dare meet his beautiful blue eyes and words fail me. *Why, oh, why does he have this effect on me?* It was not this way before. My brain lacks rational thought in his presence.

"I must see to Mother and Father."

"Are we still to meet in the wood after midday?"

"Yes." My face flushes at the thought of being alone with him. Few things have brought me more happiness the past days than the hours we spend together.

Stopping, Holden bows, turns on his heel, and takes flight. I watch him, noting how the sun shines through his golden wings. *Focus, Titania.* A queen cannot be distracted by such things as amber wings and muscled backs. Looking to the doors before me, I swing them open and enter the passage.

I am glad for the weekend days of rest and to have fewer fae in the castle. My wings itch with new growth and the sense all are watching me. Brighter green, changing to a crisp, spring-yellow green, the sheer structures have begun to replace the frayed, burned ends. It is so at odds with my blazing new red hair, which is also a side-effect of my magickal expulsion from Lower Earth. And, of course, there is the matter of my face. I hear the rumors, whispers in the halls. They think me a witch or wizard, say the adornments magnify my senses. If they only knew the truth.

This thought leads to more worry for the trial the High Council called for. Many judges will be in attendance. *What if they learn my secret? What if they learn of Mother's gift of foresight?* Powers that manifest in our realm historically only manifest in the lines of the Ring Keepers. Discovery of gifts in others could spark a full inquiry, not to mention fear—nay, even hostility—towards those who may demonstrate gifts. Disruption of the balance of power could upend our realm. Me, a female queen, rising to the monarchy at but fifteen and unwed, with the responsibility for a kingdom on my shoulders, causes strife enough. The last thing I need is more eyes on Aubren and my reign.

Reaching my parents' quarters, I slip through the door. Mother sits in front of the window, her light hair shining in the sun, and Father is at his desk, reading. With Father engrossed, I flit to Mother and, landing beside her, kiss her cheek.

"Good morning. Are you enjoying the view?" I slide my palm into hers and squeeze her cold fingers. The texture of her skin, so soft and thin, as if a stretched parchment-thin pastry dough, seems ready to rip at any moment. I wonder how much time her body may have left in this realm. Tears pooling in my eyes, I watch her face, offering silent prayers for a response.

Why I still hope, even expect, one will come, I do not know. Tucked away in my mind, in my heart, a glimmer of faith remains. If I just say the right words, play the right song or poem, perhaps recite a key memory. Part of me believes when I fulfill my purpose hers will be realized as well. Her trance will be broken. She will return to us. That pressure weighs on my shoulders. The need to end the evil ones. Ever since I secured my reign by besting Ethan, I have felt the yoke of that burden. Not only for my mother's sake, but for the prosperity of the realm.

"She loves spring. The grass is quite green this year, do you not agree?" Father crosses to us.

"I love how the sun shines on the dew in the morning." I look from his wrinkle-ringed green eyes to Mother and squeeze her hand. "Do you love how the sun reflects off the droplets as well, Mother?"

"Morning? Ha." Father strokes his gray laced mahogany beard. "It is almost midday. I thought you would have breakfast with us, but Alfreda said you were still asleep. How late into the night did you work? Or did something else occupy your time?"

I imagine a defense a normal mother may make. *Leave her be. She needs her rest.* But Mother's blue irises stay glued to the window. I smooth my riding skirt to my leg. "We were planning for the solstice celebration. I rose early but had tasks to finish."

"Of course. Planning with Holden, I am sure." Father's eyebrows creep up.

"Also Quinn. Should we all walk together this morning?"

"No, take your mother. I am engrossed in my reading." He describes the ancient text tracing the lineages of the witches.

"I am grateful for your help, Father. The more we know of Sonia and her line, the better prepared we can be. Have you learned anything useful yet?"

Replying with a negative, he saunters back to the desk. I lift Mother's hand, and she rises from her seat. I hook her elbow in mine and we walk through the passages, out to our favorite garden, into the orchard, and then to the meadow. The evaporating dew forms a haze over the field, creating the sense that we walk through a dream. But this is my life, and the scenes that come at night appear to be more of the things of nightmares. As we enter the forest, I talk to her of plans for the solstice celebrations, my apprehension about the High Council trial, and the animosity between Quinn and Holden—more specifically, Quinn's seeming hostility or jealousy.

Having nothing else to speak of, my mind wanders. For the most part, I have accepted, even become grateful for, what transpires during our walks. I could have died in Lower Earth. But the goddesses granted me time, and I will value all of it. I use these moments with Mother to reflect, brainstorm, and wonder what advice she may have given. The trial will be. I cannot change that, only prepare for what they may decide. But I will not live with the unease between Quinn and Holden. It is not healthy for me and does not make for a strong kingdom.

Having made my peace, I recite the names of the flowers for Mother. We weave between the trees, and I listen to the sound of the forest, the babbling of the brook, the songs of the birds, and the breeze tinkling through the leaves. I savor the soft moss underfoot, moist air on my skin, and warmth of the intermittent sunlight on my wings. The smell of earth, our soil, Aubren, surrounds me. It harkens memories of our many walks in this wood. I exhale. *Holden is not your only happiness. We are safe again.*

Rounding back to the castle, Mother and I pass through the orchard to the garden. I commit to her my pledge to speak to Quinn about Holden this day. A towering rose bush with huge white blooms beckons me. Approaching it, I lean over to smell a flower. Its sweet aroma fills my nose, reminding me of May celebrations. I close my eyes, picturing the lunches in the garden and teas on the verandas we enjoyed when my brothers still lived. How happy we had been.

A tear escapes my lid and rolls down my cheek. As I swipe it away, movement in the flower catches my eye. A brown grasshopper emerges from between the petals. Mother's hand darts in front of me and snatches the bug. Pressing her fingers into her palm over and over, she pulverizes the insect, and I stare in shock as she squats and mashes the brown and green goo remains of the animal into the dirt. Standing, she spits on the soil and twists the toe of her shoe into the spot, grinding the parts of the bug into the ground.

Startled out of my trance by her repetitive stomping, I wrap my arms around her shoulders. "Mother, Mother, it is gone. It will not hurt you."

Her eyes cut to mine and the glaze returns. She blinks and her eyeballs quiver in their sockets.

I fear she may be having an epileptic fit or seizure. We need help. "Alfreda—"

Wings spreading high, mother spins in front of me and clutches my arms. Her nails dig into my skin. "More to come. You need them."

Grip loosening, her eyes roll back and her knees buckle. Winding my arm around her back, I catch her as she slumps into my embrace. I nestle her head in my lap and stroke her cheek. Her skin feels ice cold under my touch. Squirming out of my vest, I lay it over her. I glance up to see Alfreda hurrying towards me.

"Heavens be. What happened? One of the gardeners said they heard you call my name."

"I do not know." My side ticks, and tears fill my eyes. "There was a grasshopper on the rose and—"

"She had a premonition, right?"

"Yes. I have not seen her move that fast or with such fury since…" I cannot bear to speak of it aloud. Not since the day my brothers died. When their bodies were brought to the courtyard, she ran to each, flinging her arms around their torsos and hugging them with all her might. Father and Alfreda spent an hour prying Mother from Rigel's frame.

Alfreda runs to get water, and I rock Mother in my arms, grateful for the tall hedges that shelter us from view. Her face appears the color of snow, but her breaths seem even and her heartbeat strong. *More to come. You need them. What more is to come? More grasshoppers? I need the grasshoppers? Or someone else? I had been talking about Holden and Quinn when the fit started. There was more danger to come, and I needed Holden and Quinn to help me stop it?* My mind races with interpretations of her words.

Returning with a pitcher of water and a cloth, Alfreda pats the cool towel on Mother's forehead. "What did she say?"

I keep my eyes trained on her face. "I do not know. It was—"

"You are keeping secrets from me now?"

"No, I…" I meet Alfreda's hard stare. "She said, 'More to come, you need them.'"

"If only there could be more context and details to these omens."

Mother twitches in my arms, and her eyelids rise. But there appears to be no recognition in her stare. I squeeze her to me, relishing in the fact that she has woken. For as long as she draws breath, I will hope for her to return to her former self.

Standing, I support Mother's waist. Step by step, we creep through the garden paths towards the castle entrance. With each footfall, Mother's back straightens, her wings returning to their normal slacked state on her back. Glancing at her face, I recognize the return of the normal haze of her state, eyes glazed and darting this way and that, with so few blinks you would think her eyes would shrivel and dry into raisins.

We escort Mother to her chamber and take her to the bed. Rolling back the down coverlet, I rest her on the mattress and remove her shoes. She spins her legs up and lies back as if repeating the act from a preset routine. I tuck the covers under her chin, and she closes her eyes. Seeing her still looking so pale, my breath catches in my lungs. I force an exhale.

Alfreda's warm arm wraps around my waist. "She will be okay, dear."

"Her skin is so pale, so cold and thin. It seems as if she could evaporate into thin air any moment." Tears fill my eyes. "I cannot lose her. Not before…"

I bury my face in Alfreda's chest. A queen should not cry, but my tears come like waterfalls from my lids. "I want to be able to say goodbye to my mother. I have to bring her back. She seemed so close today. I do not understand. The grasshopper set her off somehow."

"She hates those things. Always has. Hated that they eat her flowers. I would guess that triggered her."

Hearing someone enter, I blink the tears from my eyes. I raise my head to find Father before me. I explain Mother's episode as he kneels in front of her. Thoughts swirl in my mind. *What is coming? Is it indeed Holden and Quinn that I require? Who else could it be? They came here to help me fight the kobold, and together, we defeated them, secured this kingdom and our realm.* My stomach turns. *Could there be others? Have the evil spirits of the deep bred more armies?*

"Titania, I am sure you have much to attend to." Alfreda lays her hands on my shoulders. "We will watch your mother."

My mind darts to Quinn whom I told I would shoot with in the meadow. "You will come get me if anything changes. As soon as she wakes?"

"Yes, yes. Go. Splash your face with some cool water." She pinches my cheeks. "Your mother will be fine."

I nod and, patting Father's arm, leave them to watch her. Walking through the stone passage, I try to clear my mind, silently reciting my list of chores for the day. But my brain worries for Mother. *What if she gets sicker? Titania, you cannot tarry on these thoughts. Take things as they come.*

Chapter 2

Determined to stick to my plan, I wash my face with cool water in my chamber. I exit the castle and jump into the air, bound for the meadow. The wind in my face and the sweeping view of the land and my kingdom from that height clears my head. *You are Queen, and a queen must persevere.* Seeing Quinn in his shooting stance, my mind races again. *How do I broach the topic of my displeasure at his behavior towards Holden? Just be honest. It has always served you well.* Taking in and releasing a deep breath, I descend to the field.

"I thought perhaps a troll absconded with you, cousin." Quinn lowers his bow.

"I was enjoying my walk with Mother too much to return to the castle."

"You are more patient than I believe I could be."

"Do you not think yourself a patient person? You seem to love your father. I cannot imagine you do not feel even more love for your mother."

"I believed myself to be a patient fae before coming here." He hooks an arrow in his bow string.

Lifting my quiver and bow from the ground, I ready my arrow as well. "And now, cousin? Tell me. You do not seem happy anymore."

"I am and I am not." He lets his arrow fly, and it lands on the second-most inner ring.

Releasing my shaft, I turn to face him and wait.

He holds my gaze for a second. Taking a breath, he explains that while he feels he has more purpose now, he struggles with the stress of being a good leader and knowing what is right and wrong, how only time will tell if our actions will be seen favorably or with dishonor.

His green eyes bore into mine. "I know not how you make decisions so easily, stand the pressure."

I lay my hand on his chest. "You follow your gut, that is what you do."

"May I speak freely?"

Lowering my arms to my sides, I brace for what may come next. "Of course. I hope you know I always want your honest thoughts."

"Something I admire in you, cousin." He grips both my hands. "You are so smart, so beautiful... Why do you pursue this relationship with Holden?"

I reel in my first instinct to demand that it is none of his concern. How dare he pass judgment on my personal affairs, my happiness. *You are a queen, and Quinn is an advisor on your council, and a cousin. Speak to him as such.* "He is smart, and brave, and a prince."

"You cannot give your heart so freely."

I study his face. "So, you are worried for my feelings?"

"And how it may look to others."

"Neither of us are spoken for. And it is too soon to know the extent of what may be between us."

"You must think about what is good for Aubren. He is but a youngest son."

I want to shoot fire from my eyes at him. *What is good for Aubren? I think of it with every breath. How many times must I hear it? I expect such from Father but from Quinn as well? What if you could give him just a small jolt of that electric magick?* Wriggling my hands from his grip, I release my breath.

"I know that, cousin. Little else occupies my mind. But right now, Aubren has no need for anything. I am but sixteen and not even half a year into my reign."

"But we could need allies. You want to further your cause? Continue to work with the witches of the trinity? You need other countries on your side."

"I thought you did not favor interaction with the witches."

"I do not. But this is how you gain support in our realm, by making alliances. Lindleton has the highest population of fae and is one of the oldest and most conservative kingdoms. If you could garner support there, others will follow. You have power, a power many will want. Use your position to make the best match for Aubren."

Power. I wonder if he suspects. *No, he could not, right?* "I have not seen other kingdoms offering their aid. Only you and Holden stayed to help."

"Because your father invited us to."

My blood boils as I recall how Father and General Kane plotted behind my back to have me engaged. I ball my fists but hold my tongue. I must know his complete line of thoughts, and lashing out at him will not garner open discussion.

Quinn grasps my arm. "Just go this banquet season with an open mind. Do not limit your options by chaining yourself to Holden."

"Is this why you hold animosity for him?"

"He hangs on your every word. Agrees with your every thought. And how could he not? Even before your transformation, you radiated light, warmth, power. Now, you shine." His eyes grow round. Releasing my arm, he steps back and lowers his gaze to the dirt.

My face warms with his assessment. It almost seems as if he favors me as well. This could be the root of his displeasure. That I chose Holden over him. But another matter concerns me. I do not want puppets around me. I have always seen Holden as strong, independent. If he has misrepresented himself, I need to know. *Would you have sensed that? Perhaps* you *are under his spell just as Quinn accuses him.* I must be wary of this.

"Do you not think Holden honest?"

"I believe love can make one do many odd things."

The skin of my cheeks flames anew. "Thank you for your honesty, Quinn. I value that above all."

Returning to my shooting stance, I let an arrow loose.

Quinn resumes his shooting as well.

I fire my arrows at the target until my muscles sear. Then, I switch arms because my newest endeavor is to learn to use my nondominant side with as much accuracy as my dominant one.

As that arm tires as well, I take my leave. I jump into the air and make for the dense forest south of the castle. Two of my most trusted guards, Grant and Timothy, trail me until I spot Holden, his fair hair now loose around his shoulders. My guards drop to the forest floor as I push forwards. Above the canopy, I spread my wings and float down to the bank where he waits. I cannot help a smile spreading wide across my face.

It has not even been a week since I escaped Lower Earth, wanting to see no one more than him. My lips tingle with the memory of our first kiss that night. So few days have passed, and yet, we share so many new memories. The night spent discovering the coral reef, trip to the whatever falls of Elita, and then to the snowy peaks of Lindleton play through my thoughts. Feet landing on soft grass, I slide my quiver to the ground. "I hope you have not waited long."

"I would wait for you forever and a day." His sparkling blue eyes meet mine.

My cheeks warm, and my heart skips a beat. I bite my lip, wondering at the intensity of his words of affection and longing to be at his side every moment of every day.

His eyes hold mine. "You doubt that I would?"

"No, I could never doubt you. I am just… So much has happened, and there is so much to come. I feel a bit overwhelmed."

"You were shooting with Quinn, and he has, I am sure, been speaking against me. I wondered why you were late." Spinning away, he lifts a rock and chucks it into the brook.

I lay a hand on his shoulder. "It was not just him. I was with Mother."

Turning back to me, he grasps my palms. "Has she foreseen something? Is that what has you unraveled?"

Taking in his wide, light eyes, so full of concern, I know I cannot keep things from him. "Yes, but honestly, right now, it is this. Us. It feels wonderful and scary at the same time."

"Of course, I cannot speak for all, but I would say that is how love is. Exciting, joyous, and equally terrifying." His eyes drop, and he releases my hands.

"Have you been in love before?" He is eighteen, a year and a half older than I, and by not being saddled with the traumatic experience of losing one's brothers, I imagine he had a normal adolescent experience. Perhaps he has been in love multiple times. Or, at the very least, in many relationships. Being quite handsome, I can imagine many fae would pursue him.

"Were you not in love with Foster?"

Backing to a boulder, I climb atop it and sit down. "I believed myself to be falling in love with him. I was heartbroken when he left. He was the first fae I ever cared for that way."

"I know that feeling well."

He proceeds to tell me of a girl, a princess from Willhelm, he met last festival season. She befriended him, and he assumed they shared a mutual affection. Then he learned she favored his brother, and her father courted an agreement to have them married. My heart aches thinking of the pain and betrayal he must have felt.

"From the second my brother began to pay attention to her, she never gave me a moment's time." Holden kicks at the grasses in front of him.

"That is horrid. Did you tell your brother you liked her?"

"He knew. She was beautiful, and he was quite proud to steal her away. Plus, he is older than I. It was also an advantageous alliance as she is the eldest daughter of a brother of the king of Willhelm."

"So, they married?"

"Not long before I came to Aubren. That is why my father allowed me to be away in the army and brought me here for your coronation."

I slide to the ground. "I am glad you came."

"As am I." He holds my gaze.

My head swims, wondering where this relationship will lead us, if I should consider Quinn's advice. Looking into Holden's eyes, holding his callused hands, I think of the bond formed over the past months. With my brothers gone and Mother absent, I have few to trust, and fewer still to call friend. None that make my heart thump, butterflies fill my stomach, and tensions ease, somehow all at once, as he does. *And I need him. And Quinn,* my brain pings.

"You look deep in thought. Tell me what happened with your mother and Quinn."

Tugging at Holden's hands, I jump into the air. "This meeting is supposed to be a respite from court drama. I do not wish to think of Quinn or anyone else but you."

He hovers before me. "Your wish is my command, Que—"

I wave a finger in the air. He grabs it and brings it to his lips. Wrapping the other arm around me, he pulls me into his chest and kisses my lips. Tingles flutter over my skin at the feel of his warm, soft lips. As the kiss ends, I open my eyes to find we are twirling up. Tree branches rustle overhead.

"Where shall we go today? Should we hunt for faerie crosses in the brook?"

Nodding, I slide from his embrace and shoot through the trees. Dodging trunks and branches, I find my worries for Mother, alliances, the trial, and festival season whisp away. The green of the leaves, bed of ferns below, bursts of color from flowers dotting the landscape, rush of wind in my ears, calls of birds flitting from our path, and chill of humid air washing over my skin immerse me in forest life.

I recall the scene I had played over in my head many times before deciding to fight for my throne: a thatch cottage hidden in a copse of trees, a small garden outside, Mother sitting on the porch, Father chopping wood. The girl who dreamt of that simple life is gone. *Is the woman that replaced her happy?* With a burst, I thrust myself through the canopy, up over the forest. Spinning, I look out to the sea, then over the farmers' fields, and south to the desert. My land, my kingdom.

Holden stops beside me. "I thought we were going to the stream."

"I needed a moment."

"Is something wrong?"

"No, everything is right."

"Good. Then I will race you to the bank where the river turns." Holden drops into the trees.

"You will not win." I dart after him.

I could beat him, but I am content to lag behind, watching his golden wings beat in strong, swift strokes, catching and reflecting rays of light that penetrate the dense foliage. If I listened to Quinn, I would not let myself go on like this, my hormones and affections flowing so recklessly. *Stop.* I admonish the thought. *Should you not be happy? You were two seconds ago. Allow yourself to be a girl in addition to queen.* Refocusing on the forest around me, I descend to the bank. I land beside Holden on the soft, cool moss.

"You let me win." Holden's smile widens.

"How else can I have time to watch you fly?"

"Are you admiring me or critiquing my form?"

"I am not wearing my crown, so I am just a girl noting a handsome fae."

"I love seeing you like this." Tugging at my waist, he pulls me to him. "Of course, I love seeing you period, no matter what headdress you are wearing."

"And I you." I push up on my toes and give him a quick peck. "Now for the crosses."

Jumping into the stream, I rake my hand through the silt and dredge up a handful. We wade in the water, scooping up piles of dirt and rock till the sun dips in the sky. We swap stories of our childhoods, families, school, and friends. Noting the dimming light, I sigh.

"And alas, our wonderful time must end." Holden strides to the bank.

I flit to his side. Catching his hands, I lean in and press my lips to his. "Thank you for a wonderful afternoon."

"Can I see you tonight after dinner? It may be our last chance to see each other for some days."

"Yes, I still need a list of games for the celebration." My mind churns with the other tasks I must complete.

"I hope we can do more than work?" Lifting my hand, he presses his lips to it.

I focus on drying my feet as my face flushes. Jumping into the air, we circle to find my guards and, joining them, head to the castle. In my quarters, I find Alfreda folding dresses and stacking them in my trunk.

"Oh, good, you are here. Which dress would you like to wear for dinner? Your father wants everyone in attendance before they are to leave for the trial."

"And Mother is okay?"

"She is fine. No worries for her."

"Something traditional, like Mother always wore, double-breasted, high-neck top with long sleeves and an A-line skirt." I slide from my vest and douse my skin with a wet towel.

Alfreda stands upright and stares at me.

"What?"

"If your mother could hear you now. You have grown into a brilliant, strong woman, and I am so proud of you." Tears pool in her eyes.

"What brings this on? This morning, you scolded me for being young and determined. Plus, we do not know that Mother does or does not hear us. She very well may." I slide my pants to the floor. Tugging a top over my head,

I cross to the mirror. "Are you worried about Mother's premonition? Is that what has you crying at the drop of a pin?"

Approaching, Alfreda lays her hands on my shoulders. "I worry because of all of it. Her bodement, the trial, your obsession with the witches."

"What happened to having faith? They will see reason. The council will give him a slap on the wrist and send him back to his post." Thinking the goddesses would never allow anything to stand in the way of my destiny, I study my reflection.

What will they say of the jewels on my forehead? It is bound to be discussed. *Will the elders think me a wizard? Or a witch?*

I wrap my fingers around Alfreda's hand. "Do not fear. All will be well. You will see. Aleem, Holden, and Quinn will be back home in two days' time, none the worse for the experience."

⸺⊰⊱⸺

STROLLING TOWARDS THE SMALL dining room, Alfreda and I pass the grand hall. Through the open doors, I catch a glimpse of Holden and Quinn at the head table. Quinn appears deep in conversation with an advisor, and Holden throws his head back, laughing at something Grant has said. I smile, hoping my dinner with Father and Kane does not run too late. Knowing Quinn, he will hold them all in the hall until well into the night, so I may not have time with Holden.

Finding Mother, Father, and General Kane in the small dining hall, I kiss each of their cheeks and take my place at the head of the table. I realize the family meal had been a good idea. It has been a long time since we have gathered our makeshift clan together. I study each of their faces. So much is the same, but even more is different. Father and Head General Kane no longer sit on pillars in my mind. Sadness descends as I remember their treachery. Father has been easier to forgive, but Kane's second offense deepened the chasm between us. There was one time I would have called him uncle. Now, I have my guards spy on him day and night.

"Did you enjoy your target practice with Quinn?" Father lifts a bite of meat to his mouth.

"Not really. His thoughts only increased my stress."

Swallowing, Father pats his lips. "He is very opinionated. You are well matched, make a good pair in that regard."

I picture steam shooting from my ears, flames gushing from my eyes and alighting his beard. *A pair? He still thinks I should marry Quinn?* I take a deep breath. "There is no match between Quinn and me. He is my cousin and heir presumptive, also a trusted advisor, but nothing more, Father. And it is an advisor's job to speak freely so that a ruler may hear all sides of an issue. So, I appreciate his candor."

"What will you do with Quinn once you have an heir? Toss him aside as a bad apple? And what, pray tell, did he have opinions on that has you so defensive today?"

Resting my palms on the cool wood before me, I smile. "Father, this is a social affair. Let us talk about opinions after the meal."

I look at Mother and lay my hand atop hers. "Mother, are you feeling better?"

Mother's gaze shifts from her plate to the fire. I withdraw my hand and lift a bite of potato to my mouth.

"It is going to be a grand festival season. Your plans for the solstice look magnificent." Alfreda raises her wine glass.

"To the solstice." Kane lifts his chalice.

Hoisting my charger, I clink it to Father's, Kane's, and Alfreda's in turn. Hesitating in front of Mother, I note her eyes still glued on the flames. I bring the wine to my lips, remembering her latest prophecy. *More to come. You need them. What more and who?* But I shall put my faith in the goddesses and their plan for me. They have not let me down yet.

Alfreda describes some of the details for the solstice celebration, and Kane and Father add ideas.

I mention I may let the advisors ring in as well.

Father agrees it is a good use of their time. He ends his oration with the suggestion that I should be using my energy to see to the accounts, which have not been surveyed in a while. And what contingency plan I should make in case they rule against Aleem, decide to strip him of his title.

I fight rolling my eyes. There cannot be a single meal without the two of them critiquing me. "I need no plan. The trial serves as a fact-finding query. Aleem, Holden, Quinn, and you will tell them what happened. You and Aleem sided with me for a reason. It was a fair vote with only Regin and Quinn who opposed. The rest of the judges, as well as Aleem, sided with me. The High Council shall judge well. Aleem assured that I was able to defend our realm. They will see that."

"But you pressed Aleem to go against the High Council ruling, and he acted treasonously. There must be some answering for that." Kane holds my gaze.

"And I will accept whatever decision they make. I cannot imagine they will side against the oldest Keeper in the realm. Aleem's reputation is spotless, as is yours, Father."

"But they did not ask me to attend the conclave." Father slumps in his chair.

"The others will testify as to your vote. I am not worried, neither should you be." I say the words but my stomach turns. *Would they really replace Aleem? And with who?*

Kane shakes his head. "I miss being young and naïve."

"I told you there was much to worry about." Alfreda wrings her hands.

I stand. "What if I play? Music always lifts spirits. Let us retire to the study."

We pass the grand hall, and I long to be dancing with the masses to the tune of a fiddle. I note Holden still sits next to Grant. In the center of the jig circle, Quinn stomps to the beat, seemingly enjoying himself for the first time in months. I wonder if my absence allows him to feel more carefree. The thought saddens me because I have done everything in my power to ensure his happiness in my kingdom.

Dark hair and purple wings catch my eye. I note Abeetha's form behind Quinn. Why I allow Gunther's family liberty in my castle, I do not know. I am too soft. I should send them all to Willhelm. Refocusing on the soft skin of Mother's hand, I make a turn towards my parents' quarters. We settle in the study, Mother and Father in front of the fire and Alfreda and Kane on either side. Pulling the harp to me, I pluck at a string to test the tuning. It rings true, and I start a melody. Not an uplifting jig, but a sweet melody like one Mother used to play for me as a child. I watch her face but, seeing no reaction, focus on the strings.

Kane stifles a yawn, and I end the tune. Making excuses that I am tired, I bid them goodnight and wind through the halls to my study. I must pen my story. Sliding the manual for the kobold from my shelf, I read through the last entry. I recall how Foster and I discovered the kobold's hiding spot by shooting arrows across the cave's entrance. It feels like a lifetime ago, and yet, not six months has passed. Dipping my quill in the ink, I record the date at the top of a new page.

Thinking how that day started, I realize I should record the story, not only in the histories of the kobold, but in those of Lower Earth and in the journals of our interactions with witches and vampires, *and* vampire-witch hybrids. My head spins with the thought that these hybrid creatures may number many more than we could know. *What if someone else sought to raise an army as Sonia did?*

We were not put in this realm to defend against all evil, just that which threatens from below.

As I pen my story in the last journal, a hear a rap on the door. Seeing Holden's face inch through the opening, I smile.

"May I come in?"

"Just you?"

"Yes. I believe Quinn is enjoying the festivities for once. I escaped without his notice." Holden slips into the room and stands with his back to the door.

"Please, sit. I want you to read my accounts of our interactions with the kobold and witches. See if you would add anything more." Ending my sentence, I sign my name and spin the text towards him.

Sliding into the seat beside me, he flips to the prior page and starts to read.

Unable to sit still any longer, I cross to the window and look out over the meadow. The dim light from the moon above the ring causes the green of the grass to glow with a hint of purple.

"You did not write of your transformation."

I note an owl swooping low over the grass, after a mouse I imagine. His wings make no sound as they propel his body over the field. "This is not about me. It is about the magick kobold aided by the evil spirits of the deep, the magick of the rings, and the witches."

"I believe you will have more to write after the High Council trial."

Father's and Kane's warnings pinging in my mind, I voice my fears. "If the council rules against Aleem, I am sure Gunther and Ethan may try and take advantage, paint me unworthy as well, or do whatever it is that delights traitors."

"I see you still hold animosity." Holden joins me.

I turn to face him. "Sorry, I saw Abeetha in the hall, and my nerves are frayed after dinner with Father and Kane. I believe they aim to have me worry more. As if I do not have enough unease on my own." I proceed to tell Holden of Father's and Kane's concerns.

"You have not spent much time with him this week. It may be hard for him to know your fears."

"But of course I would worry for Aleem. He knows how important he is to me."

Holden wraps his hand around mine. "Should we finish plans for the solstice celebration? Will that put you at ease?"

"I decided to request final opinions from the advisors. I only need your ideas for the games, and my mind will be at rest for tonight."

Snatching up a quill and paper, he writes five items. *Hunting. Archery. Shot put. Discus. Croquet.* He smiles wide and lifts the page. "These should make everyone happy. What should we do? Is the air calling to you?"

"It is."

Closing the history texts and adding them back to the shelf, I jump to the windowsill. We take to the sky. I beat my wings, climbing higher and higher. At the ring, I peer into Upper Earth, my wings aching to be pushed to their limits. My muscles long to sear with wear to escape the mental angst. I cannot see the stars for the dense canopy of dark leaves above. I imagine them blanketing the sky that night, not so many months ago, when we followed the stream of souls to Italy. There have been many challenges in the six months of my reign. I will not let the High

Council, or whatever things my mother sees on the horizon, stop me from protecting my kingdom and our realm. It is my destiny. I can feel it with every fiber of my being.

"Thinking of fleeing to the human realm before the council passes judgment?"

"No, just remembering the stars."

"They were magickal, were they not? I had never been above at night before." Holden kisses my cheek. "Tell me what your mother said."

"Not now. Should we fly south?"

"Your wish, my Qu—"

I press my finger to his lips. "Let us race."

"You will not win." Holden grabs my wrist and kisses it.

Tugging my hands from his grip, I shoot down to the water, and we weave back and forth from the beach out over the ocean. Looking into the deep blue water, I long to be immersed in the warm nothingness, silence. I focus on the air around me, the constant rush of wind against my skin. Following the coast east and then south, I let the smell of the sea, the spray of tiny droplets pelting my body with each beat of my wings, consume me. Turning west, we press forwards. By the time we land on the southern tip, I am soaked.

"You let me win, again." Holden beats his wings, and water sprays out from the tips.

I turn my back to him and snap my wings together, sending a flood of droplets his way. He hops into the sea and scoops his hand into the water, flinging handfuls at me. I leap away, catching only the tail end of the turret. His laughter, low and sweet like the sound of a jug flute, carries in the wind like a lullaby. I let my wings fall slack and land beside him as he tromps onto the beach.

He entwines his fingers with mine. "We could always go live with the merfolk if you have had enough with the likes of the High Council."

"The merfolk? Truly?" The idea harkens my vision of the tiny cottage in the wood.

"I would follow the woman I love anywhere."

My breath catches in my lungs. Smiling, I find my voice. "The woman you love?"

He cups his hands around my face. "I have no other words to describe the feelings I have for you. I love you."

Hearing the words from his lips, the *woman* he loves, harkens such different emotion than it did with Foster. He seems a boy compared to Holden, a prince in his own right, and eighteen. A man, and an equal fae, one who has been, and could continue to be, a true partner in all ways.

"You do not feel the same?" Releasing me, he steps back.

I grab his arms. "No, that is not it. No one has ever called me a woman like that before."

"That was not the most important part of what I said."

"I am surprised. I did not expect to feel this. So sure. Like it sits right inside. I thought I should feel scared, or giddy, or butterflies, but it just feels solid. Like this love has always been inside me, and now, I have someone to share it with. Almost like breathing. Knowing I love you is effortless. I love you, Holden."

"And I, you." He presses his lips to mine and warmth spreads over my skin. As the kiss ends, his light eyes hold mine. "And if they will not accept you as you are, we will run away and live with the merfolk."

Chapter 3

"You really have this merfolk plan in your head, do you not? Why not Upper Earth? We could aid the witches of the trinity," I say.

"I should think you would want to be closer to your people. Ready to resume your mission when an opportunity presents."

"Then it shall be with the merfolk."

I look out over the water. The way the bits of light bounce off the tips of the waves mesmerizes me. Holden wraps his arms around my middle. His warmth envelopes me, and I believe I will always feel safe and loved in his presence.

He kisses my cheek. "I do not wish to speak these words, but it is late, and I must rise early. I want to be well rested for the trials."

"Of course." I spin to face him and push up to my toes, planting a kiss on his lips. "I shall miss you."

"And I, you, my love."

—◇◇◇—

Sleep does not come after Holden's confession of love and my worry for Aleem. Perhaps I should have trusted

Regin with my secret. Then he would understand. Perhaps if I go to him, he will drop his grievance, say he had been rash, and he now believes the situation warranted such action. But there may still be those on the council who will say the trial should proceed. And there is no way to know if I can trust Regin with my most important secret. As Keeper of the only other ring in our kingdom, the Nariel Ring lying to the south, he holds the same position as Aleem. I should trust him.

But I have known Aleem all my life and am sure he guesses my gifts. Regin and I only became acquainted when I rose to the throne. I decide there are too many doubts. I will leave things be. Further meddling may cause more problems. Aleem made the decision knowing he could face blame, and the goddesses will see that my path is clear. I have faith in that.

I wind to the kitchen for tea and back through the halls towards my room. Passing Holden's room reminds me again of our evening and admission of the feelings between us. I know it shall never pass, but if we were to go live with the merfolk, or in my fictitious cabin in the woods, then I imagine we would be happy forever. We could enjoy a simple life with no worry for kobold, councils, advisors, or heir presumptives. *But would my conscience allow that, knowing what I know?* The answer stands a firm no.

Setting my tea beside the bed, I hug my robe to me and slide between the cool covers. I envision days of picnics beside the brook and nights spent flying over the countryside with Holden.

The sky turns dark, blacker than I have ever seen it. A face appears. Abaddon.

"Did you think I would not come?"

"Nor I?"

I spin to see Lucifer floating towards me.

"And I?" A cackling voice emits from the mouth of a dragon. Sonia.

"We haven't met." A smile spreads across a face I do not recognize. Thanatos? *Son of Sonia, father to Hunter, and—*

"But surely you remember me." Theron's face appears before me.

The images close in.

⬦

I SUCK IN A BREATH AND SIT upright. I clutch my covers. My bed. My room. My castle. My kingdom.

"Perhaps for a while."

I jump to my feet and spin around, searching for the source of the voice. There is none. I am going crazy. My dreams have become hallucinations. I wonder if this could be another form of anxiety, stress over the trial.

"But if you were to live with the merfolk?"

"Hush." Flitting to the window, I open the shutters to a brightening sky.

"What did you say?" Alfreda appears in the doorway.

"Nothing." I shoot to the next window and push open the panels. Blue sky, grass, trees, birds. *All is well.* "It was just another dream. In two days, the trial will be over, and I will have no more need for nightmares."

"Let us pray such." Alfreda sets a water jug and flowers on the table. "Will you have breakfast with your parents?"

"Yes, once I see the trial party off." Glancing at the clock, I realize I must hurry.

I dart to my closet and pull my nightgown over my head. Watching it fall to the stone floor, I think of the crystals and hope to find a way to secure two more sets soon. I tug on a pair of riding pants and fit a blouse over my head and tuck the fabric into the pants. Rounding to the mirror, I release my hair from the ribbon and let the curls fall around my shoulders. It will have to do. Shooting into the hall, I see Holden, bag strapped to his back.

He smiles as I land beside him. "Good morning. Did you sleep well?"

"No, but I hope you did."

"Nothing could be wrong as long as I have your love." Glancing around us, he turns back and kisses me. "And of course, we always have the merfolk."

I swat at his arm. "You and your merfolk. You will curse us. A cabin in the wood will do just fine. And we can hunt for faerie crosses all the day."

"I should think we will require food at some point."

"Then I will use my archery skills to procure a duck."

"Are you quite done with flirting? The party awaits." Quinn's voice sounds from down the hall.

"One should talk. I saw you dancing with Abeetha last evening." Holden strides towards Quinn.

I eye Quinn. "Abeetha? You danced with Abeetha? Daughter and sister of the traitors who tried to take my crown?"

"We danced once. She was standing alone. It would have been rude not to do such." He motions to Holden. "And why would you even bring it up?"

"You started it."

"You started it? Are we twelve?" I look between them. "Please, lay aside your differences. We all strive for the same goal: to keep our realm and that which lies above us safe from the evils of the deep. Remember that. You are my two most trusted advisors. I would like that we all be of one mind."

Quinn raises an eyebrow. "I dare say you trust Holden more than you trust me."

I steel my countenance against reaction to his brazen accusation. Recalling his words of yesterday, I realize I have not broached the topic of Holden's agreeing with all I propose. *Could it be that Holden's motives are less than true? And have I let Quinn's doubts be my own?*

"I trust you in different matters. Do not let these be our parting sentiments. Thank you both for representing me and our kingdom. God's speed to you."

Quinn's eyes soften. "Sorry, cousin. It was too late a night and too early a morning."

"Rest well on the journey." I kiss his cheek.

He exits into the courtyard, and I spin to face Holden. "Was it really just one dance with Abeetha?"

"That I saw."

I watch Quinn as he loads into the carriage, praying the dance was as he said it was.

Holden's arm winds around my waist.

Peering about the space, I push to my toes and kiss his lips.

"I will miss you."

"And I you. But it is only two days."

"Yes, and then we will have the solstice celebration to look forward to."

Catching sight of motion in the courtyard, I step back from Holden. As it stops, Aleem exits the carriage, and I wind outside to greet him. Placing a kiss upon his cheek, I ask about his health and of his wife and family. Then I offer best wishes for a quick and fair trial. I wish that I could inquire as to the ring crystals, but the council guards sit in the carriage waiting with the first, second, and third judges. Another carriage with Regin and his third judge joins the caravan. I recognize his group with a wave, and the entourage sets out.

Watching until they are out of sight, I turn and survey the empty courtyard. I enter the empty hall. As does Saturday, Sunday serves as a day of rest, and without Holden and Quinn, the castle feels quiet, desolate. Images of Abaddon, Lucifer, Sonia, Thanatos, and Theron flit through my mind. The second pair of my most trusted guards, Adam and Nicholas, wait halfway down the passage. Approaching them, I invite them to share breakfast with me, Alfreda, and my parents. I pray this will keep Father from pestering me with worries, but I make a mental note to spend more time with him over the next two days. With Holden gone, I will have ample time to fill.

As I hoped, breakfast passes with light chat about families and weather. I walk with Mother and Father in the garden afterwards. I do my best to talk to her as I would when Father is not present, but it is not the same. Still, I share my fears for Aleem and what the High Council will decide: Will they side with Regin? How political is the group? Regin is not without esteem. Although Keeper of the lesser ring in the kingdom, he has served as such for almost twenty years, a stint which makes him well known on the council.

Spending the rest of the day hunting on horseback with Adam and Nicholas, I dine with Mother and Father and play the harp for them in the study. By dark, I have little energy to think of anything save sleep.

I find a wooden box sitting on my bed when I reach my chamber. Thinking the situation odd, I call for Grant.

As I bend to lift the box, Grant swipes it from atop the mattress. "Have you gone mad? You know not what this is."

One of the council guards clears his throat. "If I may? Alfreda left it for you. I heard her talking with Sara, the baker. She said Aleem's wife, Merry Mae, had a page bring it to the castle."

Grant narrows his eyes. "Nicholas, go fetch Alfreda. We will make sure of this story."

The box held away from his body, Grant exits into the passage. Within seconds, we hear the beating of wings, and Nicholas arrives with Alfreda. She corroborates the story, noting she had not looked inside yet. Asking us to stay well back, Grant sets the box on the floor, unfastens the latch in a slow fashion, and lifts the lid.

He draws a small scroll from inside. "Someone go get a taster."

"Grant, I believe you are being a bit dramatic." I reach for the parchment.

He leans away. "One can never be too sure. Does Merry Mae knit?"

Alfreda and I look at each and shrug. The taster arrives, and Grant hands the fae the scroll, ordering him to taste it.

"You want me to eat the scroll? It is likely that any poison on paper would be slow acting or dangerous if inhaled."

Grant sets his hands on his hips. "Then read it and take it somewhere to dispose of it."

The taster takes a few steps back and unties the bow holding the parchment. Opening the document, he reads aloud. "Dearest Queen Titania, I had this yarn spun, and the color reminded me of your hair. Aleem and I have been so grateful for your friendship, I made this shawl for you to show my appreciation. All the best, Merry Mae."

"See? It is perfectly safe." I step towards the box.

Grant blocks my approach. He lifts the garment from the box, holding it at arm's length. The red threads glisten in the candlelight as if they are spun with scarlet silver. Squishing the shawl in his hands, he turns it over and over, inspecting it.

"It is going to be threads when you are done." Alfreda scolds.

"It seems to be safe." Grant hands me the wrap.

"This is so beautiful." I lay the shawl over my shoulders, noticing the odd weight. "I will write a note right away inviting Merry Mae to tea tomorrow to thank her. It will help us both pass the time."

Alfreda's eyes dart to the council guards. "Are you sure that is wise?"

I spin towards my study. "Well, I will at least write to thank her, and perhaps I will have both her and Aleem to supper once the trial has ended."

Penning the note at my desk, I leave it with Grant to find a page to deliver it on the morrow. I enter my chamber, hugging the soft garment to me. As I close the door, my hand runs across a bump in the yarn. Removing the shawl to inspect it, I find it littered with lumps of thread and realize these may be the source of the weight. I squeeze the ball of yarn in my hand to find it rock hard. *Rock.* I fly into my closet and alight on the stone floor. Prying the strands back, I find that my thought is right. Merry Mae has knitted the twelve ring crystals into this shawl for me. I bless Aleem for his cunning.

But what to do with the garment? If I hide it and it is found, it will raise suspicion. Opening a trunk, I tuck the shawl under a jacket of the same thickness. Once the trial is over and the guards leave, I can extract the crystals and hide them under the stone of my closet.

Sleep comes fast, but I wake with a start as the same images from the night before dance through my brain: Abaddon, Lucifer, Sonia, Thanatos, and Theron. I must find a way to enter Upper Earth and speak with the witches of the trinity. I need to know if Hunter lives and what happened when they traveled to Lower Earth.

But those worries must wait. For today, I have solstice celebration planning to attend. After breakfast and a short walk with Mother, I enter the small hall to find the advisors sipping tea and conversing.

"Queen." Bran steps forwards. "We did not expect to see you so soon. Are you sure you are ready to work on affairs of the state?"

"Of course I am. We have celebrated with a tour of the kingdom, I have had several day's rest, and I now wish to continue with my duties. Please, gentlemen, let me know what I have missed." I motion to the table.

We review the accounts, army status, and early crop reports. Little appears different save one farmer reporting a small group of locusts that ate the leaves from the bushes of a berry patch. *Locusts…* My shoulders shiver. I imagine thousands of the dark insects Mother smooshed with her foot.

When I express concern, the advisors assure me the scientists have weighed in. Although early in the season for grasshoppers, the wasps, who feed on locust eggs, will check the locust population, as often occurs.

With these issues solved, we turn to the planning of the solstice celebration, and by the end of the day, we have formal orders written for invitations, food, candles, flowers, and fireworks. We tour the shed where the games are kept. Accounting for fae assigned to each task, we leave all the directions with the respective parties.

I insist the advisors stay for the evening meal. Each accepts the invitation, and Father and General Kane join us. While part of me tires of the task of seeking out each advisor, asking as to their family and villagers, I feel more connected to my people, just as I experienced on the tour. *Before.* Yes, before the trip was interrupted by the incident with the trinity witches and then Regin's accusation of treason against the High Council. I smooth my skirt. *All will be well.* Still, I wish there were some way to know what happened today, what discussions were held, how the other Ring Keepers would judge Aleem.

"You seem lost in your thoughts." Father walks me to my chamber after the meal, music, and goodbyes.

"I am thinking of the council and what they will decide."

Taking my hand, he covers it with his other. "I am told you spent the whole day with the advisors, seeing to affairs of the kingdom and planning for the solstice."

"You have people reporting to you of my activities?"

He lifts an eyebrow. "It was once my kingdom and my castle. I cannot stop thinking of it."

"Does it make you sad not to be involved? I would be happy to have you in our talks."

"No, it is as it should be. I have enough with my research."

"The witches. What have you found?"

"Only lots of stories, some horrific. But none of significance to what may be occurring in Lower Earth now."

"Tell me."

"It is late. And I should attend to your mother. I shall tell you another time."

"Okay, Father. Give Mother my love."

I kiss his cheek and slide my hand from his palms. Approaching my door, I note the presence of the council guards. *Ugh!* How I desire them gone. *One more day,* I tell myself. I shut out the anxieties, for I will never sleep if I do not. Inside my room, Alfreda has urns of hot water, and I lift one after the other, pouring the steaming liquid into my tub. Lowering myself into the bath, I can think of no better cure for a long, fretful day. Save to be with Holden, perhaps. I smile. Tomorrow, tomorrow *night,* we shall celebrate the end of this ghastly affair.

⬥⬥⬥⬥

THE DRAGON, ABADDON, LUCIFER, *Thanatos, Theron.*

I pop my eyes open. The room is pitch black, so I reach for the tinder box lying on my table and light the candle. The dancing flame casts odd shadows on the wall, and I hug my covers to me. I note the time: four. It will not be light for another hour, but with my heart pounding in my chest, I doubt I will sleep again. Swinging my legs off the side of the bed, I retrieve my robe.

Cold stone greets my soles, and I shiver. Candle in hand, I exit my room, nod to my guards and the council guards, and proceed to the kitchen for tea. Next, I make for the library and find Father's stack of books. Noting they came from Lindleton, the kingdom lying under Europe, I open the top one, inscribed with Sonia's name. The date of the last entry reads September 21, 2017, the fall equinox, not quite nine months prior.

Sonia appeared in the sky this night. I could hardly believe my eyes. How did she escape her entombment? And worse yet, the being with her, I believe him to be a hybrid. They are siring them again. Nothing good ever comes of

Sonia's hybrids. Although I believe this one may belong to her son, Thanatos.

I run my fingers over the images. The same faces that woke me. Theron. The hybrid they write of is Theron. Thanatos sired Hunter and Theron. Like two sides of a coin, good and evil. I say a quiet prayer to the goddesses that Hunter still lives. *Thanatos is Sonia's son?* I turn the page to the prior entry, penned seventy-two years prior, and read of how the witches cast a spell to put Sonia to sleep. Bending over, I can hardly believe my eyes. At six thousand years old, they expected her to die in the coma.

Her physical body should be dead now, but it is not her form I fear, it is the power contained in a soul that has persevered over six thousand years. My mind swirls with the idea. I read page after page of her acts against the vampires. I realize most fae believe vampires to be evil as well. Those beliefs have been hard for my father's generation to let go of. We are still forbidden to form alliances with them. Although a hybrid, Alena forms the trinity. The witches and fae must recognize that. Perhaps she will herald a new peace between us all.

The door creaks open, and Father's face appears in the doorway. "Do not read those. They will haunt you as they do me."

"Is that what has you up at this hour?"

"Well, that and the sun." He points to the window.

I note the beam of light between the shutter panes and close the text. "Finally. Should we get breakfast, perhaps eat in the courtyard?"

"Eager to start the day?"

"I am ready for this day to be done, our fae called to the trial returning home where they belong."

"You sound so sure they will be found without fault."

"I cannot see it any other way. We need to continue the battle against the dark souls that live beneath us. If the witches have the same goal, why not aid them?"

"When you are older, you will understand."

"I pray I do not. We will not defeat these spirits alone. There are too many of them now."

One of his eyebrows pops up, and I realize I have said too much. But there is no way to take back my words.

"You never told me who you saw that day in Lower Earth."

"Or who I see every night in my dreams. Abaddon, Lucifer, a dragon I believe to be Sonia, Theron, and Thanatos."

His knees buckle, and he reaches for the table.

I catch his torso and scoot a chair behind him. "Father, what happened?"

Wide eyes meet mine. "You are right, daughter. If there is a trinity in addition to Abaddon and Lucifer, we may all be doomed."

Chapter 4

"Why have you not shared this before?" I slide into the chair beside him.

Finally, he realizes the enormity of the situation, but it had not been my intent to burden him with my nightmares. "It is nothing, Father. Stress over the trial, I am sure. Once the trial is finished and all returns to normal, I can go to Upper Earth, find out whether Hunter lives, and speak with the trinity about what has passed."

He shakes his head. "This should not be your concern. You have a kingdom and a realm to protect here."

Ahh! My brain screams in frustration. If I hear those words one more time, I may go mad. I grip his arm. "But do you not see, Father? They are one and the same. To protect our realm, we must deal with these evil souls. I believe the witches of the trinity can help. If we all work together, we shall find a solution. Otherwise, the demons will continue to send monsters like the kobold from the deep."

"But it is impossible. A soul cannot cease to exist, even an evil one."

I kneel beside him and lower my voice to a whisper. "How can you believe in *The One* and not know that somehow these demons can be ended?"

His eyes soften. "Yes, I believe in *The One*, a fae to end all evil. That fae may very well be you. Why else would a fae speak as you do? Think as you do? Have such radical ideas?"

"Holden believes there may be multiple ones, that the witches of the trinity may be their one."

"And this is why he pledges himself to you?"

My face warms as I remember Holden's confession of love. "I believe so. But my ideas are not so radical. The fae of my generation do not believe as yours did. We see the beings above: witches, vampires, merfolk, werewolves, humans, and we see them as *beings*, not sired from light or darkness, but from the universe."

"It may be such. It is not for me to judge. The Creator, or the goddesses alone, knows the souls of beings. I only know that they are eternal."

"Well, perhaps they can be expunged from Lower Earth, entombed, or turned to the light."

He lays his hands on his belly as gurgles emit from his middle. "Oh, to be young and so full of ideas again. But I believe breakfast should be my next task."

"Let us sit in the light and not think of such heavy things." I say the words but have little hope I will ever pass a second of my life not thinking of my purpose in this realm.

Standing, I offer my arm. He grips the sides of the chair and pushes to a stand. We wind to his chamber to fetch Mother and then to the courtyard. Fruit and pastries greet us, and I realize that by tomorrow, I will be having breakfast with Holden once again. For today, I am glad there is much work. The advisors in charge of livestock and crops are to present their full reports of the plantings and new births.

After the meal, I walk with Mother, as is our habit, then find the advisors in the study.

Bran sits in front of stacks of ledgers and proceeds to show me the reports on amounts of land farmed for each crop in every village.

By midday, I fight to keep my eyes open and suggest we take a rest for a meal. I flit to my room and splash my face with water. Hearing voices in the hall, I exit to find Foster arguing with Timothy.

My heart skips a beat. For Foster to dare show his face here, something must be amiss. "What is the matter?"

"Queen, I must speak with you. My father has fallen ill, and I wish that you find the finest of medicines in all the realm. I believe you have what we need." His wide eyes do not leave my gaze.

His words make no sense. And if something had befallen his father, I would have been alerted. Alfreda knows I want such news. "Let us speak in the study."

"Alfreda said they may be in your chest."

Confusion fills my mind. "You spoke with Alfreda?"

"Yes." He motions to my room. "We should hurry. He is most sick."

Foster corrals me through the door and towards my closet. "The High Council guards will be here any second. They are bringing you to stand trial for treason as well. Aleem sent me to get the crystals. It will not look good if they are found in your chamber."

Shadows pass over the floor, and I look to the window to find the sky darkened with a battalion of fae. I grab Foster's arm, meaning to give him directions with haste.

He lays his hand atop mine. "I know what to do."

"What do you mean?"

"I heard you. I do not know how you did that. But I heard your request in my mind."

My powers?

"Go, quick."

Leaving him, I exit into the hall to find all the guards gazing out the window.

"I saw fae approaching from my window. Do we know who this is?"

Timothy pushes open the pane, jumps to the sill, and blows into his horn. Grant, Adam, and Nicholas are beside me in seconds. Grabbing my sword, bow, and quiver, we march out to the courtyard to greet the visitors.

"I do not believe you are at war, are you, Queen?" One of the council guards flanks Grant.

"We are not. And I do not expect hostile fae, but one can never be too careful. Who knows what the spirits of the deep will cast upon us next." My heart thuds in my chest, praying Foster accomplishes his task.

"Queen, stay back." Grant blocks my path with his arm as the others proceed before us.

It is not a minute before the battalion of fae land outside the castle gate, dressed in council uniforms.

"What in heaven's name?" Grant mutters under his breath.

"Here to charge me with treason. Foster warned me just now."

"How many do they think it takes to escort you back to the council?"

"They mean to search the castle, I believe."

"Preposterous."

I see my guards open the gates and allow ten of the council guards to enter. My side ticks as they cross the courtyard. I force a smile and survey the men. All eyes fix on my forehead. I lift my chin. "Gentlemen, to what do we owe the pleasure?"

The front guard lowers his gaze to mine. Clearing his throat, he retrieves a scroll from his pack. "Queen Titania, an order from the High Council."

He offers me their decree. Opening it, I scan the lines.

*As the High Council has reason to believe Queen Titania of Aubren entered Lower Earth without such authority, and further allowed a dark being of Upper Earth to pass through our realm, endangering all—*I scan to the last line—*Queen Titania of Aubren is hereby charged with treason against the realm and is ordered to appear before the High Council at once. Further, it is ordered her castle be searched and attendants and guards questioned.*

My face flames with heat. *How dare they? Charge me with treason after I saved the realm from being overrun by the mutant kobold?* I release a slow breath. "Of course. Whatever the High Council desires. I will come with you now. I have nothing to hide."

I spin to face my guards. "Grant and Adam will travel with me. Timothy and Nicholas, see to Mother and Father.

Do *not* leave them unattended. Until I return, former King Oberon will rule in my stead. All of you are witnesses to such."

Out of the corner of my eye, I catch sight of General Kane approaching. Praying Foster has achieved his goal, I repeat my orders to him. "I do not believe I will be away long. Please send word if there are any concerns."

"My queen." Kane bows to me.

"Heavens, is it true?" Alfreda's voice sounds from the crowd gathered behind me.

Catching sight of her pushing through the castle fae, I sigh. Poor woman will probably die of anxiety over the drama I put her through.

"Titania." She wraps her arms around my middle. "I do not have a bag for you."

I pat her back. "All will be well. There is no need. Take care of Mother and Father."

"I will, of course." Stepping back, she curtsies. "Blessed be."

"Blessed be." I nod to her.

I wonder at the fact that it is her I am most anxious for. Mother and Father will be fine. My kingdom and castle will be fine, especially with my special guard in place. An incident like this weakens me in the eyes of those who may challenge me. But we will hear of any plot to take my throne. I shall only be gone a day, two at most. And once the council knows all, they will pledge support to my cause.

Turning to the High Council guards, I indicate I am ready. We take to the air, Grant and Adam at each side.

Clearing the castle tower, I catch sight of a red-headed fae. *Foster.* From the height I am unable to discern anything from him. I reach out with my mind, wondering if my magick may aid me, but hear nothing. *How inopportune a gift,* I wonder. But I shall not begrudge a gift that has saved my rule and my life twice. The goddesses will provide that which I need to accomplish what I am destined to do.

My castle, the gardens, the meadow beyond, and the forest become a miniature landscape as we climb. I beat my wings in slow, strong strokes, calming my anger with each breath.

How can they not see that I saved our realm from the kobold and possibly prevented further such invasions by aiding the trinity witches? And does every generation feel thus, frustrated with the old guard who do not seem to be able to think in new ways?

I should not fear, for the goddesses supported me thus far, and they will continue to turn the hearts and minds of those who do not understand.

Assured by those thoughts, I turn my deliberations to what is ahead. I recall the names of the council mediators, their posts and kingdoms. It will be to my benefit that I bond with them, appeal to their sentiment. The desert looms, and we leave my kingdom, crossing into Hilbron. Our Kingdom of Aubren, occupying the eastern half of the land lying under Australia, shares a long western border with Hilbron. Many fae may not notice or know the exact spot, but I fly these borders often and know them by heart.

Hilbron's desert occupies much of the land, with fae residing only near the western coast. Their population is but half of Aubren's, being chiefly fisherman. But I doubt I shall eat seafood tonight. Further into the desert, light reflects off a structure. Formed over six thousand years ago of mud bricks of the desert sand, the stone shines like a diamond on a sand blanket. Our forefathers felt the location would help keep their deliberations secret. Crossing the desert on foot would mean sure death. Anyone approaching from the air could be spotted with ease.

As we draw near, I marvel at the architecture. It appears smaller than I remember from childhood. A perfect circle with concentric rows of benches plunge into the brown barren landscape, some hundred feet into the sand. A single arched entry and aisle leads down to the entrenched stage. I swallow, knowing I shall soon be dead center, the object of every attention. Descending, I see a single fae beside the opening. His light hair and bronze wings are unmistakable. *Holden.* My shoulders relax. He, Aleem and his judges, and Father all believe in me and the role I may play in our histories. The others will too.

The council guards land, and I touch down behind them. The grand arch rises some fifty feet above me, and I scan the hundred plus fae waiting inside.

My stomach turns and side ticks. *Breathe.*

Motion catches my eye, and my attention turns to Holden.

Holding my gaze, he bows in front of me.

Frustrated by the need for formality, I offer my hand. "Holden, my Fae at Arms, rise."

"Queen Titania." He kisses my fingers. "May we—"

"Prince Holden, your place." I look up to see Holden's eldest brother, King Luther, exiting the arena.

Monarchs do not usually attend High Council proceedings. Of this, I am sure. *Why is he here? Holden's place?* As my Fae at Arms, he should be at my side, but we stand on Luther's land, and Luther is Holden's king.

I raise my chin. "King Luther, it has been lovely to see your kingdom from the air. And I appreciate Prince Holden greeting me."

Luther spins away, and his raised wings block his face from my view. "Holden."

Holden's face turns bright red, and his wide eyes hold mine as he backs away then turns to follow his brother.

Beside me, Adam and Grant close ranks. My heart races. *Luther treats me as an outcast? Has he already passed judgment, or does he fear affiliation? What of innocent until proven guilty?* Hunter sided with me in wishing to aid the trinity. And he will defend me.

Mother's premonition crosses through my mind. *You need them.*

What if Luther forbids Holden to return to Aubren? My lungs catch at the thought of losing him. *No, this will not be.* I cannot bear even to imagine this fate. A group of fae cross through the arch to me. Red sashes cross their white robes. I fight a cringe as I behold the garb of the council leaders.

The head mediator reaches me first, his eyes fixed on my forehead. "Queen Titania, we are ready for you."

I scan the faces before me. All eyes fix on the stones protruding from my brow. Heavens be, Alfreda had been right. They will see nothing more than my differences. But Keepers and judges are gifted with special powers. It is not so different than that. None of them have been to Lower Earth and come back alive. To my knowledge, I am the only fae who has. They should be heralding my cunning victory. Ignorant old fae. *Titania, your stubbornness,* a little voice reminds me. *And pride and greed.*

Forcing a smile, I curtsy. "Thank you, Keeper Zekial. I appreciate the opportunity to apprise the High Council of my experience in person."

He glances to those beside him. "You have read the decree, correct?"

"I have." I keep my eyes trained on his face.

"Then let us begin."

The nine mediators turn towards the entrance.

Releasing a slow, deep breath, I follow them to the tall arch.

The council guards block our way as we try to pass under.

The mediator before me spins to face me. "No guards, only you."

I look at Grant then Adam. "All will be well. Please, wait for me here."

Grant nods, and my guards step out of the line.

I lift my chin and fix my eyes on the center stage. Proceeding down the steps, I see the arena rise around me. I place my hand on my sword, praying to the goddesses for wisdom and courage. My heart thuds in my chest as silence settles over the crowd. A vulture calls from above, and I curse the dark creature. I have done nothing wrong. I am a hero to this realm.

My stomach rolls and breath catches as we reach the center stage, and I take in the sea of white around me. It is dotted with splotches of color, and I recognize the faces of each monarch of the nine kingdoms. My survey ends with the contingency from Aubren. Keeper Regin, who brought the charges against Aleem; Aleem and his judges; and finally, Quinn, who stands chin high and shoulders back.

I have no idea what has passed in the last day and a half but guess it cannot be partial to me considering the charges. *Has Aleem been cleared, or did they take his position?* He still wears the robe of a Keeper, as do his judges. *Have they transferred the blame from him to me?* For such an act cannot go unpunished or every fae of the land would be at their folly to ignore the orders of the High Council. But therein lies the problem. No fae would ever think to. It is not in our nature, save for me, perhaps. We are followers, keepers of the realm, protectors of the weak and vulnerable. And fae never put others in harm's way. *Nor did you,* my psyche affirms.

Zekial motions to a bench.

I raise my wings and let them fall in a slow, controlled fashion and sit down. They shall see this young queen will not be bullied or intimidated by their air of judgment. I focus on Zekial.

The other mediators sit on a long bench that forms an arc behind him. Above me, the rest of the fae settle in the pews, and a hush falls over the space again.

Zekial winds behind a lectern and opens a thick, leather-bound book. He dips a quill in ink and lifts his face to mine. "Tell us, Queen Titania. Start at the beginning. How did you come to the decision first that you should lead the kobold into Lower Earth? Second, how did you escape from that space? Lastly, why did you ignore the order of this High Council, and Fae Law, by opening rings for the witches of Upper Earth to pass through our realm?"

I start my story, projecting my voice so all may hear, telling them of the idea to lure the kobold into Lower Earth so they would be lost forever. Then, I relay the ever-so-slight white lie that the evil spirit Lucifer, or whoever he was, slammed me against the ring, and it released me back into Middle Earth. I repeat it just as I have each time I was asked.

"And the stones on your forehead? Explain those." Zekial prompts.

"I had markings on my forehead before, as many fae do. When I landed in the forest, hair and wings singed from the heat of passing through the ring, they were there. I have no explanation other than that."

He inquires if I went into Lower Earth with no escape plan. I guess they must know all these answers as Aleem and Regin would have explained such. I detail how I started to open the ring with the crystals, but they were lost when the evil spirit attacked me. Noting the Keepers seated above me hold conversations with their neighbors, I know this is the story they have heard before.

"And why would you open our rings to a vampire-witch hybrid? This creature could have decimated our entire fae population."

The arena falls silent again, and I stand. "Alena is not just any vampire hybrid. She is a witch of the trinity of witches. I knew if they wished to enter Lower Earth, it must be for good reason. It is not just Lucifer and Abaddon that preside there now. Three powerful fallen witches have joined them."

Voices rise again. Zekial pounds a gavel on the lectern. "This is not of our concern. We defend our realm and guard Upper Earth. What happens in either place, after we have done our best to fulfill our purpose, is none of our concern."

I see nods of consent throughout the rows.

You will be the crazy fae queen who aims to defeat all evil. You will not succeed. It is not possible. Lucifer's words slither through my mind.

"It has been asserted by Keeper Regin that you forced Aleem to open the rings. Do you refute this?"

"I hardly forced Aleem. We voted. Keeper Regin and his first judge, as well as Quinn, voted against opening the ring. Aleem, his three judges, Prince Holden, former King Oberon, and I were in favor."

"But Prince Holden served as your Fae at Arms. He was pledged to you. If Regin's other two judges had been present, they would have sided with Regin as well. They have testified such."

I ball my fists. "Quinn serves as my heir presumptive, so some would say he is in my service as well. I did not force any opinions. I have not punished those holding different ones from mine. And do you not respect the opinion of my father, who served as ruler of Aubren for over thirty years?"

Zekial's eyes narrow. "The rings were opened at your suggestion. It was your idea. You put this realm in jeopardy."

I imagine him standing over me, crooked finger pointed at my face. He may as well be doing this. They did not come into this arena with open minds. *Fair trial? Where are the goddesses?*

Standing, I begin to spin, hoping to see even one look of understanding. Hard stares meet my gaze. Turning back to face Zekial, I—

"I cede my post. It was my lapse of judgment. You see her conviction. I am an old man, and this position, the burden of the job, takes its toll. I forgot my role as upholder of the laws of this council. I cede my post, as does my first judge. It was our fault not to check the ambition of a young monarch." Aleem's hoarse voice sounds over the arena.

No, my brain screams. He cannot martyr himself thus, ruin his legacy after such a respected career.

"Especially for a crazy girl queen," Lucifer whispers.

"Appoint Regin's first judge in my stead. He is ready to rise. Trained by Regin, he will serve the realm well."

No. Regin's first judge in charge of my ring? It shall not be such. I will never fulfill my destiny with these short-term thinkers controlling my kingdom. The goddesses must stop this. The High Council will see reason.

Regin stands. "I assert Ishmel is ready."

Heavens be. This is madness. "There is no need for Aleem to cede his position. He was not at fault, nor was I. I am sure Prince Holden, even Quinn, testified as to the safety measures taken when we allowed the trinity to pass through."

"And did this supposed trinity achieve their goal? Are we any safer than before you jeopardized all the fae of the realm?" Zekial steps around the lectern towards me.

"I do not know. We have not been allowed to learn more because of your rules."

"So, you observe them *now* when you fear action against you?"

"I was not charged by Regin. I respect them because there is no pressing need to do otherwise."

"So, you admit, if *you* decided it was important, you would ask for them to be opened again."

"Yes, to defend this realm. Stop those that may threaten the lives of holy creatures."

"Holy creatures? And do you propose a vampire-witch hybrid is a holy creature?" Zekial steps to within two feet of me.

"I judge beings not for their physical state or heritage, but on their intentions and actions."

"And how can you know the true heart of this vampire girl? Is there a way for you to truly know her soul? The witches' souls?"

Spit lands on my face. Ignoring it, I hold his stare. "There is not."

His eyes cut to those sitting above. He rotates a quarter turn, then another, and another, and back to face me.

"But is there not a way to know their minds? You also broke our tenets when you entered Upper Earth with your soldiers to fight alongside the trinity and their vampire army."

This holds as a more egregious offense than the others, I assume. Our Fae Law, millennia old, has held that we are forbidden to interact with vampires on the tenet they are soulless creatures of the darkness.

"A witch known as Sonia cast souls of fallen witches into vampires, stealing their lives from them. Surely you know this already. If Sonia means to end the vampires, who would be next? The mermaids, the wolves, us? Sonia is one of the souls now in league with Lucifer. She must be stopped." I look up to the fae gathered with me. Surely, they will understand this logic.

"We know of Sonia and her magick. But what she does to vampires is of no consequence to us. They prey on innocent people. We should be aiding Sonia in that regard."

"Centuries ago, perhaps. Very few of them now. There are humans that commit murder. I do not see you zipping to Upper Earth to stop this."

Zekial's face reddens, nostrils flare.

I feel the heat from his body. *Why do I anger him such?* I lower my chin. "You are right. We are forbidden to commune with the vampires. Perhaps that decision was in haste. I held compassion for Hunter's case. I fear that Sonia has grown too powerful and that her goals are not pure."

His lips form a slight smile. "Yes, and when the kobold came, you were not there. You were aiding the witches of the trinity."

He does not like me, means to remove me from my throne. That is why the other monarchs have been summoned. They would not stand for having a ruler cast away by the High Council. But if they see it as just, they will accept it.

"Those in my army will attest that I arrived within an hour of the attack. Further, there was no way for my soldiers to prevail. There were ten kobold for every one of my soldiers. My leading the kobold into Lower Earth saved hundreds of my soldiers, hundreds of fae."

"I believe we have heard all. Is there anything you wish to add on your behalf?"

What can I say that will sway them? They know all the facts. There is nothing more. My head swims, but I plan to say my piece with slow, definitive words. I will not appear as the insane girl they have perhaps heard rumors of. "The safety of my people, this realm, and my duty as a fae, defending Upper Earth from the evils of the deep, are my every waking thought. As you have witnessed, I would give all for my people, even my own life."

I raise my eyes and scan the crowd. Solemn faces meet my gaze.

Zekial clears his throat. He rounds back towards the mediators. They rise and approach, speaking in hushed voices.

I raise my chin and fix my eyes on the top of the arch. It will not do me well to try and discern their words. The goddesses have given me what I needed to fulfill my duties thus far.

The group disbands, mediators taking their seats and Zekial stepping to the lectern. "Titania, the High Council will deliberate your sentence. Word will be sent once we choose a verdict. Please, stay within the borders of Hilbron. Aleem, you and your judges may take your leave as well."

My eyes cut to those seated above me. I dig my nails into my palms and refocus on Zekial. "Of course. I shall enjoy the villages on the coast while you deliberate."

I stride, step by step, around the seated mediators, onto the walk lined with the Keepers, my head high. I smile and duck my chin as I meet each gaze. *Is this the right thing to do?* I have no idea, but I will not give them the satisfaction of seeing my fear. *What if they do remove Aleem and name Ishmel Keeper of the Daintree Ring?* Surely, they will not find guilt with me though. Because if I am found at fault then Aleem, his three judges, Holden, and Father would be guilty too. Once the Keepers stand too high above me to read their faces, I train my eyes on the opening.

Grant slides to my side as soon as I exit the arch. "What happened? What did they decide? We could not discern anything."

Hearing footsteps behind me, I see a group of fae led by Quinn approaching. Regin's judges follow him as well as Aleem's. Holden brings up the rear.

Quinn greets me with a kiss and smile. "Cousin, you spoke well today. May the goddesses be with you."

"Do you really mean that?"

"You think I would have you found guilty? Removed from your throne? I do not wish that. You made a bad decision. That does not make you a bad ruler or guardian of our realm. I pray you know that my allegiance lies with you."

Guardian, I favor that term. I wrap my arms around him, hugging him close. "It is good to hear, cousin."

My muscles relax with his touch. It seems odd that this embrace brings me comfort. Perhaps the tenet rings true. Blood holds thicker than water. I raise my head, and my eyes meet Holden's.

His gaze drops to the floor as guards wearing his father's insignia join him.

Releasing Quinn, I step back and force a smile, trying to ignore Holden and the other judges and guards milling about.

They, too, will witness that I have nothing to fear from the High Council. "I would like to enjoy the coast. I have not been to Hilbron in a long time, but I remember the wonderful markets of Leeward."

Quinn and my guards stare at me with wide eyes.

I look between them. "Have you not been to the western coast before? It is magnificent."

"Of course, as you wish." Grant steps towards me, shedding his cloak. "Perhaps you may wear this?"

Daring not to speak it with so many around, I realize his intention. He does not wish for me to draw a crowd. I guess many have heard tales of the singed queen, expelled from Lower Earth and now endowed with rocks embedded on her forehead. I take the garment and, turning it wrong side out, fix the hood low over my brow. Motion catches my eye, and I see Holden and four guards take to the sky. I guess his brother has forbidden him to be in my presence. Steeling my emotions against the anger, hurt, and fear, I focus on those around me.

Adam wears his cloak inside out, and Quinn produces a traveling cape to cover his green vest. Ignoring my side tick, I jump into the sky, grateful Hilbron's capital lies south. King Luther will see. I shall be cleared of the charges, and all shall be well. We head due west and then cut south, landing at the outskirts of the village. Weaving through the town, we reach the wharf where vendors' carts line the squares. With the midday crowd, my shoulders release their tension.

I may be any girl out for a stroll with her brothers, or at least one brother. Quinn and I have similar enough coloring with our green wings.

With light undersides and dark exteriors, Grant and Adam sport the traditional color of warrior's wings. The dark sheen of their wings transforms from brown to purple to blue depending on the angle of light. Not that one could discern these colors now with Grant's folded tightly to his back and Adam's covered by his cloak. Those, too, would draw attention to them as military fae. These positions, like most in our realm, tend to be passed from father to son.

My thoughts skip to Foster and the shawl. I wonder if I judged him too harshly for siding with Kane. Perhaps I should not have been so quick to condemn. Such an unlikely soldier, but he seems true. For the goddesses would not have allowed him to hear my thoughts if he could not be trusted.

Clutching Grant's cloak around my neck, I refocus on the village before me. The air smells of salt, and gulls circle and call from the sky. Bells toll from ships' decks. Carts' wheels clack against the cobbled streets. Hooves pound on the grooves in the stone, worn from decades of use. I approach a vendor. Ribbons of every color line the sides of her wagon. Thinking back to my little cabin in the woods, the one where Father, Mother, and I might escape to if my title were to be stripped, I decide that a small room overlooking the sea may also suffice.

Quinn's arm hooks though mine. "What do you want? A ribbon for your hair?"

His touch startles me, and I again force my thoughts to the present. There is no need for worries of a life banished from society. The council will decide rightly. For now, I shall enjoy my afternoon of freedom from worry of evil spirits, crops, and my future.

I pour my energy into my best smile and lift a ribbon from the cart. "I love this deep green."

"And it shall be, cousin." Quinn produces a coin from under his cape and hands it to the woman.

"May I?" The woman holds her palm out.

Placing the ribbon on her hand, I study her face. She closes her eyes and mumbles a few words. Popping them open she extends her arm to me, twisting her hand to let the silk strand fall to my palm.

"A blessing for the road." One eyebrow shoots up. "And warning. Beware of those who seek to pass judgment."

My shoulders shudder. As if I do not have enough worries of my own. *Those who seek to pass judgment? The High Council? Does this mean I am to be found guilty?*

"Come, cousin. There are many other carts." Quinn wraps an arm around my back.

I hook my arm around his waist. I will not think of it. We stroll through the streets browsing the wares, buying trinkets—a doll for Grant's daughter, a toy boat for Adam's son, and snacking on fruits as if there were no cares in the world. We dance with the fiddler, adding coins to his case. As the sun sinks low, we walk along the shore. I jump to the top of a stone wall, savoring the warm rays on my skin, the heat the cloak holds next to my body. The waves swell, crashing with thunderous roars below me. I breathe in the salt air, heavy with the smells of the day's fortunes.

I spin to face the others. "I believe we should find some dinner. Some wonderful seafood and ale."

"How will we know when the council has decided?" Adam squints at me.

I point to guards posted around the dwelling behind us. "I know you noticed our company. I am sure they will alert me."

Beside a butcher shop, two figures back to the shadows. *Did they think we would not see?*

"Do not fret, friend." I point my toes and proceed along a thin strip of stone as an acrobat on a rope. "All will be well. You shall see. Have I not endured harsher challenges?"

"Nay, you have. Come down. I have no money left to buy you a new dress and myself a new cloak if you fall in the sea." Grant posts his hands on his hips.

I jump to the street and hook my elbow through his. "How soon you forget I can fly. Let us find a warm tavern."

Quinn and Adam flank us, and I realize this may be what my life would be like if my brothers lived. We could mosey through Capitolshire, or any other village, whenever we liked, buying whatever our hearts may desire. But this is enough. I shall be happy with what the goddesses have provided. And they have always given me all that I need.

We pass an alley, and a cold breeze rushes over my face. It reminds me of the air of Lower Earth—moist and cold against my skin. Motion catches my eye, and I see figures running through the passage towards us. I grip Grant's arm tightly and, under my cloak, slide my dagger from its pocket.

Chapter 5

THE LEADER OF THE GROUP SHEDS his hood, and when I see a blond head, I realize it is Holden.

My heart soars. He has not forsaken me. *Why would I ever doubt him?* His devotion is proven, sentiments announced. *What more could I ask?* Abandoning Grant and the others, I skip to Holden. His arms wrap around me, and I am home. The smell of his hair, like wheat and honey, and the warmth of his body, fills me.

"I am sorry, so sorry." Running his hands down my arms, he grips my fingers. "Luther has forbidden me to be seen with you until your innocence is upheld."

"Is he still with the High Council?"

"Yes. I have heard nothing yet. Are you okay?" Removing my hood, he traces a finger down my cheek.

"Of course. We have passed the day exploring this beautiful village and are headed to find supper."

"Marta's Tavern is quite nice. Tell them you are a friend of mine."

I place the cloak over my head. "I do not believe that is a good idea."

"I see your wisdom in that. We should know something from the council before nightfall. I will find you afterwards." His hand wraps around the back of my neck.

I wish we were alone in my forest, worrying for nothing. "Thank you for coming."

"I hated leaving you like that. But I want to respect my brother's wishes."

"I understand your dilemma." Detest it, but I know the duty to family.

"I hate this." He presses his forehead to mine.

Raising my chin, I push to my toes and kiss his lips. I savor the feel of his soft skin on mine, the tinge of salt. My hood falls to my back, but I do not care. He wraps his arms around me. Footfalls on rock catch my attention.

Adding one quick kiss to his lips, I step back.

"Cousin, Prince Holden, your coverings." Quinn's tight eyes widen. "You draw attention I am sure will not be good for either of you."

He cocks his head to the end of the alley where a group stands, gawking at us. Little light filters into the passage, but perhaps it is enough to illuminate a fair-headed prince and my jewel-endowed brow.

Cheeks flaming, I tug my hood over my head. I must get my emotions and impulses under control with regard to Holden. *But how can I when every cell of my body, every neuron of my mind, longing of my soul, celebrates being with him?*

Holden grips my hand. "I will see you tonight."

"Yes." I release his fingers as Quinn tugs at my arm.

We trudge down the alley, Quinn's arm firmly around my back. I glance back at Holden's retreating form, unable to breathe. *You must believe all shall be well.* Not only for your sake but for the realm. I exhale and force myself to stay in the present. Holden loves me. He would never forsake that. Also, he believes in the cause to end these evil spirits as much as I. Fate, the prophecies, they both lie on our side. *And you are a queen. A queen.* This fact brings me back to the current moment.

Quinn rebukes me in hushed words as we tramp towards my guards. Anger rolls off him stronger than any wave in the ocean.

Snatching my cloak from his grasp, I plant my feet. "Unhand me. Why are you so angry? I have done nothing wrong."

"You risk detection. And it would not end well for you or Holden."

I know he speaks true, but my heart needs something different than my brain. I struggle to rein in the part of me which cannot lose another loved one. I wonder whether Quinn's frustration comes from more than just the current moment but do not wish to think of his apprehensions about Holden either.

Taking a slow, deep breath, I raise my chin. "Thank you, cousin, but I am quite capable of walking without assistance. Let us forget this and find some supper. We are all in need of a good meal."

And some wine. But I must remain alert. I still have the High Council to face this evening. At least, I hope I do. There will be no sleep for me tonight if not. And then perhaps some ale or other fermented drink may be just what I need. But I will not let my mind linger on that possibility either.

Reaching Grant, I hook my arm through his and continue our pursuit of dinner. It is not long before we come across a pub crowded with fae. Quinn disapproves, and we march on. We pass two more that do not suit him, but a small inn overlooking the water finally fits the bill. We choose a table at the back, far from the fire. Little warmth reaches us, and salty wind streams in from around the huge windowpane. I hug my cloak to me and look out over the ocean. The dimming light over the water and the colors it creates more than compensate.

Our fish is delivered on a wood plank, steaming with smells of lemon and herb. Topped with potatoes and vegetables, and served with hunks of bread, we want for little in the meal. I can think of few times when I have enjoyed such an exquisite seafood dish. Perhaps at a solstice celebration. I realize the scant crowd may be due to the cost of a such a meal. I would guess fae only spend for such on special occasions. Even with the fine taste and having missed my midday meal, I can stomach only a few bites of the fish and bread. I favor the coffee for its warmth and energizing qualities. The others leave little to waste, however.

"You treat us too well." Grant slaps Quinn on the back as the waiter leaves with the coin.

"Tis a hard job to follow such a queen. We should all be treated now and again," Quinn answers.

I note his sly smile and realize he jests. "I believe I treat you very well." Smacking him on the arm, I chance a dig myself. "If I am such a problem, you may go back to your navy in Bedham. I am sure there are some merfolk to protect us from."

Grant snickers. "Yes, why do you keep a navy there in Bedham?"

Quinn chuckles. "The elders still remember when the merfolk decided the humans posed a threat and tried to overtake our realm."

"Flying creatures will best swimming creatures every time." Adam downs the last of his coffee. "Why did the merfolk go back to Upper Earth?"

"Our navy drove them away." Quinn shrugs. "They did not expect that we would have such a fleet."

"That, and the fact that the seas are not as plentiful as Upper Earth. Nor do we have adequate light in our seas," I say.

"There was that, too." Quinn admits.

Motion at the door catches my eye, and I focus on the two fae at the entrance dressed in High Council guard attire.

I knew they would find me when it was time. So much for my anonymity here.

They exit without engaging us, and I decide they are not so horrible after all. Except they, and the council, represent all that fuels my nightmares of late. If only I were able to confer with the witches of the trinity, learn what passed that fateful day when we witnessed Hunter's lifeless body rising from Lower Earth and passing into Upper Earth.

What dark souls still hold power, and how can we limit them?

Rising, we thank our hosts for the fine meal and exit onto the street. Following the guards out of the city center, we take to the air. As before, I skirt King Luther's castle in favor of a longer route to the arena. Approaching, we find many Ring Keepers arriving as well. I surmise they dismissed for a meal and return for my verdict.

My stomach tightens at the idea that they could find me guilty, take my crown, or banish me to icy Willhelm, or worse yet, clip my wings. *No,* I remind myself. There stands no precedent for that. Nor is there history of a ruler being charged with treason. *However, leave it to you, Titania, to be first in so many things. First female monarch, first fae to escape Lower Earth, first fae to disregard a council edict—nay, two council edicts. But what of your power? You have not been blessed with such to waste away in some deserted land. No, the goddesses will ensure you are given the tools you need to protect this realm.*

If the High Council knew of my power, what would they do?

I find it equally likely they would seek to curtail my freedom with the knowledge. For we always fear what is not understood. Not that I comprehend or can control my gift any more than they. I only know that it manifests when most needed. That gives me faith I will be given that which is required to prevail against any enemy.

I follow the lead of our council guard escorts, landing to one side of the entrance. They motion for me to stand against the wall as the throngs of Keepers enter the coliseum. Although Aubren has only two rings, and therefore two Keepers, rings serve a given area, a population of fae and humans. Larger kingdoms with a greater population of fae living in Middle Earth and humans living on Upper Earth protect many rings. Bedham, to our north, maintains five: Chastam, lying under much of southern Asia, has thirty-seven; Willhelm, north of Chastam, has thirty; Lindleton, lying under Europe, has thirty; Rotuga, below Africa, has twenty-six; Elita, under South America, the same; and Borean, below North America, has fifty-two.

Seeing Aleem, I search his face for any hint of what they have decided.

He holds his countenance steady until flashing a warm smile and wink as he passes.

Does this mean I am to be found not guilty, or is the gesture for reassurance that all will be well despite the outcome?

Regin files in next. Wearing a smug grin, his eyes never leave the head in front of him.

I note the absences of both Keepers' judges.

Following, the monarchs file in, one by one, with King Luther bringing up the rear.

Last, the mediators appear.

Zekial stops and motions me ahead of him.

Quinn squeezes my elbow and whispers, "All will be well, cousin."

With his words, my confidence rises, for he is the most conservative of those I trust. No matter that just days ago I was unsure of his allegiance. Today, he has been by my side when I needed him. I have always held that he speaks true. Not what I would wish him to say, but always what his heart and mind believes. This reminds me of the words I did not want to hear, that Holden *would* say what

I wished him to. *Had he done that today? Told me what I wanted to hear, that he would see me tonight?*

Butterflies bouncing in my stomach, I raise my chin and step into the procession. *Breathe, Titania.* In out, in out. Left, right, one foot before the other.

A pit forms in my stomach as I wonder if I will see Holden this night. For I want nothing more than to fall in his arms when this is over, to sit in front of my fire and drink wine until the wee hours of the morning. And not with just Holden, but to have Quinn, Grant, Adam—nay, even Foster and Alfreda—there to relish in my release from these charges. My mother's words ring in my ears. *You need them.* And this never felt more right. For I crave their company almost as if they are my true family.

I desire them, not only to aid in defeating the dark ones lying beneath but to shore up my very soul against those that will tell me it cannot be done. And if that is selfish, let them count me among the greedy as I proposed to Holden. For in this moment, every nerve, every cell of my being, believes I am the chosen one or *a* chosen one. A fae that can do as no other may be able to accomplish feats unimaginable, even defeat the dark souls persisting beneath us.

We reach the center of the arena, and I spin in a slow circle, focusing on each face, hoping to confirm my supposition of innocence. The expressions of the would-be accusers give away nothing as to my fate, and I count this as a positive. *Would not they be regarding me with contempt or pity if I were to be found guilty?* I turn to Zekial.

His eyes graze up and land on me. He takes a deep breath. "Titania, there has been much debate about your actions. Your service is valued in the realm."

I take in each word, my breath catching on his last sentence. It feels like there may be a *but*.

"The courage you showed in being willing to sacrifice your very life to defeat the kobold invaders is nothing short of the epitome of being a fae."

They understand I would do anything for this realm. My soul rejoices.

"But you are young."

Thud. My heartbeat reverberates in my ears.

"Still learning the ways of our people."

Thud. I hold my breath, waiting for the worst.

"Aleem made a good decision in ceding his position."

No.

"He will be replaced by Ishmel, First Judge of Regin. Aleem's first judge will serve under Regin."

No!

"You are hereby sentenced to one year's probation. I will relinquish my Keeper's position to serve as your guardian. You shall have High Council guards trailing you day and night. These will ensure there are no more lapses in protocol."

Lapses in protocol? I guess this may be the best way to acknowledge my guilt without saying it. *One year?* But time is of the essence. *How am I to work with the trinity if not allowed to access them?* These creatures of the deep will not just lie in wait until I am ready to fight. They will come at us again. *How can the goddesses allow this? How does this help me? Or the realm?*

I will not let them know any of this affects me. I ball my fists and raise my chin. "Thank you, Mediator Zekial. I welcome your company in Aubren."

Zekial tips his head. "This matter is now closed. I thank each Keeper for their service and bid them safe travels to their kingdoms."

It kills me to stand there as the Keepers file from the rows, one after the other. I take deep breaths, in and out, trying to ease my anxiety. After what seems like an eternity, the mediators rise and take their leave.

Zekial informs me he must prepare for the move to Aubren.

I assure him adequate quarters will be made ready. As we exit, he calls to four guards, giving them instructions as to my continued surveillance. *Blast them.* Perhaps I shall make their stay so boring and miserable they decide I am not in need of reform and depart early.

Quinn's eyes, wide as saucers, track me as we take to the sky, trailed by the council guards.

Anger, humiliation, shame, and despair boil under the surface of my skin. *What shall become of my reign now? Where are the goddesses in this? And when shall Holden return to Aubren?* I need his council now more than ever.

I press forwards, flying faster than I ever have before. I cannot be in my kingdom, my castle, my study, quick enough. Zekial's instructions had been clear. They are to track my movements, not my every word. What I plan, say, think, or do behind closed doors will not be monitored.

My mind spins at the thought of informing Father, admitting my error in judgment to him. But he sided with me as well, as did Aleem and Holden. *Where is the justice in this?* I find none.

How am I to prepare for the millions of possibilities of attack blind? I need to know what happened to Sonia, Thanatos, and Theron. I cannot go a year without this information. It will drive me mad. *The crazy fae queen*, just as Lucifer predicted. And now, with the High Council's rebuke, my reputation teeters on the brink of ruin.

What do you care? Yes, why would I take heed of this? I have no need for them or their opinions. My kingdom stands secure. Quinn waits in the wings should anything befall me. We want for nothing. If they make me an island, I will be such. And they shall see, when evil knocks on their doors, I will be the one to save them.

The familiar sight of my forest, meadow, and castle gardens, although dark with night, eases my tensions. But I find the building itself brings no joy. I shall have to face Aleem, Father, Kane, the advisors, Alfreda, and Mother with my shame. *A fine legacy you have provided for your family. What if Holden's brother orders him to cut ties? Will Quinn abandon me as well?*

Sharp pain shoots through my side as my lungs contract. Such a familiar yet almost forgotten feeling in the past months. Foster's face appears in my mind. *You only have these attacks when you feel out of control.* His words play though my thoughts. *But what control do I have? I am not free to move about as I would like. Why would the goddesses forsake me?*

I grip my side as I land in the courtyard. A horn sounds, announcing my arrival, and I want to rip the instrument from the soldier's mouth.

"Tell them to be quiet. Fae are sleeping." I bark at Grant. "Call for Father at once, and meet me in my study. Quinn, follow me."

"What has happened?" Quinn skips to my side as I enter the castle.

"Shush. We will speak when there are no ears to overhear." My side ticks again as I rebuke myself for being so rude.

I stride down the hall as fast as I dare, past the grand halls, king's study—wondering why I still call it that—and Holden's room, and my side catches again.

You cannot have a breakdown in front of everyone. You will not have an episode, period. I shall not allow it. You can figure out how to clear your name, remove the stigma, prove you are worthy of holding your position without oversight. All will be well.

Reaching my study, I enter and release my breath. Quinn shuts the door behind us.

Setting my palms on my desk, I let the soft grain and cool timbers be my every thought. I look out over the meadow, noting the dim light on the grasses turning the green into purple, just as it does each night. *Nothing is different. You are still Queen of Aubren.* Except everything is changed, and I must accept this.

"How bad is it?" Quinn whispers.

I spin to face him and rest against the desk. Taking a deep breath, I relay the council's decision.

"This is not so bad." He steps towards me. "A year, maybe less, if they see there is nothing to be concerned with."

"That is what I thought. I will make everything so exceedingly humdrum that they will leave of sheer boredom. The evil spirits lying below us will not stop plotting, and I have no idea how powerful they have become. Perhaps I shall enlist my private guard to spy from abroad."

Sitting on the edge of the chair, Quinn takes my hand. "Cousin, I beseech you. Do not follow this course. Once Zekial witnesses there is no need for his presence, he will leave, perhaps in six months, maybe even three. Surely you can lay your quest aside for this short time."

"But what of Ishmel? I have no crystals. No way to assure the safety of this kingdom and Middle Earth without the ability to pass between realms."

"One year. Do their bidding for one year, and they will forget all that has passed. Your reign is new. Enjoy the solstice and the festival season. This will get you to the fall equinox, and then we will have harvest season and the winter pageants."

"You think I can be entertained by parties and gaieties when evil spirits lurk just under our realm?"

"Try, cousin. For the sake of your rule. You must think long term. It is harder when you are young and all seems so immediate. But consider what is best for your rule and kingdom five years from now, ten, twenty. That you sat a year doing the council's bidding will pay off in the future."

I weigh his opinions. Logic tells me he speaks true. But my heart beats as though it has broken. *Ker-thump, a lump, bump.* It skips and stutters. I hold my breath as the episode passes. The goddesses have abandoned me. There is no other way to see this. Perhaps I had been wrong. *What crazy girl would believe she is The One to end all evil?* A deranged child, that is who.

A rap on the door brings me out of my mental spiral. *You can fall apart when you are alone. Never before.* I call out, inviting my visitor inside. Father's form appears in the doorway, and I motion him in. Head hanging, I admit what has befallen me.

He lifts my chin. "But would you now, knowing what you know, make a different decision?"

I hold his gaze. "No, I would not."

"We sacrifice much for what we know to be true."

"But do I know it, or am I just a crazed young queen who thinks she has all the answers?"

"What if you had not let the witches pass?"

Kicking out a chair, I sink into it. "I know not. For I know not what they accomplished. Only that they fight the same battle we do."

"Then you shall persevere, whatever it takes."

I do not want to hear it and do not believe it this second. All my fight is gone. If the goddesses want me to fight for good, they should provide the means. I see none.

"Go. It is late. Let us not talk of this. It shall be as Quinn says, the most mundane kingdom in all the realm. Not even my own citizens will want to live here when this year is over."

"Titania, you are being dramatic." Father goads.

"Quite the opposite, Father. I am being pragmatic and practical. I will accept this sentence with grace and humility and go about my duties as queen in earnest. You shall see. All will be well."

"Why am I more fearful now than just a moment ago?" Quinn's wide stare holds mine.

I kiss his cheek. "Never fear, cousin. I will not smear our family name further, you have my word. It is late. You should both sleep. We will finalize the solstice preparations tomorrow."

Instructing Quinn to ask Alfreda to draw a bath, I latch the door behind them. Even though I am sure Holden knows of my fate, I start a letter, penning all my thoughts and fears. Rage burning, I write three pages before stopping. I throw the quill to the desk and stare at the pages. *What would they say of this in Upper Earth?* Oh, yes, the word is cathartic.

Perhaps this would be why fae choose to live in the human realm. *For how are we to know those faes' minds when every mention of them gets stripped from our records upon making the choice? What if I decide to join the trinity?* Perhaps I would be of more use to the goddesses in that realm. Maybe this is what they are telling me.

Every muscle in my body aches with wear. I am too tired to think of this now. Crumpling the pages, I throw them into the fire. I look at my clock, seeing it is after ten. I should have a bath and rest. But I will not sleep without knowledge of Holden and his plans. I start a new letter.

Prince Holden,

I bid you well. I am sure by now you have heard of the High Council's decision. Please, know that your place as Fae at Arms stands as it did before.

Your Queen,

Titania

My heart aches as I fold the page, and melting wax, I pour it over the edges. I press my seal into the warm drop and blow on the form until it cools. Despite the late hour, I ask the letter be delivered with haste and the page to wait for a response. I should have word from Holden before midnight. Sitting behind my desk, I bounce my leg. Even sight of the meadow with glowing dew forming on the grass gives me no comfort.

Alfreda appears in the doorway. Her wide-eyed look angers me, and I want to throw my candle at the wall. I do not need her pity. Still, I will not take my self-hatred of the moment out on her. *Self-hatred?* Nay, my loathing for those sitting on the High Council and the goddesses. They are the source of my rage. *How am I to go through festival season, inviting them to my castle, hosting them with drink and wine, when I despise the action taken against me? How am I to have faith the goddesses will guide me, provide that which is needed to secure my realm and the world above us?*

"I am okay, Alfreda. You need not pity me. I am sure Father has told you what passed, and I guess every fae in all the realm knows by now. I should plan to host Aleem and his wife for dinner tomorrow. Ensure that he is taken care of. Also, we must ready a chamber for Zekial."

"Of course, ma'am." She curtsies.

"Ma'am? And you are bowing to me now? Please, stop. I am not a China doll. I do not need your worry. This, too, shall pass. I endured the death of my brothers"— *guilt over not being able to save Rigel*, although I dare not speak this—"silence of my mother, Gunther and Ethan, and the evil souls of the deep, and still, I sit here, the true and rightful monarch of my kingdom. The decision shall not rule my psyche. I shall do as Quinn suggests. We will go on as if nothing has happened."

"Of course, miss."

"Glory be, Alfreda, I have a name." I stand. "Is my bath ready?"

She wrings her hands one over the other. "I am sorry, Titania."

"As I said, Alfreda"— crossing to her, I wrap my arm around her waist—"I am fine, all will be well. You shall see."

Chapter 6

THE WATER WARMS MY ACHING muscles, and lavender soap releases the salt, grime, and scents from the day. Still, soaking in the large tub gives my restless mind no relief. Dressing in soft pajama pants and top and tightening a warm robe around my waist, I ask Alfreda to bring the lists of preparations for the solstice. They look in order, but I double the fireworks and flowers requests and brainstorm how to pass the week and half before the holiday. *What would torture dear Zekial the most?*

I must see to Aleem and the transition of his first judge to Regin's compound. Then, I should help in planning Ishmel's rising ceremony. Following, we shall need to ensure all the protocols for the rings stand clear and have Zekial's approval. My mind floats to the shawl Aleem's wife left. I find it crystal-less and folded neatly at the top of my chest, sure Alfreda righted all after the council guards' search mayhem.

I wonder what Foster did with the ring crystals. Aleem must have given instruction. *The goddesses gave me the power to make my wishes known to Foster but did not assure I would have the power to complete my purpose? The* quandary baffles me. I continue with my lists. Perhaps we shall visit each shire leading up to the solstice, deliver fireworks and other party favors for their celebrations. Jostling along in a carriage for a week may be most uncomfortable for an older fae like Zekial.

Rebuking my pleasure of planning Zekial's suffering, I note the time. Almost midnight. I should have word from Holden soon. I cross to the window and gaze out over the meadow and to the sky. Standing there will not help the message come faster, and I go back to my lists. I should also review all the accounts, take stock of the crops and animals, get a water report, and receive updates on the building projects. Also, I shall rekindle my physical training regime.

My muscles being quite healed from the Lower Earth experience, it seems time to resume combat practice, fencing, weightlifting, riding, archery, and flying drills. Perhaps I shall also increase my study of potions and histories, maybe even revive my harp lessons. *Fantastic. But when shall there be time for Holden and me? Of course, he may accompany me in many of these pursuits, but how will we steal away for time together?*

A rap on my door has me flitting across the room and yanking open the panel. Smiling at the sight of Holden's seal, I thank Timothy and, closing the door, bounce to my bed. I sit cross-legged and slip my finger under the hardened wax, peeling the pages apart. Gladdened to see a lengthy letter, I begin to read.

Dearest Titania,

My brother apprised me of the council's decision. I know it came as a surprise and shock and wish I could be there to comfort you. Although I also know that you would hate that. I picture you in your room making plans and lists as I write this.

It is with a heavy heart that I write the next lines.

My breath catches. Tears well in my eyes. I know what he is going to write. He will not come back. Because the goddesses have forsaken me. That, or I have believed wrong about my fate. *Who was I to think I could be a savior to my people, anyway?* Blinking, I force myself to focus on the words on the page. Teardrops fall to the sheet, and I draw in a breath, steeling my emotion against what I know will come next.

I have told my brother that I intend to return to Aubren.

I swipe my tears from my eyes. Perhaps there is hope.

But Mother expresses she misses me and begs me to stay for the solstice. I have never been away from family for the holiday. I know we had many plans for celebrating the holiday together. I am sorry to disappoint you in this way but would very much like to be with my family through the solstice. I will return to Aubren soon thereafter.

With apologies, love, and devotion,
Holden

New tears spring to my eyes. My chest heaves. *No, Titania. Ten days. He said he will come after the solstice. You can bear to be apart from him for that long. Would you begrudge him time with family when they still live? All will be well. He shall return.* I set the letter on my table and snuff out the candle. Lying down, I pull my covers up around my chin.

All will be well…

———

DARKNESS. BLACK. SONIA MORPHING *into a dragon, Thanatos, Theron, Abaddon, Lucifer. "It cannot be done. You will go crazy trying."*

I bolt up to find my breakfast on the table and curtains open. Bright light pours in from around the windows, and birds call from the fields. A dream. A nightmare I thought would end with the council decision. Yet the evil of Lower Earth still haunts me. *These stories come from your own psyche. You terrorize yourself.*

Throwing the covers off, I decide to rid myself of the dreams with distraction. The goddesses have made clear they do not wish me to pursue this battle, and I shall not. I have much work without putting the weight of the fate of the universe at my feet. I sit and eat my eggs and fruit then dress in riding clothes.

Winding to my parents' quarters, I greet Father and walk with Mother in the garden. I gather the advisors and review plans for the coming weeks. Then, I request they assemble information for all the reports. They leave with light feet and renewed vigor, it seems.

Quinn even compliments my attention to such details. "It seems stress is a powerful motivator for you, cousin." He hooks his arm in mine as we exit the grand study.

"Have you not observed such before?"

"You are right. It should have been evident. I must ask, have you heard from Holden? I would expect you to be most anxious about his return."

"Yes." I pat his arm. "He will enjoy the solstice with his family and return afterwards. Who would want to be away from family for such a holiday? Your parents will join us for the celebration, correct?"

"But of course. They arrive a week from today."

"Splendid. It will be good to see them." I flash him a big smile and pray it conveys all is well. For this is my forte, holding my head high and pretending to be unaffected by events swirling around me, to be strong and confident.

But you are strong. You have proven it over and over. I boost my own psyche. *Yes, yes I am. Goddesses or no goddesses, I will thrive.*

We greet Aleem and his wife in the courtyard. He grips my hand as he walks with a bent back and faltering steps. I support his elbow in mine.

I have much to convey. I will be quick, but you must listen closely. I freeze at the sound of Aleem's voice in my mind. I know Keepers, judges, and their lines possess powers but had not been apprised of all of Aleem's. *Smile at me if you can hear me.*

"I am most happy you came." I pat his arm and flash him the biggest smile I can.

It shall work well, then. Support me to the hall. The crystals Foster took from the shawl… He has hidden then in the woods in a cave at the bend in the river. He searches for another set so you shall always have access to two. I know the next year will be trying, but you must keep faith. His eyes bore into mine, and I fear he can see into my very soul.

Refocusing on the passage ahead, I summon the power that manifested when I was able to communicate my wishes to Foster. *You have sacrificed much for me, and I am grateful. But the goddesses have forsaken me. They do not wish me to pursue this. And even if they did, how can I with guards of the council with me night and day?*

He squeezes my fingers so tightly I fear they will break. *Your mother has visions. They have always been true. Heed them.*

I shall. I remember her latest premonition and look forward to Holden's return.

Releasing my hand as we reach a small dining hall, he continues ahead of me to the table. Once Father and Mother join us, I salute Aleem for his service to our kingdom and the realm. I request that he serve my court as scribe and historian for as long as he wish. To my pleasure, he accepts the position and gift of a home just outside the castle walls.

I end the meal with another toast. We move through the passage to the courtyard. As I bid him farewell, Aleem grips both my hands. *There is one last thing. My son, my former first judge, now Regin's first judge, he will serve you. Seek him out if needed.*

My head aches with the force of the words flowing from him. Forcing a smile, I kiss both his cheeks.

Appointing Alfreda to see to their move and transition, I watch as they load into a carriage.

Can it be the goddesses are finding ways to help me after all? Do I dare trust any other with this? Especially one who is to serve Regin? And could this be a trap? One meant to ensnare and prosecute me further?

I will take no action to obtain the crystals or seek out Foster or Aleem's son unless there is no other choice. And for now, I see no eminent danger. Thus, I shall stay my course of torturing my new guardian, Zekial. He and his guards shall find no fault in me.

After spending the afternoon riding with Grant and Adam, shooting arrows with Quinn, and then fencing with Timothy and Nicholas, I bathe and dress to welcome Zekial.

Father, Quinn and I greet Zekial at his carriage in the courtyard. We whisk him right into the small dining room for drinks and supper then to the royal study for dessert and music.

I catch him nodding off more than once during my harp number and am happy to have achieved my goal. We will invite him to dinner every night, and he shall be so worn that he will crave a vacation from my presence.

After the meal, we escort him to his chamber. His rooms lie in the hallway with Quinn's, facing our private courtyard used for meals and entertaining. I point out the view as being one of the best in the castle, and he appears most pleased. Departing, I say I look forward to our breakfast at sunrise, and his stare widens for a second. I know I am achieving my goal. *How do those of Upper Earth put it? Kill them with kindness?*

THE NEXT MORNING, I BREAKFAST with Zekial and Quinn, steal an hour to walk with Mother, and then convene with Zekial and the advisors. We begin with the crop and animal reports. The farming advisor notes several more incidences with locusts. He reports they attracted wasps by moving blooming flowers into the fields. The wasp larvae all but decimated the locusts, and the few remaining flew west.

"How many fields were lost to the locusts?" I stiffen my back, remembering Mother's reaction to the brown grasshopper in the garden.

The advisor studies his notes. "Three additional fields in the western portion of the kingdom."

"Make sure the farmers have the help they need to replant, and repay them for their losses. And you confirmed the locusts have gone west? Out of our kingdom?"

Assuring me they have seen no insects in the past two days, he reads the names of the farmers affected. Foster's farm is among those with lost crops. I make a mental note to visit these families on my upcoming kingdom tour. Then, I add another task to the list, instructing that we should alert King Luther just in case the locusts survive the desert. I would find it surprising, but they have shown odd patterns and resilience this season. *Disgusting bugs.* My shoulders tremble.

The sun wanes low in the sky as we adjourn the advisement session. I invite Zekial to shoot with Quinn and me in the meadow. As we finish, Ishmel arrives. Greeting him, we show him and his wife to their chambers and leave them to ready for dinner.

"Did you see Zekial? He is about to keel over with the wear," Quinn whispers as we walk towards his room.

"Then I am achieving my goal. Let us make sure to have entertainment for the weekend." I squeeze Quinn's arm.

His eyes light up. "We can hold a party for Ishmel's rising."

"Is this tradition?"

"I will research."

"You do that, cousin." I kiss his cheek as we reach his door.

My guilt flares that I relish in such hideous folly, but the child in me delights in my vengeance. Still, I am taking better care of my kingdom than I ever have, so no one could slight me. Entering my chamber, the empty table I spy dampens my joy. For I wrote to Holden last night and hoped to have a letter from him. I wonder what he may be doing: hunting with his brothers, walking gardens with his mother, or dining with family and friends late into the night. There may be little time to pen a message. And he deserves such a holiday after his challenging year.

AND SO, THE DAYS FOLLOW WITH the monetary advisor's report taking a full day, Ishmel's rising ceremony, making him Ring Keeper of the Daintree Ring, and the day of celebration following. Each night, I find my table and desk empty. It gladdens my heart to think of Holden occupying himself with family events, however. I imagine them drinking and talking late into the night.

Packing my days distracts me from missing him as well as wondering about the witches and the status of the evil beings below me. *When shall they strike again? Will I have the power to stop them without access to Upper or Lower Earth? Why have the goddesses forsaken me?* These thoughts swirl in my mind. The sky calls to me, and I take late night flights with whichever guard serves me. I try to ignore the council guards trailing us, for they remind me of my loss.

Monday, we depart for the south and our tour of the kingdom in a caravan of carriages loaded with festival goods for the villages. I invite Zekial to fly with me and beg forgiveness as I abandon the cart and take to the sky. My guilt peaks as the caravan, bouncing along the rutted road, becomes dots on the landscape, but it is not guilt enough for me to stop the trip. Approaching Westshire, I spot a barren square in the green patchwork quilt of fields. Foster's farm grows in my view as we spiral downward.

I spot his sister and mother, Nissa and Jasmine, hanging laundry on the line beside the house.

Foster and his father, Matthew, trudge behind plows, turning under the nubs of dead stalks in the field.

I wonder if any others would find time to assist them with their own crops to mind. I make a mental note to allocate some troops for aid.

Nissa spots us and, abandoning the wash, runs inside, darting out again, dolls from my prior visits in hand.

I land beside her, and she flings her arms around my neck. I wonder if there is ever a better feeling in the world than to be loved by a child.

"Where are Prince Holden and Quinn?" Nissa searches the skies above.

Holden's absence weighs heavy, but I push the feeling aside. "Prince Holden is visiting his family in Willhelm for the holiday, and Quinn is at the castle. Hopefully, you are not too disappointed to just see me. I brought you a present."

She bounces as I shed my pack and produce a doll with hair of strawberry, just like Nissa's; a pink silk gown; and golden wings gracing the doll's back. Kissing my cheek, Nissa whispers in my ear, "Now I have three, and they shall guard our realm just like you, Holden, and Quinn."

"That sounds like a magnificent idea." I kiss her forehead.

Her mother waits behind her as I give Nissa another hug. Seeing the council guards land behind me, Jasmine curtsies then, with apologies, envelopes me in a hug as well. Her arms feel warm and strong, and the scent of lye surrounds me. Thoughts of my mother flood my mind, and I wonder if I shall ever feel my mother's love like this again.

"It is wonderful to see you, Jasmine. I hope our visit is not an imposition. I wanted to wish you a happy holiday, and we desired to tour the fields."

"No, not at all. It is always a treat to see you, Titania. Although, you spoil Nissa. Her friends are most jealous of her dolls of silk from the capital."

"What are little girls for but to be spoiled?"

"You know you do more than that for our daughters." She hooks her arm in mine and turns us towards the house. "You inspire them to dream of doing things we never even knew we desired. Come have some tea."

Hearing the carriages approach, I thank her for her hospitality and divert our path to the drive.

Foster and Matthew land beside me as the caravan stops.

"Who have you brought with you this time, Titania?" Foster kisses my cheek.

My face warms with his show of affection. I realize that after all we have been through, perhaps we are now friends as the gesture suggests. At least, I still count him as one I trust. It seems odd that he now holds one of my deepest secrets: the location of the ring crystals.

His father hugs me as well, and I realize, outside the castle, this family may be my closest friends. They feel as family to me. It saddens me that I do not have such relationships with aunts, uncles, cousins, nieces, and nephews, but for the time being, I will adopt Foster's family as such.

Zekial exits the carriage, and I introduce him to Matthew, Jasmine, and Foster.

Jasmine offers Zekial tea, and I head to the field with Matthew and Foster.

The locusts chewed every leaf from the plants, and only stalks and browning branches stand. Matthew notes he aims to till under the vegetation to fertilize the soil for next season.

I promise additional hands and funds for the lost crops. We find the farm advisor correct in that not a single locust can be found, and the wasps, having devoured the larvae, moved on as well. I wonder what an overpopulation of wasps could hurt and hope it is not worse than swarms of locusts devouring crop plants.

Bidding the family farewell, my entourage heads into the village of Westshire, distributing candies to the children and fireworks to the adults. Before night falls, we visit two more townships. I hope that being away from the castle and Holden's empty room brings me relief from missing him, but all I can think of is our last kingdom tour, when we met up each night, stealing away every moment possible together. I wish it could be such now. But perhaps the worst moments occur at the breakfast meal when I look across the table and see no one but Zekial.

We travel another day south to the Nariel Ring. Regin and his judges host us for supper. Then we cut north, arriving back at the castle two days later. With preparations for the solstice well underway, it provides little time to think of Holden or my demons until darkness falls and all is quiet. I lay staring at the stone wall that separates my room from his, a hole growing in my chest like none other I have felt before. *Three days.* Three days, and I shall look upon his face again. I picture his light eyes, golden hair pulled tight against the back of his head, and wings of sun-kissed straw and reread his letter.

Being home gives me some sense of grounding as I sit gazing out over my meadow, eat my breakfast, and then walk with Mother in the wood. We spend the day greeting visitors, advisors and their families, military officers, and judges from the shires. My eyes cut to the sky as I wonder if Holden will change his mind and appear any second. A horn sounds, announcing a royal guest. Double checking the completed guest list, I speed to the courtyard, praying that maybe Holden, and perhaps his brothers as well, decided to spend the solstice eve with us.

The carriage displays the crest of Bedham, and a fair-headed woman steps out. Aunt Cassia.

Instructing Alfreda to fetch Mother and Father, I check my instinct to fling myself into Cassia's arms. Still, I cannot restraint myself in giving an extra tight hug and kiss to each cheek of the woman I remember with such warmth.

"Aunt, I did not know you were coming. This brings me such joy, and I am sure it will Mother as well." I look upon her face, so much like Mother's, and tears form in my eyes.

"I hoped you would be happy with our hasty decision. If my presence pains you, we can go."

"Oh, no." I wipe the tears from my cheeks. "These are tears of joy."

"Let me look at you." She holds my hands out. "What a beautiful woman you have become. I am sorry we have not visited sooner. The threat of the kobold provided too much risk to come for your coronation."

"I understand. Are you here alone?"

"Mother," a voice calls from the carriage.

I look around Cassia to see three faces peeking around the carriage curtain. I skip to the coach as three blonde heads spill from the door. I greet each of them with a hug, calculating their ages. Gatuika, the eldest daughter, at a year younger than I, would be fifteen; Makani, fourteen; and Isla, thirteen. Memories of our many days spent building forts in the forest, playing in the stream, and play acting our weddings circle in my mind.

I have not seen them since my brothers' funerals, almost four years ago now. *Four years… What did I used to say?* Mother would spend a year mourning each of her sons. Perhaps maybe there is hope with Cassia's arrival. Maybe she will be the one to bring Mother out of her mourning.

"I cannot believe you are actually queen." Gatuika hooks her arm in mine.

"Neither of us would have dreamt this as children. Let us find rooms for you. Perhaps there is one near mine." I fold my hand over hers, thinking the only room left may be Holden's empty chamber beside me.

The space could work. If they plan to stay beyond the solstice, I could move them to emptied rooms once other guests depart. Two more days, and I shall see Holden again. Surely, I can withstand forty-eight more hours, especially with my cousins as company. We wind through the halls, finding Alfreda looking for my parents. As I guessed, Holden's chamber is the only empty room left. She dispatches helpers to move two cots into Holden's room, and I lead my company to the space.

"May I see your room, cousin? It must be so grand. I cannot imagine being a queen and having anything you would like." Isla flits to my side.

I show them my study and bedroom, and the girls brainstorm how they would decorate it with velvet curtains and silk for the bed. Invading my closet, they ask if I have a separate room just for my ball gowns.

"No, this is all."

"If I were queen, I would have a dress of every color." Isla lifts my emerald dress from the hanger.

Watching them, I wonder why I see them as girls. Gatuika is fifteen, but a year younger than I. Father made me queen at fifteen. But they seem so different from me. Crossing through my bedroom and seeing my crystals overhead, the answer comes. *They have not been touched by death and evil.*

As Isla opens my trunk and notes the plain wool blanket, Cassia scolds them, saying she would guess a queen's job is much more than hosting parties and wearing beautiful jewels.

But I do not want to think of my predicament as ruler and the fact that essentially my wings have been clipped of any freedom to do as I see fit. "Should we find Mother? I know she would be eager to see you all."

Cassia's wide eyes hold mine. "Of course. How is she?"

"She is well."

Seeing my cousins with their mother brings all that has been lost to my attention. Still, I should be grateful. Mother is alive, and she aids me in her own way. At least the goddesses have given me some insight in her premonitions. *Before.* Before *they allowed the council to put Ishmel in Aleem's post, move his first judge to study under Regin, and place Zekial and his guards in your castle to watch you day in and day out.*

We wind through the halls to my parents' chamber and, not finding them, proceed to the courtyard. Mother and Father sit, drinking tea with Victor, Father's cousin from Bedham and father to Quinn, and Victor's wife.

Father stands. "Grace, look who has come! Your sister, Cassia."

Mother's eyes stay frozen in their sockets, trained on the garden beyond.

"Mother, look. It is Cassia. She and my cousins have come to celebrate the solstice with us. Is it not grand?" Taking Cassia's hand, I place it in Mother's.

Cassia kneels beside Mother and kisses her cheek. "It is good to see you, sister. I have missed you."

Father calls for more tables, chairs, and tea.

I wonder how long I can sit and look at Mother being so stoic in the presence of her sister. I listen to the conversation and shake my head and smile as if in a dream. But if only this were an illusion, it would be a nightmare most welcome compared to the evil creatures I see each night. But the goddesses will reveal all one day. It will be clear why we endure such tribulations. Our pain shall not be in vain. Or it will, and none of this will matter in the least because in the end, our lives could be random events plundering together as a brook falling over a waterfall. I rebuke my thoughts. I shouldn't think such although it does seem as if the goddesses have forsaken me.

Unable to endure the scene any longer, I offer to take my cousins on a tour of the castle grounds. I catch sight of Quinn standing outside one of the worker's homes as we wind around to the farmyard. His back to us, I do not see who he is speaking with at first.

"Who is that?" Gatuika hooks her arm in mine. "He looks most attractive."

"That is my cousin, Quinn."

"Your heir presumptive? He is more handsome than the rumors speculate. At least this side of him. Will you introduce us?"

Laughing, Makani takes my other hand. "Yes, I am so tired of light-headed fae."

As we near Quinn, I realize who stands behind him.

Abeetha. Her dark hair and purple wings grate my every nerve.

Has Quinn taken the opportunity to sneak away to speak with her while I have been occupied? I hoped it was as he had said, a random dance, but this scene shows me something more.

Smile reaching his eyes, hand wrapped around hers, this relationship seems formidable.

Chapter

I

ABEETHA'S EYES CUT TO US and grow wide. She deflects her gaze back to Quinn, and he turns to look our way as well. After another few words to her, he spins and starts towards us.

I wish Gatuika to be older so I may distract him with her beauty. As it is, I have no one to offer as a substitute for his attention. If only I had friends like a normal fae.

"Cousin Quinn." Pulse racing, I call to him as he nears. "Come meet my cousins from Bedham."

"I am most happy to meet your cousins." He bows.

Making all the introductions, I ask him to join us for the rest of our tour. We wind past the soldiers' courtyard with the girls gawking at the warrior's muscled arms and then to the meadow to shoot arrows. Me, all the while, seething inside. *How could he start a relationship with her, the daughter of a traitor who tried to have me removed from my rightful throne?*

"How about hidden passages in the castle? Do you have any of those?" Isla asks as we make our way back to the rock structure.

I wrap my arm around her waist. "Well, they would not be secret if I told you, would they?"

Her wide eyes hold mine. "Do the stones in your forehead hurt?"

"No, they are like your wings or hair. You may touch them if you like."

She runs her finger over the smooth stones and ridges gracing my brow. "Did it hurt when you were ejected from Lower Earth? And what did you see there?"

"Isla, do not be rude. Mother said we were not to pester her." Gatuika slaps her sister's arm.

"It is quite alright. It was a very odd experience." I recount the dark void of the space and my story of how the magick of the ring ejected me. "It was more like a large shock of lightning."

"And what of Prince Holden?" Makani takes my hand. "I hear he is quite handsome and that you are close."

"And this is when I shall take my leave." Quinn bows to each of the girls and then to me.

"I will see you for dinner, cousin." I hold his gaze, hoping he realizes how wrong he is to pursue Abeetha.

Watching him walk away, I wish I could shoot lasers into his brain for being so stupid as to pursue her. *How could he trust her? Spend time with her? When it is likely she encourages attention for treacherous reasons, to be close to him to plan some sort of coup on my rule.* I would rather him court anyone but someone from Gunther's line. *And how could he lie to me about their relationship?* I make a mental note to enlist Alfreda to help me find some suitable girls to introduce to Quinn.

"Why are you angry at Quinn? Is it because he was talking to that maiden?" Makani squeezes my fingers.

"Is it that obvious? And yes, she is the daughter and sister of the ones who tried to take my throne."

"Ooh, scandal!" Gatuika exclaims. "But tell us of Holden. Are the rumors true? Does he court you?"

"I guess one could say that."

"But what would you say?" Makani inquires.

"I would say he is a very fine Fae at Arms." I wink as we enter the orchard.

"You are no fun. I want a wonderful wedding to attend." Isla slouches down on the grass.

"I am only sixteen. It is best to wait till seventeen to wed."

"I believe you have broken all the rules already, cousin," Gatuika says.

"I am quite good at that."

As we pass into the garden, I inquire about their lives, school, friends, and interests. I note Gatuika to be much like me, technical and exact, while Makani seems quiet and reserved, but Isla acts and speaks without a filter.

She rambles on about Gatuika's affinity for singing, Makani's love of the flute and playing it while alone in the forest, and Isla's own favorite activity, swimming.

I admit to my love of water as well and promise we shall walk in the wood for a dip in the stream the next day.

"I wish that we could stay with you always." Isla spins through the door as I hold it open for her.

"I would think that you would miss your friends and school."

"But it is so small, and your kingdom has so much more to explore, so many more people. I wish to see it all." She flits to the windowsill.

"Well, you are quite the adventurer. Your family is welcome to stay here as long as you wish."

I LEAVE THEM TO DRESS FOR dinner and wind to Quinn's room. But marching the long halls gives me time to think. *What good comes from yelling at him, forbidding him to see her?* Perhaps another approach would be prudent. One he took with me: show concern, warn him about giving his heart too quickly. Instead of the hard blow I had thought to deliver to the door, I make a slight rap.

Opening the door, he rolls his eyes. "Why did I know this would be you?"

"You looked happy with her." I can scarcely believe the words that pass from my mouth.

"And I am sure you are here to end that."

"You know that I distrust his family, but I have said time and time again I want you to be happy here. I must caution you as you have me. Be careful with your heart."

"She is not her father or brother. She had nothing to do with their plots. I have spoken with her about this. She hates what her father did. She lives with her sister's family. She came to the castle grounds to see her mother while Gunther was out hunting. You, of all people, would know what it is like to be estranged from your family at a mere fifteen."

I will never trust Gunther's family, but Mother's words ring in my head. *You need them.* It is not only for some ominous prophecy that I want Quinn here. He is a friend, a support, when I have so few. He is the only one I would trust with my kingdom. Tears spring to my eyes. "I am sorry. I am too emotional of late. But take the advice you give to me. We go into festival season. There will be princesses lined up to court you, especially as heir presumptive. Please, keep an open mind."

He wipes a tear as it escapes my lid. "I promise I shall for festival season, cousin. I will write to her just now, before dinner, and tell her such."

"Thank you." I grasp his hands. "You are as a brother to me."

"And you as a sister to me." He kisses my cheek. "Now, let us forget this and celebrate the solstice as such."

"Yes." I rub the water from my face. "I believe I have let my frustrations from the past week overwhelm me. I will see you at dinner."

Squeezing his fingers, I release his hands. As I walk back to my chamber, with a smile for each fae I pass, I motion for Timothy to draw near and instruct him to have Grant and Adam called to my study. It has been too long without a report from my special guard. Someone should have seen the relationship between Quinn and Abeetha growing.

I pace my study, waiting for Grant and Adam. Hearing no news of significance from the guard, I instruct them to ask Foster to watch Quinn. Foster would not be suspected as he is not a new face to court. Grant and Adam look between each other, and I question their side glances.

"Foster is our best spy. We have him watching Regin in the south," Grant divulges.

"And who watches Gunther and Ethan? Cannot Foster be here to watch Gunther, Ethan, and Quinn? Besides my own hot-headedness and lack of impulse control, Gunther and his family stand as the biggest threat to my reign."

Adam shakes his head. "Do not rebuke yourself. You did what you must for this realm. Others will come to see that."

"You have more faith than I. Tell me you have someone capable of Foster's level of skill watching Gunther."

"Yes, Henrick sees to Gunther and Ethan. We will enlist others to watch Quinn and Abeetha."

Dismissing them, I stare out my window into the meadow. How I wish to be with Holden and assured that all will be well. I pen another letter to him, saddened that I have received none in reply to those I have sent every day. I unwrap his note and read the last words—*with apologies, love, and devotion.* Yes, what we have is more than a passing fancy. We are well matched. A tap on the door brings me out of my thoughts. A page holds a scroll, and I fight the impulse to snatch it from his hands.

Thanking him, I close the door and lean against the panel. Unwrapping the document, I find Holden's handwriting.

Dearest Titania,

I am sorry that I have not written in many days. My brothers and mother occupy my time from sunup to sundown, hunting all day and dancing till the wee hours. My head hits my pillow exhausted each night. Still, it is your face I long to see. Mother beseeches me to stay for the festival season, but all I can think of is returning to you. I will see you soon, love.

Your devoted,
Holden

I hug the scroll to my chest. Two days, and I shall look upon him again. Bathing quickly, I pin my hair up and slip on the dress Alfreda left for me. Tonight, we host our guests in the grand ballroom. My side ticks as I recall the ill-fated events held in the hall before. *Grant and Adam would know of any subterfuge*, I assure myself. *The holiday will not be marred.*

I slide my dagger into my boot and exit my room. Knocking on the door to Holden's chamber, I find it opens with the pressure of my hand. I peek in to find a blizzard of fabric with gowns gracing every surface.

"Titania, you must help me choose a dress." Isla grabs my hand and tugs me towards a chest.

I find it overflowing. "How many gowns did you bring?"

"I wish I could wear dark colors like you, but my skin would look like bleached flour." She holds up a light blue satin. "Should I wear this tonight or tomorrow?"

"The blue matches your eyes. I like that one."

Gatuika emerges from the dressing closet wearing a lavender gown. "Just tell her which one or we shall be in this room all night."

"This is a favorite as well." Isla snatches a silver dress from the floor.

Thinking Holden would laugh for days at the sight of the room, I focus on Isla. "You should wear the silver for the solstice. The blue is beautiful for tonight."

"Thank goodness. Can we go now?" Makani, wearing a light gold dress, rises from a chair.

Arm in arm, we march through passageways lit with a hundred candles. The grand hall already filled with guests, I greet as many as possible as we wind through the tables to the front. I smile at the sight of Quinn seated to the right of my throne and Father to the left, followed by Mother and Alfreda. All those I hold dear gather with me. *How can I not count myself blessed? For, in the end, is it not those we love that hold most importance?* I imagine the cottage in the woods and Holden's proposal of living with the merfolk. As long as our realm stands and I have these fae to gaze upon, I should want for no more.

We dance until the wee hours of the morning, and sleep comes the second my head hits the pillow. Still, I wake to the image of Lucifer's sinister face. *I am still here.*

Pressing my fingers to my lids to erase the vision, I open my curtains to the light of morning. The smell of sweet nectar surrounds me. I dress in riding clothes and open my door to find ropes of flower garland lining the passageway. The solstice, the celebration of light, will be a most perfect and needed reminder of the gifts bestowed on our realm. *Yes, count your blessings. For the past year saw you triumph over your foe, and you have your family here surrounding you. Holden shall return tomorrow, setting all right with the world.*

We breakfast in the courtyard, and I walk with Mother, Aunt Cassia, and my three cousins through the garden and into the meadow. Afterwards, we ride horses through the wood and shoot arrows with Quinn and our guests. I love seeing the castle grounds filled with so many fae, and my excitement for the festival season grows. We have not had such a crowd since my brothers' funerals, and it harkens a rebirth of sorts. Quinn will find a beautiful fae maiden to fall deeply in love with, and he shall be most happy, I am sure of it.

How could I doubt the goddesses when I have so much to be grateful for? Holden and Quinn may be all I need to save our realm from the evil below, just as Mother foresaw. But for today, I decide to put these thoughts aside and embrace the celebration.

"Queen, may we have some time?" Advisor Bran approaches with two other advisors as we start a game of croquet.

I signal for Quinn to join us and, handing my mallet to Gatuika, gather with the advisors under a tree. Bran informs us that the swarm of locusts must have survived crossing the western desert. They decimated several fields in southern Chastam.

"Are you sure they were the locusts from our kingdom? Across the sea? How could that be?" I ask.

"The scientists confirm they have the same markings as those seen in our farmlands. The insects have morphed to a swarm, making them hardier," Bran answers.

"But our realm has had outbreaks of locusts before. It is not that uncommon," I say.

"Yes, but this is not a trivial thing. The last catastrophic locust outbreak nearly starved the whole realm. If not for the flood, we would have abandoned Middle Earth."

"Well, gentlemen, there was a flood. The goddesses saw to our safety. And they shall again. But we are not anywhere near losing all the crops in Middle Earth. We will send our scientists to Chastam to aid them tomorrow. I am sure there will be a solution, be it wasps or some method of deterring the insects."

I thank the advisors for their time and bid them join us in the games. We commence with croquet and enjoy badminton and polo. By time to bathe and dress for the celebration, I need a nap, but as soon as I lie down, thoughts of Holden pop into my brain. *How much more wonderful would this day be with him at my side?* Abandoning the need for rest, I prepare my gown.

Opening my door an hour later, I find Quinn, hand up, ready to rap on the panel. "I have come to escort you to the celebration."

"How thoughtful. Thank you, cousin."

Seeing Holden's room empty, we wind through the halls to my parents' chamber.

Mother stands inside, dressed in a golden gown. She looks like an angel.

I kiss her hand and tuck it around my arm. We proceed to the courtyard, Mother on one arm, Father on the other. Long tables line the space, and I greet the advisors, Aleem, General Kane, my guards, the High Council guards, and Zekial. Castle staff and villagers mingle through the tables, finding empty spaces.

I wind around the head table to my chair. Lifting a goblet, my breath catches in my throat when a hush falls over the crowd. These are my people, my kingdom, and they trust me with their very lives. Swallowing, I fight tears.

Forcing my arm above my head, I lift my chin. "To the goddesses! Blessed be."

"To the goddesses! Blessed be." All gathered lift voices and glasses.

"Let us all celebrate our blessings." I sip the wine, and a chorus of cheers sounds from the crowd. Sitting, I lift my fork and salute those before me.

The dinner proceeds with trays of fruits, cheese, meats, vegetables, and all sorts of sweets being passed along the tables. I watch all the faces, trying to savor the images of my people happy and carefree. After the meal, we carry the tables to the edges of the courtyard, and a band starts to play. I open the dances in a jig with Father and all joining in. We form a huge circle and weave in and out of each other to the beat of the music.

Circling back to Father, he passes my hand to Quinn. As another song begins, Quinn cedes his position to Grant. I meet his gaze and force a smile, thinking if Holden were here, he would have been my next dance. As it is, I pass the hours dancing with Alfreda, my cousins, and my guards. I am dancing with Adam when a huge boom sounds overhead. I look up to see flashes of light exploding in the sky.

"The fireworks." I grab Adam's hand.

I weave through the crowd to find Gatuika, Makani, Isla, and Quinn, and we jump into the air. Landing on top of the castle roof, I train my eyes on the sky, waiting for the firework show.

Bong. The clock in the highest turret sounds the first stroke of midnight.

A dark cloud forms above us. A hush falls over the audience below and the music wanes.

"What is that?" Quinn steps to my side.

"Fog?" I squint my eyes to focus on the mass.

Waves of black churn inside it as if it is a pot of boiling liquor.

Faces in the crowd spin to look at us.

With the second stroke of midnight, I instruct Grant to have them proceed with the fireworks. Whatever caused the cloud will dissipate with the heat from the explosions. The form grows larger, spreading over the castle and all the grounds to the forest. With the third gong of the clock, I wonder if I shall have to light the wicks myself. I peer over the castle wall, down to the meadow.

Hearing pops and whistles, I am assured the fireworks have been lit. Hundreds of balls of light rise into the dark mass. It appears they have fired all the explosives at once. I cover my ears, waiting for the noise.

Boom, boom, boom, boom. Bright blazes of light erupt in the sky.

The crowd below cheers, and the music restarts.

With the explosions, the cloud appears to dissipate. Hearing a pop in the meadow, I look over to see more fireworks being lit and am relieved they were not all launched at once. It would not be a very climactic show to have them boom off all at once and then have nothing left. Feeling something fall into my hair, I look up to find ash raining down on us.

"What is this?" I hold out my palm to catch the cinders.

Quinn lifts a piece from his jacket. "Is this…?"

I snatch the flake from him and examine it. "This is a wing."

Catching more falling residue, we confirm our suspicions. A locust swarm hung above us, and the fireworks shred them to pieces.

"Spread word through the crowd. The residue is ash from the fireworks. The pyrotechnic shot too many off at once. We have to avoid panic at all costs. Nothing is going to mar this night."

As my guards jump over the wall, I spread my arms and spin around. "Is this not amazing? The goddesses have blessed us with embers from heaven."

"You are crazier than me, cousin." Quinn takes my hand.

I grab Gatuika's hand, and we form a large ring. We skip sideways, rotating the circle around the roof. As the last stroke of midnight tolls, I jump into the air. The others follow suit, and we spin in the sky. Alighting in the courtyard, we join the rest of the dancers. I stomp my feet as hard as I can, trying to remove any evidence of the locusts. This shall be a long night of clean up.

Passing whispers to Grant, I have him round up the advisors. I thank my lucky stars that Zekial and the elders have retired for the night. It seems even the council guards have taken the holiday off as I have seen not one of them the whole day. Seeing my cousins occupied with flirting with soldiers, I sneak away from the festivities.

I join my advisors and guards in the king's study. "Gentlemen, what is said in this room, this night, must stay in this room. We do not want to cause panic. We will work through the night to remove all trace of the locust debris. Tomorrow, we will gather the scientists and farmers to investigate the origins of the swarm."

Having no questions or comments, I disband the meeting. Exiting the castle, I think I have never wished for rain as much as now, but the rainy season is months away. I weave through the throngs of fae dancing in the courtyard to find my cousins.

Gatuika, Makani, and Isla dance in a small circle with Nicholas, Timothy, and a few other guards.

Again, I thank the goddesses to be blessed with such faithful helpers. After joining in one more dance, I herd my cousins inside, using the excuse that their parents may be quite mad with me if the girls witness the drunken soiree these festivals inevitably end with.

I leave Nicholas to watch their door and gather as many guards as possible. We weave through all the walks, batting our wings to clear the slag. I wind into the garden, blowing the embers into the plant beds. At least the remnants will serve as fertilizer. I note to ensure the gardeners water everything well tomorrow.

Entering the meadow, I find it, too, is coated with dust. I pray a breeze will clear most by morning. My thoughts jump to the village streets where little wind may penetrate. Finding Grant and Adam, I enlist them to help inspect the town. Upon exiting the castle gates, we find no trace of ash or debris.

I post my hands on my hips. "This is odd."

"Perhaps they were attracted by the light and noise. The cloud did not form until the first firework exploded." Adam stops in front of me.

"That is a good theory. At least we do not have more work to do."

"After witnessing the events of tonight, I may not sleep for days." Grant's shoulders quake.

"Do not be dramatic. We have had locusts before. The scientists will figure something out."

Chapter 8

Shedding my dress, I bemoan that Alfreda will scold me for soiling it. If only I had thought to change before clearing the paths of the pieces of those wretched creatures. *Why would they hover over the castle in that fashion? It must have been the noise and lights that drew them, perhaps the smells of the feast. Do locusts even have a sense of smell? Well, I shall leave that to the scientists.*

My nerves frayed, I sit on the windowsill, listening to music and revelry drifting from the courtyard. I think of Holden doing the same and thank the goddesses I shall see him tomorrow. As my tension eases, I trudge to my bed.

I am not sure why Lucifer's hot breath and gruff voice surprise me each morning. I kick off the covers, thinking he will become as a background, a fly to be swatted away. *You have no hold over me. For I shall prove you wrong. I will not be the crazed, deranged girl bent on following some fabled prophecy.*

Rising, I cross to the window and fling back the curtains. *You will see. I can be most happy. I shall enjoy watching the fae of my kingdom go about their normal lives and serve them as any good ruler would. For it seems that is what the goddesses want as well.*

Dressing and proceeding to the main courtyard, I confirm our endeavors to keep the locusts secret were successful. I wind to the garden for breakfast and enlist Cassia to walk with Mother and me. Next, I gather the advisors and our top scientists. They report no other instances of locust swarms, save the ones yesterday in southern Chastam and ours the prior night. I count this as good news and bid them study all they can about the insects and prepare a report for me. They retreat to the library, and I go to find my cousins.

I spend the day with the girls, distracting myself from thinking of Holden by participating in games, horseback riding, and archery. By nightfall, I can stand it no longer and believe I shall just fly to Hilbron myself. Just as my mind is made up, a page arrives with a letter. Waving him away, I tear off the bow.

Tears form in my eyes as I read the words.

I am sorry to be detained further, but Mother's family lingers with us after the holiday. I know not for how long.

I let the page fall to my desk. *A few more days, Titania.* Too wound up for anything, I jump into the sky. Pushing my wings to their limits, I soar up to the barrier separating us from Upper Earth. How I wish to fly through the ring and coast over their cities, glide under their stars.

MONDAY DAWNS WITH THE SAME nightmare, and I dread the day ahead. Reports, preparations. *But you still have your aunt and cousins. They shall entertain you.* Cassia and I leave Mother in her room after a walk, and we start out in search of the girls.

"I do not know how you endure seeing your mother each day. It breaks my heart and frustrates every nerve."

"I love her. And she and Father are all the family I have left."

"I hope you count us family again. I sense you hoped I would help her. I am sorry it did not happen."

I wind my arm in Cassia's. "How long will you stay?"

"A few more days. I did want to ask you a favor. My daughters love you so much, love being here, and we have few visitors in Bedham for the festival season. Would you host them this summer?"

My mind spins. *Me, an appropriate host?* Stifling a laugh at the thought of me being considered anything near a suitable guardian, I check my composure. "May I have a day to think about it?"

"Of course. I will not mention it to the girls."

A page lands beside us, and Cassia bids me goodbye.

"Another swarm, near Westshire." He belts out between sucking in breaths.

I jump into the air and twist through the halls to the library where Quinn and the advisors are gathered with the chief scientists and farmers. They apprise me that a field in the farm next to Foster's was decimated just this morning.

"Where did they come from? Did they hatch overnight? How long does it even take them to transform from larvae to bug?"

Plopping into a chair, I demand to know all about the insects.

They believe the locusts traveled overnight, for the farmer woke to find them covering his crop. I listen as they throw out theories and suggest they investigate the scene firsthand. The scientists agree on the course of action, and I leave orders to alert me when there is more information.

I am not two steps out the door before Quinn calls my name. He motions me to the side of the window as a group passes us. "We could use your help in strategizing what to do about these swarms."

"How am I to help? The scientists and farmers are the experts here."

"You are the smartest fae I know. Your instinct is unrivaled as far as I am concerned."

"These are grasshoppers, Quinn, not some army we need to slay."

"But they could be."

"Or they could be gone next week."

"I do not understand. When it was the kobold, you would not rest until you solved the problem."

"Again, completely different things. We are not anywhere near the grave situation we faced with the kobold. They were bigger than us and aided by magick. These are bite-sized arthropods. What would you have me do, play a tune on my harp to lure them into Lower Earth with me?

Because my prior stunt is serving me so well right now. This is not something I can fix."

"You befuddle me."

"And you do not understand anything."

"Help me understand, then."

I take a step back. "I am going to spend time with my cousins. I will see you at dinner."

He crosses his arms over his chest. "Right, you will not enlighten me because you do not trust anyone. Except for Holden. But he is not here."

Spinning, I stomp away. *How* dare *he. I am to trust him when he is part of the reason I have no power right now? What am I supposed to do about a ton of bugs, anyway? I cannot control my magick. And even if I could, I cannot zap away a million bugs that I have no clue from whence they come or where they shall strike next. And should my powers be used in that way? Who am I to disturb natural processes?*

Plus, there stand worse catastrophes, like deciding whether to host my cousins. If I say no, I risk alienating my aunt and her family, but being responsible for three teens on top of my normal duties, and trying to figure out how to get Lucifer out of my head, does not seem feasible.

If only Holden were here to help me figure all of this out. I march to my study and start a letter. I write all my thoughts, my anger with Quinn, frustration with my aunt, Zekial, the council guards, festival season, Lucifer, the locusts, and every trivial detail standing in the way of me feeling the least bit successful. Breath evening out as I pen my name, I wonder if I should send the note. But if he is to be away, he may at least send me ideas via letter.

Foot bouncing, I think about my cousins. I love being with them. They serve as the sisters I never had, but I cannot play games and ride with them every day. *Perhaps I may carve out time for them, but will each one of them not need individual attention as well? You are not their mother. They want a vacation, that is all.* As with most things, I know it will not be enough for me to leave them to fend for themselves. Perhaps I could give them jobs. There are many tasks in hosting the festival dinners, menus, seating charts, and flowers to be arranged. They could help in these duties. Looking out over the meadow, I decide to sleep on the decision. In the morning, I shall walk with Mother alone, talk it out, see where my feelings take me.

Motion draws my gaze, and I spin around to see Alfreda inching through the door. *Have I not ignored her as well this past week with my cousins and aunt here?* We walk, arm in arm, to dinner, me vowing to be present in the current moment.

⸺❖⸺

I DRAW OUT THE EVENING, taking advantage of the last night with my aunt and possibly cousins. Mother still sits catatonic, and even with my hope waning that she will ever return to us, I feel happy. At least I have a relationship with Cassia and my cousins again, and Alfreda will forever be family.

A scroll lies on my desk when I return at midnight. I flatten the page and read Holden's message. He writes that he misses me, but time spent with family can never be replaced. I realize I know this more than most. What I would give for one more day, even hour with my brothers?

So, even as their presence may bring more work, I decide to accept hosting my cousins.

———

BREAKFAST BRINGS NEW CHALLENGES as I realize much of my alone time may be spent with Gatuika, Makani, and Isla in the coming months. *How am I to foster relationships with them as well as attend festival guests and spend time with Holden?* New doubts arise as Alfreda and Quinn list our schedule for the week's end. At least Holden will return soon. Together, we tend to complete tasks with greater speed and gaiety. I put it in my mind to try this tactic with Quinn as well. Start fresh with him. *For you need him, too*, I remind myself. *Your mother has said so.*

Cassia seems so intent on walking with Mother I feel I cannot begrudge the request. Me on one side, leading Mother, Cassia hooks her arm through Mother's opposite elbow, chatting away as if nothing is wrong. I cannot look at Cassia's tight-drawn smile, for her pain seems to lie just under the surface of her gay veneer. Letting my thoughts wander, I picture a day integrated with my cousins' presence. Breakfasts, flights around the kingdom, hosting festival dinners, them at my side in the receiving line.

Mother stops, and I refocus on her.

Cassia runs her hand down Mother's arm and takes her hand. "Are you okay, sister?"

With Mother's eyes fixed on the path in front of her, I follow the line of sight. A brown grasshopper sits in the middle of the walk. I bend to sweep it away.

Mother slaps my arm away, and her foot lands atop the critter. Twisting her shoe into the dirt, she pulverizes the insect.

"Mother, it is quite alright." I run my hands down her arms.

Her eyes hold mine. "More to come. You need them."

I squeeze Mother's hands. "I know, Mother. Do not worry. It is just a small grasshopper. But all will be well. You are safe. We all will be safe."

"Why did she do that? What is she talking about? I thought she never spoke." Cassia backs away.

"Only on rare occasion and only a few words."

"I cannot be here any longer. I am sorry. This is too hard." Cassia spins and jogs away.

Wrapping my arm around Mother, I guide her back to their chambers. I pace her bedroom as Alfreda settles Mother under the covers. Her prophecy haunts me. *What am I to do?* I have no direction, no aim except hosting fluff parties for dignitaries I do not even care for. And there seems no way to contact the trinity witches.

These grasshoppers terrorize Mother as much as my inability to rid Lucifer from my brain plagues me. Quinn's words trek through my mind. *Your instincts are unrivaled.* As unnecessary as I may be, I might as well commit to solving some problem. *Fine. If nothing else, I will distract myself with these stupid insects.*

Leaving Alfreda to tend to Mother, I stomp to the library and approach Quinn. "I am ready to help get rid of these cursed locusts."

"Sit down, cousin." He pushes a chair my way.

We spend the day listing all their predators, charting where the locusts have struck, and noting which crops they targeted. I study the map, realizing the swarms follow the same pattern as in past plagues. Dry conditions cause their solitary versions to congregate, transforming them to the swarm variety.

"The egg stage is at least ten days and non-flying stage almost a month, correct? So why are we not seeing any herds of locusts on the ground? That is what we need to be looking for. To stop them before they form a flying swarm." I pace the aisles between bookshelves.

"The farmers are trying to attract wasps to eat the larvae. But they have not been successful in killing all of them." Quinn follows me.

"What about spiders, lizards, birds, foxes?"

"Birds will eat the crops as well, and how do we attract that many of them?"

"Upper Earth seems to have this figured out. How do they control the swarms?"

"Chemical pesticides and fungal pathogens."

"Well, chemicals are not an option. But we could research the fungal pathogens."

"The council is not going to let you use any technology from Upper Earth."

"They will if their food is threatened. We should create a taskforce with the kingdoms affected. Send word to Hilbron, Chastam, and Rotuga. I am happy to host the meetings."

"Yes, of course. Any battle to distract yourself with." Quinn rolls his eyes.

I place my hands on my hips. "What does that mean?"

"You are upset about Holden's absence and the council's imposition into your life. Plus, Zekial and his guards keep you from seeking out the trinity. Therefore, you have decided to focus on an acceptable foe."

Throwing my hands up, I march away. "This is what you wanted, Quinn! But think what you will. I will figure out a way to end this locust crisis."

I pass through the library doors into the hallway to find Gatuika, Makani, and Isla waiting against the wall. They rush to my side.

Gatuika grabs my hand. "You have to talk to Mother. She told us to pack our things, that we are to leave tonight. Please, speak with her. We want to stay with you for the summer."

The day spent in the library allowed me to ignore the problem with my aunt. Now I had to face it. "I did not know you were aware that she asked me if you could stay."

"Please, let us." Makani wraps her hand around mine. "We will not be a bother, we promise. And we can help you. We aid Mother in planning parties all the time."

"This is a big responsibility, and I have not dealt with teens before."

Isla's big blue eyes bore into mine. "It is so boring in Bedham. And we could learn so much from you. You know better than any the plight of a royal girl. We need your help and guidance."

"Let me think about this more and speak with your mother. I am sure she is most upset. I do not want your family to leave with ill feelings."

"What did happen, if we may ask?" Gatuika spins in front of me.

"My mother is not well, as you have seen. She did something to upset yours. Let me go talk to her."

"Thank you." Gatuika squeezes me to her.

I wind through the halls to Cassia's room, finding her tossing clothes into a trunk. "Aunt, can we talk about what happened this morning?"

Setting a dress atop the pile, she smooths her skirt and nods. I motion to the table, and we take seats opposite each other. I fold my hands in my lap, waiting for her.

She cuts her eyes to the window. "I was under the impression that Grace never spoke."

"As I said, she rarely does. And even then, her sentences make little sense. She does not like the brown grasshoppers for some reason. This is the second episode where she reacted that way to one."

"That is why we must leave. It is not safe here. Evil targets this kingdom." She leans forwards, then with a sigh, relaxes against the chair back.

I wonder if she means to say more or if she guesses Mother's gift. It would be risky to expose Mother in this way, for my secret lies just a step away.

"I did not realize the girls knew you were going to ask me if they could stay."

"What did they say?"

"They begged me to talk to you and to agree that they could stay."

Tears fill her eyes. "I worry for them. Our kingdom is small, and our family so big. It will be hard to find them suitable matches. Many will flock to your castle for festival season, but I cannot risk their lives in this fated kingdom."

I rise and cross to the window. "They will come to see the female queen who escaped Lower Earth, the monarch admonished by the High Council."

"May I offer some advice? I believe your mother would want that."

I turn to face her. "Of course. I will take any wise council I can receive."

"Win them over. Show them you are a refined, beautiful queen, not the notorious rebel they have painted you to be."

"I should rather be a revolutionary than sit and make small talk with men who think less of me because I am a woman."

"Well then, display your other skills, riding, hunting, archery, fencing, whatever strategy you were cooking up with Quinn today to manage the locusts. Show them you are an equal."

"I *am* an equal. And you, nor your girls, are in danger here. This I can assure you. But it is your decision whether you stay or go. I hope we part as friends."

Approaching, she takes my hands. "This is nothing personal against you or your mother. It is just hard for me to see my sister as the frail recluse that she is now."

"Thank you, Aunt. Your daughters are most welcome if you will allow them to stay. They say they are good at planning, and I could use the help."

"Can you assure me that if there is danger you will send them home?"

Refocusing, I hold her gaze. "I will. I have my own special guard. Your daughters will come to no harm in my kingdom."

A sly smile spreads across her face. "Yes, I have heard of your special guard. I had hoped to meet Holden."

My face warms. "He shall return by the end of the week. You can meet him the next time you visit."

She kisses my cheek. "Then I shall leave my daughters in your capable hands until the end of the festival season."

"It will be my honor to host them."

The door bursts open, and Gatuika, Makani, and Isla flit to us, throwing their arms around their mother and me in turn.

I ask Cassia to stay the night, and she agrees to wait until morning to leave. I leave them to make arrangements for their stay and weave through the castle, looking for Alfreda. We decide on rooms for the girls in the next passage over from mine. This way, they will be close but not directly beside me.

"I just do not know what you were thinking to agree to something like this." Alfreda wrings her hands as we inspect the rooms. "Teenagers can be lots of trouble. Your plate is full as it is, with the High Council breathing down your back, and now the locusts."

I lay my hands on her shoulders. "Alfreda, they have promised to help with the festival season dinners, so they will aid you as well. And I doubt they would do anything to jeopardize their stay here. Plus, the locusts will be gone in no time. Quinn and I worked on it all day, and we are gathering a team from all the kingdoms affected to design a unified plan."

"I am glad to see you getting along so well with Quinn. You have so few you trust. I feared his relationship with Abeetha may anger you."

"You know about them? Do you rebuke me for my misgiving?"

"Rumors run rampant in the castle. And you have much to be wary of."

"I am not sure I trust Quinn at all. I do believe he wants what is in the best interest for this kingdom. I will put my faith in that at least." My shoulders shudder as I picture Ethan's dark purple wings hovering over me, remember the searing pain that shot through my body as he broke my leg, and recall sleeping on the cold floor of the dank dungeon.

Alfreda shakes her head. "We do not choose who we love."

"Perhaps not, but he has known her for only a couple of weeks. Their bond cannot be that strong."

"What did you think the first time you laid eyes on Foster?"

Releasing her, I giggle. "You think he is a good comparison? After he betrayed me?"

"Perhaps not. What about Holden?"

"I thought him handsome but arrogant. I did not like him right away. Our friendship formed over time, and I grew to love him. But Quinn has so many choices. He will see. Someone will catch his fancy, perhaps even Gatuika. She will be sixteen in just months."

Alfreda wraps her arm around my waist as we walk from the room. "He is eighteen, nearly nineteen. She is a child to him. He needs a woman. This I know."

"Fine, make a list for me of those that will visit during festival season that may catch his fancy, and we will be sure to place them together at the table."

"So, you are a matchmaker now?"

"The High Council decided I am not good for much else. I might as well be nanny and cupid for the summer."

Laughing, she slaps my bottom and points me to my chamber to change for dinner.

⬥

I NOTE CASSIA'S TENSE POSE as we walk through the garden with Mother the next morning. Still, Cassia tells Mother the girls will stay for the festival season, and Cassia will visit again at the end of summer. We wind to the front of the castle where her carriage waits to take her to the harbor. She hugs Mother's rigid form and, smiling tightly, kisses each of her cheeks. With a kiss to my cheek and long hugs for the girls, Cassia climbs into the carriage.

Isla grabs my hand as soon as the coach is out of sight. "What shall we do today?"

"What would you like to do?"

"Could we explore the forest?" Makani asks.

"Yes. Have you hunted for faerie crosses before?"

"We are finding brown rocks?" Gatuika rolls her eyes. Why can we not go to the market?"

I glare at her. "You will see. They are very special faerie crosses. But, of course, you may go to the market any time you like. Just do not go alone. We could all go

141

together tomorrow to look for ribbons or silks for the party this weekend."

We find the girls suitable wading clothes and, after showing them my faerie cross collection, take to the air. Flying above the orchard and meadow, we wind into the trees. I weave through the trunks to the river. Being there reminds me of the hidden ring crystals, and I wonder if Foster has found enough for another set. I imagine it would take quite a while and realize his other duties would prevent such excursions. Perhaps I could appoint another to watch Regin. Only the goddesses know when the crystals may be important, and I would trust no one else save Holden.

Holden… I look to the sky as I sift through a handful of dirt, so adept at searching for the cross-shaped crystals, I know them by feel. A spray of water lands on my face, and wiping it off, I stand upright to assess from whence it came.

Isla stands, hands on her hips, looking at me. "Where are you?"

"Sorry, being here has me thinking of many things. I used to come here with my brothers. They helped me begin my collection of faerie crosses."

"You were drooling. You were thinking of Holden." Makani laughs.

"And what if I were? That is not so wrong."

"I cannot wait to meet him. I hear he is handsome. Perhaps he has a younger brother that I may meet." Gatuika hops to the bank and rests on a stump.

"He is handsome, but if you had studied his family, you would know that he is the youngest of his siblings."

"Are you kidding? That is the most boring part of our instruction. The begats. Who cares who birthed who?"

"Well, you should care if you would like to help me play matchmaker to Quinn and arrange to meet wonderful fae who may be of interest in the coming festival years."

"I could marry this year. Many fae marry at fifteen." Gatuika dips her toe in the stream.

I stand upright. "I guess you could, but your father may have something to say about that."

Motion catches my eye, and I look up to see a red-headed fae descending to us. *Foster.* My heart issues a thud. His presence can only mean one thing: Something is wrong.

"Who is *that*?" Gatuika springs to her feet.

"A friend. A very good friend." I jump into the air to intercept him before he reaches us.

Sweat beads on Foster's face, and I realize he must have had either a long or fast flight. "What has happened?"

Hi eyes cut to the left and right and focus on me. "Not here. In your study."

"Foster—"

"Titania, trust me in this."

"Fine." I zip above the trees and then remember my cousins.

Dashing back to the stream to make apologies, I ask Grant to stay with them in the forest. I dart back to Foster. His creased brow gives me no comfort. I zip ahead of him, for I cannot look at his countenance for another second. My heart races in my chest and breaths become shallow as I imagine all the things that could befall me. *Regin further plots to remove me from my throne? He has convinced Zekial of my madness?*

Every cell of my body wishes to fly directly into the window of my study and demand Foster tell me all, but that would seem odd. As it is, he could be any other soldier. I left the castle with two guards and am returning with two. I land in the courtyard, greeting those gathered. I force myself to walk through the passageways at a normal pace, which just now, with my heart beating out of my chest, feels as though we trudge through molasses.

My ears buzz, and lines around the periphery of my vision blur. I dig my fingers into my palms to focus. *Breathe in and out. You make this worse than it could be.* Foster's news may very well be good. He could have found the second set of crystals. Smiling at the High Council guards, I enter my study, wave Foster in, and shut the door. I pour two glasses of water and hand him one.

Thanking me, he chugs the whole charger.

I motion for him to sit, and he sets his pack on the floor and slides into the seat.

As his breath evens out, he looks up at me. Wide eyes holding mine, he opens his mouth and closes it again. He runs his hand down his pant leg and shifts in his seat.

"Foster, whatever it is, just say it. You, better than any, know that I am not a glass doll."

"The High Council. The reason they ruled such is that Gunther wrote a letter and delivered it through Regin detailing your anxiety condition and holding that to be the reason he challenged your reign."

"Regin and Gunther are aligned? Gunther has made a move to remove me from my throne again? How did you learn this?" The ribbon vendor's words echo in my mind. *Beware of those who seek to pass judgment.*

Foster lifts his bag from the floor and produces a scroll. "I intercepted this just yesterday."

"Yesterday? Why am I just getting it now?"

"I wanted to make sure we had all the evidence to charge Gunther with treason."

"And do you?"

"Yes."

"Okay, well done. Thank you. We should take this information to the judges now." I start towards the door.

"Wait." He catches my arm. "Sit down, there is more."

"I do not need to sit down. Whatever it is, out with it."

His Adam's apple bobs in his throat. "You know that since Aleem has trusted me with things…" He holds my gaze.

"What?"

He releases my arm. "I thought that you may hear me. I guess it does not work that way."

I squat down and take both his hands but hear nothing in my mind. I whisper, "Is this about the crystals? Have you found enough for another set? Because I was thinking that we should divert your energy to that."

"No. It is not about the crystals. It is about Holden. I have just come from Hilbron."

Releasing his fingers, I stand. "Who authorized you to go there?"

"We thought it best to confirm—"

"We? Who is we?"

Rising, he motions to the chair beside me. "Please, sit."

"I will not sit until you tell me what is going on."

"There were rumors, and I had to confirm them for myself."

"For goddesses' sake, out with it, Foster." My head spins. *Luther has joined ranks in having me removed as well. Holden told them of my powers and our theory that I may be The One. No, Holden would not betray you in that way. But in a drunken moment? Or if he decided his family trustworthy, wanted to enlist their help in finding a way to contact the trinity?*

His cheeks slack, eyes widen. He reaches out to me.

I back away. "Tell me now."

"Prince Holden has signed an engagement contract with a princess from Lindleton. Princess Lily, the first daughter of King Hector."

My stomach lurches. It cannot be so. Contracts like these take weeks to form. He wrote to me just a day ago saying he would return.

"Please, sit. You look ashen." He takes a step towards me.

A hum passes between my ears. I grip the chair rung. As I lower my body to the seat, Foster lifts his chin. I follow his gaze to the window. Five fae approach from the west. Wings of the one in the front shining like gold in the light, he wears the green tunic bearing my crest.

Holden.

"You are wrong. Look, it is Holden, wearing my uniform." I jump to the windowsill and into the air.

Holden and those with him slow as I approach. Seeing his sweet, handsome eyes, the cleft of his chin, hair like straw pulled back in a tight bun, I want to fling my arms around him and welcome him with the longest kiss ever, but many eyes track us. I study his face and find no hint of tension.

Foster is wrong.

Chapter 9

His eyes cut to the council guards and back to me. He bows low as we hover there. "Queen, it is good to be here. I have missed your fair kingdom."

"As I am sure it has missed you." I smile at him.

Approaching fae catch my eye, and I realize they are my cousins and Grant. "Let us proceed to the courtyard. I would like you to meet my cousins. I believe it is about time for the noon meal as well."

Spinning to face the castle, I see the tables set in the courtyard and Mother, Father, and Alfreda approach. Once we are on the ground, I introduce Gatuika, Makani, and Isla to Holden. He compliments each in turn, and their faces blush from the adoration.

Quinn exits into the courtyard and crosses to us. "Holden, you are just in time to aid with the locust problem. The delegates from Chastam and Rotuga arrive tomorrow."

"Yes, we have been fortunate in Hilbron thus far, but I hear they have done some damage in other kingdoms."

"As well as here." I take my seat at the middle of the table.

Quinn sits to my right and Holden to my left. Heart beaming with pride, joy, and a renewed feeling of completeness, I look down the table at Mother. Yes, we are together again, my trusted colleagues and me. She need not worry about her premonition being fulfilled. I have who is required for my endeavors. Now, I just need the goddesses to help me find a way to be rid of Zekial and the council guards, for this moratorium on traveling to Upper Earth to be lifted, and for them to allow me to speak with the trinity about their experience in Lower Earth. Then my head shall rest easy on my pillow.

Lunch passes with Holden sharing stories from Hilbron's solstice celebration, us sharing our odd fireworks display, and Gatuika's rendition of how boring hunting for faerie crosses is. As the meal ends, others trickle away, and the girls take their leave to clean up from the morning's adventure.

"Should we bring Holden up to speed in the library?" Quinn lays his napkin on the table.

"My study may be more appropriate." I want to tell Holden about the swarm of locusts on the solstice, an event I would not dare pen in a letter to him.

"May I have time with you first?" Holden stands and offers his arm.

After a kiss to Quinn's cheek, I hook my arm in Holden's. Strolling into the castle and down through the passage, I whisper to him of my afternoon in Leeward, time with my cousins, and Mother's repeated reaction to the grasshoppers. I end with the description of the swarm that hovered over the castle the night of the solstice.

I spin to face him. "But you are here now, and all is right with the realm again."

"Shall we?" He motions to my study.

My stomach flutters and heart races at the thought of finally being alone with him after the joyous, yet long, lunch. I nod to the council guards as we pass. Not even they can dampen my mood this day. Entering, I see Foster's bag, scroll sitting therein. I bend to pick it up and hold it out to Holden.

"Foster found—"

Holden drops to one knee, and my heart issues a thud. Words catch in my throat.

His eyes fill with tears. "I love you with all my heart. You have made me the happiest fae in all the realm."

My heart flutters with joy, and I step towards him. He holds up his palm, blocking my advance. With his other hand, he unhooks his sword and places it on the stone. Stripping his tunic, he lays it at my feet.

"What is this?" I retrieve the vest from the floor.

"My heart will be forever yours." Water streaks down his face, and he swipes it from his cheek.

Standing, he wraps his arms around me. I stand there, frozen in his embrace, sucking in his scent. I press my lips to his bare chest and push up on my toes to kiss his lips.

Releasing me, he cups his hands over mine. "Forever yours."

His words are but a whisper on his breath. He presses his lips to my forehead and steps back.

Then I see it in his tight eyes, balled fists. Foster's information rings true.

Hmmmmm. My brain pulses. The sound of laughter wafts up from the garden, and I look out of the window to see my cousins flitting over Zekial and his guards as they amble along the path.

He looks up at the girls and then towards me.

Swallowing, I step back, pressing my palm to the tabletop behind me. I force a smile. "So, it is true. You are to be married to Princess Lily."

His eyebrow tips up. "You heard?"

"Foster came with the news just before you arrived. I did not want to believe it." I turn my head and look out the window. For I fear if I look upon his face, I shall never be able to do what I know I must.

"Congratulations. I wish you happiness. Alfreda packed your things in a closet when we needed the room for my cousins. I will have her arrange to deliver them to Hilbron."

"Do you have nothing else to say to me? I leave for Lindleton tomorrow."

Heart ripping to shreds, I keep my eyes trained on Zekial. I channel all my emotion, the love, the sorrow, the pain, the anger, into my hatred for him. "I love you. You know that. But we always knew this could happen."

"Titania, please. We must speak of this. Have closure. I beg your forgiveness. You know if I had any other choice. But—"

"But Lindleton is the most populous kingdom in the fae realm, and your kingdom, Hilbron, is the least. Your family needs this alliance. Again, I offer you and your family congratulations." I fold the fingers of one hand into my palm and dig my nails into the flesh.

He steps towards me. "Look at me, yell, hit me, anything besides this."

Zekial resumes his stroll, and I savor the feel of my wet palm, my nails digging into the open wounds. Flesh, blood, life, and death. "I said that I love you, and you know that I do. What more do you want from me? This is where our story ends. I will be forever grateful for your service, for standing by my side and aiding me in defeating the kobold. All I want from you now is the courtesy of walking through the passageway with me, a smile on your face, out into the courtyard where I will announce your engagement, thank you for your service, and watch you fly away. Please, tell me you can do that."

"Whatever you ask, my queen." Dipping his chin, he backs to the door and opens it.

Summoning a breath, I wish it would feel like fire in my lungs, anything that would divert the pain in my soul to a physical outlet. I raise my chin and pass through the doorway into the hall.

"I am no longer your queen. Please, never utter those words to me again." I slide a handkerchief from my pocket and hold it to the wounds in my palm.

He walks just a step behind me, and for this, I am grateful. For if I had to look at him, see his features now, his bare bronze chest, squared chin, blue eyes, knowing what he has done to us, what he has done to me—nay, what the goddesses have decreed for us—I would surely collapse to the ground and never wish to rise.

Why have the goddesses forsaken me? My mother foresaw it. *I need him. And who shall I trust with my deepest secret? And what of my alliance with Hilbron? How shall I foster that now?* His brother seems to hold no love for me, whether it be because I am female or rash, I cannot know. Perhaps now that Holden has done the right thing, acquiesced to his brother's bidding, we may resume our cordial relationship. I shall focus on that, garnering ties with leaders of all the kingdoms, making them see I am just like them. And it will commence tomorrow with the delegations from Chastam and Rotuga.

With these kingdoms as allies, my enemies will see that I cannot be brushed aside so easily. Starting with Gunther. I squint as we exit to the courtyard. Asking a herald to sound the bugle, I wait for everyone to gather. I catch each eye and smile, praying my face portrays a calm, even, happy façade. Quinn exits the library, and I motion for him to join us. I lace my fingers in his, first, glad I chose to mar my left palm, and second, praying he will buttress me if I start to waver.

Seeing Zekial, Alfreda at Father's side, Mother, and my cousins all staring, I swallow. "Prince Holden has come to us with happy news. He is to leave tomorrow to join his betrothed, Princess Lily, in Lindleton. We praise him for his service to this kingdom, nay, this *realm*, for aiding us in defeating the kobold. May happiness grace him for the rest of his life."

Quinn squeezes my hand and releases it. Stepping behind me, he crosses to Holden. I stand there, muscles rigid, smile plastered on my face as others approach then curtsy or bow and offer muted congratulations. I focus my gaze above their heads, to the woods. For this whole horrid affair to be over, to be pressing through the air, darting wide tree trunks, is all I want right now.

"Cousin." Quinn's voice sounds in my ear.

I blink to find all eyes fixed on me. I motion to Holden. "To Prince Holden! Godspeed."

Out of the corner of my eye, I see him dip his chin and jump into the air. I fix my sight on the ground, only raising my face when Quinn whispers Holden is gone.

"Cousin." Quinn's wide eyes hold mine.

"There are urgent matters. Find Foster." I gather my skirt, wondering how we need to approach the matter of Regin's treason.

"Perhaps you need to take a rest?" Quinn's arm wraps around me.

"No. You, Foster, General Kane, and Father need to meet me in my study, now."

As I enter the passageway, Alfreda pulls me into a hug. She whispers apologies in my ear.

I wriggle from her grasp. "Have Holden's things sent to Hilbron at once. And make sure the girls do not pester the elders in the garden. Send them to the market to get supplies for the weekend's dinners or have them arrange the seating chart. I will finish with business in a couple of hours and can find them then."

My skin crawls as I march to my study, thinking every fae gawks at me, wondering if I shall break down. I will not give them that satisfaction. I am a queen. Crossing into my study, I stop short at the sight of Holden's sword and tunic. I dip to pick them up and place them in the corner. That should symbolize what I must do with my feelings. I must store them in a corner until—

A rap on the door diverts my attention, and I look up to find Father, Foster, Kane, and Quinn standing in the doorway.

"Good. Everyone is here. Foster is now my Fae at Arms. Kane, get him the appropriate uniform. Foster, please take your evidence, I am not going to even touch it, to Ishmel and his judges at once." If you had asked me what I would say before those words passed my mouth, I could not have told you.

"Perhaps this is a hasty decision. Foster is only a foot soldier, has not even been trained to lead." Kane turns to Foster. "No offense to you."

"None taken. But, Titania"—he clears his throat and holds my stare—"Queen, also, I cannot achieve my goals with this post."

Flustered, I point through the doorway. "It shall be Grant then. Grant"—I wave him towards us—"you are now my Fae at Arms. Please alert the guard of the change in leadership. Foster, go!"

Foster kneels, lifts his pack and retreats from the room. With a bow, Kane follows him. I summarize Foster's findings for Father, Grant, and Quinn, my eyes landing on Quinn.

"We must finish preparations for the locust conclave tomorrow."

I giggle at my words. "A locust conclave, indeed. It sounds as if we are inviting the locusts for a weekend in the country." Laugher rolls out of me, and I find I cannot stop. I double over.

Father rests his hand on my back. "Are you quite alright?"

Catching my breath, I stand upright. "Yes, but this may not be a bad idea. We could lure them all to one spot and trap and kill them somehow."

"With what? More fireworks?" Father chuckles.

"A flock of birds?" Quinn wonders.

"Where shall we get that many birds? I believe the wine from lunch has affected us all."

"I am sure there will be a solution." Patting my shoulder, Father backs from the room.

Grant bows and follows him out with my instruction to secure a proper uniform for himself.

Quinn clutches my hand. "I am quite concerned for you. Today was a big blow."

I suck in a breath, and my side ticks. I want to scream, ask him if he would like to gloat over my misfortune. Because he and Father alike warned me of this. They told me not to give my heart so freely. Look where I am now. I cannot break down. I have a kingdom to run.

"We should finish the schedule in the library."

Quinn releases my fists and lifts his palm to find it smeared with blood. "What is this?"

He grabs my arm and lifts my left hand. "Why is your kerchief bloody?"

"It is a cut from the stream this morning. I forgot to bandage it."

"You lie. Your hand was fine at lunch." Unfolding my fingers, he reveals the slices in my palm. "Titania, you did this. Please, do not hurt yourself. I know—"

I place a finger over his lips. Water fills his lids, and I know he loves me. Not the kind of love like Holden and I had. Perhaps Quinn thought that once, but all I see in his face now is true kinship.

"Let us not say more of this. I thank you for your compassion. We have work to do."

We finish the schedule in an hour, and I take off to hunt for the girls. I find them in the market, securing items on Alfreda's list. We go from vendor to vendor, making sure to pick the very best vegetables, meats, cheeses, and flowers. It feels good to be away from the castle, and I wonder why I do not come into the village more often. As we take turns pushing the cart over the cobbled path to the castle, Gatuika hooks her arm in mine.

"Are you very sad about Holden? I know you want to put on a good show for others, but you can talk to us."

"Thank you, cousin. Thank you all." I grab Makani's hand. "I am glad you are here. We shall have a wonderful summer together."

"We could move back into the room next to yours, so you will not be so alone." Isla sets the wheelbarrow down.

Sliding from my cousins' embraces, I lift the handles. "It is a small room for three people. Perhaps I shall knock down the wall and expand my quarters. Everyone is always saying I should have a bigger space."

"I think you should do it. We can help. It will be a wall-bashing party. That is what Mother has us do when we are upset about something. She gives us a mallet and brick and has us bash away on it. What do you usually do when you are upset?"

"I like shooting arrows and flying over the countryside."

"You can imagine Holden's face on the target." Isla skips ahead.

"I am not mad with him. There is nothing to be done about what happened."

Gatuika hooks her arm in mine. "It is so unfair."

"What will be even worse is if we are not back with this cart before dinnertime. Alfreda will have our hides." I cannot let my brain entertain thoughts of Holden for too long. It feels unfair beyond belief that we cannot be with the one we love because of the assumed need for so-called alliances. No, I do not blame Holden. I curse the goddesses for it feels as if fate has forsaken me.

"Got it. You are in denial." Gatuika slides her hand from my embrace.

"I am not in denial. I will just keep busy until I cannot lift another finger. Then I will sleep, wake up, and do it all again." And this is how I shall get through the festival season, deal with the locusts, become matchmaker for Quinn, and watch my cousins flirt with who they may.

Upon our return to the castle, we help Alfreda store the food for the weekends' dinners. Instructing the girls to change for dinner, I find Foster waiting outside my study.

"I do not like the look on your face."

"And you will not like what I have to tell you."

I usher him into the room. Ignoring the sight of the green tunic and the tick in my side, I spin to face him. "Out with it. I do not expect anything less than unfavorable news given my luck of late."

Motioning for me to sit and taking a chair across from me, he describes how Ishmel found Gunther guilty of no wrongdoing. Because all that Gunther testified was true, Ishmel and his judges found no fault with the actions, nor with Regin's.

"I am sorry. I thought that since there was an insinuation that Gunther expected payment, it would be enough to bring charges."

"An insinuation, but no proof?" I gaze out the window.

"I should have waited to catch Regin in the act of compensating Gunther. They are still being watched. We may get the evidence yet."

"Regin would be tipped off by Ishmel. Ishmel would never let shame come to his father. Do not worry for this. Zekial and the council will see that I am a capable leader. All will be well."

I speak the words, but I do not believe them. *For how can I when the goddesses have forsaken me, stripped me of my freedom, and taken Holden from me? But you may regain your liberties. Cling to that.*

"Thank you." I rise.

He stands and starts to open his mouth.

"If this is about Holden, do not speak the words. You were right. I thank you for your service. Please, join us at dinner. You shall be seated on my left." I tell him this although he only reminds me of the love that I have lost, first him and now Holden. I shall not give my heart with ease again.

At dinner, I focus on the conversation, and we stay up late into the night playing instruments, singing, and dancing. My wings drag the stone as I trudge towards my chamber. All cooperated in distracting and amusing me, which I am sure was their plan. I keep my eyes facing forwards as I pass his room. The lingering pain, the absence of him, the hole that I fear will open up and consume me is so close under my skin.

I will write it all out as I used to do for my brothers. One day it will not hurt so much. I know that to be a lie. The pain lingers. But I have learned to live with it. I stop as I reach my door. Light from my study window catches my eye, and I turn my head to find a scroll upon my desk.

"Where did that come from?"

"A page brought it just after you left for dinner," Nicholas responds.

Crossing into the room, I shed the ribbon and open the page. Holden's script looms on the parchment, large and dark.

Dearest Titania,

Although I do not deserve it, I beg your forgiveness. Please, know that I fought this outcome with my every cell. My words to you were true. I will never love another.

No signature graces the bottom of the page. Rolling up the sheet, I hold it to my chest. Tears form and, blinking, I swipe them away. I rise and lift his tunic and sword from the stone, hugging them to me. Although I would rather stand and stare out over the meadow all night, I force myself to walk into my room. I gaze upon the rug where we picnicked, remembering the first time I let myself be attracted to him, how we danced around the stack of blankets to fictitious music. Sitting shoulder to shoulder with him, trying to solve the mystery of the kobold. Our flights high above my kingdom and through the woods, and the sight of him the night I returned from Lower Earth.

I bring the vest to my nose and suck in his scent, like fresh hay on a summer day. How cruel for the goddesses to take him from me when he was all I had. Yes, I may have Quinn, and I may be surer of him now, but still not fully, like Holden. And Foster… He and Quinn would still, most likely, stop me from serving my purpose if it meant harm to me. Father and Kane seek to marry me off, see me pregnant and fat to preserve the line.

I look at the wall and think of my cousins, how they suggested crashing it down. Lifting my arm, I start to fling the sword at it but stop. The hilt, the blade, he labored for hours forming. I cannot mar his memory. I shall take the saber to my tomb. Setting the scroll on my table, I climb into bed, one hand clutching his vest the other, his sword. *I forgive you, Holden.* I let the tears flow until there are no more.

⸺◈⸺

WAKING, I FIND LIGHT POURING in my window. *What? No nightmare? No Lucifer whispering in my ear?* I release my grip on Holden's tear-soaked vest. *But also, no Holden.* I stare up at my crystals. *Where have the goddesses gone?*

No one questions my late morning as I confirm readiness of the sleeping quarters for the locust conclave guests from Chastam and Rotuga with Alfreda, check in with Mother and Father, and find the girls shooting arrows with Quinn in the meadow.

"Did you knock down the wall yet?" Isla skips to me as I approach.

"I thought about it."

They make me promise they will be present when I make the first strike.

—◇◇◇—

THE GROUP FROM CHASTAM arrives first then the Rotuga contingency. I eye one of the soldiers. With a white beard and small stature, he seems familiar, but I know I have never met him. Perhaps he attended the council meeting. Shrugging off the sense of déjà vu, I note the courtyard where we will share the midday meal and take my visitors to their rooms.

At lunch, I scan the table, taking in our mismatched group, and realize these kingdoms have not sent their best teams. Neither kingdom sent a member of the royal family, and there are only a couple of scientists, officers, and soldiers, not even one general among them. *Are they really that concerned about the locusts? It appears not.*

I wonder if these men even have decision-making power. *Do they have authority to pledge fae or resources to the cause?* I hoped to come away from the conference with a definitive plan. I tell myself not to make assumptions, smile, and join in the random conversations.

We convene in the study to list all the tactics possible to destroy either the larvae, nymph forms, or flying locusts. Bugs in their flying forms seem hardest to take on, so we focus on the other life stages. The only challenge lies in finding them in these states. In dense jungles, they may be hard to locate. Still, with no other immediate threat to our realm, I see no reason for not allocating troops to the goal.

As we discuss each idea, odd sounds interject, filtering into the library windows at random. First, the sound of a flute, then a harp, a trumpet, a fiddle, and then, they synchronize, harmonize into a song. A most joyous tune, but loud and boisterous. I wonder if the band practices for the festival dinners. The speaker raises his voice to be heard over the music.

Quinn starts to rise, and I lay my hand upon his arm, gather my skirt, and slink from my chair. Tiptoeing out of the room, I turn my head each way, trying to discern from which direction the music emanates. With no indication, I cross outside into the courtyard. I realize the sound comes from the highest turret of the castle some four stories above us. I cannot help but smile for it sounds like such a joyous tune. Motion catches my eye, and I see Alfreda running towards me.

"Madam, I am sorry. I was coming to find you. I am not sure what to do. I told them to find something to occupy their time, to entertain themselves. But I was not sure what to do with this." She lifts her palm.

Clasping her hand, I give it a squeeze. "It is alright, Alfreda. I will speak with them. It has been a long time since we have had young spirits in the castle. I am quite sure no one will hold them ill will."

I enter the passageway and start the climb to the top. I could fly, but I am quite enjoying the music and break from tedious theories and suppositions about how to deal with the locusts. The stairs circle the outside of the round tower. Halfway up, I chance a peek over the edge, and cool air rushes over my face. Hugging the wall, I let my fingers trail over the cold stones, and I think about generations of family members who graced this stairway. How my brothers and I would sneak up to the high tower room to evade adult oversight, spending afternoons putting on plays. They would bring their swords and teach me to fence because Alfreda had disallowed it, thinking it inappropriate for a female fae.

As I step onto the top landing, the rock beneath my feet vibrates, radiating into the balls of my feet. *How can three girls create such a symphony?* Turning the knob and swinging open the heavy wood panel, my breath catches in my throat. A breeze hits my face, and my hair and skirt swirl around me. A lyre harp floats above my head, strings vibrating as if being plucked by a hand. A fiddle and bow hang above it. To my right, a flute lies suspended in air, a trumpet hovers opposite me, and banjo is on my left. Between them, globs of liquid—I cannot even find words to describe them—morph into different shapes: a star, a heart, a rabbit, a butterfly.

The instruments and blobs swirl in a circle with slow, mediated precision, like a carousel. I look down to see

Gatuika, hands raised as if directing a band; Makani rotating in slow circles; and Isla moving her fingers and hands around each other as if forming shapes in clay.

"What is this?"

They spin to face me. Liquid falls from the air, splashing over our bodies, and the music stops. The instruments hang in the air as if suspended by invisible strings. Air hovers around my skin as if I am encased in a cocoon.

Gatuika's eyes grow wide. "You could hear us?"

"Could I hear you? The whole castle, probably the entire village, could hear you. We cannot hear ourselves speak in the study. What? How?"

Makani's hands perch on her hips. "Gatuika, you said you figured out the sound boundary."

Isla's eyes narrow, and her face shines red. "Yeah, Gatuika."

"How many instruments do you see? This is a lot of work." Gatuika crosses her arms over her chest.

My heart thumps in my chest. "Girls, come here."

I hold out my hands and, eyes to floor, they approach. When they look up, their gazes seem to plead with me.

I swallow. "You were doing all this?"

Chapter 10

LOOKING BETWEEN EACH OTHER, they nod.

"How? No, I have a room full of scientists, officers, and soldiers from Chastam and Rotuga downstairs. I cannot talk about this right now. It must be later, somewhere safe."

"We thought you knew. If we do not practice our magick, it will leave. I am sorry. I thought I could mask the sound." Gatuika squeezes my hand.

My head swims. "Knew what? No, we cannot do this right now. We will find a way tonight. Perhaps a slumber party."

Isla lifts an eyebrow. "And wall bashing?"

Dropping their hands, I lift my finger. "There will be no wall bashing, and there will be no more of whatever happened here today. Not in the castle. I will figure out a way to sneak some fae here so others will see band members exiting the tower stairs, but until we speak again, please, find something normal to do. Not *you* normal, normal teen fae normal. Buy some dresses, do your hair. Alfreda will give you coins if you need."

Tears form in Gatuika's eyes. "I am really sorry, cousin. We thought—"

I wrap my arms around her. "It is okay. I am not mad. Everything will be fine."

Hugging Isla and Makani, I exit the room and close the door behind me. Heart racing, I lean against the cold rock wall. I place my palm over my heart. *They thought I knew? Knew they had magickal powers? Did Cassia think I knew? Does she have powers as well? Is that how Mother knows things? Is that why I have my gift—if that is what one would call it?* Of late, it feels like a curse, for it has brought me nothing but ridicule and judgment.

I jump into the air and shoot to the bottom of the stairs. In the passageway, I find Alfreda, hand to heart, pacing.

"Why are you soaked, and how did they get so many people up there without me seeing a soul? Those are the sneakiest teens I have ever laid eyes on."

Smiling, I wrap an arm around her shoulders. "They were playing with water. I believe they met friends in the village and had them fly up, one by one."

I realize this may not be a problem Alfreda is equipped to handle. Circling to my quarters, I find Grant and inquire as to Foster's whereabouts. My guard informs me Foster went south to monitor Regin. I sigh, realizing it must be Grant I put my trust in now. Pulling him to the side of the hall, I whisper directions to him. It works in my favor that the secret passages enter into the tower.

I duck into my room, blotting my hair and shedding my wet dress. Approaching the library, I find Quinn and the others exiting to the hall.

He indicates they listed many good ideas, and we should firm up the plan and schedule the next morning.

Feeling relieved not to be stuck in meetings for the rest of the day, and that I may have some time to deal with my cousins, I inform Quinn we will ride in the woods till dinner time. I feel I may go mad if I cannot sort out the holes in my knowledge with haste.

I spin around just in time to see Grant escorting a group of six random teens, all carrying instruments, out of the tower stairwell. Gatuika, Makani, and Isla file out, followed by Adam.

I join the end of the procession, winding through the front courtyard, under the main arch, and outside the castle walls. We thank the stable and farm fae for their service, reward them with coins, and have them circle back to their work sites.

Asking Grant and Adam to fetch Nicholas and Timothy as well, I gather the girls and make for the stables. The stable hands never like it when I arrive unannounced, but I assure them we can saddle our own horses. My cousins' wide eyes tell me different, but I demonstrate the process then help each with their bridles, girths, blankets, and saddles. Once I am assured all fits securely, we mount the horses and start out. As always, two council guards trail my four escorts, but I know how we shall hide our words.

Pressing my horse to speed across the meadow, I enter the forest. The girls follow as we meander through the trees to the stream. I look up to see my escorts and council guards hovering above the canopy. Stopping at the bend in the river, I slide from my saddle. The girls do as well, and we knot our skirts and enter the brook. The cold water washing over my feet quells my nerves.

I bend over and grab a clod of sediment from the riverbed. Searching through it, I ask my cousins to tell me their story as they hunt for crystals. Surprised I know nothing of the family history, Gatuika starts at the beginning.

Unlike the gifts bestowed on the judges' lines, magick in our family passes from mother to daughter. Women in my mother's lineage have guarded the secret for generations for fear they would be shunned or cast away.

Gatuika grips my hands. "But now that you are a monarch, you have the power to change all that."

Isla jumps in front of me. "What is your power? It is super strength, right? Tell me I am right, for I will win our wager, and they have to wash my clothes for a year."

"No. I do not have any powers."

Makani narrows her eyes. "You lie. You could not have bested Ethan or escaped Lower Earth without some form of magick."

"I believe I am the one asking the questions. I need to know everything you know."

"Your mother did not tell you? Wait, when did…" Gatuika bites her lip.

"My brothers die? My mother fall silent? Just months after my twelfth birthday."

Makani shakes her head. "She should have told you. Our powers, if we have any, manifest around twelve years of age. On our twelfth birthdays, our mother told us about our heritage, about what we may experience. And when our powers started to emerge, we trained to grow and control them."

Gatuika takes her sister's hand. "Do you know if your mother has a gift?"

Bending to pick up another handful of mud, I sift through the rocks and, not finding any of value, let them fall to the stream. *Perhaps I could develop my magick so it would be of more use to me.*

"You will not tell us? We have trusted you with our biggest secret. You must have faith in us. We would never betray your confidence. Because we are cousins first, but also because it could cost all of us our freedom."

Faith is not an easy thing for me of late. I look up at her. "And that is why your mother wanted you to stay with me? Because she believed you would be safe here? That I knew and would keep your secrets?"

Makani scoops up a pile of rocks. "We did not lie. We want to meet others beyond those few that may come to Bedham. But also, yes. We assumed that because you knew our secret, we would be safe, and that you may offer some additional training. Our mother has not been gifted any abilities."

"I am afraid you will be disappointed."

"You truly do not have any powers?" Isla looks at me wide-eyed.

"Maybe your mother does not either, and that is why she failed to tell you. She thought that you both lacked the gift," Gatuika says.

Anger swells up inside me. *Why did Mother neglect to tell me?* Father said she saw the kobold kill my brothers *and* me. She knew she possessed the gift and yet said nothing. I remember my twelfth birthday as if it were yesterday. We planned a party in the courtyard with all my friends, but the kobold attacked in the south, and Father and my brothers, along with all the other soldiers, went to battle. The whole kingdom nailed their shutters closed and did not dare venture outside for fear of the winged monsters. Perhaps with the danger and hysteria, Mother forgot. Or perhaps she did not want to burden me further. My mind circles back to the present. *You have guessed that perhaps your gift had been familial before,* I remind myself. All of this should not be such a shock to you. *But can I trust them? What if* they *could help* me?

I look between the girls, wondering if there is more. I have to know everything. "As you can imagine, all of this comes as quite a shock. My faith in my mother is shaken. Even before she fell dumb"—I pause as I realize it may have been her choice—"she neglected to enlighten me that we may have gifts. What if it is too late for me?"

Gatuika grabs my hand. "We may be able to help you if you trust us."

"Yes, two of the witches of the trinity had no clue of their heritage. They did not develop their powers until they were seventeen. And you are but sixteen." Makani takes my other hand.

"You follow the witches of the trinity? Are we part witch?"

Isla holds her palms out flat. Tiny droplets of water rise from the stream. "Every fae who has any free time whatsoever watches the witches of the trinity. That is, when we are allowed to do so. It does not matter what we are. If we neglect the gifts of the goddesses, it would be blasphemy."

Many things they say disturb me. *Do I commit blasphemy by blaming the goddesses for my plight?* But the need to know if Hunter lives trumps all else. "What else do you know of the trinity?"

"I know"—Gatuika's smile widens—"that if Hunter were not in love with Alena, I would go to Upper Earth and glamour him to be mine forever."

"Hunter is a strong witch. You could not glamour him." Makani sprays water on Gatuika.

"Then he would fall in love with my beauty." Arms stretched wide, she spins around.

Isla drops her arms and the droplets fall to the river with a splat. "I would marry Jude. He is much more handsome and sweet." She cuts her eyes between us. "If he were not in love with Camille."

Makani places her hands on her hips. "I favor DJ and would need no glamour. He would see how special I am and fall in love with me instantly."

"He is half vampire. He would eat you." Gatuika splashes her sister.

I wave my hands in the air, trying to rein them in. "Okay, I get it. They are very handsome. But do you know if Hunter lives?"

"Oh, that." Gatuika drops her eyes to the river. "No, Mother was so freaked out about the whole Lower Earth thing she forbid us to go to the rings after that. And then the council—"

"But I am sure all that will be cleared up soon. The goddesses would not leave you in such a state." Makani's wide eyes hold mine.

"Would they not? I do not believe the goddesses favor me anymore."

"That is too sad to bear." Isla envelopes me in her arms. "I will not believe it."

In the distance, I hear the sound of the gathering horn. I look up to see the light dimming and realize it is time for the night meal. Instructing them to pack their things and move to the room beside me after dinner, we saddle up. The meal passes with our guests enjoying dancing. Seeing all entertained, I steal away to ensure my cousins' move proceeds smoothly.

Approaching the door, I stop short.

Holden stands in front of the fireplace.

You have gone mad with exhaustion. My chest tightens. Closing my eyes, I open the doors to find the girls shifting clothes from trunks to hangers. If one more burden befalls me, I believe I shall buckle under the pressure.

"This is an amazing room." Isla flits to me. "So much bigger than our last."

I force a smile and survey the chamber. Three small beds line the wall where the large one once stood. Leaving them to finish their chore, I wind back to the celebration. With my new knowledge, I will rest easier with my guards outside their room. Plus, if further shenanigans ensue, at least they will be near.

I realize I did not ask how out of control their powers could get or if they manifest without warning. *No, that could not be the case.* Otherwise, I would have seen it in the six days they have been here. *But would I?* The girls said if they did not use their powers, the magick would fade. My heart skips a beat as I think I may not have access to my power when most needed. Now that it seems the goddesses have turned from me, perhaps my magick will as well. I must do everything to ensure my powers. *That is, if you still believe your destiny lies in defeating the evil spirits of the deep. Otherwise, what does it matter?*

I shudder. *Have I lost complete faith?*

It is okay to believe such. The voice sounds as if someone stands behind me.

Spinning around, I see no one in the dark corridor. I hurry to the banquet room as bumps rise on my skin. I have gone mad.

"Are you quite alright, cousin? You look pale." Quinn greets me.

"I did not get much sleep last night, and it has been a long day. I believe I shall turn in."

Looping back to my chamber, I press open the door to my lightless room. Glow reflecting from the meadow highlights Holden's green tunic hung over a chair. I light a candle and, crossing the room, lift the vest to my face, sucking in his smell.

Perhaps it does contain magick, demon repelling magick. At least for one more night, I will believe in that. I lift the sword from the corner and climb into bed, setting the blade at my side and clutching the fabric to my chest. I stare out the window, my brain swirling with the day's events. Mother should have told me about our lineage. I am really angry with her. *Can I hold this against her?*

Would I have shared that secret with my daughter? If she had told me of her gift, perhaps she knew she would have to reveal the things she saw or heard: that my brothers would die, that *I* would die. *How could one lay that burden on a child?* No, I do not blame her for that choice.

I do not let myself imagine the relationship we could have had if fate had not taken my brothers and her from me. Instead, I picture my power radiating from my hand, illuminating the sky. Odd how I do not even know what it is. Isla controls water; Makani, wind; and Gatuika, sound. *But what did I do when I shocked the kobold looming over me? Or when power shot through my muscles, enabling me to best Ethan? What about propelling myself from Lower Earth?*

Is it an electric energy? Am I summoning it from inside or channeling it from elsewhere? And how do I discover the source? My cousins said they watched the witches of the trinity hone their powers. Perhaps I should let my cousins tutor me. *Can I trust three teen girls? You are but a year older than Gatuika,* I chastise myself. *And you shared your secret with Holden. He could blab it to his family or his wife*—my throat closes with the thought—*and the whole realm may learn of it.*

I spread my fingers, willing the magick to manifest.

Nothing.

I think about the energy, how it felt coursing through my nerves, muscles. Each time it manifested, there was an outlet: the sword I thrust into the kobold, Ethan's body, the ring. I place my other palm opposite the first, leaving a small gap. With every ounce of my brain, I imagine energy flowing from one hand to the next.

Nothing.

Thinking again about when my power released, I note danger had been a factor. Quinn would not like this train of thought. Each time, my very life was threatened. Of course, I know this, had recognized it before, assumed the goddesses only interceded when they saw no path for my survival. But the goddesses are gone now, and I must learn to realize this magick myself.

But how will I with Zekial's presence and the council guards trailing me night and day? You wait them out, that is how.

I WAKE NIGHTMARE FREE ONCE again and stretch my wings. Lifting the tunic and sword from the mattress, I rest the weapon in the corner, tunic hooked on the pommel. I believe it makes a fine decoration, a reminder to keep my heart guarded.

Breakfast is buzzing with discussion of completing plans for controlling the locusts. Seeing Alfreda walk Mother to the garden, my mind pings with guilt. There has been little time for me to give her of late. I promise to make time on the weekend. With the meal's end, we convene in the library, penning strategies for curtailing the locust populations at each stage of their lives. With jobs clear, we draw the meeting to a close before the midday spread.

I invite everyone to join us, but all request packed lunch baskets. They seem as eager to join in the first festival weekend in their home kingdoms as I do to start mine. I excuse myself to find Alfreda to alert her to the changed plans and rush through the passage.

"Queen! Queen Titania," I hear a voice call. Turning, I find the white bearded soldier from Rotuga who seemed so familiar.

Looking one way and then the other, he motions me into a side corridor. Bowing, he stands upright. "May a have a moment's time? I had hoped to steal you away last night, but you retired early."

"It has been a busy week." I force a smile, wondering again where I had seen this odd-looking fae. Long white mustache and wide middle, all he would need was a beard to pass for the Santa Claus figure of Upper Earth. "Have we met before?"

"No, Queen." He dips his chin and diverts his eyes again, scanning the space. Looking back to me, he whispers, "I am Alemayehu. I, too, encountered the witch they call Hunter in Upper Earth."

"That is why I recognize you. I saw you in Hunter's thoughts."

"Aye, I suspected you did. He was most intent on finding aid. But I could not risk going against the rules and aiding the hybrid beings with whom he associates."

"Wise given my current situation."

"Yes, I learned of that as well. I thought you may want to know that Hunter lives."

My heart soars. Not only for Hunter, but for Alena and Camille. It feels as though a weight lifts from my chest, and my breath comes a bit easier. "He is alive? How do you know?"

"I am a believer, obsessed with figuring out the riddle of the trinity's goals. I saw before they ordered the rings guarded by the council."

The word believer seems odd, but I am more intent on learning all he knows. "What else did you see? Did they break the curse? How did they break it? And why did they chance traveling to Lower Earth? And once there, what did they achieve?"

"I believe the curse is broken but could not confirm it. The witches of Michael's coven were moving against Hunter. Whatever passed in Lower Earth, the coven stopped the attack."

"So, what of Sonia, Thanatos, and Theron?" Their images flash through my mind, and I wonder if I have cursed myself to enduring the nightmares again.

"I know not."

Frustration crowds my brain. "What did you mean that you are a believer?"

"I believe that the kobold that attacked your kingdom were aided by magick of the evil spirits and that these evil spirits lie beneath us plotting to overtake our realm."

"Why would you not? This is a fact."

"You do not know?"

"Do not know what?"

"Most say you imagined the kobold were aided by magick."

"Imagined? But my father, the generals, and the soldiers all saw."

"The fact that Gunther staged the robbery of your crystals signaled to most that it was improbable that the kobold were invisible, that you created the story."

"But I saw it with my own eyes, as did many of the soldiers. Our ring crystals were taken with no detection by the Ring Keeper.

"Many soldiers saw, or just the one with you? It was dark, no? And some say your father had your Ring Keeper remove the crystals to spur you to become the hero."

My face flames. "That is ludicrous. My father would never. This is why they assigned Zekial to watch me? To make sure I am a suitable ruler?"

"I saw Hunter's mind as you did. I know how powerful Sonia is, and if she is in league with the demons of Lower Earth, the goddesses help us all. The problem is that we have not been threatened by these evil spirits in generations. That is how they gain foothold. They wait until no one believes, and then they strike. And who would blame the goddesses for not coming to our aid? Leaving us to fend for ourselves? No one offers prayers anymore."

Is that my problem, I wonder? I have not prayed to the goddesses since learning the High Council would hold the trial. I was too distracted with Holden, stealing every moment with him. That is when my nightmares began. Still, mere days missed of prayers should not anger them to the point of abandoning me, throwing me to the likes of Zekial, or taking Holden from me when I have done all in my power to honor the gifts I was given, even being willing to sacrifice my own life.

"Queen."

I refocus on the fae in front of me.

"Yes, Alemayehu. Forgive me. This issue weighs heavy on my heart."

"I am sure. Be strong, young queen. There are those of us who believe, and we will be ready to fight with you when it is time."

Voices echo in the corridor.

He lifts my hand and kisses my fingers. "Forgive me, for I cannot be seen with you alone."

"Of course, go. And thank you. You have done me a great service." I point him to the secret passage and instruct him on how to exit.

As soon as he slips away, the heaviness hits me like a brick. *Everyone thinks me a fraud? Father a liar? How could this be? Would my guard not hear these rumors?* Henrick watches Gunther and Ethan, Foster watches Regin, four stay on my service, leaving six, and their ears may not reach behind closed doors of far kingdoms. I clutch the windowsill. My breathing comes heavy, and the space tilts on its end.

No. I grip the rock, digging my fingers into the stone. *You will not give in to this anxiety spell. You will show them all, goddesses included, that Titania, Queen of Aubren, is quite worthy of respect and honor.*

Chapter 11

I LIFT MY PALMS TO SEE THEY are bloody. *Drat.* Winding to my room, I clean my hands and pocket a few extra kerchiefs. I zip to the kitchen and order the lunches. Lunch, my neglected family, and welcoming the group from Willhelm for the festival weekend, I focus on these chores. Taking slow, deep breaths, I wind through the passages, exit into the front courtyard, and wish happy travels to the locust conclave guests.

Alemayehu winks at me as he takes to the sky.

My stomach turns. *No. You will not think of it.* It is festival season. All the royals will come from each kingdom. *Nine weeks. You have nine weeks to convince all of them you are sane and capable.* Then Zekial will leave, bored to death of counting chickens and lambs, and all will be normal again. *Except you will be alone. No. You will not think of that either. For now, you have your cousins.*

"Where were you, cousin?" Quinn whispers in my ear as he secures his arm around my waist.

"Helping with the baskets. I needed to wash up."

"What should we do before we welcome our guests from Willhelm? I think a mini-holiday is in order."

I smile. "Perhaps we should picnic in the meadow and shoot some arrows. I need to prove you are not quite as good as me yet."

"I will take that challenge." He rubs his palms together.

Rounding up the girls and securing a basket full of fruits, meats, and cheeses, we make for the meadow.

Zekial watches from the garden courtyard as we aim our arrows at the target.

Even with my distress, I find I am still a bit better aim than Quinn. It saddens me that this makes me glad. *Why should I need to be more proficient than him? Feel special in some way? Because you feel you having nothing right now.*

I summarize Alemayehu's confession for Quinn as we shoot.

He cuts his eyes to my cousins, asking if we should discuss such in front of them.

I propose they may be of help in listening for opinions of me, and this prompts them into planning ways to spy. It reminds me of the task of matchmaking for Quinn, and I note to conference with the girls before the dinner tonight. I hope there will be at least one beautiful, fair-haired princess from Willhelm to catch Quinn's eye.

Little sun reaches the land, and the fae of Willhelm tend to be of light coloring. With white to blond hair, translucent wings, skin of milk white, and blue or golden eyes, they appear almost iridescent. As a child, I remember thinking them like angels of the human books. Even with their borders stretching from the north coast of what is Asia to Europe of Upper Earth, their kingdom remains sparsely populated. In winter, they remain indoors for months. It is there I wish to banish Gunther and his clan for good.

I shall not let myself think of any negatives this weekend. Our relationship with each kingdom, including Willhelm, needs to be solidified. Withstanding Alemayehu's warning of the nonbelievers, they grow abundant crops of wheat, and we exchange vegetables for their grain often. Plus, if we ever wish to drop our criminals on Willhelm's frozen tundra, being on good terms will help.

Of course, if I list who may make the best allies, Lindleton, lying under Europe, and Borean, lying under the United States, rank highest. More fae live in those two kingdoms than all the others combined. Even with our standing as the first fae kingdom, of the nine, we hold second to last in size and fourth to last in population. And now, with my reputation tarnished, I imagine my battle for securing a better reputation to be an uphill one. Oh, but if I were a sheep of a male monarch, following the age-old traditions, maybe they would hold me in higher regard. If only I were not cursed with this inner fire, perhaps I would find favor with them.

After lounging on the blanket with our meal, we take to another round of target practice until my arms sear. *I must remember to do more of this.* I am sure there will be plenty of chances, while entertaining guests, with such contests. I remind myself to let others win. Finishing, we return to the castle to dress to welcome guests. I ask the girls about the seating chart and possible introductions we may make for Quinn.

With sly smiles, they show me how Quinn is seated between Princess Marta and Princess Nika, being sixteen and seventeen, respectfully.

I hug them and thank them for their help.

—◇◇◇—

AN HOUR LATER, I STAND, fighting the urge to scratch at the skin under the delicate lace on my arm. My outfit, a traditional green silk gown with long lace sleeves, neckline spanning from shoulder to shoulder, a tight bodice, a V-waist, and an A-line skirt, annoys me to no end. Alfreda argued with me for an hour about the skirt, but I would not bend. She favors the poufy skirts, and I will wear nothing of the sort. It serves as torture enough to wear this dress as it is, so thin and sheer, leaving me vulnerable. At least I have my boots with my dagger, which she abhors as well, but she is not queen.

Eyes on the road, I await arrival of the royal family of Willhelm, for they will fly to an inn, change into their best frocks for the evening party, and travel here by carriage. Part of me resents these traditions, finding them unnecessary and stuffy. The other part of me clings to them like a child, wishing back the years when I would stand, barely able to keep still for the excitement of seeing all the fae dressed in their most elegant gowns and suits.

As is tradition during festival season, the princes and princesses travel to visit each kingdom in turn. Thinking this saddens me further, as we have no one to visit other kingdoms. Sight of the carriages brings me out of my spiral, and I straighten my shoulders. Quinn and my cousins by my side, I walk to the lane to welcome our guests as they exit their coaches. The stream from the carriages line up oldest first: Prince Abram and his wife, Princess Mina, a princess in her own right from Chastam; Princess Beatrice and her husband, Prince Rolan, also a prince in his own right from Chastam; Prince Maxim and his twin, Princess Nika; Princess Marta; and the youngest, Prince Kirill.

The others dip their chins and kiss my cheeks, but Kirill bows low and, taking my hand, kisses my fingers. As he stands upright, I realize him to be taller than me. My face flushes as I meet his translucent blue eyes, take in his high cheek bones and wide chin. I scan the line of royals, their skin of ivory, punctuated by the darker fae of Chastam. I introduce Quinn and my cousins in turn. Picking up my skirt, I lead them through the flower-filled halls to the inner courtyard, now alight with lanterns strung over the space like a blanket of stars.

From the corner, a string quarter starts a tune, and servers lay finger foods on long tables.

This hour is meant for drinks and conversation. I look over the scene with terror. *What am I to talk about?* Shaking my head to remember my protocol, I turn and smile at Abram and his wife, Mina.

"I am so happy for you to be here. Tell me, how are your father, King Ivan, and mother, Queen Ria?"

He replies they are well and send me greetings.

Seeing Mother, Father, and General Kane, I head their way .

Abram greets Father with a firm handshake and pat to his shoulder. They converse as if they are old friends asking about hunting successes.

"It is just like men to huddle together about such things." Ria leans into me.

Yes, just like them. To completely ignore that it is me, not my father, who sits on the throne. I engage Princess Beatrice and Rolan, asking about their activity of late. Rolan asks about the locust conference with Chastam and Rotuga, and the group falls silent.

"We constructed a plan to combat them in each of their life phases and will begin next week," I answer.

"It was sweet of you to host the taskforce." Prince Abram dips his chin to me.

I bite my tongue. *Sweet? To host?* Expelling a breath, I smile. "Yes, well, the first swarm struck our countryside, and I hope to prevent more destruction. It seemed important to launch a coordinated attack."

"Against the hideous bugs, yes." His tone rings serious but the edges of his lips turn up.

Silence ensues. My rage festers in my chest. *How dare he mock me.* "I guess it would seem more pertinent if your wheat crops were threatened. We should talk of prettier looking things at a party. Dove hunting is quite popular in Willhelm in summer, is it not? Tell me of your latest quests."

"Doves are a rarity. That is why they are so treasured and the hunting such good sport. I manage to bag a few a week. But I should commend you on your latest victory, your triumph over the kobold."

I have thought of this as I let arrow after arrow away. *How to sway them to realize that I am not crazy, and the kobold did have magical powers? And that Father engaged in no subterfuge?* I lift my chin.

"Yes, it was quite an experience, as you can imagine." Brushing my hand across my brow, I lay my hand on Father's arm. "It was good King Oberon and his generals were able to discover the kobalds' abilities. Their work helped me form my plans. Did you read my father's accounts of the stolen ring crystals?"

Wide-eyed, Abram looks from me to Father and back. "I do not believe I have read those accounts."

"Copies were sent to each kingdom, correct?" I turn my head to Father.

He clears his throat. "Yes, I made sure of it. The kobold of late were not the same as those that attacked before. They were able to steal the ring crystals without leaving a trace. We should all be wary of such magick."

I want to hug Father. He played his part as if we rehearsed it.

Prince Abram clears his throat. "I will make sure to read your account when I return to Willhelm."

Yes. You do that, please. I wave a palm in the air, hoping to catch a server's eye. "But this is a party, so we should all have more wine and speak of happier topics."

"To Titania." Prince Abram lifts a glass once they are refilled. "To her victory and assured resolution of the locust issues."

"To Titania," the others repeat.

I smile and raise my glass to each in the circle.

The conversation turns to sport, fashion, music, and dance.

I glance around to find Gatuika, Makani, and Isla with Quinn, Prince Maxim, and Princess Nika. All their faces wear smiles, and relief washes over me. The festival season will end in success, and all will be well. Convincing everyone I am not mad and finding love for Quinn would solve two problems. Perhaps these events will not be as horrid as I thought. *As I imagined without Holden. Holden…* I must not picture him dining with Lily in whatever kingdom they celebrate a festival dinner this night.

The dinner bell chimes, and Father wraps his arm around my waist as we meander to the front table. "I assume I got my lines right?"

I smile at him. "Yes, Father. Thank you."

"I would do almost anything in support of you and this kingdom. You know that, do you not?"

My side ticks as I expect a but or a request to come next. "Of course, Father."

"Then please, make yourself as available as Quinn seems to be doing."

Forcing a smile, I whisper in his ear, "I will dance, and I will be polite, but if you press me in this, I will take you to Willhelm and leave you in the frozen tundra myself."

He blinks. "Understood, daughter."

And I do exactly that. I dance with everyone who asks, even though the fifteen-year-old Prince Kirill asks me multiple times. At half past eleven, I round up Gatuika, Makani, and Isla, thinking that removing them from the party before it descends into debauchery gives me the perfect excuse to retire for the evening.

"Quinn talked with Princesses Nika and Marta, and danced with them as well." Gatuika reports.

"That is very good." I take her hand. "And tomorrow will give them more time to connect. Although I doubt Quinn would like living in Willhelm after the temperate climates of our kingdom and his home in Bedham."

"Perhaps a princess from Willhelm would want to come here. She would be elevated in title because he is heir presumptive."

"But as soon as Titania marries, he will not be. Right, Titania?" Isla looks up at me.

My breath catches in my throat, and I swallow. Tears threaten. How am I ever to find another like Holden, a prince in his own right, so full of life, so devoted? I am not sure I can ever give my heart again.

Makani slaps Isla's arm. "Why would you say that? So soon after…" Makani takes my free hand. "I am sorry. She did not mean to mention marriage or love."

"Do not dismay for me." Dropping Makani's hand, I reach out to Isla. "All those I need are right in this castle."

Leaving them in their room and shutting the doors to mine, I lean back on the soft wood. Except they are not. *He* is not. Mother said I needed him, and I need him, and he is gone. I slump to the floor. The stone is cold and hard, but I care not. *Make yourself available.* Father's words ramble through my brain. *To whom? Why? For alliances?* I have no need for a fake marriage that provides me a thin string of a promise of protection. No, the goddesses willing, I am the only protection we need. *But are the goddesses still so inclined?*

I hold out my palm, concentrate with all my might, flail out my fingers, and thrust my arm out, again and again. Nothing. Pushing on the stone, I stand, shed my gown, don my nightclothes, and retrieve the tunic and sword from the corner. *Damn you, Prince Holden of Hilbron who I shall never marry.* As tears fall to my sheets, I lay my head on the pillow.

———

MORNING COMES AFTER A dreamless night. I almost kiss the tunic in thanks, but think I should be spitting on it, damned fate of the goddesses. Willing those thoughts from my head, I draw the curtains and dress.

Games follow breakfast in the inner courtyard along with activities like archery, fencing, and a hunt in the afternoon.

Prince Kirill trails me throughout. While his presence feels somewhat safe—I would much rather talk to him than someone who could be a match for me, like his older brother, Prince Maxim—I fear Kirill may get the wrong impression.

I watch Quinn with Princess Nika, hoping that will be a fruitful relationship. At dinner, I note them smiling and talking, and she is his first dance. As a new tune starts, I catch motion at the entrance to the castle. Apologizing to Kirill, I make my way to the door.

Grant is bent over with Adam, listening to the words of a page.

I recognize him as hailing from Westshire.

They bow as I reach them, and Grant takes my arm and leads me inside. "There is a swarm that descended upon a field just minutes ago. What should we do?"

"Exactly what we planned to do. Let us go, *now*. You"—I point at the page—"rush back, gather as many as you can, get lots of water, and start digging a trench around the field."

The page shoots into the air, and I do as well, bound for my chamber. Inside, I shed my gown and dress in a riding skirt and vest. Exiting, I find Quinn and three more of my guard waiting.

"Should I come?" Quinn inquires.

"No, we will have enough fae. Make sure the girls are cared for. Ask Alfreda to tend to them."

I leap to the windowsill, hearing something that approximates him accusing me of breeding the locusts myself just to get out of enduring the party. Taking to the air, we rush south and west to Westshire. Even in the dim light, I can see the darkened mass from the sky. Approaching, the hum of the bugs rises. To call it a hum offends all hums. The sound emanates from the ground like a sharp grate of metal on metal, rising and falling, almost in synchrony.

Bumps form on my skin, and the hairs of my arms stand on end as I land. I clap my hands over my ears to block the deafening sound. We are waved inside the farmhouse.

Fae pack the dwelling, twenty deep. They report the trench almost finished and buckets posted at intervals alongside. The back door opens, and a brown-winged fae confirms the tasks complete.

We file outside and receive torches.

Wide eyes greet me as I am passed mine.

"Queen, you…" His mouth hangs open.

"I have come with the others to help end these wretched creatures."

Touching our torches to a lit one, we file down the trenches. With the signal, we touch them to the nearest plants, producing a ring of fire.

I shield my face against the heat and roar of the flames.

As the fire spreads like a wave crashing in on itself, bugs and smoke fill the air.

I watch the sky as many locusts escape into the dark.

"Follow them." I jump into the air.

But the winged creatures disperse, and their bodies disappear against the night sky.

Still, we managed to kill many, and I count it a success. Tomorrow, we will search the woods and adjoining fields for the creatures and their eggs. Returning to the ground, we guard the field until the fire is out. I huddle with the others as the embers die, instructing all that can to meet at first light.

"Do you not have to see your guests off in the morning?" Grant asks as we fly back to the castle.

"Quinn and Father can do it. I can write them apologies and thanks for the visit after tomorrow's task is complete. What monarch would risk her country's food supply to stand, smile, and wave as fattened guests make off in carriages?"

"Well said, Highness, and that is why we follow you." Adam dips his chin.

Ignoring the last of the revelers, I peek into the girls' room to find them snoring. Leaving instructions to wake me well before first light, I fill the tub and wash the soot from my face and wings. I take up the vest and sword and climb into bed, muscles relieved at the feel of the soft feathers underneath them.

"Did you think it would be that easy?" Lucifer's hot *breath drenches my neck, and the words hiss over my ears.*

I sit up with a start and fling the sword and vest to the floor. My talismans fail me. *Drat you, Lucifer. Hunter is alive. I will be proved sane and capable and we will come for you. I know not how, now that Holden has left, but I will uncover a way, one morrow, somehow.*

Dressing hastily, I leave instructions with Alfreda, the girls, Quinn, and Father.

Grant, Adam, Nicholas, Timothy, and I, trailed by Zekial and two council guards, set out for Westshire. Nearing the farm, we find the field of ashes.

A young fae, I guess him to be not more than thirteen, follows a mule with a plow, tilling the ash under the soil.

Some forty fae gather beside the cottage. Landing, we join their ranks.

Charting a map, we parcel out sections fanning out from the spot, a league in every direction, each parcel to be searched for locusts and their eggs. We leave out the heavily wooded areas because the locusts tend to lay their eggs in the open sand.

I describe the egg pods the swarming females bury and the foam that will help us locate them. My skin crawls when I think that one female may lay twenty-five eggs.

With instructions to return at the midday hour, we head out, Grant and Adam with me. As I assumed, Zekial and his two guards follow, and I put them to work as well. At least their presence makes for faster inspection. Seeing no evidence of the bugs in our section, we span out farther into the desert. We spot no locusts but find a few egg pods buried in the sand. Burning these, we press on, scanning every inch as we take step after step into the dry desert.

As the rendezvous time nears, we place the wasp attractants at the edge of our inspection zone. I produce small cups of wax filled with clover honey from my bag and set them every ten yards or so to draw the larvae predators to the spot. Accomplishing this task does not render the same sense of satisfaction as the previous night, but it is not as if we could inspect the whole country. *Or could we?* It may be possible in Aubren, but in Rotuga, and Chastam especially, where their vast kingdom reaches two-times-three-thousand leagues, it would take a large number of fae. I will leave such drastic measures as a last resort.

The other teams report seeing no locusts and finding only a few egg pods.

Where did the creatures go? I decide not too many of them escaped but wonder if they dispersed or reconvened and will move again as a group. Continued dry conditions make the environment ripe for their gregarious forms to persist. I make a mental note to mark my calendar when we return to the castle. Their eggs hatch within ten days, and the bugs remain in crawling nymph form twenty-four days before transforming to fliers. This makes thirty-five days till they can mate and lay twenty-five more eggs per female. But twenty-five by twenty-five makes six-hundred twenty-five which means two locusts make six-twenty-five in twenty-five days and over fifteen thousand in fifty days. Fifteen thousand locusts can do much harm.

In the last epic outbreak, the swarms covered village-sized areas, wiping out crops meant for thousands of fae in one day. We do not even approximate that magnitude. *You have strategies, so trust in that.* I console myself.

IT IS MIDAFTERNOON WHEN WE return to the castle. My body craves rest. But seeing the girls rush to greet me, I cannot help hearing all their news of how Quinn talked to Nika the whole evening and Kirill switched his attention to Makani once I left.

We find Quinn in the meadow, practicing archery, and I hear his report as well.

After enjoying a quiet dinner with Mother, Father, and Alfreda, we gather in the study for music.

I escort the girls to their chambers afterwards and summon Grant for news from my special guard.

Foster finds nothing askew with Ishmel and Regin, and Henrick reports no new subterfuge from Ethan and Gunther.

I hold my breath for news of our Willhelm guests' opinions of me.

"Our spies report they expected you to be quite mad, crazy with odd ideas, but they found you pleasant if not a bit intense," Grant says.

"That is not so bad. And I believe Abram will read Father's reports on the kobold. If I can repeat this with each delegation, I will win them over, or at least convince them I am not an insane fool, and that Father is a true soul."

"You realize the group from Lindleton will arrive in five days. And that Holden is likely to be included." Grant holds my gaze. "Also, I hear Prince Mikel seeks a bride."

I want to huff and stomp my foot and tell him, "Of course I know all of this." Because I do, and I do not want to be reminded. I must come up with a plan to deal with Holden. Perhaps, in this one instance, I will have the male fae hunt while we females sew in the garden. The idea disgusts me almost as much as the locusts do. *No, I will surround myself with my cousins and never be alone.*

Excusing Grant and the guards, I turn to Quinn. "Princess Rose is sixteen. Perhaps she shall be very lovely."

He slits his eyes. "Are you matchmaking for me now as well?"

"As well? Were you not doing the same?"

"Your cousins were set on pushing Marta and Nika on me. It was quite obvious."

I march around him. "But they were quite beautiful. And you seemed taken with Nika."

"She was quite nice, although tied to her kingdom. I am sure we will both find our true mates someday."

"I need to get letters out to Chastam and Rotuga about the locusts still."

"I will leave you to it." He dips his chin and backs out the door.

It is well after midnight when I climb into bed, dreading the feeling of isolation that has haunted me since Holden's departure and the nightmare I know will come. Even though I long to have his smell surround me, I leave the tunic and sword in the corner. They should not even be here. I should burn them. But such a beautiful weapon. *Could I use it? Is it wise to be reminded of his love when I shall never have it again?* The chasm opens in my chest, and my breathing becomes labored. *You cannot break down, Titania.* I grip the sheets. Curling up in a ball, I allow the only acceptable release: letting the tears stream down my cheeks.

⬦⬦⬦

MORNING DAWNS AS I KNOW it will, with my silent scream in the void.

Lucifer wrestles Holden's sword from my grip and hurls it towards him, sending it straight through his heart.

"You think the goddesses took him from you. They did not. I did."

Chapter 12

"WHAT DO YOU THINK DREAMS mean?" I pop a strawberry in my mouth as Quinn sits down beside me at the breakfast table.

"I believe they can be a mirror of our psyche, help us work out issues which may be hard when awake. Perhaps they even give us answers that are there, but we just cannot figure them out with the many thoughts that crowd our mind in the day. Have you a dream you need deciphered? Tell me."

I lean over and whisper in his ear, "Just Lucifer again, as always."

Alfreda, Mother, Father, and the girls join us for breakfast.

As we eat, letters arrive from Chastam and Rotuga, and my knee bounces with apprehension. Still, I force myself to wait for the others. As soon as Alfreda lets her napkin fall to the plate, I stand. "It is nice to see you all this morning. Quinn and I must meet with the advisors. Have a good day."

"Titania." Father rises from his seat.

"Yes?" I wave Quinn ahead.

Father points to the path, and I fight rolling my eyes.

Halfway to the garden, I can bear it no more and demand he share whatever thoughts weigh on his mind then and there.

"You have not walked with your mother in over a week. You need to make time for her."

I know it to be true. But has he not seen all that I have been doing? Hosting festival dinners, entertaining the girls, battling locusts, and he believes I should make myself available for love as well?

Taking his hand, I smile up at him. "I will try to make some time this afternoon, or at the very latest, tomorrow morning."

"Thank you. You know how she likes your walks in the morning."

"Of course." Forcing a smile, I kiss his cheek.

Turning back to the castle, I hurry along the path. *How does he know or not know what she favors?* Her expression never changes, eyes never lose their haze. It seems shocking to see her even lift a fork to her mouth. For that serves as her only activity save sitting, sitting, and staring. I berate myself. That provides cause enough to keep her active and engaged, so her mind and body do not wither altogether. With renewed resolve, I enter the castle.

The day races by with updates from advisors and farmers and penning notifications to be copied and posted in all the village squares. As Chastam and Rotuga alike report small swarms, the advisors feel we should delegate the army's time to the cause.

I warn that even if we eradicate the pests from our kingdom, swarms could travel from elsewhere.

Still, they think it best to use the army.

As we have no other foe at the moment, and I figure it may look good to Zekial that I do not rule with an iron fist, I agree. I send a messenger to call Kane, his generals, and the officers to meet with me the next day. I notice the light dimming in the sky as I finish the last task. I stretch my arms. My muscles beg for release.

"I could use a long fly after today. Or a large glass of wine." Quinn closes the ledger in his hand.

"Both would be good." My stomach turns as I realize there are only three more days to prepare for Holden's presence. "But I need to walk with Mother. Perhaps after dinner we may take a jaunt around the kingdom?"

"You want me to go flying with you?"

"Of course. Why not? Perhaps we can invite the girls as well. They have not seen the kingdom, and it is quite beautiful at night I believe."

"You have never asked me to fly with you before."

I lay my palms on the table and hang my head. "Why is this such a big deal?"

"You have not been flying for pleasure since…"

Looking up at him, I shrug. "Since?"

"Since Holden. I do believe this means your heart is healing, cousin."

"That is not true. I went flying with the girls just last week. And since when do you keep track of my comings and goings?"

"Into the forest. Not beyond. The only people I have noted you to go on long jaunts with are Foster and Holden."

Wishing I had something to snatch up and march away with, I stand there. *How am I supposed to respond to such a comment?* And it is the first time he has been so bold as to mention Holden since he left. *Flying, up so high you almost reach the barrier.* I can think of no greater joy save that of loving someone, being loved completely. To see the land from such a height—small lights shining from homes the size of peas, green fields, purple in the dim light, the desert sand glowing gold, faint diamonds reflecting off the top of waves—had become my escape, my release, my zen. To mar that experience by including others who may not appreciate it, or who I do not trust, to honor the experience, is a line I will not cross.

Have I decided I trust Quinn completely, or is he making something of nothing?

I grab a handful of my skirt. "Well, join us or not. It is your choice."

Marching from the library, I slam the door behind me. *Trust Quinn after he would not side with me to aid the trinity? But he did not know the gravity of the situation. What if I did tell him all? You would tell him before you divulge your secret with your cousins who share the same gift? No, I would not. Further, he courted my enemy's daughter, and he would probably have me married off to some prince from a distant land just to make an alliance, just like Father. But perhaps not since Quinn could then lose his standing.*

And why does he stay? Out of duty to family? He had few prospects in the small kingdom of Bedham as a distant cousin to a queen, a mere officer among officers. Here, he holds clout, position, respect, even power. Who would not want that?

All these things spin in my head as I amble through the halls to Mother's chamber. *And what shall I talk to her about?* We cannot converse in confidence as we did before Zekial and his guards lurked about. Knocking on her door, I force a smile.

I find her sitting in front of the window. Kneeling, I ask if she would like to walk. With no response, I lift her hand. She rises as I hook it in my arm. I fold my hand over hers, and we wind through the halls, out into the courtyard. In the garden, I tell her of our efforts to combat the locusts. How the first festival weekend stood a success, and that we would welcome the royal family from Lindleton the coming weekend.

Perhaps the locusts will return in force, and I shall have excuse to be away the whole weekend. Sad that I should wish for a swarm of the destructive pests. Facing Holden, having to smile and converse with him and his betrothed… Even thinking of it makes me feel as if I will die. My breaths shorten and side ticks.

Mother stops in her tracks. *Does she sense my anxiety?* I wrap my arm around her shoulders and lay my head there. She stands still, stoic as a soldier. I imagine her hand stroking my cheek, whispers of consolation. A tear forms in my eye, and I lift my head. Perhaps a flight will do me good, clear out my sadness.

Urging her forwards, I take a step. She follows suit, and we return to our accustomed pace, a slow meander through the paths of the garden. As we reach the border with the orchard, she shivers.

"It is cooling and almost dinnertime, let us go back." Placing both palms on her shoulders, I twist her around.

The silence grates me, so I describe the girls and their personalities, all of them so loving but in different ways. Gatuika with an air of duty; Makani and her quiet, drawing compassion; and Isla with her sparks of energy that cannot be ignored. I talk of our afternoon in the village and how they help Alfreda. Were ears not so close, I would chance telling Mother of their powers.

Not as long as the High Council watches me day and night, day in and day out. My anger flares again, and I remember my plot to make them miserable. Perhaps the girls would be helpful in this endeavor. Waking the old fae before dawn, making noise outside their windows late into the night, ensuring the menu included foods they did not like, and ensuring the water is cold for their baths. How delightful, and shameful, a thought.

At the evening meal, my leg bounces under the table while I manage polite conversation. My thoughts and emotions on overdrive, the skies call to me. Bidding goodnight to Alfreda, Mother, and Father, I round up Quinn and the girls. We jump into the air, flying low over the meadow, then rise to meet the height of the trees. As is my habit, the journey must be a circle, and I head west to the border then straight south. We lose the High Council guards, with their slow wings and weak muscles, before we reach the Nariel Ring.

From there, I point out Mt. Kosciuszko, where the kobold hoarded our ring crystals. We swoop into the desert, and I take in the dry air and scent of sage. Bordering the forest, we find the desert pea and sweet fuchsia.

Fording the small strip of lush jungle, we plunge to the beach and swoop out over the water. Salt spray pelts my face, and all else falls away. *Bam.* And then the memory of the merfolk hits me. The merfolk, the people to be mine and Holden's refuge.

Everything good about the trip explodes. My muscles ache with wear, the wind agitates my ears, and high pitch of the gulls' cries echo in my head. I have to be home. Speeding as if my very life depended on it, I leave the others in my wake. Looking back, I see Grant and Adam trail from afar. *How could I have thought this a good idea? What an utter fool I am to think I could have happiness ever again.* Water pours from my eyes, and I fear it will never stop.

Everything blurs, and if not for my inner compass, I doubt I could make it home. But home for a fae harkens from our cells and pulses through our veins like a lifeforce. It draws us when we roam. Even this knowledge brings thoughts of Holden, so far from his birthplace. *How am I ever to live without him? Can I stand in front of him as if my world is not ending?*

Seeing the lights from the castle, I clear my eyes and make large, slow, sweeping circles to the courtyard. I spin around to wait for Grant and Adam, thinking Quinn and the girls may be quite angry with me. *Why would they not be?* I let them down. Abandoned them. Same as I am falling short of many of my duties of late to Mother, Father, Quinn, the trinity, and perhaps even the goddesses.

Grant lands beside me. "Is something wrong? You took off like mad. Did you sense danger?"

"No. I am tired, and it is late. I wanted to be in my bed. I am sorry." I fight tears as I watch for Quinn and the girls.

They appear as dots in the sky and descend to us. Quinn lands and leans over, hands resting on his knees.

"Cousin, you amaze me still with your speed."

"I apologize. My muscles needed a release."

I turn to the girls and take Isla's hand. "What did you think? Is the kingdom, with the dark jungles and blazing gold sand, not amazing?"

"All I want to know is how you are able to fly so fast. And can you train me to do such?" Isla swings our arms between us.

"That was amazing." Makani spins in the air.

"That *was* quite a trip." Gatuika's wings slump to the ground.

Relief washes over me as I realize they are not angry with me—or do not appear to be. Further, given Makani's and Isla's energy level, Makani could buoy herself with the wind, and Isla may use the water to do the same. But Gatuika would have no advantage. Unless a sound wave could do more than produce sound. I make a mental note to study the physics of such.

"My muscles feel drained as well. I believe we all need hot baths and a good night's rest." I tussle Isla's hair. "With lots of flying and good amount of protein, you can be as fast, perhaps even faster."

Tonight, I am glad we took the extra energy of fashioning two additional tubs for the girls' room. I leave them to their baths, and although the wait seems forever for the water to heat, the payoff is great as I sink into the steaming tub. I lay my head back and pray to the goddesses, tears streaming down my face. *Please, give me the strength to welcome Princess Lily and Holden with grace and proper demeanor.*

———

JOLTING UPRIGHT FROM A DEEP sleep, I punch the air. "I do not care what dominion you think you have over me. Lucifer, Abaddon, whoever you are, will not best me, you will not best the fae. For we have always prevailed."

But this is different, and you know it. With Sonia, Thanatos, and Theron, we can, and will, be your end.

"Damn voice." I slap my head. "Out with thee."

"What was that?" Huge smile and raised eyebrows, Alfreda enters the room.

Does she always have to be so happy?

"Why are you so gay?"

"Your cousins are amazing planners. With their help we got four days of work done in one."

I rise. "I will make sure and note your praise to them. Arrange fencing lessons for them today. I have a day full of meetings with the generals."

———

AS I EXPECT, KANE AND HIS men loathe the idea of purposing troops for the locust hunts. I am glad the forethought to have the advisors and scientists present came to me at breakfast.

Two of the advisors had returned to their shires, but four, including Quinn, join the discussion.

"If we have no crops, none of us will have food for the winter," Advisor Bran says to Kane. "Then we will be more vulnerable than ever."

Kane shoots a pointed stare at me. "Queen, may I have a word outside?"

"Of course." I flash the room a big smile as murmurs rise.

He follows me into the passage, and I spin to face his tall figure. He motions me down the hall, and I proceed.

"You cannot be serious that you entertain these hysteric requests from the advisors. We have lost a mere three fields." He hisses into my back.

I turn to meet his query, trying to figure how to convince him. I cannot just say this is for show. *But is it? Is my only motivation to prove that I am an amenable ruler? Do I believe it may be an overreaction? Yes, but what if these steps are needed? Only history will tell.*

Lifting my chin, I meet his wide gaze. "This may seem rash, like reacting to panic. But what if it is not? These creatures multiply by twenty-five every generation. Two become fifteen thousand in sixty days. What if this does become a realm catastrophe as before the flood? What would history say then? All would look at us, where it began, and ask why we did not do more to prevent the tragedy."

His cheeks go slack. He shoots his eyes up to the ceiling and back to me. "The men will not like scanning for tiny nuisances day in and day out."

"Make it a contest. Reward those that find insects and egg cases. Impress upon them what could come to pass if these pests are not stopped. The rains will not come for months, and even then, the scientist say that once in swarming form, they will not change back overnight. Only a long, cold winter would end them, and we are not assured those here."

Resting his hand on the windowsill, he nods. "I see your reason. I do not like it, but I shall follow the request of the advisors and direction of the scientists."

"Thank you." I lift my hand to rest it on his sleeve but stop, remembering his prior insubordination.

"You are changed, less rash, headstrong."

"I hope you mean that as a compliment." I motion towards the library where the others wait.

"Yes, of course." He dips his chin.

He opens the door, and I pass through, thinking I will not be so acquiescent in other matters. With issues concerning the evil spirits of Lower Earth, there will be no compromise.

But you cannot win. Lucifer's voice scurries through my mind.

But you will see. I will find a way, I reply.

Kane convinces his general and officers of the gravity of the situation, and they fall in line.

We dismiss the advisors.

The scientists instruct everyone on collecting specimens and how to note the location where they were found.

I spend the rest of the day plotting out hectares and organizing soldiers into teams.

We estimate with three hundred, we can span eighteen-hundred feet, about a third of a mile. With one and a half million square miles to cover, much of it in dense jungle, the task will take four weeks.

One mating cycle, I realize. *Will it be enough?*

Thinking this needs to happen faster, I ask Kane to recruit future soldiers, teens who may have time before their schooling starts in fall. Feeling an irrational wave of fear, I circle back to the plots, reorganizing them to fan out from the location of the swarm attacks rather than beginning in the north. If each landowner searches their own property, the soldiers can concentrate on natural areas, cutting down what needs to be inspected. Still, it leaves a lot of dense jungle in the interior of the kingdom that will challenge the soldiers. I think about the vast canopy of branches, lush undergrowth, and thick bed of decaying leaves and branches. It seems an insurmountable task, but search of the ground will have to suffice.

Besides, as the advisors noted, there are no other threats now.

Except the crazy voices in your head and weekend with Holden and his bride to be. No. All shall be well. In forty-eight hours, the contingent from Lindleton will be gone. Hopefully, within weeks, Zekial will leave with his guards, and I can figure out a way to contact the trinity.

I walk with Mother, talking about the flowers and birds we see. Then we sup with our now bulging makeshift family. Afterwards, I play a song on my harp and insist the girls entertain us as well.

Isla chooses the flute, and we dance to her delightful jig.

Makani joins her sister with a fiddle.

As our bodies wear, Gatuika takes up a violin.

I rest on my chair back, intrigued to see what tune she may choose. *For is it not her gift to control sound?*

She sits at the front of her stool and holds the bow above the strings. Lowering her chin to the lower bout, she touches the bow to the strings and pulls it down.

Tears well in my eyes at the perfect hollowness of the low note.

The ballad starts slow, with minor chords, as if telling a story of a lonely fae. It picks up and weaves a second, quicker rhythm and ends in a fast bravado of notes I do not believe our finest violin player could rival.

As she strikes the last chord, water overflows my lids. I cannot remember a more beautiful song played, since… *Since Mother.*

I reach over and take her hand, searching her face. Her head does not turn. *But did her eyes widen and narrow a hair?* I abandon the quest for a reaction and rise from my chair, congratulating Gatuika, Makani, and Isla on their talents.

⸺◈⸺

THE NEXT DAY, AFTER REPORTS, I spend with the girls and Quinn, practicing fencing then archery, and taking a brisk fly to the midpoint of the kingdom and back.

In the evening, the girls apprise me of their market list, and I promise to join them in the village outing the next day. I crawl into bed, yet again, so tired I have not the strength to think of anything but my head on the feathers. I glance at the tunic and sword in the corner, knowing I must pen some lines, rehearse what I shall say so I do not slip. In this, there can be no mistakes. I pledge myself to enroll Quinn's assistance in tackling the task on the morrow.

AT BREAKFAST, I KEEP TO MY promise and set a meeting with Quinn following the midday meal.

After a market trip with the girls and a quick lunch, I pace in my study, waiting. Everything I write sounds trivial or callus. *How can I speak to them, speak to* him, *as if nothing has passed?*

Quinn finds all my speeches acceptable. "You do not even know that she is aware of your relationship with Holden."

His comment catches me off guard. I open my mouth to protest, *but he is right. All the realm may know of my triumph over the kobold and treasonous acts of allowing the witches passage to Lower Earth, but of our love? Would he tell her? I did not know that Holden had been in love with another until...* I cannot finish that thought because it was just over a week ago that he said goodbye *to me.* My brain jumps to the next conclusion before I want it to. *He got over* her, *and although he pledged to love me forever, he may very well have fallen in love with Lily.*

"You look as if you may be ill. What passes through your mind?"

I cross my arm over my stomach. Blinking tears away, I study the page.

"Welcome, Princess Lily, Prince Holden." I look up at Quinn. "Do I have to say more? I cannot lie. I will not be glad they are here or grateful they have come. To say, 'I am happy you are here' or 'thank you for coming' would be lying."

Quinn takes the page. "I believe just saying welcome will be perfectly acceptable. And I will be right at your side to jump in with conversation."

"Okay, well, it is settled." I place the page on the desk and smooth it to the surface. Still, my stomach lurches at the thought of gazing upon his large blue eyes, golden hair, and perfect mouth. *Ugh! Blasted festival season.*

"And I shall run interference with Prince Mikel should he approach."

"Why is there need for that? I can take care of myself."

"You wish to be courted by Lily's brother? To end up in the same family as Holden? How torturous would that be?" Quinn asks.

I stare at him, thinking we have never spoke so openly. *I guess this is what comes when you spend day in and day out with someone.* "No. I wish never to set foot in their palace."

He sneers and wriggles his nose. "I hear it is quite pretentious with the whole thing made of white marble. Who do they think they are? For we are of the first line. This, the birthplace of the fae."

A chuckle escapes my lips, and I double over. "I cannot believe you said that aloud. Please, tell me it was for my benefit."

"Of course."

"But your ire should not lie with King Hector's family. What of Holden's father? What would you say of him?"

"I would spit at his feet." Leaning out the window, he spits into the dirt.

I cover my mouth, trying to contain the giggles. Tears form in my eyes as my laughter works itself into a frenzy. I gasp for breath. Swiping my tears, I hold his gaze. "It is good that I have you and my cousins."

Even with this release, my brain will not settle, and I request another night flight.

Quinn takes us north, and we loop around the shores of the isles of their kingdom of Bedham, swooping from the beaches up to the mountain tops. The memory of the sky of Upper Earth dotted with millions of stars tempts me, but because the High Council guards trail us, we dare not venture near the rings.

I settle into my bed, praying the goddesses will give me strength to endure the next seventy-two hours. *Really forty-eight,* my mind pings, *a bit less, because they arrive after noon Friday and leave before noon Sunday.* There will be many distractions, games and hunting. *All you need do is avoid him.* I stare at the tunic and sword in the corner, and the tears come again.

How could the goddesses take him from me? After my brothers and mother? Perhaps that lays too much blame. Could they not intercede, at least? And now to have my free-dom garnished?

⸺◈◈◈⸺

A HUM FILLS MY BRAIN, THE vibration and volume rising so high I feel my ears may pop. Sitting up, I look out over the meadow. All appears still, and I flit around, trying to discern the source of the noise. It seems to come from all around me. I note my clock reads ten after two, the witching hour.

I tug on riding pants and a vest and stuff my dagger in my boot. Exiting into the passage, I find Nicholas, Timothy, and two High Council guards. Taking Nicholas and Timothy aside, I ask if they hear the buzzing sound. They express they do not, and I wonder if it could be a headache or allergies from flying over the ocean and so much vegetation.

Crossing back into my room, I down a glass of water. I lay, head propped on extra pillows, but alas, the whir will not subside. I go to the window, and the pitch changes. Thinking of Mother's words, *you need them*, I snatch Holden's sword and jump over the sill, landing on the ground with a thud. I sense no evil as I did when the orbs of spirits passed to Upper Earth. Still, something stirs. *Do I dare chance a visit to the rings?*

Gathering Nicholas and Timothy, I jump into the air, circling the castle.

The council guards trail us, and I guess they think me mad.

Still, I loop slow and steady in an ever-widening path. I close my eyes and still my brain, hoping to find a pattern, an area where the sound is louder, anything that will point me to the source. As my eyes adjust to the darkness, I notice a faint light emanating from the woods. I cut west over the trees, making a zigzag pattern over the forest. The glow increases as we approach the stream. Reaching the place where the stream bends, I hover above the thick canopy, the whir in my ears almost deafening now.

I hover close to Timothy. "There is something down there."

"But I see nothing," Timothy whispers, "hear nothing. Are you sure you do not have water in your ears? Perhaps the spray from the ocean?"

"No, it is not that." My heart races. *Lucifer? Abaddon? Sonia? Could they have entered our realm without detection?* I cut my eyes to Nicholas and back to Timothy. "Stay here. Whatever is down there may not be of this realm."

"Should we call someone?" Timothy opens his mouth as if to say more but shuts it.

Holden? Foster? Quinn? No, it is just me holding Holden's sword. I lift the metal scabbard. "If I do not return in half an hour, get backup and come searching for me."

"Half an hour? Are you mad?" Nicholas grabs my wrist. "Kane would—"

"What would Kane do? Have me detained and dethroned as he attempted before? If he had succeeded, we would all be dead. This is why I formed *my* guard. I need you to trust me."

"Fine." Nicholas releases me. "But a quarter hour and no longer."

Taking a deep breath, I plunge through the canopy of leaves. Underneath, a blaze of light almost blinds me, and I shield my eyes. *What in the goddesses?* Bumps form on my skin, and my hairs stand on end. I hover, muscles taut. Then the sound of music reaches my ears. *A violin? Harp? Fiddle? Flute? No! The girls! Why would they? They will be detected!* My mind screams. Closing my eyes, I let the waves of magic guide me to the source.

"We knew you were lying." Isla's voice startles me.

Opening my eyes, I find the humming has stopped and the glow has muted. My surprise and anger bubbles over the surface. "What are you doing? My guards and the council guards are just above the trees. You could be discovered at any second."

"Do you know nothing?" Isla jumps into the air spins in a circle. "It is the witching hour. All magic is hidden save from those who share the gifts. That is how we are sure you are lying now." She lands in front of me, her eyes wide. "You have to tell us what your powers are."

I look from her to Gatuika and Makani. "Hidden? Like no one else can see or hear?"

"Exactly." Makani takes my hand.

Biting my lip, I tug my hand from hers. "I do not have power. It is the goddesses' power. They give it to me only when there is no other way."

"Like to best Ethan or escape Lower Earth?" Gatuika urges.

"And to save my life from a kobold. One killed my brother in front of my eyes. It was about to kill me, but a blast, like lightning, shot through my sword, into the creature, and killed it. I have tried to awaken the power, make it manifest, to no avail."

"But we can help you." Makani takes my hand. "There must be a way for you to learn to control your power."

"Yes, the witches of the trinity did." Isla grabs my dagger and holds it up to my face. "Cousin, try, or I shall slice your arm."

She lowers the blade and touches it to my bicep.

"Are you mad?" Makani bats the blade away. "That should be a last resort."

"You heard her though." Isla paces in front of me, eyeing me like her prey. "It only manifests when she is about to die or is scared she is going to die."

"Or lose her crown." Gatuika's eyebrows lift. "Why did the goddesses not help you with the High Council?"

I slump to the cold grass. "I told you. The goddesses do not favor me anymore. I know not what I did to cause them to turn away."

Makani kneels before me. "What evidence do you have of that?"

"The council watches me day in and day out. There is no way for me to know what transpired in Lower Earth." I look at them, wondering if I should tell them of Lucifer, Abaddon, and Sonia. "There are evil spirits waiting to take our realm and the one above us. The trinity knows them as well. I believe, if we can work together—"

"We would love to help the trinity." Sitting, Isla hooks her arm through mine.

Lowering to my side, Gatuika takes my other hand. "There must be a way."

"Not at the present. I am watched day and night, and Holden is gone." I offer my palm, and Isla lays the hilt of the sword in it. "This is all I have left of him."

"What does Holden being gone matter? We do not need men to fight for us. We do not need them at all."

"My mother sees things, knows things. She said I needed them, Holden and Quinn." I raise the blade. "But this is all I have of him."

"Then maybe it is enough." Isla raises her shoulders and lets them fall.

I rise. "I assume you are practicing magick here, at the witching hour, to avoid detection."

They nod agreement. I release a long breath. "I must go. Nicholas said he would follow in a quarter hour."

"And that, too, is the magick of the witching hour. They will think you gone but minutes. Stay and practice with us." Isla raises her palms, and droplets of water rise from the stream.

"Not tonight. But soon. Next week. Perhaps when my head is clear."

"We can come into the forest every night if you need. We will work with you until using your power is like breathing, right?" Makani raises her eyes to each sister in turn.

"Well, I do want to meet a charming prince still." Gatuika smiles. "But yes. We will help you."

"Thank you. I should go. And please"—I hold their gazes—"be careful."

With nods of agreement, I leave them in the clearing, praying they will be safe. If there are evil spirits lurking about, the girls may stand a better chance against them than me anyhow. I push through the canopy to find Nicholas and Timothy just where I left them.

The council guards draw close.

Chapter 13

"So?" Timothy inquires. "What did you find?"

My mind races. "A doe giving birth. I must have heard her cries."

Timothy's eyes narrow. "A doe? She let you help her?"

"A leg was caught. But I turned the fawn. They will be well." I rub my free hand on my skirt, trying to make it look like I may have washed in the stream.

Nicholas shrugs. "You always have had a sixth sense about animals."

"And the buzzing in your ears?" One of the council guards questions.

"The cicadas are quite loud in the wood. My ears tend to be sensitive."

I pray my explanation is enough as we fly back to the castle. Feeling the hum of the magick restart, I smile, and my psyche dares to hope. I grip Holden's lance with all my might. Perhaps, with this sword and Quinn, the premonition will be fulfilled. *And can Holden not speak to the nonbelievers?* He witnessed the kobold. So everywhere he visits, he may enlighten them as to the magickal abilities they displayed. Maybe he does not need to be with me to satisfy the omen, only champion my cause. *Should I write to him or talk to him to confirm that he can help in this way?* My side pings as I remember his squared chin. Even this small bit of optimism does not lessen the pain in my heart.

And Quinn… I cannot lose him. With a split-second realization, I know what must be done to ensure I do naught to damage that relationship. If the goddesses take him from me as well, fine. But I will not be the cause of his departure. I tell Nicholas and Timothy to have the officers of my guard meet in my study at first light.

I know I should not, but I take up Holden's tunic and clutch it to me as I lie down. *Why do I torture myself thus? Because. Because it is too much to believe I no longer hold his love.* Thoughts of him and the girls swirl in my head as I fall asleep.

⸻

Now I know about them. They are not safe.

I bolt up from sleep at the sound of Lucifer's voice in my head. I cram my fist into my pillow.

Be gone. You are not real.

I release the tunic and sword and push up on my palms. Darkness still covers the meadow. I change from my wrinkled outfit into fresh blouse, vest, and riding skirt. Rifling through my dresses, I try to choose the perfect one for greeting our guests from Lindleton. *Not purple.* I rake away the light violet dress. *Red is too bold. White? Never. Light green? Ivory?* I decide to ask the girls for their opinions.

Rounding from my closet, I run smack into a soldier. My heart skips a beat as I take in his broad form. *What is he doing here?* I plunge my hand in the side of my boot and swing the blade up in front of my face.

"Titania, it is me." Foster's voice emits from the helmet. He sheds the headwear.

Gasping for breath, I double over. "What are you doing in here?"

"I heard you were gathering the guard's officers. I wanted to speak with you before you met with them."

"Is there news? Something I should know?"

"No, all is quiet. If Regin planned to reward Gunther for his information, I have not found proof he did."

"What of the crystals?"

"I secured an additional second, and they are with the first."

"Very good." With the realization that Holden can still champion me and this win, I count two blessings in the past day.

"Why have you called a meeting?"

Wondering if he shall side with me, I lift my chin. "If there have been no signs Quinn has been in touch with Abeetha, I am going to tell them to stop watching him. He is with me almost all day, and I do not wish to spy on my friends."

"So, you trust him now?"

I cut my eyes to the floor and back to his. "Not with all."

"Good. Hold your secret near your heart, Queen." He lays a hand on my arm.

Looking into his blue, blue eyes, noting his fair skin, I only see a faint resemblance to the soldier boy he had been when we met six months ago. Bulging muscles ripple down his neck, across his shoulders, and down his arms and torso. With a few creases around his eyes, they hold more assuredness, less wide-eyed wonder. He has become a man. *And one you may trust,* my psyche adds.

"I will go soon to retrieve the crystals." I realize the witching hour and my magickal cousins may be the perfect cover.

"Where will you put them? Is not it safer to leave them where they are?"

"You are probably right." I say these words although it pains me not to have at least one set in my possession. I have been nowhere near a ring in three weeks and will not be given a chance as long as the council guards me.

A rap on the door sounds.

Foster slides his helmet on, and I cross to open a panel. Seeing Grant, I step back to let Foster out ahead of me and find him gone. Wondering at his stealth, I follow Grant into my study. They report finding no offenses with Ethan's or Gunter's activities and no evidence Quinn contacted Abeetha. This news warms my heart, and I direct them to cease watching Quinn. I instruct them to listen for opinions of me that our guests may share, and we end the meeting.

Passing the girls' door, I hear no sound and decide to let them sleep. I find Quinn at the breakfast table alone. I almost ask him if I should contact Holden about speaking in my defense, but I think better of it. Perhaps that inquiry will lead to questions I do not want to answer.

He holds my gaze. "Are you ready for today?"

"No, but there is not much to be done about it. I did shorten my speech to one word, welcome."

His eyebrow shoots up.

"Someone will announce them, and I will say welcome."

"Well played, cousin." He smiles and lifts a biscuit from the platter.

Mother and Father join us, and I walk with her after the meal. I wish I could tell her more of my cousins and how I believe her premonition is fulfilled since Holden may champion my cause from afar and I possess his sword. I guess that since she has not felt it necessary to repeat her words, perhaps she knows this. All of this warms my heart. *Yes, maybe I shall never love again, never find one to replace Holden, but I pray the goddesses have decided I may be of use for something besides hunting insects, counting crops, and attending festivals. I rebuke the thought. Should I not be grateful for the position I hold? Is it not enough to serve my people?*

⧫

THE GIRLS SELECT A GOLDEN GOWN for me from their collection for the evening. It seems a bit much for the first night of the festival weekend. When I protest, Gatuika pulls a brilliant green gown lined with emeralds from her trunk.

She lays it across her arm. "This will be for tomorrow. It was my mother's. If there were ever a need to wear such a gown, it is to show Holden, Lily, and all their family that you are a strong woman."

My side ticks when I realize this weekend may not be as bad as it gets in my path forwards with Holden. Monarchs are expected to attend the weddings of royals. They are even scheduled not to conflict. Which means I will have to stand and witness them joined, see the ribbon of marriage binding their wrists together, watch as they weave ribbons around the marriage pole. My stomach churns.

"Are you quite alright?" Makani asks.

"Yes." Folding my legs under me, I sit down on the cold stone. *Focus on today. You may find some excuse to miss the event and send Quinn in your stead. Perhaps the locusts will swell in number, and you will be needed here.*

I bathe and have my hair curled and piled atop my head with white flowers. As the hour draws near, I pace my room. *You are an adult, a queen.* I admonish the butterflies churning in my gut. Hearing the bugles, I strut from my chamber and gather the girls. I hold Gatuika's hand as we proceed to the main courtyard to greet our guests from Lindleton.

Quinn, in a double-breasted coat of gold and white, stands to my right and the girls to my left, where Holden would be. I force the thought from my brain.

Two carriages stop in front of us. Three fae exit the first coach and approach us. *Drat, I seen none brought for introductions.* The three bow in turn.

"Prince Arimas, Princess Greta, Prince Mikel." I dip my chin, acknowledging them. "Welcome. We are excited to have you in Aubren."

Prince Arimas and Greta greet me with a bow and curtsy.

"We are glad to meet you and see your fair kingdom again." Mikel, sporting a tight haircut, as is their style in Lindleton, smiles.

"I hope you will enjoy your stay."

"I am sure we will."

Motion diverts my attention to the second carriage. I see a tall, fair-haired fae exit. With hair cut short against his head, I wonder if there is an extra guest. My breath catches as I see the ring on his outstretched hand. *Holden.* His arm out, I note the pale skin of his muscled forearm. Fingers hang in the air.

A hand, slim and white, tipped with perfect alabaster nails, glides from the carriage. The fingers clasp his. A foot descends, small and slender, fit into an ivory slipper. Then her head emerges, with hair of spun hay draped in curls around her face, falling past a perfect white neck, and landing on trim shoulders. Her dress of white silk fits to her body as if seamed seconds ago.

My eyes cut to her face to find large, round eyes of sea blue and full, pink lips. *Lily, could there be any other name for such a creature?*

She smiles at him, and his face echoes her sentiment, eyes holding her gaze.

I swallow and release Gatuika's hand, binding my palms together in front of me. My stomach twists, turns in upon itself.

As they walk towards us, he looks from her face to the ground and back, her face to the ground and back.

I cannot tear my eyes from the scene. *Do not look at them. You know what he said. How he would always love you.*

The world blurs around them, and they are engulfed in a fog. Biles rises in my throat.

TsssssssK!

A lightning bolt emits from my left palm and jolts into the other. Pain shoots through my right hand and up my arm, and my heart thumps in my chest. My breath catches. I freeze my spine, holding it erect, straight as a statue. Quinn flinches, and I cut my eyes to him and back to my hands, daring a peek at my palms. I find the tiniest line of smoke rising from my joined hands. I smile. When I raise my eyes, the world appears crisp, clear again. Smiling wider, I raise my chin. *No, the goddesses have not forsaken me.*

In front of me, Holden bows low, so low I see the back of his head with his hair cut short, neck shaved clean, and flowing locks gone. The bow is overpronounced, too sweeping for a prince greeting a queen.

I wonder if he means it as reparation, an apology, to beg for forgiveness. But he grants me no way to discover this because he looks at Princess Lily again.

She curtsies.

"Welcome." I dip my chin to her and then him although his eyes stay locked on her countenance.

"Welcome." Quinn steps forwards, offering his arm to Holden.

Holden's eyes widen, and he lifts his arm to clutch Quinn's. A second later, Holden's hand holds her elbow again.

Quinn spins towards me, rolling his eyes.

So that is how it is to be. Holden will have hardly any interaction with either of us. Well, I will show him. "Princess Lily, Prince Holden, congratulations on your engagement."

"Thank you." Princess Lily beams. She holds out her slim left hand, bearing a ring with a pearl as wide as her finger. "Is it not beautiful?"

"It is. You must be so happy." I look at Holden, but his eyes do not stray from Lily's face.

Behind them, a girl clears her throat.

Princess Lily slides closer to Holden, allowing the girl to approach.

"Princess Rose, welcome." Balling my right hand into a fist, I offer my left hand to the slight girl. She so favors Lily, with ivory skin and golden hair, I would guess they were twins, save for Rose's smaller size.

"And please, meet my father and cousins from Bedham." I walk them down the line introducing Father, Gatuika, Makani, and Isla.

Isla hooks her arm in Rose's and volunteers to show her to her room. The girls flock around Rose, leading her inside.

"Let me show you to your quarters." Quinn motions for Lily and Holden to follow.

As planned, I am left to escort Princess Greta, Prince Arimas, and Prince Mikel to their chambers. We have readied the wing at the opposite end of the castle for their group to avoid any unwanted interactions. I ask of their trip from Lindleton as we enter the passageway and stroll to the far wing.

"Your jungles are so dense." Greta peers out the window.

"This wing is the most shaded from the sun. I thought the temperature would be more comfortable for you."

"We appreciate that." She fans her face. "I already feel as if I stand over a hot steaming bath."

"The nights cool off considerably."

I show Prince Mikel his room and then Greta and Arimas theirs. Exiting back into the passage, I half-scamper, moving as fast as I can out of the wing. Ducking into an enclave, I unfold my right palm. The center holds a black circle ringed by red, puffed skin blistered as if poked with a red-hot iron just from the flames.

"What are you doing?" Quinn's voice startles me.

"Oh." Moving my hand behind my back, I skip to him. "Just admiring the ferns. They seem so lush this year."

Quinn steps around me to the window and leans out. "Those are elephant ears. Are you sure you are well? What is behind your back? Let me see your hand."

He holds out his palm, and I open my left one for him.

Folding his arms over his chest, he steps closer. "The other one."

I produce my hand, palm down.

He swirls his finger, indicating I should turn it over.

Rolling my eyes, I swivel the palm face up.

"What have you done?" He grabs my fingers.

"It is a burn. I burned myself curling my hair. I need some salve for it. I was going to the kitchen just now."

He narrows his eyes. "There was a spark in your hands when Holden approached. You did not have a flint and steel in your palms did you?"

"No! I would not do that. That is madness. Ask the girls. They will tell you." My heart races, wondering if I could speak with them before he does. Or if the girls may hear my wishes as Foster did the day the council guards arrived.

"Okay, and you do look amazing, much more beautiful than that waif of a girl Holden is marrying. I cannot believe he would not even look at you. What a coward. He should be stringed up."

I place my uninjured hand on Quinn's arm. "You are sweet to say so, cousin. But he did not choose this course. We all have responsibilities."

"That makes him even more a coward to not to stand up to his father. You are too gracious to him. If he had not left and you needed an alliance, I doubt you would have married just to make it. I imagine you would cut out your heart before you did that."

He does not know how true that is. The pressure in my chest builds. I must divert the topic. "I should see to this burn before the party begins."

Giving his arm a squeeze, I head towards the kitchen to retrieve some salve.

Alfreda catches me, and another round of drama ensues.

Kissing her cheek and hugging her shoulders mid-sentence silences her, and I count my lucky stars. I make for my room to check my appearance, praying there are no notes from Holden. He has said his piece, and I hope against hope that he is done.

The girls tumble in my room as I check my rouge in the mirror.

"Quinn said you burned your hand." Isla lifts my bandaged palm.

I place my finger on my lips and gather them to me. Describing what happened, I relay that the goddesses saved me from complete humiliation.

"No." Gatuika shakes her head. "You saved yourself. And this is good because now we confirmed pain will coax your powers to life."

"It may not work if we are alone." Makani ponders.

"We have a weekend of festivities to host, so this must wait till afterwards. But yes, please, ponder how we may goad my powers to emerge."

We finish our inspections and proceed to the inner courtyard. My eyes rake over the crowd, finding Holden with the group from Lindleton. My side ticks at the sight of him, and I tighten the grip on my burned palm. I focus on my goal for the evening: to ensure all the royals know I am sane. Greeting Father, I lead him over to their group.

"Oh, it was just as hot there as it is here," Greta says.

Arimas hugs his wife to him. "I heard your festivities were cut short last weekend."

"Yes. We had a swarm of locusts descend on a field not far from here. But we, like Chastam and Rotuga, are doing all in our power to quell their numbers."

"I heard you put together a consortium of sorts."

"Yes, it was very productive. I believe our methods will be successful."

"And we should toast you on your victory over the kobold." Mikel lifts his glass.

The others follow his lead, and I raise mine to theirs. "It was quite the challenge as a new monarch. But the goddesses were on our side."

"And some quick wit, I would say." Smiling, Mikel tips his charger towards me.

"Or a very risky, unnecessary move." Arimas raises his eyebrows.

I hold his gaze. "You would have hundreds of your soldiers die?"

"You would risk their monarch's life?" He swivels towards Quinn. "Oh, I forgot you have an heir presumptive waiting in the wings. I am sure that would not cause problems at all. As if your kingdom had not experienced enough drama already, what with the challenge to your throne."

All the rumors stand true. Lindletons exhibit much brash honesty, bordering on rudeness.

Father tugs at my arm, but my mouth is already open.

Arimas's charger thrusts up, and wine sloshes from the glass, covering his white jacket front.

"Oh, my goddesses." Stifling a laugh, I plunge my hand into a fold of my dress and produce a kerchief.

Snatching it from me, Greta presses the fabric to his surcoat. My eyes catch motion behind them, and I look up to see Gatuika, Makani, and Isla, faces beaming with joy.

"It will be fine." Arimas shoos her away. "As I was saying, I would think your main focus should be the stability of your kingdom."

My anger quelled by my cousins' intervention, I smile. "I see your point. But again, you would have hundreds of your soldiers die? Risk the kobold taking your rings and moving to the next kingdom to do the same?"

"You think too highly of them. They are not that intelligent or organized."

My rage surges. "Yes, no creatures have tried to take our realm before. Not the merfolk or trolls."

"Oh, yes, I forget. These are magickal kobold." He chuckles and downs the rest of his drink.

My eyes cut to Holden, whose gaze is fixed on the ground. I ball my fists. "I believe Holden would also attest to our accounts of the magick of the kobold."

Holden turns to face Arimas. "Yes, I was here for the second battle and witnessed Titania's success in trapping them in Lower Earth, but I did not see their magick. I believe Titania's father, King Oberon, penned the accounts quite thoroughly."

How dare he act as indifferent as the rest of them. I raise a leg to take a step towards them, meaning to face down our doubters with fierce animosity.

Father grips my arm, holding me in place. "Perhaps you do not respect the company gathered here. I fought the kobold some half dozen times in my twenty-year reign. I know those creatures inside and out. My histories were sent to each kingdom. Surely, the firstborn of his line would know these accounts. Or do you not find such things important in Lindleton? Perhaps you are too busy lounging in your cool Mediterranean air. Forgive me, daughter. I believe I tire of this company." He lifts his chin, spins, and marches off.

I hold my shoulders square. "I believe my father said that very well. Perhaps we should all toast to a kobold-free realm. Thanks be to the goddesses who ensured our safety."

Quinn hefts his glass into the air. "And to your bravery, cousin."

"Of course." Arimas holds my gaze for a second and lifts his charger. "I should excuse myself to find a new jacket."

The dinner bell rings, and I thank my lucky stars to escape that conversation. I wonder if I can last through the next day and a half of their company. At this point, I miss the kobold, and we are to host six more sets of royals, possibly all who think the same as Arimas. *Goddesses help me.*

My hand throbbing, I can focus on little else. I down a second glass of wine and keep my eyes trained on my right side where I have placed Quinn and the girls. I hope to avoid all contact with the Lindleton royals, but Mikel finds me as the dances start.

He offers his hand, and I place mine in it.

"Thank you for your kind words before." I smile.

"We are not all the horrible brutes my brother would have you believe us."

"He was quite convincing."

"He believes everything our father says."

"So, your father, your king, thinks I am mad as well?"

He blushes. "Perhaps that was not the best use of words."

A snippy Upper Earth comment enters my brain. *You think?*

"I find you very beautiful."

Is he kidding? I force a smile. "Thank you."

"Excuse me." Grant's face appears before me.

Making apologies to Mikel, I follow Grant to the edge of the dance floor.

Mikel trails me, and I repeat my excuse for ending our dance.

"I wish to be of assistance. Unlike my brother, I have read all the accounts of late."

Forcing a smile, I repeat my desire to speak with Grant alone.

Bowing, Mikel backs away.

I roll my eyes. *As if he would be invited to my private conversations.*

Pulling me towards the castle doors, Grant stops before the opening. "There are two swarms. South of Westshire."

"What? It has only been six days since the last incident! Where are they coming from? And *two?*"

Marching into the castle, I tell him to gather General Kane and Quinn. I change into my riding gear and meet them in the study. We plan out how many soldiers should be sent to each location, and I jump to my windowsill.

"You are leaving?" Quinn stares at me with round eyes.

"You would have me stay here and be ridiculed by Arimas?"

"No, go. Just be careful of your hand."

I lead the soldiers around the castle so as to skirt the courtyard holding our guests. Still, the music drifts to my ears, and I imagine Holden looking up. My chest tightens as I remember our victory together just over a month ago. I swallow back the bile in my throat, the sadness threatening to consume me.

"Queen, may I join you?" A voice sounds beside me.

Now dressed in leather pants and vest, Mikel hovers in the air.

"Your brother approves?"

"I am eighteen. My brother has no say over my actions."

I want to send him away. This is my escape, and his face reminds me of all I have lost. How selfish that I treat a catastrophe to my advantage.

"If you wish. Stay by my side, and do exactly as I say."

Flying towards the field, I realize that months ago I might have been attracted to a fae who prefers action over passivity. That is how Holden won me over. *Did Holden calculate all that to woo me? Was I his best option at the time and now he has moved on?* No, I will not ask myself such questions. *He is true. He never gave any reason for you not to think so.*

Except he looks upon her as he did you. And with no note of explanation. You did not want apologies from him, remember? My mind swims with new questions. *Had I imagined our love? You always do this,* another side of me argues. *Become paranoid to excuse your fear and pain. You know what you had was true. And now it is gone. Deal with it.*

"Tell me the plan," Mikel shouts over the growing sound of the locusts.

I startle at his voice, barely audible over the buzz. As we swoop down to the farm, I summarize our strategy.

We land amongst the soldiers and cart buckets to the side of the field.

They douse the grass, and we dip torches in oil, lighting them in the fire. We spread out in a ring around the field, each several paces apart, ready to light the plants.

I lift my arm, white bandage reflecting the light of the torches.

Silence.

The whir of the insects ends.

I look out over the field to see the locusts rising into the air. Their wings catch the light of the torches, and a golden mass floats above us, churning like waves in a sea. A crow calls, and birds swoop along the edges.

The cloud climbs.

Chapter 14

"What do we do?" Grant asks.

"Follow them." Dropping my torch in the bucket below, I instruct ten soldiers to tail the swarm and alert us when they settle again.

My mind spins. *Did they realize we about to set them ablaze? Did we have information that they feared or were they deterred by fire before?* Inspecting a plant in front of me, I find not even half the leaves eaten. *Perhaps we were successful in saving this crop.* A locust drops from a branch to my foot, and I fight the urge to fling it off. Cupping my hand, I grab it and stow the bug in my pocket. It will be good to compare the insect to the others collected.

A bright light catches my attention, and smoke rises from the next hillside. At least the other team was successful in burning that swarm, but I am not sure which outcome is better. We saved this field, but the locusts escaped. If we cannot find their landing place and destroy their eggs, draw enough wasps to eat their larvae, or predators to eat the nymphs, they will continue to multiply. *And how did their numbers swell so fast? Where did they come from?*

This will be a long night. Flying to the castle, I wonder if setting up torches in fields would keep the locusts from landing. Or perhaps we want them to land so we can burn them or have a flock of birds waiting to consume the bugs. I shudder at the thought of the wretched creature in my pocket. Even further, thinking of the group from Chastam and how they described eating the non-swarming form of the creature. *Ick.*

Mikel trails us to the library, and for as much as I detest his presence, I will not send him away. Perhaps he intends to spy, take reports back to his brother and father. Well, Mikel will find no insubordination or treason against the council here.

Even at the late hour, I gather the scientists to inspect our sample insects. After study and conferment, they are reported to have the same markings as those in the swarm of last week.

"But how could they multiply so fast?" I pace the library floor. "And why did they flee? Last week, there was no indication that they cared for the torches. And the other swarm did not start at them."

I grab a piece of parchment and pen our findings to be sent to Chastam and Rotuga with word that we have no news of incidences from them. I resume my traipse from one end of the library to the other. *Think, Titania. You must prepare for every outcome.* I instruct that soldiers be sent out at first light to trail the burned swarm and as many doves as possible gathered at the castle farm. With the late hour, I decide we should retire for the night.

Putting my head on the pillow, I stare at Holden's perfect tunic. For as much as I thought I wanted no communication, I do now. I want him to tell me he is as miserable as I am, that he thinks of me day in and day out, that he will always love me and wishes our lives could be different. Cradling my hand to my stomach, I let my tears fall. The zap of magick serves as the only plus for this day. I pray to the goddesses tomorrow will be better.

⸺◈◈◈⸺

SEE? YOU ARE POWERLESS AGAINST US. Lucifer's voice plays through my dream.

I lift my bandaged hand into the air. "But I will not be forever."

Even with only hours of sleep, I wake from the dream energized. Even with the heaviness the sight of Holden's tunic and sword evokes, I have hope again. Not for finding love, but for my magick and ability to combat whatever evil Lucifer and his band of spirits throws at us. *Yes.* I roll my eyes as I rise. If we could only get rid of the swarming two-inch insects, then we may be able to focus on real threats.

Grant reports the swarm from the prior night disappeared into the dark sky, and my positive vibe wanes.

I pen a message to the kingdoms, warning of the swarm that escaped.

Quinn lectures at breakfast that I should not go to the front lines of the locust scene like every cell of my body craves doing.

I know he is right. I must host these guests, show them I am a sane and balanced ruler. Even if it means I have to burn a hole through my own head. *Oh wait, Lucifer already tried to do that and failed. Yes. If I can escape death in Lower Earth, I can handle anything.*

I know it is wrong, but my injury buoys me through-out the day. Smiling, conversing about art, culture, and fashion, all things I care little for, I do.

Grant feeds me updates on the progress of the sol-diers hunting remnants of the burned swarm and Nicho-las's efforts to round up birds.

I shoot arrows and pretend I am not that good. I lose in croquet and fencing, all to appease and compliment our guests. *What is the phrase of Upper Earth? Kill them with kindness.* If nothing else, my sense of irony led the voices in my head with full force.

Dancing after dinner, I cannot avoid Mikel. But thankfully, many of my soldiers divert his presence. I watch Quinn to distract myself from the hole the sight of Lily and Holden threatens to carve in my tough exterior.

Quinn dances with Rose and my cousins, entertain-ing them with jokes and tricks.

I dread the sight of my room, Holden's sword in the corner, and the goodbye I must bid him the next day. As the party wanes, I wind to the girls' room, down a glass of wine, and curl up on their couch.

I OPEN MY EYES AND TAKE A second to get my bearings. No Lucifer. *Wonderful!* Slinking from the room, I bathe and dress in a forest-green gown. We eat breakfast in the garden with our guests.

Lily and Holden are seated at the far end of the table on the same side so do not enter my line of sight often.

Still, I know the moment is coming, and my stomach and chest tighten as the meal ends.

Waiting in the front courtyard, my foot taps the stone.

Quinn grabs my arm and makes bug eyes at me.

I fold my hands behind my back. At least I acclimated to Holden's short hair and doting demeanor. I do not expect anything less from this official sendoff.

The youngest, Rose, leads the line of royals, hugging the girls, curtsying to me, and offering her hand to Quinn.

He kisses it, and she expresses her hope to continue their wonderful conversations via letters.

I give him a sideways glance as Lily and Holden approach.

Lily leans towards me and kisses my cheeks. "Thank you for hosting us in this difficult time. I look forward to seeing you at our wedding."

My breath catches in my throat. I swallow and form a smile. "I look forward to it as well."

I force myself to look at Holden's face, but his eyes cut from Lily to the ground. Quinn's words echo in my head. *Coward.* But I cannot feel that way about Holden. I can only interpret his gestures as a heartfelt apology. *For would I want to stare into those eyes again, knowing he can never look at me as he did? No.*

Mikel follows. He kisses my cheek, and I want to deck him. It was bad enough for Lily to show affection as if we were familiar, but I pray Mikel does not assume we are tied in some way.

"I hope you will write of your progress with the locusts."

"Of course. Your father will get updates."

"Perhaps you misunderstand. I would hope that I could write to you as well."

Goddesses help. I force a smile. "Of course, but my schedule tends to be quite taxing, as you have witnessed."

His eyes drop and pop back up to my face. "Of course. I look forward to seeing you at my sister's wedding."

"Thank you." I dip my chin. How I am to get through that wedding, I have no clue.

Princess Greta curtsies in front of me, and Arimas offers his arm. "My father confirms the facts about the ko-bold. I am sorry to have offended you. I believe we may be contemporaries in a short while and hope to forge a good relationship with you and your nation."

"Thank you for your sentiments. Your apology is accepted. I look forward to many successful years in our realm."

"As do I." He dips his chin.

He joins the line his family formed behind him. Each of the males dip their chins, and the females curtsy.

We return the gestures.

I watch Holden, and as before, his eyes cut from Lily's golden head to the ground and back. Part of me wonders if I shall find a letter after their departure, some sentiment from him. I hope for it and I do not.

The groups load into their carriages, and I release a long breath as they clammer away.

"I cannot believe Arimas apologized." Quinn turns to me. "Well done, Titania."

"I am not sure I handled Mikel as well."

"If he were not from Lindleton and his sister were not marrying"—he hesitates—"Holden, I would think you might favor him. He is tall, fair, and energetic, just like Holden. Of course, now Holden only seems to be a slithering coward. You are probably better off with the likes of Foster."

I grab my green gown at the skirt and plant the other hand on my hip. "I will hear nothing else about my courtships from you."

"That is good because I do not wish to discuss Princess Rose, either."

"Did you like her? Should I be inquiring about a meeting with King Hector concerning her?"

"You? Arrange my marriage? You are barely sixteen and two years younger than me."

"But I am your queen, cousin." I hold his stare.

"And that you are." He dips his chin. "And none softened from the bruising you took this weekend, I see."

I exhale and take his hand. "I am sorry, cousin. My last nerve is frayed. If you favor her, you know I would support you."

"Believe me, even if I did think her amazing, I would never marry into that kingdom. Not after how Arimas treated you."

"At least he apologized." I turn to the castle. "It was more than the royals of Willhelm did."

"But they were not as rude."

"True."

We wind to the library to hear reports from the scientists and soldiers tracking the locusts. No kingdoms report spotting a swarm. The samples returned from the burned field matches those found from the swarm that spooked. The scientists puzzle as to how the creatures repopulate so quickly. Further, the inspection of parcels yields no findings.

"They cannot be coming from nowhere. What of Hilbron? We share a long border with them. Are we getting any cooperation? Any reply from my requests?"

The advisors report none, and I stand even more bewildered. "So, either Hilbron does not care, or they will not help?"

"Perhaps both." Kane contends. "There have been no incidences in their borders. Perhaps they do not see it as a threat."

"Could we at least request access to inspect for ourselves? They have miles of desert where the locusts can land, blend in, and lay eggs." I look between Kane and the advisors.

They agree yes, and sitting, I start a letter to King Luther. I have half a mind to fly there and ask him myself. *Everyone else we have spoken to takes this seriously, even the High Council, so why not him?* They grow few crops but also have a small population. I think to highlight that they often request grain and vegetables from our kingdom but leave that out. Penning my name to the end, I instruct the page to wait for a reply.

We send word to the farmers to light torches to protect their fields. Because we have worked past midday, I invite all gathered for lunch in the courtyard. Looking at the girls, I am saddened this has not turned out to be the joyful, carefree summer they expected. I make it a goal to spend the afternoon with them. As we finish the meal, the page returns with a message from King Luther.

He will not read the message until his work week begins.

I want to fling something across the table. *Have these people no sense of duty?*

Placing my napkin on the table, I motion for Quinn to follow me. "Who does he think he is? How can he not see that this could be a realm-wide catastrophe in the making? I should go to him."

"What is there today will be there tomorrow. Take a break, and get your mind off everything. You had a stressful weekend. You should rest."

Rest is not what I need, but I know he is right. If I push, Luther will likely dig in his heels. "I need to do something fun with my cousins, anyway. Would you like to join us for a ride or shooting in the meadow?"

"I will retire to my quarters for a rest."

"Okay, cousin." I kiss his cheek. "Thank you for your service this weekend. I appreciate your counsel and support."

"What of my comedic breaks?" He smiles wide.

"Those helped as well." I wink at him.

I gather the girls. We change and ride into the wood. Stopping at the stream, I commend them on a job well done with Arimas and the wine. I know it to be wrong, but the pig very well deserved it. *How can he think himself worth more than a hundred soldiers?* A leader's job is to protect the people, not use them as shields.

Putting these thoughts out of my mind, we wade in the rocks, searching for crystals and splashing about. They whisper to me, inquiring when we should practice magic. I indicate that we should retire to bed early and wake during the witching hour. Making apologies for their drama-filled week, I receive ridicule.

Gatuika rests on the bank, dipping her toe in the water. "Are you mad? All of this is perfect. We are so sheltered from the rest of the realm, it is good to know the politics. And all the personalities are quite intriguing. Like a drama series of Upper Earth."

"Intriguing. That is a good word. I have to admit, I was rather sheltered as well before rising to queen."

"We heard how you put Arimas in his place. So impressive," Makani says.

They tell me all they overheard during the weekend, and I am most grateful to them. We discuss next week's visit and how we may find someone who catches Quinn's eye.

"Mikel seemed to like you." Isla smiles wide.

"Perhaps." I let out a long breath.

"I am sorry." She hooks her arm through mine. "I reminded you of Holden."

"It is what it is."

"You will find love." Isla hugs me to her.

I relish in her embrace. *So young, so innocent.* But once a heart is broken, I wonder if it could ever mend. *Yours healed with Foster. But no. He was different. I had not been sure I could see a life with him. I did with Holden.*

⸻◈◈◈⸻

Splat!

A wave of water knocks me off balance, and I stumble back.

Isla draws wave after wave from the brook, batting me this way and that.

I block my face and fling out my hand, willing my magickal energy to rise and block her.

Nothing.

"Again." I hold my palm up.

Thump.

I land on my bottom as Makani sends a blast of air at me. Holding the air current, she pins me to the ground.

I focus on my hand, my arm, my heart, willing my power to emerge to stop her.

Nothing.

Jumping up, I spin to face Gatuika. She deflects the sound of the raging stream at me, and I cup my ears against the pressure. I fling out my arm, focusing all my thoughts on blasting her.

Nothing.

"This is not working." She releases the spell. "You would not use your magick to hurt us. And you know we are not going to really hurt you."

Makani circles my drenched form. "Your power emerged when you were almost killed, almost dethroned, and almost ridiculed."

A smile spreads on Gatuika's face. "When she was in emotional pain over Holden. Holden is the key. Remember Holden, Titania?"

"That is cruel, Gatuika." Isla's wide eyes plead with her sister.

"But it is true." Gatuika circles me. "He left you. And he became another person. Maybe he never loved you. Maybe all he said was a lie. Perhaps you were his best option, and he found a better one."

I shake my head as tears threaten to form. *How could she guess all my fears, insecurities?* "No, he loved me."

"Let the pain come." Makani coaxes. "Tell us everything. How you fell in love, what he promised you, how he betrayed you."

My stomach turns, and I swipe my tears away. "He promised if we could not be together here, we would run away and live with the merfolk."

"And now he is gone forever. Will marry another." Makani grips my shoulders. "You shall never know his loving gaze, warm embrace, again."

Water gushes out of my eyes, and I fall limp in her arms.

She pushes me away. "No. Make the pain stop. You have the power to stop it."

"No, this is sick. Do not tell her to hurt herself again," Isla shouts.

"Do you want your powers, or do you want to be sad forever? Believing you are shunned by the goddesses?" Gatuika stands shoulder to shoulder with Makani.

"They would not forsake me." I straighten my spine.

"Would they not?" Makani lifts an eyebrow. "Your mother said you needed him. And he was taken from you. Your love, your soulmate. You may never find that again.

And your freedom stripped by the High Council. You have nothing left, really, Titania."

I let her words wash over me. *She is right. She voices all my fears. I am nothing now.*

"Poor Titania." Gatuika skips around me. "She will be a forgotten queen in forty years, unloved and useless."

Seeing Isla bury her face in her hands, I take a deep breath.

I will not die alone and forgotten. I will not leave this realm to the wiles of the monsters of the deep. Something inside me says I can best them. *You are powerless against us.* Lucifer's words play through my brain.

I raise my chin and lift my palm. Focusing on my core, I draw in a breath. Willing the power, the hurt, the anger, and the rage into a little ball, I push my arm out straight.

Nothing.

"It is no use." I slump.

"You do not want it enough." Gatuika jeers.

A high pitch shrill cuts through the night, piercing my eardrums, and I drop to the ground. I grab her ankle, willing a tiny shock, anything to make her stop.

Nothing.

"No." Isla's voice sounds through the tone. "We are done for tonight. We will try again tomorrow."

"Gatuika, she is right." Makani's voice enters my sphere.

The wood falls silent, and I lift my head. Exhausted, I place my palms on the ground and push up. "She is right. We should brainstorm ideas and try again tomorrow."

SEE? YOU KNOW THE GODDESSES have forsaken you. Lucifer's hissing voice sounds in my dream, and I bolt upright.

Perhaps they have. I am not sure of anything anymore. I need perspective. I need Mother. Perhaps if we walk through the wood, we can be out of earshot of the council guards, and I can bare my soul as I used to on our strolls. *Would I even bare all to her? How Holden left me? How I am a laughingstock in the realm?* All of it seems almost too much to withstand. I cradle my healing palm in my other hand.

Why am I so hard on myself? Why must I always push the limits? Because you must, for your brothers. I draw in a centering breath. I cannot, I *will not* squander the gifts given me. Time. Time they did not have. Time to love, time to find my fate, and time to serve my people and my realm. *For is that not every fae's purpose? Especially that of a leader?* I let gratitude fill my thoughts. I have Alfreda, Mother, Father, Quinn, my guards, my cousins, and Foster. Thanking the goddesses, I flit from my bed.

MOTHER AND I VENTURE INTO the woods, and I begin to whisper all my thoughts to her. I forget that I harbored resentment against her until I tell her of my cousins and their abilities. Clutching her hand around my arm, I press on. The High Council, Holden, Quinn, Foster, the locusts, royals from Willhelm and Lindleton… It all comes gushing out like a fountain.

Her eyes stay trained on the path ahead, but for once, I welcome it. No judgment or opinions. It just is. And this feels normal, routine, as if the High Council never ruled against me. But it did, and I have no power against the evil spirits that haunt my dreams each night.

Acceptance. My mind holds the word as I leave Mother in her room and round to the library. I cannot change what is. Faith that I will have that needed to fulfill my purpose is an issue left for another time. Entering the library, all eyes fix on me.

Quinn lifts a scroll from the table. "From King Luther of Hilbron."

"Have you read it?"

"No. It is addressed to you."

Slipping the ribbon off, I scan the text.

With incidences in Aubren less than the fingers of one hand, I do not feel this rises to the level of a viable threat. I do not give you permission to enter my borders and risk bringing hysteria to my people.

Drawing in a breath, I roll the page and fix the string on it. "King Luther does not see a viable threat. He will not allow us within his borders."

"Perhaps if I wrote to a scientist there, note our odd findings," the chief scientist says.

I look at Quinn, and he shakes his head. "We will do what we can do within our borders and work with those from Chastam and Rotuga."

"There were incidences on Madagascar and Sri Lanka."

"Those are islands. Were the other swarm attacks not on the mainland?"

They confirm my memory.

"As to our soldiers progress?" I look to General Kane.

He reports they have reached as far south as a quarter way across the kingdom. The desert heat requiring longer rest and water breaks.

I suggest they search at night with torches, and he says they will investigate the approach.

Advisors report a roundup of almost eighty doves, and I propose they make it a thousand.

Pulling out a chair, I sit down. I hate feeling ineffective.

We move to other topics like crop yields, animal counts, and festival reports. The advisors count our first two weeks of hosting as successes because the royals from each kingdom were enlightened as to the traits of the most recent kobold we battled.

"The Boreans tend to be more open-minded." I offer an opinion of the next guests we are to host. *And there are two sisters, one sixteen and one seventeen. Perfect for introductions to Quinn.*

"They are the youngest and largest kingdom. Their people harbor adventurous and rebellious spirits like yourself, I have heard. More fae from Borean choose to abandon Middle Earth for Upper Earth," Advisor Bran says.

"I imagine they blend well in the United States. Many vampires and werewolves weave into their societies." I venture a guess at the reasons behind the choice to live in Upper Earth, thinking perhaps you learn to shut out the voices of so many thoughts around you. In the few times I have been in that ream, the cornucopia of mental activity was overwhelming.

⸙

EACH WITCHING HOUR FOR THREE nights, the girls and I venture into the wood. They try many forms of mental and physical torture, only stopping short of putting my life in grave danger. But my powers never ignite, not even a spark.

With the impending visit of the royals from Borean, we shop in the village Thursday and turn in early. I am wakened by a blaring trumpet alarm and slide into my riding clothes.

Grant stands outside my door. "The locusts are outside Westshire again."

"Westshire? Even with all the torches? How many fields?" I look west, out over the meadow, to see plumes of fire and smoke rising into the air. They must be burning the crops. Jumping onto the windowsill, I take to the air. By the time I arrive, three fields stand empty, and fae douse the last of the flames with buckets of water.

"We caught some live ones." A major approaches with a lantern box.

"Thank you." I take the glass container from him.

I stare out over the smoking fields. Seven fields ruined thus far, three in one night, and the last two attacks just six days apart. Holding up the lantern, I study the insects. To me, they all look the same. The scientists will analyze if all the markings match the prior ones. Perhaps we can experiment with these and find a poison or discover their mating and life cycles. It seems our best shot at combating these pests.

Jumping into the air, I leave the locust container in the library and return to my chamber.

I toss and turn all night, wondering if other kingdoms experienced attacks as well.

Stop thinking of them as attacks, I reprimand my mind. *They are insects with no strategy or scheme. Their nature reacts to harsh conditions, that is all. What if they were more pleasant looking, like butterflies? Would you think so ill of them? Yes. If they ate our crops I would.*

Seven fields represents about five percent of the kingdom's harvest.

Where could these insects be hiding for six days? Do they hover in swarms above the oceans? Scurry under the leaves of the forest floor? Burrow into the sand of the desert? The scientists say they can live up to five months, continuing to lay eggs throughout their adult stage. No wonder their numbers swell such.

At first light, I round to the kitchen and fill glasses with every powder I can think of: flour, fine sugar, salt, soda, lye, and leavening powder. Carting them to the library, I place them on the table with the container of locusts. I realize the insects may need water as well as sustenance and pick some leaves from the garden still heavy with dew. I sit down and pen the news and our next steps to our taskforce partners in Chastam and Rotuga then a new letter to King Luther, requesting again that we be able to search his land.

"I thought I may find you here." Quinn enters with a tray of pastries. He stops short as he reaches me. "What are those?"

"Our test animals."

"Now they are animals? I only see bugs. And what are these?" Quinn moves my bottles to the edge of the table as he sets the platter down.

"The poisons."

"What?" He shakes his hands in the air.

"Well, they are not poisonous to us, but I am hoping something that will not harm the plants will kill the locusts."

"Smart thinking." Grabbing a muffin, he sits beside me. His eyebrow turns up as he views my page. "King Luther again?"

"It is worth a try. I do not know why he detests me so much."

"Well, you did involve his brother in a battle against evil demon-dragon creatures. And let us not forget the trinity witch escapade. And the High Council ruling."

I pen my name and set the quill in the ink jar. "Holden did all of that of his own accord. And Luther sided with us before."

"Before you were charged with treason."

Chapter 15

"I SEE ZEKIAL AND HIS GUARDS every minute of my waking hours. You need not remind me of that."

"Are you sure? Because you are with your cousins very often, and they are obsessed with the witches of the trinity."

"How would you know that?"

"That is all they talked of when they first arrived. He is more handsome than Hunter, or Tyler or DJ are more handsome than him. You could send them back to Bedham to be your spies."

"I would not endanger my cousins in that way, and we have rarely spoke of the trinity after their first days here. We speak of girlish things: our hair, our dresses, what prince has caught their eye, and who dances with whom. They are a comfort to me."

He holds my stare. "Now that *he* is gone."

"You may say his name."

"I felt something that day you greeted him. A shock from your arm. And then your palm was singed."

My mind spins, hunting for an explanation. "Really? It must have been my gown, silk rubbing on silk can often spark."

His pupils roll to the sky. "You must think me daft or paranoid. Silk."

"Perhaps you need a vacation, cousin. Take today off. I can handle the scientists myself."

"I believe I shall do as you suggest." He kisses my cheek and, spinning, walks from the room.

I munch on a muffin and try to think of additional pesticides but am stumped aside from metal dust. The scientists trickle in, and as all assemble, I present my suggestions.

They laud my thinking and suggest additional poisons for the pests, oils and noxious herbs. News comes from Chastam and Rotuga of more swarms on the islands mirroring Madagascar and Sri Lanka. They note the same pattern as us, six days between attacks and the bugs becoming undeterred by the torches.

I answer with plans for our research and that we will report after the weekend.

"This can be figured out this weekend, correct?" I scan the faces.

Looking between each other, they nod.

Glancing outside, I realize the light shines brightly. The clock reads past midday, and I invite them for lunch. With the late night and early morning, my energy wanes. I search out Mother and Father and walk with them through the garden. My chores secured, I wish I did not view walks with my parents as such sometimes, I draw a bath and assess my wardrobe.

———⋘⋙———

I SEE HEADS HANGING FROM THE windows as the carriages stop before us. The royals from Borean spill from their coaches, chatting excitedly. I look at Quinn and then the girls and refocus on our guests.

With swift strides, the tallest male crosses to me, bowing deeply.

A female trails him and copies his gesture.

"Prince James?"

He nods. "And this is my bride, Princess Wendy."

She curtsies and holds my gaze. "It is true! You have stones on your forehead."

I touch the stone at the center of my brow with my index finger, realizing they have become part of who I am. It has been but six weeks since I escaped Lower Earth and they rose from my skin, but I rarely think of them. I see my guests from Willhelm and Lindleton in a new light. I look different, not like them, and perhaps naturally one that should not be trusted.

Smiling, I laugh. "Yes, it is true. Odd, but real."

The shortest female approaches, finger up. "May I?"

Wendy closes her palms around the girl's shoulders. "Kate, your manners."

"It is fine. See?" Rubbing the stone on my temple, I lean down.

Kate sets her finger on the jewel. "Do they hurt?"

"No, not at all. They feel like fingernails."

Taking Kate's hand, James proceeds to introduce his younger siblings: two girls of almost equal height, a boy, a girl just a bit shorter, and Kate. I add in their ages—seventeen, sixteen, fifteen, fourteen, and twelve—from my study of their family, now assigning names and faces to my memory. Introducing them to Quinn then my cousins, I send the youngest two girls off with Gatuika and her sisters. Quinn and I show the others to their quarters.

WHEN MY FATHER AND I stage our inquisition as to their opinions on the kobold, James and his brother, Maxwell, react with excitement. They have read all our texts and crave our insight as to the monster's origins. Relief washes over me, and I realize these opinions may not reflect that of their father. But it would be rude for me to inquire, or at the very least, tip them off as to my intention of bringing up the subject.

"So, do you know how they gained their magickal abilities?" Maxwell asks.

"From Lower Earth, we believe. The spirits are able to either control them or breed them."

"Lucifer? You speak of Lucifer?" Maxwell leans in closer. "You believe he is real? Like flesh and blood. More than a spirit?"

"I battled him in Lower Earth. He is very real. Can take physical form."

"Our father thinks you dreamed it. Lucifer made you imagine your experience," James says.

"I have nothing other than my memory and these." I touch my finger to a stone on my forehead.

"What do you think Lucifer will do next?" Maxwell inquires.

"I believe the queen has much more pressing matters than to lounge around guessing what these supposed evil spirits will do next."

I jump at the sound of Zekial's voice. The man moves with such stealth he must be a ghost. "Yes, the locusts. Our scientists are experimenting with poisons as we speak."

"We are lucky thus far. The insects have not traveled so far west as to reach Borean." James steps aside to make room for Zekial.

I motion to the new pens for the plants and insects. "I pray we can stop them before they infect your lands."

"And we will be most grateful." James dips his chin.

Steering the conversation to the games of the next day, I watch Quinn with Marta and Sara. I hope one may interest him. With hair of brown, skin of cream, and wings of gold, they are beautiful girls. *More like his coloring. More like Abeetha's.* Picturing dark hair and purple wings hovering over me, I shudder.

We meld well with our guests from Borean, and I find myself enjoying the weekend.

Maxwell lingers at my side often, so I make sure to never be alone with him. Even if he is my age, just entertaining the thought of being courted makes my stomach turn.

⸺⬦⸺

MONDAY DAWNS WITH US EAGER to hear progress of experiments from the scientists. They report the dry agents either had no effect on the insects or caused the plants to wilt. A light oil derived from grape seeds, especially if mixed with pepper extract, caused the insects to stop feeding but caused no harm to the leaves. With no other source of food or water, they died within a day.

"But were they weakened from the oil? Such that they could not fly?" I inquire.

"That is not known," the chief scientist admits.

"What of poisonous plants? Belladonna, hemlock, wolfsbane, or foxglove?"

"All not poisonous to the insects."

I slouch in my seat. "Well, we could at least protect our own crops, and perhaps the locusts will die of starvation before they can reach another food source. Can we try that?"

The scientists agree to order batches of the grapeseed oil and distribute them to farmers. I suggest printing the recipe for growers to create themselves if ingredients are available. In addition, I ask that they round up supplies to deliver to far ends of the kingdom where it may be hard for carts to travel.

Kane reports no findings of the insects, either in larvae, nymph, or adult form in any significant numbers. I fear we hunt for a needle in a haystack, but I order the searches continued. Seeing Zekial sitting at the far side of the library, I hope he approves of me doing more than sitting and wondering what dear Lucifer may be planning next.

For I know what not he plans. His voice and image come to me each night.

He aims to kill me.

But how remains a mystery.

—◆◆◆—

"Titania," Quinn calls as I stroll towards my quarters after the meeting.

"Yes, cousin?" I stop, welcoming his company as I have not had time to speak with him about the royals from Borean.

He motions ahead of us, speaking of the success of the weekend.

Noting how gracious and open the Borean royals seemed, I chance asking if he enjoyed time with Marta and Sara.

He responds that they were quite nice, but his face shows no excitement for the topic. At least we have the guests from Elita visiting next.

I remember their dark hair, olive skin, and colorful wings from hosting them years ago. Their vibrant colorings bewitched me, and I wonder if they may Quinn as well.

We cross into my study, and he closes the door behind him. "I would like to speak with you about a private matter."

"Of course." I spin to find him on one knee before me. My breath catches in my throat.

His eyes hold mine for a second, and then his chin drops. "I need to ask your forgiveness."

Nerves on the edge of hysteria, I lock my fingers together at my waist. "Stand up. You are my cousin, my heir presumptive, and an advisor, you need not bow before me."

Grabbing the tabletop for support, and standing with slow, halting movements as if his appendages weigh a ton, he widens his shoulders and takes a deep breath.

"I love Abeetha." His words are but a whisper.

My mind reels. *Abeetha?* I trusted him. He pledged himself to my reign.

"How?"

"You know how love works. I tried to look at another, keep my heart open, but I cannot. She is the one."

I lift my chin, wanting to fling a candlestick at his face. "H*ow*? How do you even know? When have you spent time with her? How can you know what her ambitions are?"

He takes a step back. "We have written and met in the farmyard, late at night, most nights over the past two weeks."

Digging my nails into my palms, I swallow. *I trusted him.* "Marry me."

"What?" His eyes grow wide.

"Marry me, and you shall be King of Aubren."

"You would give me Aubren so that I would not marry Abeetha?"

"No, I would give you equal standing with me."

"You do not even love me."

"I do love you. You know I do."

"As a cousin. Not as a wife. And I do not love you that way either. Why would you even propose such?"

I chance my hunch. "But you did love me that way, in the beginning, did you not? When Father asked you to stay."

He sets his jaw. "Perhaps I was attracted to you. But that ended long ago."

"You find me so hideous?"

"No, that is not… It does not matter. I love Abeetha. Why would you want to marry me?"

"I need you. You are my friend, and I need you." I do not want to go as far as to tell him of Mother's premonition but will if I have to.

"You will not lose me as friend or cousin."

"You know that is not true. That is why you started this conversation on one knee." Motion catches my eye, and I turn to look out the window. Zekial and his guard pass underneath. *Like flies drawn to the sugar of drama, the old fae must have a sixth sense.* I close the shutters, cross back to the table, and light a candle.

"You will marry me, or you will take Abeetha and leave this country. I care not where you go, but you will no longer be welcome in my kingdom."

"Abeetha is no threat to you."

"You have twenty-four hours to make your decision. I do not want you to leave your chamber until you come to me at this time tomorrow."

"You will keep me imprisoned?"

"No, I will ask this of you on your honor." For if I see his face again, I may cut his head from his neck. Fury builds within my center.

"Please, do not leave things this way. We are cousins, friends."

I look at the wood panel shutters, thinking if he does not stay, I shall never trust another soul for as long as I live. Not even the goddesses. "I have said I need you. And you know I would not say that, would not offer you so much, unless it were of the utmost importance to me, to this kingdom, and this realm."

"I know you are very spiritual. Can you explain more?"

Making myself look into his green eyes, I chance what truth I dare share. "I believe the goddesses want you here to help me."

"The goddesses want me to help you? With what? The locusts? You have scientists, advisors, and generals."

"You know there are more to come. The kobold were just the beginning. The spirits of Lower Earth will not rest."

"And we have always bested them before. You cannot tell me that you believe I am required to help in such a matter. One like Holden perhaps."

Hearing his name unlatches something inside. I bite my lip and cut my eyes to the ceiling to keep tears from forming. "That is what I believe. It is your choice. Now, go and contemplate your choices."

"Titania." He steps towards me.

Bang. Bang. Bang.

"Titania!" Grant's voice sounds through the wood door.

Backing, Quinn swings it open.

Grant's eyes cut to me, then Quinn, but my guard charges ahead. "They found a patch of locust larvae in the desert."

"They did? Let us go." I raise my hand and, seeing red blood stains, pop it closed.

As I pass, Quinn grabs my arm.

"Go, Quinn. I will see you tomorrow."

He opens his palm to reveal a handkerchief.

Taking it, I hold his stare. "See? You do love me."

All I can think of as we fly south is that I asked Quinn to marry me. Me, marry? Us, marry? But if the choice is between that and losing him, there lies no other path. *Where have the goddesses gone? How could they take Quinn from me as well? And if we marry, will I ever trust him truly?* His words echo in my ears. *You do not trust anyone but him.* No, I do not trust anyone. Period.

"The soldiers were setting honey to attract wasps," Grant yells over the sound of the wind. He summarizes that they found the breeding ground just after daybreak and had been working all morning.

"Good. Hopefully, we can prevent another swarm."

I focus on my beating wings, the feel of the hot, humid breeze hitting my face. It is a half hour before I see the green fields and meadows give way to brown grasslands dotted with trees. In another half hour and some, we descend into the center of the wide desert. Confusion fills my mind as I take in the scene below.

Soldiers stand in a line.

As we near the ground, I see the sand spotted with black dots. I land to find hundreds of thousands of wasps, spread across the landscape like a carpet, wings frozen, as in a lifeless state.

"What happened?" I approach General Kane.

"I do not know. The honey worked, attracted thousands of the wasps. They seemed excited about the larvae but started dying not long after consuming them."

I watch as additional wasps fly towards the area. "First, stop attracting more wasps. Put the honey away. Bring tools or use swords to dig up all the eggs sacks we can find. Then we will burn them all."

Requesting Grant's sword, I start raking through the sand, hunting for eggs and larvae.

The soldiers follow my lead, and we spread out over the area. Our grid starts at the north end of the patch and moves south. I crisscross the sword through the sand in front of me, uncovering egg pouches. Rocks, small scrubs, and grasses litter the area, but as the light wanes, we find fewer and fewer cases.

I halt the mission when we march a hundred feet, finding none.

I instruct the soldiers to set up a burn perimeter, and we light the egg sacs, larvae, and wasps afire, starting in the north and moving south. With little ground cover to burn, the fire dies behind the front line. The few outbreaks that form we douse with sand. My arms sear with wear as I look out over the blackened desert. Questions plague my brain.

Why did the larvae poison the wasps? Have we ever witnessed such before?

"May I have my sword, Highness?" Grant offers his palm.

I hand it to him, grip end first, and he wipes it on his pant leg.

"Home?"

"Yes, home." Although I would rather descend into Lower Earth again than face the aftermath of my actions of the day.

The job of destroying the locusts proved successful this day. Fighting my demons, however, may be an insurmountable task. *I asked Quinn to marry me? What had possessed me to do such?* Would that I could ever love him as Holden, it may make sense. But even as I see Quinn as handsome, he has never stirred emotion in me like Foster or Holden.

The flight provides me with no relief. I descend into the meadow and trudge through the winding paths of the gardens. *How am I to sleep with such weight on my shoulders?*

"May I, Queen?" Grant's voice captures me from my spiral as I enter the orchard.

"Yes?"

"Tell me what passed. If there is one you should trust, you know it is me."

I cut my eyes to him. "You are married and have children, correct?"

"My eldest is just a year younger than you."

Leading him into the orchard, I spill all of it. I tell him of my mother's premonition and how I offered Quinn my hand in marriage.

"But you do not love him."

"You know as a royal I do not have privileges others do."

"You seemed so different. The first woman monarch. I thought you would marry for love. I hoped you would."

"I *was* different. And now, they have made me one of them. Into their own likenesses. Never pushing the boundaries or trying anything new. Never believing in anything I cannot see. My faith is gone as well. And who would you have me marry? Holden is gone. Royals from all the other kingdoms think me mad."

"You are young. There may be another. You cannot know your future."

"I do not know whether to pray Quinn accepts my proposal or hope that he does not."

"I will say prayers for you tonight." Gripping my shoulders, he kisses my forehead.

I watch him walk away. Eyeing the dark branches and then the rows of trunks surrounding me like bars on a jail cell, I sense my chest tighten. The hole in my chest, the one forged by Holden, now bored deeper by Quinn, threatens to consume me. *Thud.* My heart echoes between my ribs. I double over, arms hugging my middle. I sink to the ground and pull my knees to my chest. *Breathe in, breathe out.*

I know not how long I sit there, but another thought forms. *You are a queen. Rise, and be a queen.* Pushing off the wet grass, I stand. I march towards my chamber, peeking in the girls' room and seeing them asleep. I enter my study and pen today's findings. *Dead wasps?* Leaving the letters to be copied and sent to Chastam and Rotuga, I head to the library. All the texts on the locusts have been gathered on one table, and I skim through, looking for references to wasps.

"So, this is where you are hiding?"

My pulse races at the sound, the voice all too familiar. "You are very quiet."

"I told you I am very good at my job." Foster's lips form an irresistible smile. "Grant said you were here."

"Do you not know it is bad manners to sneak up on a lady? Worse, even, on a queen?" In a swift motion, I yank my dagger from my boot and point it at him.

"And such a dangerous queen indeed." His eyebrows peak.

"Do not mock me. I am not in the mood." I refocus on the book in front of me.

"Grant also mentioned that." Foster glides into the seat next to me.

Cheeks warming, I peer up at him. "Why are you here? Is there news of Ishmel or Regin? Perhaps of Ethan or Gunther?"

"Do you regret trusting Quinn now?"

"Did you know he was courting Abeetha again?"

"No, Henrick was watching Ethan and Gunther, but no one watched Abeetha after you ordered we leave Quinn be."

"It is fine. What is done is done." I say the words, but my heart pounds in my chest. I have sealed my fate. I will be miserable forever. Whether Quinn chooses Abeetha or me, I lose.

You were doomed the second the High Council ruled against you. This just seals the coffin. There is but one hope. If Quinn stays, and Holden decides to come to his senses and speak about what happened with the kobold, Mother's premonition may be fulfilled.

Chair legs scrape on stone, and I turn to find Foster on one knee.

"Do not marry him. Marry me. I beg you, Titania."

Chapter 16

If one more fae bows before me, I fear I shall free their head from their form. "Get up, Foster. I no more want to marry you than I want to wed Quinn."

"But you offered to make him king? Why would you do that?"

"Grant should not have shared that with you. What does it look like if my Fae at Arms leaves to marry a princess in Lindleton, and then, just weeks later, my heir presumptive flees to marry the daughter of a traitor?"

"It looks like a royal is fulfilling his duty to his country, and a man fell in love with a woman. Just as I am in love with you."

"Our love has been over for months, Foster. Why are you even thinking this?"

"Because I have always loved you. You know that. My heart could not bear to see you with another."

"So, you will leave me if Quinn accepts my proposal. Is this what you are saying?" My stomach turns at the thought of losing yet another. Especially one the goddesses seem to trust. For I have no other explanation of how I came to communicate with him without spoken words.

"I am saying it would be a great burden. As it was to see you with Holden. You loved me before. You cannot tell me that is completely gone."

Looking at the books in front of me, I press my hands to my temples. My fingertips graze the jewels in my skin. "It is late. Go, Foster. This conversation never happened."

He stands. "It did. And I will remember. And you will as well. I love you, Titania."

I know he is gone by the absence of warmth from his body. No sound crosses my ears, and I wonder if he may have some magick of his own. Standing, I cross to the window and open the panes of glass. Cool, sweet air rises from the garden. I stare out across the meadow, surprised at how different the scene looks from this side. The grass reflects a blue hue rather than the purple I am used to. Movement from below catches my eye, and I see a fae jump across a path at the edge of the orchard.

Studying the scene, I find another set of wings, purple wings, those of Abeetha's family. And green wings on the first fae means Quinn. *Abeetha and Quinn. But if I were a fly in a bush.* Gathering her in his arms, he holds her for what seems like forever. I duck down so only my eyes peek over the window ledge. Scanning the castle walls, I realize this would be the only window to view them from. Smart, dear cousin.

He releases her, and they sit, shoulder to shoulder. If only I had Gatuika's skills of modifying sound just now. I cut my eyes between the couple and the clock.

They speak for five minutes, and then he presses his lips to hers. After another quick kiss, he takes both her hands. Releasing them, he backs away and slips behind a hedge.

Abeetha sits there, fingers to lips.

Whether she is in shock or happy, I cannot discern. *Was the kiss a goodbye kiss, or a we will be together forever kiss?*

Can I disrupt my cousin's happiness? I said I wanted him to be content here, but however selfish it may be, I cannot lose him. I must try all to keep him at my court. Returning to the table, I continue to search for information on wasps and locusts.

⸎

A DOOR CREAKING OPEN, footsteps on stone, voices. I lift my head to see my advisors filing in with the scientists.

Carrying two large scrolls, Bran stops at the table. "Queen, you are already here. We were looking for you. We could not seem to find Quinn, either."

Smoothing my skirt, I stand. "Quinn will be taking a day of rest. Is there news?"

He lets the scrolls roll atop my pile of texts. "These are from Chastam and Rotuga. They each report six swarms."

"The insects multiply quickly." I motion for everyone to gather around a map as I mark spots of attacks.

Describing that I found nothing about locusts being poisonous to wasps, I ask what the scientist think.

They have never seen this either but confirm the few nymph and adult forms found in the area match those from before.

"But how can they be of the same line and have different qualities? Are you sure?"

"Their exterior markings are exactly the same. We find no differences in the insects from the beginning of the swarms."

"Okay." I pace to a shelf. "Are all the crops doused with oil? And we have sent the oil recipe to Chastam and Rotuga? Were the fields attacked treated with the pepper oil?"

"Our farmers completed the oil treatment yesterday, but farms in Chastam and Rotuga had not been treated."

"That is good. We will assume our fields will be protected until we have information otherwise."

I ask for reports on acquiring birds. We have accumulated almost a thousand. *A thousand mouths that could be fed.* But they provide space for the birds to breed and nests to replenish numbers in the forests. If the oils do not kill or at least deter the locusts from devouring the crops, we will use the birds. I cut my eyes to the clock. It reads half past nine. In three and half hours, I will hear Quinn's decision.

Asking the scientists to continue their study, I take my leave. Seeing Mother and Father ahead, I flit up to them and offer to take Mother for a walk. Father transfers her arm to mine, and I cup my palm over her cold fingers. It is all I can do to walk in silence through the garden to the orchard and to the wood. Worry eats at me as if the locusts thrive inside my skin. *How could I be so rash as to order Quinn to marry me or leave?* My personality is killing me.

Still, I do not speak to her. I find I am too tired to even let the words pass my lips. *Goddesses.* I do not even know what to ask for.

—◈◈◈—

AFTER LEAVING MOTHER IN HER chamber, I find the girls prepping the seating arrangement and menus for the next festival weekend with Alfreda.

Noticing I wear the same frock as the day before and smell of smoke and muck, they send me to bathe.

Even this activity brings me no respite from my gnawing stomach. I request lunch in my room and look between my crystals and the clock, waiting for my sentence. *Will I wed my distant cousin, or will my closest friend abandon me?*

At a quarter till one, I move to my study. With the shutters still closed, the room is dark and dank. I open the window to welcome a breeze. Leaning on the windowsill, I note each activity within my view.

The scientists hover over the locusts' cages. Barn hands lead horses across the meadow. Soldiers mill about the courtyard.

I think of my training and how neglected my muscles are, that I have not shot arrows in three days. This only leads me to thoughts of Quinn and Holden. *How have things gone so wrong?*

Because of your need to control them is the only answer I find. *But was I not gifted for a reason? Did I survive a kobold attack to lead armies against battalions of bugs?* Perhaps I did. I back to my chair and sit down at the desk. I lift the quill from the ink and start to make circles on a page. Round and round, my life spins round and round with no purpose.

A rap on the door brings me from my depressive reverie.

Be a queen. Standing, I spread my shoulders and straighten my back.

"Enter."

Seeing his round wide eyes, I pray he does not kneel. It will be the death of him as well as me.

I lift my chin. "Tell me."

Tears form in his lids. "I love her. I want to stand by you, aid you in defending the realm, but I will be miserable, as will you. You must know that to be true."

Turning to the window, I cross to close the shutters. I press my hands to the soft wood as water pools in my eyes. "I know. I wish you would stay though."

"I will stay here if you allow us to marry."

The hole in my heart turns to anger. I exhale. "It cannot be so. Her father is a convicted traitor. I will allow you to take her to Bedham where you can live the rest of your lives together."

"She begs that her mother and father are allowed to come with us. They will live under our roof."

Is he mad? "No. I cannot allocate resources to have Gunther watched in Bedham. But her mother and sisters may visit as they please."

"May Ethan and Gunther at least travel for the wedding?"

I dig my nails into my palms. *Do not be rash and cruel.* "Yes, for three days, escorted by my soldiers."

"I would hope you would attend our wedding as well."

I want to, to stand and witness his happiness, but then I picture her form, with the dark hair and deep purple wings. Think of sitting across from her family at a wedding celebration. It cannot be. Still, I will keep my pledge to slow my pace and show kindness.

"I will think about it. Keep me informed of your plans, and I will make a decision." Fists clenched, I give orders that he should pack this afternoon and leave after the evening meal. At that supper, I will announce his engagement and upcoming wedding in Bedham, omitting his bride's name. He and Abeetha should have separate carriages that will be escorted to his home estate.

"Tonight? You wish us to leave tonight? What of the work on the locust problem?"

"I have many scientists and advisors, as you reminded me." I hold out my palm, glad to have left no cuts. "Give me your tunic."

He lifts an eyebrow. "Will you take my sword as well?"

I want no memory of this friendship. What might have been if he had stayed. How his departure may alter the path of history. For that loss, compounded with Holden's absence, may send me to my grave.

And a fiery grave it will be. Lucifer's voice trickles through my head.

I shiver.

"Are you well?" Quinn steps towards me.

Swallowing, I back away. "You have served me and this kingdom well. I will miss you, cousin."

Heart feeling as though it will crack in two, I offer my arm.

He grips it and dips his chin. Releasing me, he sheds his tunic. He lays it on the table, turns and opens the door. The wind wooshes through the window and through the opening. Flecks rise from the table and soot scatters from the fireplace.

Ashes to ashes. Dust to dust.

Just as you shall be in my lair, Lucifer snarls.

Perhaps I am mad. Maybe these voices represent hallucinations. I lean against the table. Scraping the green frock from the surface, I hurl it into the hearth. I palm the flint and metal and bend to light the tunic. Orange flames consume the garment, and smoke curls up the chimney.

The door swishes open, and the fire blazes higher.

I spin to see Alfreda, hand to hip. "Heavens be, it is hot as an oven in here. What, pray tell, are you doing? Quinn said you may have some directions for me?"

All I must do is make it to sundown. "Yes. Quinn is to return to Bedham to be married. He leaves tonight, so I would like to host a farewell dinner for him. Invite all the advisors and generals."

Mouth hanging open, she stares at me. "Quinn is leaving?"

I want to yell at her. Shout not to make me repeat my tragedy.

"Who will be your heir?"

"I do not know." I stare at the paper in front of me, thinking I should pen a formal announcement, write a speech to commemorate his service.

Crossing to me, Alfreda wraps her arms around my shoulders.

I stiffen at the feel of her warm, soft skin. I want nothing more than to melt into her embrace. But then the tears would come, and I fear I cannot stop them. I need to make it to sundown. I squeeze her torso. *Do not be rash. Do not be cruel.* "Thank you, Alfreda. Your support means much. I would think there is much to plan."

She opens her arms and releases me. "Of course. Are you—"

"Alfreda, I have much to do as well." I lift the quill from the ink.

"Yes." Dipping her chin, she backs out the doorway and closes it behind her.

Throwing the page with the circles into the dying embers, I raise a quill from the ink jar. Touching the point to the parchment, I start the official decree. I form the letters slowly and surely, writing of his service to the kingdom. I end by asking all those that would like to bid congratulations and farewell to meet at the main courtyard at eight.

Grant's eager eyes greet me as I exit my study.

I raise the document before his face.

"Never fear. Your wish is granted. Quinn leaves for Bedham tonight. Hang this in the main hall."

Feeling my ribs tighten, I take slow, deep breaths. I must convene Father, General Kane, and the advisors. *But do I trust them to list a suitable heir presumptive?* I will not give it to Kane, nor any of the advisors. Perhaps to Father until he declines in health. *By then I could be…* I stop that line of thought. Two proposals in one day, and still, I have no one.

Refocusing, I wind through the halls to Father's chamber. Seeing Mother at the window, golden hair glowing in the light, I think of the girls. How heartbroken they will be to see Quinn leave. I must tell them next. I draw in a breath and approach Father at his desk.

Palms pressed to the wood, I inform him of Quinn's plans to return to Bedham and take Abeetha as his bride. I omit my marriage proposal and the drama with Foster that ensued.

Father's face transforms from rose, to bright red, then purple.

Seeing he still breathes, I brace myself for the onslaught of questions and accusations. They come in quick succession. What had I done to drive Quinn away? Did I do everything in my power to stop him? How could I let this happen?

"Father," I say in a volume just above a whisper, "this is Quinn's choice—"

"I should have forced you to marry him months ago. You have made a mockery of this kingdom with your affiliation with the witches of Upper Earth, fiasco with Holden, and now Quinn's decision to leave. Do you have any skills at all?"

Pushing off the desk, I stand upright. "Yes. It seems I have a knack for science, especially the science of invasive species such as kobold and locusts. And if you ever speak to me that way again, I will send you to Willhelm to live in the frosty tundra until your death."

Spinning on one heel, I march from the room. *Damn him.* Tears fill my lids. *Why did he have to be so hurtful?* Father should know this stands a big loss after many. I saved this kingdom when he could not. I should have known he would react this way. He ensnared Quinn with the promise of a marriage alliance. *Why would I come to Father hoping for support, even empathy, now?*

Turning a corner, I step to the wall, pressing my back to the cold rock. I close my eyes and draw in a breath.

"Titania." Father's call echoes through the passage.

I have half a mind to flee and leave him searching for hours. Wiping my cheeks, I raise my chin and wait.

He rounds the corner and drops to the stone. "Titania, forgive me. I spoke in haste. I was in shock."

"You, of all people, should know how to control your reactions. I do it day in and day out. I will not ask forgiveness for my words. You cannot speak to me that way, father or no. I am your queen now, and you must accept that. Know that I did everything in my power to keep Quinn here. He is my cousin, and I will miss him very much, especially now, knowing the little faith my father has in my skills."

He reaches for my hands and drops his palms when I back away. "I did not mean what I said. You have proved a capable, even outstanding, leader in everything that you faced. My worry got the best of me. Please, forgive me."

"Father"—I take his hand and hold his gaze—"I need people by my side that support and believe in me. If you cannot be that, please, go with Quinn, for to look upon your face and know your disappointment will be too much for me. I have done everything in my power for four years to forge myself into a strong, capable ruler for Aubren. And despite setbacks"—I lift my finger as he opens his mouth—"I am doing a good job."

"I can see that, daughter. I spoke in haste from a place of fear. Fear for you. Your mother said something."

"What? You let me go on when Mother had an episode?" I pull him to the wall. "Tell me."

"She said, 'you need them.'"

I want to roll my eyes and stomp my foot to the stone. This is not new, and I do not want to be reminded of it just now. "She has said that to me several times in the past weeks."

"Who do you think she means?"

"Holden and Quinn. But I have lost them both. The goddesses have abandoned me." Squeezing his hand, I look to the ceiling to stop the tears from forming. "But all will be well. The High Council will see I am following their rules, we will figure out how to quell the locusts, and things will go back to normal."

Releasing my hand, Father sets his palms atop my shoulders. "Heavy is the head that wears the crown. I know this better than anyone. Rest tonight and recharge for tomorrow, daughter. And please, pay no heed to my hasty words."

Thanking him, I exit the passage at the first door. I need to yell, scream, wail at the top of my lungs, find some release from this vice-like grip on my heart my grief forms. I wind through the garden to the meadow, walk through the grass, palms raking the top of the soft, feathery tassels. I know I am trailed by Grant, Adam, and two High Council guards. This is my life. But if I go into the wood, they will hover over the trees, waiting for me. At the edge of the forest, I jump into the air. I push my wings against the wind with all my might, speeding around tree trunks. I make a wide circle and land beside the brook just as it turns south.

My crystals lie hidden just on the other side. *Why did I come here? What do they represent? How do they make me feel safe? Control.* They ensure an escape, a way out. A possibility when I see no other way. They are the only thing I have faith in anymore. For if this realm does not want me, I will go to the witches of the trinity and join them in their quest to end the demons of Lower Earth.

I wade into the water and cross to the far side where the water rushes up to my chest. My wings bat in the current. I long to hold the crystals, confirm they sit where Foster alleged, but I do not dare risk it. For if the High Council guards saw me, I could lose everything. I trudge from the beginning of the curve to the end, hand scraping the branches and brambles of the bank.

Cold and worn, I let the current carry me to the opposite shore. I climb to the soft bank, wring out my skirt, and flick the water from my wings. In a few flaps, my wings dry, and with a last look at the far bank, I jump into the sky. Meeting my guards overhead, I turn towards the castle. My home, almost empty again.

Descending to the meadow, I find three forms waiting. Gatuika, Makani, and Isla rush to me as I land, flinging their arms around me, one after the other in a giant, mass hug. With their embraces, I cannot stop tears from pouring from my eyes. At least I have these three cousins. *Until the summer's end.* My side ticks. Drawing in a breath, I wriggle from their arms. "You have heard?"

"Quinn came to us. He saw you leave alone and was worried." Gatuika takes my hand.

"It is a big loss." I swipe water from my face. "But we must go on. I am happy to have you here."

Taking Isla's hand, I start to the castle. We check on Alfreda's preparations for the event, I send messages to gather the advisors and generals, and then we bathe and dress as if for a festival dinner. I choose a hunter green dress, the color of my crest. Light bouncing off the beaded bodice offsets the shimmers from my forehead.

Looking in the mirror, I take in a deep breath. *You can do this, Titania. There is nothing to fear but fear itself.*

And a few damned souls. Lucifer's voice plays through my thoughts.

Leaving the girls to help Alfreda, I round to Quinn's chamber. Arm in arm, we stroll to Father's chamber, and the three of us process to the study.

With the advisors seated around the table, Father and Kane, and the generals behind them, I stand before them and start my rehearsed speech.

"Father, advisors, and generals, I have gathered you here for news that affects my line of succession. It is with sorrow, but joy for him, that I announce Quinn's return to his home country. He has served us well but now must follow his heart home. I hope you will all join us for a farewell dinner in his honor this night."

"This night?" Bran's eyes widen, and he scans the faces of the others. "But what of your succession? If you still insist on flying off to aid the soldiers, we must name an heir presumptive."

"I agree. My father is still able and can serve as heir presumptive until his health declines. If that is acceptable to the advisors."

"But this is not a permanent solution either," another advisor says.

I hold my arms steady at my side as if comfortable and unfazed. I knew this would be a question. "Gentlemen, as we have experienced with Holden's transition and now Quinn's departure, nothing is fixed. Our minds change, our hearts change, and we can only make choices based on the information we have in front of us. If you would like a day to think through this decision, we can convene again tomorrow afternoon."

Bran stands. "What will change before tomorrow? I say we approve now and move to more important topics. If the pattern of the locusts continues, we need all minds fixed on that problem. Titania has been very instrumental in limiting the locusts so far, and she defeated the kobold, so why should we not grant her recommendation?"

The tightening in my chest relaxes upon hearing his words. At least Bran still stands on my side. I see nods of agreement, and one moves to vote, we have a second, and all vote in favor of naming Father as heir presumptive.

Congratulating Quinn on his vague transition, the advisors file out.

"Nicely handled, daughter." Father pats my back and shuffles from the room.

"He ages quickly," Quinn says as we linger at the table.

"He does. I do not know another who could be named though."

"My father. He is ten years younger."

"Perhaps, but he is not here, and they do not know him."

"You have forgiven me quicker than I thought."

I smile. "Yes, I have forgiven you, although I shall miss you greatly. But I would be a hypocrite for denouncing your actions. Would I have not done the same for Holden?"

Standing, he offers his arm. "I hope you find happiness, cousin."

I hook my hand in the crook of his elbow. "One day, perhaps."

Throughout the meal, I distract myself with everything but thoughts of Quinn and his absence. The tears will come tonight when I am alone. I will cry for myself; that I have failed the goddesses; that they have deserted me; and that the merry three that once were, Holden, Quinn, and myself, never shall be again. I compliment the food, the wine, and each dress and pressed suit. Anything to stall the moment of his departure.

But it comes.

I stand beside him in the courtyard, staring as attendants load his trunk into the carriage bound for the harbor. I wrap my arms around him and wish him well. I kiss his cheek.

He steps away and bows low. Hugging the girls, Alfreda, Mother, and then locking arms with Father, Quinn takes a few steps towards the coach. Waving, he slides inside. I see his face once more as he reclines in the seat. The car jerks forwards, circles to the drive, and travels down the hill and outside the castle walls.

I long to have them raise the drawbridge and lock my heart inside so it shall never be broken again.

The girls flank me as I proceed to my room, wanting nothing more than to shed every item that will remind me of this night, this day, this week, this month, this season, and this year.

"Should we have a slumber party? We could steal some desserts from the kitchen." Isla slides her hand in mine.

Squeezing her fingers, I thank her for the idea. With the excuse of exhaustion, I hug each one and kiss them goodnight, promising to spend time with them in the morning. *Morning.* I cross into my room. *Six days since the last locust attack.* For tonight, I will not think of it. I shed my dress and slip on Holden's tunic, burying my nose in the scent of him. I light the fire and retrieve his sword from the corner. Sitting cross-legged, I lay the lance on my lap. I stare into the flames and let the tears come.

Air gushes over my skin, raising bumps on every surface. Grabbing the sword and jumping to my feet, I swirl to meet the intruders.

Three shocked faces greet me. Doubling over, I let the sword drop to the floor.

"We stole some wine from the cellar." Gatuika lifts a bottle in the air.

Isla lays a tray on my bed. "And sugars from the kitchen."

"And we brought a fiddle." Makani rings in. "We are not going to let you be alone tonight. You may cry, or yell, or drink and dance, but we will be here with you."

Fresh tears jump to my eyes as I take in the sight of my beloved cousins. If I were not so tarnished, I could be of use to them as well.

Chapter 17

Morning dawns with silence. I lift my head to see Gatuika on one side, Makani on the other, and Isla at my feet. Three pure souls, a buffer from Lucifer's intervention in my psyche. *But do you really count yourself damned? Why should I not?* All the evidence points me to that end.

Moving as quietly as possible, I dress for meetings with the advisors and scientists. With light streaming around my curtains, I grab a pastry from the kitchen and fetch Mother from her room. I watch the sky as we walk the garden, then the orchard, my thoughts on the looming locust visit.

My bug-update session is short with my team reporting all fields covered with the pepper oil. Chastam and Rotuga made much progress as well.

I wonder if the pests will move to new kingdoms.

King Luther will not be so flippant when it becomes his food they devour. Goading myself for the thought, I end our meeting and wind through the castle to find the girls.

They sit with Alfreda, making the seating chart for our guests from Elita, the land of the colorful birds, snakes, and lizards. *So much opportunity for seeing the world missed due to my anxieties.* But such trauma to overcome. The girls and I ride after the noon meal and shoot arrows in the meadow. All the while, I keep my eyes trained overhead, expecting to see a swarm descend on us any moment.

After dinner, I leave the girls to Alfreda, Mother, and Father. I dress in my leather battle vest and head to Westshire, the frontline of the battle with the locusts. Even *thinking* we have a battalion of soldiers on the ready to attack insects seems ludicrous, but these bugs have proven unpredictable and resilient, so we must be ready for anything. Losing five percent of our crops may be acceptable, but ten percent would be taxing. And if the locusts' numbers continue to grow, goddesses help the whole realm.

We stationed battalions at four points in the kingdom. With soldiers standing guard in the northeast, southeast, southwest corners, we rendezvous at Foster's farm. Seeing the tiny cottage reminds me of the first time Father and I visited. It seems like a lifetime ago. *How could you be so ill fated as to lose two loves in six months? And friend and heir presumptive?* Refocusing on the task at hand, I land near the barn with Grant and Adam.

Seeing a familiar redhead, I draw in a breath. I force a smile as he approaches. "I was not sure you would be here."

Foster dips his chin. "Welcome, Queen. I am leading this battalion, and it is my farm."

"Leading? What about your other duties?"

"Since it has been quiet, and this is the most important task at the moment, Grant suggested I take command."

"Very well, thank you."

Torches and water buckets stand ready to be dispersed to the spot of infestation. We wait one hour, two hours, three hours, past dark. The clock tower in the village starts the ring of midnight. Frustrated and stiff, I rise from my post on an upturned bucket. I study the grey sky. As the last chime of midnight gongs, I hear them. It starts as a low hum and rises to a deafening buzz as a patch of sky over us turns black with the insects. Looking beyond our field, I see two additional swarms.

As if in concert, they descend and hover over the fields. Some insects drop from the group, landing on the plants. I hold my breath, praying the pepper oil works. Seeing the bugs rise back to join the swarm, I grow hopeful. The swarms rise, and the deafening done of their beating wings subsides. We watch as they trace west.

Shouts ring out, and soldiers whoop with joy.

"It seems this plan worked." Grant commends me.

I nod. "For the present time. But where will they go? To fields not treated in other kingdoms?"

"I guess we shall know tomorrow. It is late. Do you want the men to camp here?"

"Yes. It may be overly cautious, but we cannot risk losing more crops or the insects feeding further and multiplying their numbers."

"I will give the order." Grant backs away.

Waiting for him to return, I try not to watch Foster.

His hair is cut shorter and muscles bulge under his vest.

It makes me happy that he has risen so far in such a short time. As we take to the air, I scan for signs of swarms to the south and east. Then I turn my attention to the west. The night sky makes it impossible to discern whether dark patches represent clouds or merely darker portions on the barrier.

Landing at the castle, I hear reports from the other three battalions. No other swarms were cited. This news lightens my mood. Their numbers have not risen to an overwhelming amount yet. I pray Chastam and Rotuga had similar successes.

Worry tortures my sleep. *Will the locust attack in other kingdoms? What damage may ensue? How will their numbers be buoyed?*

⋅⟐⋅

I RISE WITH THE FIRST LIGHT and make for the study. A page finds me not half an hour later with a letter from King Luther of Hilbron. He reports three swarms devasted nine fields before they moved out over the ocean. I instruct that he be sent copies of all the precautions that have brought us success.

Nine fields devoured, I ponder. This means the locusts fed well. They may not need more sustenance for a while. Or perhaps they sense their impending doom. But the feeding may also shore up their bodies, making them able to fly farther.

Letters of success arrive from Chastam and Rotuga. Notes of distress come from Willhelm and Lindleton, as swarms devoured fields near their southern borders. As with Hilbron, we send out instructions with haste. Even though Elita and Borean lie across a large ocean, I write to them, imploring them to take precautions as well.

"You have done well," Grant says. "The pepper oil may curb their numbers."

"The insects are erratic. We have witnessed that. First, they feared the torches then they had no effect. And what of the dead wasps?"

"You cannot think to eradicate every locust from all of Middle Earth."

"If we get through the dry season with enough crops to feed our people for the winter, I will be happy. I believe the rains may cause them to morph back to their solitary forms."

I hear reports from General Kane as to their progress of searching the kingdom for locust breeding grounds. The soldiers move south, with just a fourth uninspected. Instructing him to continue the search, I ask that other soldiers be sent to aid farmers in dousing their fields with oil. If dew forms, then the pepper oil must be reapplied each day.

As the hour reaches midday, I look out over the gardens and orchard. Something is missing. *Quinn.* His merry face and aura of cheerfulness and calm. Now, all that is left is me and my neurotic sense. My thoughts turn to the insects. *Why do they not eat other plants? Shrubs? Tree leaves? Could they turn to these if we cut off their other sources of food?*

WORD COMES THE NEXT DAY that with the upheaval caused by the locusts, festival season will be suspended. I find the girls in a glum mood.

"We have no one to entertain us now. Alfreda has no need for us, Quinn is gone. This is no fun anymore." Isla huffs and falls limp on her bed.

"Yes, you just have your horribly boring cousin to keep you company now." I drag her up by her arm. "What if we practice fencing with the soldiers? I believe you may be ready to test your skills."

We round to the fencing dojo and fit them with masks and suits. My four trusted guards, Grant, Adam, Nicholas, and Timothy, spar with us through the afternoon. Having a fantastic idea, I announce that the soldiers will be our guests for the weekend and that games will proceed all of Saturday. I see Alfreda's face go white and make a mental note to pitch in to help her the next day.

<hr>

THE SUMMER HEAT MEETS ME as I rise. Finding Alfreda already in the kitchen, I appoint Isla and Makani to help with the food, and Gatuika and I help in the field with the tents.

"I cannot imagine Quinn sparring with the soldiers," Gatuika says. "I wonder what he would think of this."

My side ticks with his loss. "Actually, he was a soldier in Bedham before he came here. He may return to that."

"Have you heard from him?"

I answer in the negative, feeling somewhat guilty that I have not written him either. But he could not stay here with her.

Foster did confirm she traveled to Bedham with her mother the day after Quinn's departure. Foster left four soldiers to watch them in Bedham. I cannot imagine those men to be happy with that job, but it will not be needed always. Quinn would not be glad that we spy on them I am sure, but her family has shown several times their willingness to act against me.

I hope Quinn can be content with Abeetha in Bedham. I wonder if I would take him back if he changed his mind. That is too much to hope for. I would think he would be of much use to Bedham's King Herman as to how to deal with the locusts. Glancing at the sky, I wonder about the insects and when they will strike next. *Savor the happy times.* I refocus on the tasks at hand.

We work till sundown and dress for dinner and the celebration following. The girls look happier dancing with the soldiers than they had with royal guests. This party holds more joy for me as well. I am with my people without worry for diplomacy or what opinions they may have for me. I enjoy jigs with any who approach.

Foster offers his hand, and with mixed emotion, I accept. I cannot forget his betrayal nor the offer of marriage. Looking out over the dancers, I realize the party creates a needed distraction. *What would I have done all weekend with no reprieve from thoughts of the loss of Holden and Quinn? Only locusts to think of? Become the mad queen everyone believes me to be?* I focus on Foster's hand on my waist, his callused fingers brushing mine, and his blue eyes sparkling in the light. This, too, brings me a tinge of sadness. For I may never trust enough to love again.

We dance till midnight, when with complaints, I drag the girls to their room.

"But the party still goes on." Isla moans.

"The party with drunken soldiers." Makani bulges her eyes in their sockets.

"Yes, drunken soldiers who can entertain themselves." I blow kisses and bid them goodnight.

Shedding my gown and dressing for bed, I eye Holden's sword and vest in the corner. Retrieving them, I hug them to me and crawl into bed. *What would it be like if he were still here?* We would have slipped off to fly the countryside. I imagine the feel of the warm wind on my skin, transforming to cool vapor as we plunge into the forest.

Goddesses, why? Why has everything been taken from me? Even with these whirling thoughts, exhaustion wins.

WITH REPORTS THAT CROPS OF the entire realm of Middle Earth stand protected from the locusts by the pepper oil, I open the games for the day. We hold fencing, wrestling, archery, riding, javelin, shot put, bowling, and croquet matches, and by midnight, I fall into bed, muscles aching from wear.

Trumpets blare, waking me from my sleep. They only mean one thing: There is credible alarm on castle grounds. Heart in my throat, I glance at the clock as I tug on my riding pants. Two a.m. on the mark. I am already at the door when a fist pounds on it. Swinging it open, I find Foster and Grant.

"The orchard. A swarm just landed in the orchard." Grants ushers me to the window.

Jumping to the sill and taking to the air, we shoot to the orchard perimeter. Soldiers gather with torches and water buckets.

"It is too close to the castle and the village. We cannot burn the orchard."

"What are we to do, let them feed and devastate your trees only to be nourished to reproduce again?"

"No." I dart into the air, headed for the bird pens. "We release the birds. Get the torches and soldiers away from the trees."

Landing beside the cages, we fling the gates open. The birds squat, huddled together, and we duck inside, shooing them out. I see them rise and then, perhaps tuned to their prey, turn towards the orchard. Having no clue how many locusts inhabit the trees, we release the whole lot of them. I remember reading how the birds ate so many insects they could not fly during the great swarm before the floods.

As the birds alight on the trees, locusts fill the air. Their hum grows as they coalesce into a cloud. I fear they may target our vegetable garden and order soldiers to stand around the trees with torches. Time expands as the birds swoop through the orchard, and the locusts hover above. My stomach rolls in my torso with the cacophony of chirps and drone of the insects.

Seconds expand to minutes. With bloated bellies, the birds descend one by one to the grass.

My eyes cut to the ground and to the sky. The pitch of the insects' hum rises, and the now, I pray, diluted host of locusts moves in a wave over us, circles the castle, and heads south. Chill bumps rising on my skin, I order the bugs followed. Perhaps if they land, we could use some type of other poison on them. This brings me to the question as to whether the scientists have found a substance that harms rather than just deters the bugs.

I wait in the library for word of the swarm, but scouts report that it seems to be circling the continent. I send a messenger to alert King Luther of Hilbron. Seeing Foster and Grant approach, I rise to meet them.

With eyes cutting around me to the advisors gathered, Grant motions me away. I follow him and Foster out of the library, through the garden, and to the orchard. My breath catches in my throat. Lifeless doves lay atop the grass like a cover sewn of feathers.

"Did any of them survive?"

"Not that we have found." Foster scans the orchard.

"No one touch them. Set guards every ten feet so not a soul comes near here. Wake the scientists, all of them, now." I clutch my stomach as it threatens to heave.

Dead wasps and now dead doves? How can this be? I bend down and study the bird nearest me. Nothing seems amiss. The locusts must be poisonous. And it would lead that these birds may now also be poisonous to us. *How will we dispose of them?*

By daybreak, the scientists have no other explanation than I had come to myself. With the brightening sky, we see that perhaps only a fourth of the leaves of the trees were damaged. If not for the dead birds underneath, I could have counted it a victory. I gather the scientists, advisors, and generals, and we pack into the study to counsel. As we debate, message after message arrives from the other kingdoms. Swarms attacked other non-sprayed plants elsewhere as well, and fires set resulted in the locusts taking to the air. I thank the goddesses no other kingdoms attempted using birds.

Seeing dimming light from the window, I peek out. A swarm passes over the castle, and I open the window to hear their droning hum. *What are they doing?* By midafternoon, my brain and body crave rest, and I retire to my chamber. The girls request entry, and I wave them to my bed. Gatuika humming a tune, I fall into a restful sleep.

It is not over. We are coming for you. Lucifer's voice threatens.

I sit up with a start. Climbing over Makani, I light a candle and note the time. *Six.* Light will come soon. I tiptoe to my study and read the new letters that arrived in the night. The swarms still linger. I request Nicholas and Timothy update me, and they report the same of the swarm circling our kingdom.

I exit into the garden and wind to the orchard. Foster and Grant confer with the chief scientist at the exit to the garden, and I inquire as to the decision on how to deal with the birds. The only solution seems to be burning them, and I request they move them to the far field where they prepare the animals.

Hearing a hum, I look up to see a swarm of locusts approaching. "What are they doing? How long can they go without food or water?"

"They absorb moisture from their food," the scientist notes.

"And they must eat sometime, right?"

"Our research shows they can go without food for days, perhaps even a week."

"A week with these ghastly things flying about, and we all shall go mad. Is there not any poison we could use?"

"Spray it in the air for it to fall to the ground and potentially harm us?"

"I guess not." I plant my hands on my hips.

The hum grows so loud we cannot speak over the drone. Taking to the air, I circle to the other side of the castle to get a better view of the swarm.

"They are congregating near the ring?" I stare in disbelief. "Do they think they may get out? How do they even know the ring is there?"

"They must sense fresh air, catch the scent of untreated plant life perhaps?" A scientist guesses.

"Good riddance to them, I say. Let them pass to Upper Earth. The humans have pesticides to combat them." Grant waves his hand at them and turns back towards the orchard.

"Titania." Nicholas hovers in front of me. "Regin is reporting a swarm huddles around the southern ring as well. He wants to call a conference with the High Council, debate whether we should close the rings or let the bugs exit."

"I guess that is appropriate. It is his call. Send letters to the other kingdoms. Find out if they report the same."

All day the swarm lingers under the ring, causing an eerie gray to wash the land. The other kingdoms report the same, and the High Council convenes in Hilbron. With direction from the scientists, they decide the insects cannot gather there forever. The locusts will either pass to Upper Earth and become a human problem or start dying.

By dinner, the darkened sky wears on my every nerve, and I request we eat inside with every candle possible lit. It reminds me of the kobold and how they stole the ring crystals, causing our ring to fail. *Was it just seven months ago that I feared that our realm could be cut off from light and water from Upper Earth? It is not the same.* But every cell in my body remembers the panic.

On edge as well, the girls sleep in my bed again. The faces of those of the deep, Sonia, Abaddon, Thanatos, Theron, and Lucifer, play through my dreams.

We are here.

My eyes fly open, and I glance around, getting my bearings. *In my room, in my castle, in my kingdom, in my realm,* I repeat in my head. *Post-traumatic stress disorder, or PTSD.* If I were in Upper Earth, I would be diagnosed and sent to therapy. Here, as a fae, and a royal fae, leader of an army, perhaps it stands as a tenet of my position. No, of me, of my life. *Because how many other twelve-year-old fae have seen their brother killed before them? Or have almost been ended by the most evil one himself?*

I look at the clock to see it reads seven. It should be light out, but no light creeps around my curtains. Lifting the covers and flitting up, I cross to the window. Seeing the dank, muted colors of the garden, I round to each window in turn. I note the swarm overhead. The mass churns as if a cauldron of tar boiling on a fire. My skin chills. *How long can the locusts hold us hostage? Could there be some way to spur them to disperse? Wave them through the ring? Or break up the swarm with sprays of water? What if we exploded fireworks in their midst as on the solstice?* I dart from the room with all these ideas swimming in my head.

I convene the advisors, scientists, generals, and Zekial. Zekial always hovers, no matter where I am, but today I make a point to add him to the invitation list. As former leader of the High Council, I figure he serves as their representative here. They disregard the explosives idea because it would take weeks to make the amount needed to disperse the swarm. The scientists predict the water will expand their life cycle. It remains a question as to how we may force them through the rings.

The generals wonder if a breeze from our wings may force them into the ring. In the end, all agree this to be the safest and best course of action. I instruct General Kane to assemble all the troops and the tactic be tried that afternoon.

Sounds of beating wings joins the chorus of humming insects as fae soldiers convene in the meadow.

If I had ever thought I would summon my army to fight a herd of locusts, it would only be if I were mad. Part of me thinks to pinch myself to see if I still dream.

General Kane gives the order, and we take to the air, Foster and Grant, and of course, Zekial and his guards, fast at my side.

Approaching the swarm, the soldiers turn their backs to the bugs and hover, not two fae length away.

I watch from the side as the wave of insects undulates. Instead of moving towards the portal, the locusts approach our line.

Kane directs them to make passes at the insects as if herding them like cattle into the opening.

As the soldiers move to one side, the entire swarm turns black. No trace of definition remains as if they have turned all their wings in the same direction. Motion catches my eye, and another ebony swarm approaches from the west.

"This seems to be attracting the bugs," I yell to Foster over the drone of the beating wings.

Other swarms join the hovering insects, and I order the army to secure the castle. Hovering under the wall of bugs, I find the black barrier reaches as far as I can see in every direction. *What* are *they doing?*

We are here. Lucifer's voice plays through my mind.

I blink, trying to clear my head and comprehend the enormity of the mass of insects gathered above me. *Do they mean to all pass to Upper Earth, or have they formed a death pack, one final push to find sustenance?*

Starting from the far side, a wave of white washes over the group, turning the entire swarm into a bleached cloud.

"What are they doing?" Zekial draws near.

"I have no idea. It is as if they have one mind."

"But they are insects, bugs, and their thought processes are not that evolved."

Dark patches emerge against the chalky background. I struggle to process what I see. An image of a chin, lips, nose, cheekbones, eyes, forehead, ears, and hair forms in the swarm.

"Is that a face?" Zekial whispers.

I stare in disbelief. "It is not just a face. That is Theron."

Chapter 18

"CLOSE THE RING. CLOSE ALL the rings. Sound the alarm, now!" I shout to Grant.

Faster than I thought he could move, Zekial latches on to Grant's arm. "She has no authority to make that decision. Stand down."

"She is my queen, and I do as she commands."

Zekial's eyes turn on me. "You do not have the authority. We want these insects gone. Order your men to crowd them through the portal."

"Do you see a face in that swarm?"

"Yes."

"Yes, you agree you see a face?"

"Yes." He acquiesces.

I look at his guards. "Do you see a face?"

Wide-eyed, they nod. I ask the same of Foster and Grant, and they affirm as well.

"Do you recognize that face? Have you seen it before?"

They all assent to not having seen the male's image.

"That is Theron Michaels, brother to Hunter of the trinity of witches, son of Thanatos, and grandson of Sonia. I saw Theron in Upper Earth and then in Lower Earth. My guess is his spirit is trapped there and is trying to escape to Upper Earth. If we let these locusts through the portal, we are opening his spirit into the human realm. There, it may roam free, bringing his vengeance to the witches and endangering many humans."

"How can you be sure this is Theron's spirit? It is an aberration. It just appears as the form of a face from this angle." Zekial motions to the cloud above.

I jet down to the castle roof and wait for Zekial and his guards to join me. The image manifests the same, frozen features of a man, a man who looks just like Theron.

"Do you still see a man? The same figure as before?"

"Yes. But how can I trust what you say is true? It could be any male."

"Ask any fae who followed the trinity."

The swarm begins to rise, and I shout at Zekial, "You need to order the rings closed! Theron cannot be freed!"

"How am I to take your word for this?"

"It is Theron! That is why the wasps and birds died, the six-day pattern of attacks. They were not random. The insects are being controlled by the dark spirits of Lower Earth." *Lucifer's voice in my head all these weeks.*

"You are a witch. This is all a scam for you to take over our realm. I shall have you arrested and tried! If not for witchery, for madness, removed from your throne," Zekial yells.

Equal parts of me want to double over in laughter and spit in his face. Drawing in a breath, I hold his gaze.

"A witch? I am a witch? And I mean to take Lower Earth for myself? I have wings on my back. I was born in

Middle Earth to two fae parents. You have known my father almost all your life. The same credence runs through my veins as does yours: To protect this realm and that above from the evil souls of the deep."

"You are in league with them, or your spirit has been possessed as you propose these locusts are. How else could you have lured the kobold and escaped Lower Earth?"

I ball my hands into fists. "You only fear what you cannot imagine. That a girl of sixteen could defeat an army of evil creatures. That I accomplished this by being smart and brave alone. Do you see the kobold returning? No. They are dead. *I* defeated them."

"These are bugs, and they will die in due time."

"You do not believe that. I see the fear in your eyes, can smell the anxiety rolling off you. What evidence do you have to charge me with what you proposed? And who shall help you with the locusts? Your guards? Maybe I should leave you all to the perils that await." *Maybe.* Because I may have no better solution now that Holden and Quinn are gone and the goddesses have abandoned me.

Motion catches my eye, and Gatuika and Makani alight beside me.

"I told you it looked like Theron." Makani taunts Gatuika.

"What are you doing here? You need to be inside."

"We left Isla with Alfreda. We thought we may be of help." Gatuika's eyes bore into mine.

My palms tingle, and I stretch out my fingers, savoring the release of tension. *You need them.* Mother's words ring through my mind. *Them, my cousins, not Holden and*

Quinn. The goddesses did not forsake me. I had what I needed all along.

"Zekial, you heard my cousins. They, like most young fae, have followed the witches of the trinity and those surrounding them. They see him too."

His eyes cut to the form above and between me and the girls. "They are your cousins. They may be witches as well. You can communicate with them through your minds. You told them to corroborate your story."

I look up to see the mass of insects forming a funnel at the entrance to the ring. "We are running out of time. Pick any fae in the village. But do it fast. Because, so help me, if you do not send the signal to close all the portals before a single locust passes through this ring, I shall sound the alarm myself."

Zekial glances up to the swarm as the funnel grows, now just inches from passing to Upper Earth. "Sound the alarm."

The horns blaze, and echoes of trumpets from the south and west bounce through the realm. I sense the stillness of the air as the portals seal shut. Above us, the swarm flattens out again, and with a ripple, the entire surface transforms to black.

He shifts his weight between his feet. "I do not see the necessity in closing all the portals. It has already been a day and a half with no sunlight for the entire realm. Our water supply will dwindle within days. With the summer heat, Middle Earth will become a hotbox. Many could perish from heat exhaustion alone. Our crop yield already suffered under the reign of terror of these horrid locusts.

If it is a spirit, it is everlasting. It could starve us until we fold."

I square my shoulders. "Now you believe?"

Straightening his spine, he locks eyes with me. "Only the goddesses know the truth, and only history will tell if you are right or not. I see no other path at the moment. You have until the morning to form a solution. At noon tomorrow, I open the rings."

"Zekial." I offer my arm. "We will defeat the locusts. And this realm and the one above will be protected from the evil spirit possessing them. I promise you that."

He takes a step back. "I pray to the goddesses you are right."

I spin to the girls. "Gather your sister. Foster will see you safely there. I will come to you soon."

Turning to Foster, I offer my arm, and he wraps his palm around my forearm. "Thank you for your brave service today. Go with the girls."

Foster's thoughts run through my mind. *I will secure the crystals as you asked. I do not relish the thought of you returning to Lower Earth, but I will not stand in your way again.*

I smile to myself. For my aim had been to touch Foster so I could convey my need to him. I do not know how we will banish Theron's spirit, but having access to at least two portals will ensure I can accomplish the task. I offer my arm to Grant and then Adam, thanking and directing them to gather the advisors, scientists, and generals, as well as to assure the soldiers all will be well.

Shooting to the castle, I enter the main passageway. Corridor thick with soldiers, I weave through them, offering reassurances and praise to all.

Zekial trails me, and I wonder if he means to guard me every second.

In the library, I address the advisors, scientists, and generals, offering thanks for a job well done and promising a plan by the day's end.

Rounding to check on Mother and Father, I find Alfreda in the kitchen.

"Oh goddesses, the girls said the spirit of Theron is controlling the locusts?"

"Hush." I silence her by wrapping her into a hug. "All will be well, I promise."

She wriggles from my grip. "That means that you will risk all yet again."

"Not all. You know I would never put my people in jeopardy."

"You know that is not what I meant." Tears form in her eyes.

"This is my destiny, Alfreda." I hug her to me again. "Ask for help in the village. Many will take the soldiers in for the night."

⸺⟡⟡⟡⸺

I CIRCLE BACK THROUGH THE passages as soldiers exit into the courtyards. At my suite, I find Nicholas and Timothy guarding the doors as well as two High Council guards. Thinking they could be an issue, I flash them a smile and slip into my study.

Isla runs to me and throws her arms around my waist. "Did he really call you a witch? Will they take us, too?"

I make bug eyes at Gatuika and Makani.

And Gatuika mouths *sorry*.

"He is scared. He does not even know what he is saying." I squeeze Isla's shoulders.

Running my hand down her arm, I clutch her fingers. "But we must shore up a plan. I have one forming but believe I need help."

Waving the girls towards the fireplace, we gather around the hearth. Heads inches apart, I reveal my idea. I outline how I may need each of them and inquire as to whether they believe we can accomplish it.

"We do not need all the tools you speak of." Gatuika insists. "Only our powers."

"If we use our powers, the whole family may be exposed. I cannot risk that. I will risk myself alone."

Gatuika takes my hand. "I can create a diversion. We all can. It will be hard to discern from where the power emerged."

As Makani completes the circle of locked palms, my mind opens to their thoughts. I marvel at how even their mental patterns match their voices and personalities. Within minutes, our plan is formed. Kissing each of their cheeks, I rise and exit my study.

Seeing Foster approach, I sidle next to him, and he brushes my arm with his.

I retrieved the crystals. They are in your hiding place. His voice echoes in my mind.

Thanking him, I instruct that he round up my guard. They will be instrumental in ensuring my plan comes to fruition. Convening with the advisors, scientists, and generals, I begin to summarize my plan.

Zekial sits front and center, studying me as if daring me to create a viable solution.

I explain the tactic, the science behind it, and implements needed to make it a success. I see some heads nodding and other fae wide-eyed with doubt. Taking each question in turn, I listen as they express trepidation, fear, even disbelief at my theories. Most of the scientists see it as a sound plan in a technical sense, the advisors worry for the safety of our fae, and the generals wonder if we could construct the needed massive instrument of destruction with enough speed.

If, most add, the locusts do represent the spirit of the so-named evil spirit, Theron. But for this, I have no answer other than I can feel it deep in my bones. *What other evidence do we need save he revealed his face? For what reason?* To taunt me is all I can guess, but I dare not divulge the thought.

Looking at Zekial, I prompt him. "You are probably the highest ranking fae in our midst, what say you? Will you give us the time we need?"

"We have already passed two days without light or additional water. One more may be all we can bear."

"We will start immediately, and by the heat of the day tomorrow, I believe it can be accomplished."

"Go then."

Leaving orders to evacuate the castle and village starting at first light and to gather all the metal chainmail in the kingdom within the passages, I confer with the generals and advisors.

Workers and soldiers alike must perform their tasks inside the castle to avoid being seen by the evil spirits suspended above us. Walking through the building, we plot out the longest continuous stretch of hall to build the huge web of metal netting required. Each general scatters to gather their men and supplies.

I make for the kitchen to prepare the staff, asking them to divert all hands to feeding our workers.

As our fae begin linking chainmail sections together, I wind back to check on the girls. I urge them to have a good meal and get to sleep early. They express worry for my energy level, and while I share their trepidation, I cannot leave my workforce alone when it is I who commissioned the assignment.

Saying goodnight to the girls, I join the line of blacksmiths, soldiers, farmers, ferrymen, fishers, and seamstresses, bending metal strips to bind pieces of chainmail together. We use any metal strip solid enough to hold the heavy net together, melting them until soft enough to fold and encircle two links of chain. Then we dip the piece in water, hardening it. I gaze down the row at hands holding metal strips over canisters of open flames, and fae dipping the joined ends into pots of water, steam rising above their heads.

With the haze in the air, it seems as if I am in a dream, and I shall wake any minute. But this is real, and this is my life. Lucifer said they were coming, and the evil spirits are here, hovering over my castle, threatening my people and those of Upper Earth. *What will happen if we cannot defeat it, him, Theron, whatever form he now takes? Will he overwhelm the magic of our rings? Absorb their power? Close them forever, locking us inside to die in the heat box Zekial predicted?*

You need them. Mother's words trace through my brain again as I dip the next joint in the water bath. I realize it is not just Gatuika, Makani, and Isla I require, but all my people, all the fae. Everyone must believe and pledge themselves to the cause as our people have for centuries. Our foe become craftier, more powerful with Sonia, Thanatos, and Theron joining their ranks. We must be prepared for not only this threat, but any visage they produce.

I think about Father and Kane, how my lack of trust for them keeps me from seeking their help. Of Foster, who, even though he stood against me before, now aids me. Grant, Adam, Timothy, and Nicholas, who have guarded and supported me from the beginning. Of Quinn, who I know loves me as well. And Holden… I will not believe he has forsaken me. Mother, who helps in her own way. And Alfreda, whose heart is so true it almost breaks mine. The girls, who, as sure as blood now pumps through my veins, will have their own parts in this fight. If I must leave them, if my time has come, at least I know it will be for a good cause, in defense of my people and my realm.

Three I have neglected most with my cousins' arrival, festival season, and the locusts. Three I would least want to treat with indifference: Mother, Father, and Alfreda. They have been my world. We would spend each night in my parents' study, singing, dancing, and playing music, before my brothers' deaths. After, I played for them each night. Before… Before I rose to queen.

"Queen, your fingers." The fae beside me nudges my arm and motions to my hand.

I snatch them from the fire and plunge them in the water. Raising my arm, I find my fingers glowing red. I must take care. I cannot let my melancholy overwhelm me. *You felt none of this before, why now? Because you have no one.* Holden and Quinn lay their heads across seas and oceans. *Who will move to the little house in the wood with you should you fail here? Or run away to live with the merfolk upon your exile?* I bite my lip, knowing success or defeat may mean even worse, my end. I must be sure to tell the ones I hold most dear of my love for them.

Refocusing on the task in front of me, heating the metal nails, folding them over the ends of the webbing, lowering the pieces into the water, I wonder if I have given up. If I have lost faith in even myself. *You cannot think this way. If not for yourself, for your cousins. Do you wish them to endure the trauma, the struggle, and the fight you have trudged through? If you are to stand victorious over this evil and come out alive, you must believe in yourself. At least have trust in your own inner compass.*

Yes, I let Foster, Quinn, Kane, Regin, and the High Council eat away at my confidence and conviction. I harken the girl who fought Ethan for her crown, stood against her general to defeat the kobold, and escaped the very evil souls that threaten the realm now. Faster than I ever thought my hands could move, I repeat the motion, heat, clip, cool, over and over, as the others beside me do. We work through the night, and as the clock chimes seven,

I look to the windows. One would think it midnight on a new moon. Scanning the halls, I sense it, the fear and anxiety, and I see it in round, red eyes. Rising, I move to the window. The barrier of locusts hovers above, offering the same drone of a hum. *Not for long.*

I glide through the passageway, offering praise and smiles for each face I meet. In the great hall, bound metal netting lies crisscrossed from one side to the other and back again like a snake. *This will work.* Shooting through the back exit to the kitchen, I find Alfreda barking orders to the workers. Upon seeing me, her eyes fill with tears.

"Your hands?"

"They will be fine with some salve. Thank you for supporting everyone, and most of all, me." I hug her to me and whisper, "Do not fret. I will see you when this is done."

I fill a breakfast tray for Mother and Father and find them in their small dining room. Father complains that I should be with my troops, but I sit with my parents, telling them of the dedication displayed by everyone and my gratitude at the trust placed in me. Even though Mother sits stoic, repeating the movement of lifting food for her mouth, I take comfort in this, the sameness of how our mornings used to be. With big hugs for both, I wind to my chamber to find the girls still asleep on my bed.

I review the plan with Foster, Grant, Adam, Nicholas, and Timothy and leave instructions for them to find me when my cousins wake.

Taking my place in the line of workers again, I continue hooking together the pieces of chainmail. I keep watch on the window nearest. With no view of the insects above, I rely on the light to signal a change. None comes. I wonder how powerful Theron's spirit may be.

Foster brings word that all kingdoms report disappearance of the locusts, and I realize it can only mean one thing. They all gather above us, above *me*. And if the dark spirits can accomplish overpowering our ring, will they move to the next, and another after that? Or will Theron be satisfied with obtaining his freedom?

When crews bring midmorning snacks, I can wait no longer for my cousins and rouse them from their sleep.

"But it is still dark." Isla complains as I slide my hand over her forehead.

"It is past ten. It seems all the locusts amass here, blocking our ring." I take their hands as Isla sits up. "I hope you are all ready. Foster, Grant, and Adam will guard you in the tower. If anything happens, they will make sure you are safe."

"We will not fail our part, cousin." Gatuika squeezes my hand. "We only worry for you. What if—"

"There will be no *what if*. If my power does not manifest, then we shall pray to the goddesses the science theory holds, that enough charged particles build up and beg for release. I can already sense the current in the air. This will work."

Leaving my cousins with kisses to their cheeks and directions to eat and prepare, I gather the generals and advisors. The villagers have been evacuated, and the castle will be cleared after the noon meal save for the soldiers needed to hoist the net. I offer all praise for their fast work and release them to find shelter with their families.

"Titania." Kane approaches, dipping his chin to others as they exit. "We should ensure your safety as well, appoint another to carry the rod."

Frustrated, I draw in a breath. "Have we not been here before? I will not ask another to sacrifice in my stead. Father holds health still. And I am sure you have not forgotten the kobold. This is my honor and duty to serve the realm in this way."

"If I cannot talk you from this, I will say prayers to the goddesses for your safe return."

"Thank you, Kane." I offer my arm.

Taking it, he leans in and kisses my forehead. "I have always known you were no ordinary fae."

Exiting the study, I find Zekial and his guards approaching. I force a smile. "Gentlemen, I thought you had evacuated."

"I think perhaps the opposite should be true. The locusts only linger around your Daintree ring. Whatever the reason, the rest of the realm is safe. The council believes it best to leave the insects undisturbed, let them die of natural causes."

I want to shout sense into his aging brain. "The council? The High Council?"

"Yes, we gathered this morn."

"Without me?"

"Monarchs do not make up the council, only the Ring Keepers."

"And who of the Ring Keepers have witnessed the oddities of these insects? Only you and your guards? Have you forgotten the face you saw in the swarm just yesterday? Did you forget the magickal abilities acquired by the kobold, of which many have attested? You just missed a room full of fae who will witness to the attacks my kingdom has suffered. The evil that gathers above us will not stop at this castle, or kingdom, or realm, but will terrorize all. Would you risk that, Zekial? And if so, are you willing that your name be on that stamp in history? Me and my soldiers stand as the gatekeepers. I will not allow Theron's spirit to be unleashed."

"You risk treason against the High Council again, Queen."

"What has swayed you? Just yesterday you approved my actions."

"It is absurd that the spirits of Lower Earth use grasshoppers as vehicles for their spirits."

"Crazy and brilliant. Because none of us noticed until it was almost too late."

"I do not see them trying to escape our realm now."

"Zekial, sir." One of his guards interrupts.

"Wait till I am finished." He waves off the fae.

"But, sir, look to the window."

I spin to face the glass to see it covered with white underbellies of locusts. My skin crawls. Turning to Kane, I order him to get Mother, Father, and all staff into the tunnels below the castle, and then to line the main passageway with soldiers ready to launch the net.

"Zekial, you may stay and fight with us, or you may go below. It is your choice. I will not leave my kingdom to a siege of evil spirits."

I dash to my quarters, and with Foster, Grant, and Adam, escort the girls to the second highest tower. The insects swirl outside, and my lungs feel as though they may seize from the weight of the humid air.

"We need all the bugs back in one swarm."

"I can mimic the sound I heard from them yesterday." Gatuika closes her eyes.

The drone of the hum surrounds us and my eardrums flare with the pressure. Circling the room, I wait and watch, but the locusts remain fixed to the panes.

"It is not working. What about a windstorm?" Makani asks.

I step towards her. "Try it. We need them aggregated in one cloud."

"We must open a window though."

Looking at Foster to ensure they have door secured, I unhinge the lock and push the panes open. The locusts flood into the room. Their wings scratch like sand on my skin. I swipe them away to find another layer pelting me.

Did you not think I would get to you? A different voice echoes through my mind. *That is right. Feel free to warn Hunter. For he, Alena, and Camille are my next targets. I will start with Alena as he loves her most, as do I. Before I am finished, she will beg to join me. If only you had accepted our invitation, your loved ones would be safe now.*

Woosh!

A huge gush of air swooshes by me, cleaning my skin of the insects.

"It is working." Isla joins hands with Makani.

Gatuika grabs Makani's other hand, and the three stand with their faces to the window. I look out to see the bugs beating their wings against the wind yet still hurling backwards. Below, the grounds stand empty.

My time has come.

Squeezing each girl's shoulders and kissing their temples, I turn to their three guards. "No one comes into this room. Guard these girls as if they are your own flesh and blood. And if something goes wrong, get them to safety below with my parents."

"Godspeed." Foster offers his arm.

I lock arms with him, then Adam, and Grant. Checking that the room is clear of insects, I slide out the door. I jump into the air and speed down the center of the stairwell. I exit into the passageway and raise my dagger.

"To arms," I call, winding through the corridor, rallying my troops.

Section by section, they lift the huge net.

At the main doors, I meet General Kane.

"It is time."

"Queen." He bows.

He lifts a rod from the wall behind him.

Wrapping the attached chain around my waist, I grip the stake. I motion to two soldiers at the doors, and they swing them wide. I jet out ahead of the troops, Holden's sword in one hand and the rod in the other.

The troops take to the air, lifting the metal web into the sky. I hover under them, waiting for the right time. With a new gush of air, cool water droplets accost my skin. Above me, the insects churn and writhe against the portal. The hairs of my arms stand on end as the cool air meets the heated cloud above.

Bringing down my sword, I hear the trumpet blare. The soldiers fling the net above their heads. I dart above it and release the chain from my middle. Hooking one end on the net, I charge into the swarm, rod out in front of me. Locust wings beat against my skin. I close my eyes to protect my sight. My wings flap against the insects as if paddling through a storm of leaves.

Hissss. Spickkkk. Hisss. Spickk.

I hear the charge growing around me.

Holding the rod high above my head, I fold my wings to my back and turn my face. Stomach lurching, the sensation of falling overwhelms me, and I fight the urge to slow my descent. I hit the metal and grip it with one hand, but my speed increases. I hold the rod as high above my body as my arm allows.

Nothing.

Glancing down, I see spaces of open darkness below and realize there are seconds to execute the plan. *Where is my power? Where is science? Hot air, cold air, negative attracting positive, a charge to my rod?*

You knew this would not work. Lucifer.

Tossing the rod, I reach for the web below me with my free hand. But it is not there. Other hand still gripping the wet metal, I spin around and dive towards the net, hooking a single link with a finger. I fight to gain a handful of the metal and pray it will be enough.

"Goddesses," I whisper.

I clutch my eyes shut and squeeze my fists, praying for divine intervention. *Nothing.*

Seeing the edge of the swarm and my cousins standing in the tower below, my throat closes. I dig deep into that place in my soul. *This is my destiny. Only I can fulfill it. Goddesses or no goddesses, I will fight till my dying breath.*

Skkkkkkkkkkkkkkkk-tck.

Waves of energy flow through my arms and explode on the metal with a flash of light. Blue and white bolts of bright energy zap around me.

Chapter 19

My fingers go slack and arms go limp as jelly melting from a biscuit on a hot day. *Thud.* My heart beats in my ears. *Light. Dark. Wind across my face. Brown polka dots and a blue background.*

Bam. My lungs freeze as my back slams against a hard surface. I lift my chin and try to engage my windpipe. With a swoosh, my air sacks expand. *Breathe. Life. Perhaps. Or death? Heaven.* I squint at the bright light over me.

Shielding my eyes, I try to make out the scene around me, but the brightness overwhelms every color. Pushing up on a hand, something crackles under my palm. Shells? Wet goo seeps between my fingers. I lift my hand, but all I can visualize are cream fuzz blobs with dark splotches. Shell. Slime. *Locusts?* I am in Hell.

Flailing my hands about has no effect as the wretched matter hangs on.

A shadow passes overhead, and I squint to make out the form. A round, white object hangs haloed by orange. *Not Lucifer.*

"Titania? Titania? Are you okay?" *Foster?*

I open my mouth to speak, but my throat burns with the intake of air.

"Do not try to speak." His warm breath caresses my cheek.

"Are they?" My voices cracks. "Did it?"

"Yes, it worked. They are all blown to pieces."

"And my cousins? The soldiers?"

"Everyone is safe."

"Titania?" Isla's voice hangs in the air as another shadow enters my vision. "She is here!"

The shadow morphs into a fuzzy form that is Isla.

"Yes, that was some lightning storm." Makani's voice sounds at my other side.

"I cannot see that well." I roll over to my hands and knees, trying to get up. My muscles shake under the pressure, and I fall to my side.

"Drink this." Gatuika's voice urges, and a hand winds around my waist, pulling me to a sitting position. Something presses my lips, and sweet wine coats my throat.

"That is nice wine." I smile.

"I am not sure she knows who we are." Foster.

"Do not worry, Foster, as soon as this haze wears off, I shall give you another medal."

"Oh, thank the goddesses." Grant huffs and a large form appears before me.

"You all should be thanking the goddesses I am not charging your queen with treason." Zekial croaks.

"Our queen saved the realm from an evil spirit bent on our destruction," Grant says.

"Yes, and word is spreading that a great lightning bolt zapped from the cloud to the net and electrified all the locusts, killing them instantly. But I watched the entire maneuver. There was no lightning bolt. The spark emerged from the center of the net, from your form, Queen. For if it had been lightning, you would be dead now."

I quell a laugh, and the muscles in my side ache at the strain. My first thought is to say I am an electric queen. I am sure there is some Upper Earth song akin to that. "I am a very lucky queen indeed. Charge me with whatever you like, Zekial. Stay as long as you like, following me around. I will still do what is best for my kingdom and this realm."

"And the wind and wet air? From whence did those come? You are a witch."

"It is a good thing I am a good witch then." Giving up on my muscles, I let my arms fall slack in my lap.

"Help the queen up. She should address her army, thank them for a job well done." A shadow passes over me as Grant stands.

Hands on both sides support my arms and lift me up. My legs hang slack as I am dragged over the bed of crunching locusts. As we move, forms come into focus. I smile at Foster on one side and Grant on the other. Trying my wings, I feel them spread wide on my back. I will my leg muscles to support my weight.

Still, Foster and Grant hold each arm.

Glancing around, I find us to be in the garden. We wind into the castle and through passageways lined with staff. I smile and nod, squeezing hands as they reach out to greet me. We stop short as we near the main hall.

Mother, Father, and Alfreda stand beside the exit.

Alfreda rushes to me, flinging her arms around my neck.

As she releases me, Father gathers me in a hug. "Good work, daughter. I happy to see I am not needed as king."

I kiss his cheek. "I should not say that I am, too."

I motion to Mother, and Foster and Grant help me shuffle to her. I grasp both her hands, kiss her cheek, and lean into her ear. "It is done, Mother. The locusts are gone. My cousins helped. You were right. I did need them."

I imagine feeling pressure where her arms might lay on my shoulders, but it does not come. Releasing her, I take a step back. The great doors open, and light blinds my view. Deafening cheers sound in my ears. With Foster on my right and Grant to my left, I step into the courtyard. I scan the crowd as my vision perfects. Soldiers and villagers pack the square and the castle walls above. With a jolt of adrenaline, I flit to the top of the fountain.

Neck craning in a circle to view all, I raise my hand. Silence crashes as a wave on the sand.

"To all soldiers and citizens, let it be known this day that the evil spirit harbored by the locusts is no more thanks to the hard work of so many and the bravery of our soldiers. This kingdom and the realm owe them all much."

Foster alights beside me. With a wink to me, he lifts my palm above our heads. "And if not for the bravery of our dear queen, we may yet stand here threatened by this evil spirit. All hail Queen Titania, Guardian of the Realm."

"All hail Queen Titania, Guardian of the Realm!" Shouts ring out.

Noting the smiling faces of my people, my heart overflows with love. *How could I ever think to be deserted with them at my side? Who cares what the other kingdoms or High Council think? As long as the people that know me find me true and worthy, what else shall I need?*

A roar goes up and dancing ensues. Someone starts a tune, and all the doors from the castle swing open. Castle servers flit around with crafts of wine, handing them to any within reach. Jumping to the stone walk, I approach my cousins and gather them in a hug.

"I know you are true heroes here as well, but your secret should remain until the time is right."

"Mother would have us thrown in the cellar if she knew what we did today." Gatuika's eyes cut to her sisters.

"We should all wash for dinner." I realize that perhaps I should send a message to their parents that all is well.

"Yes, you are quite scorched." Isla picks some singed skin from my wing.

Arm in arm, we start to my quarters.

Halfway down the corridor, Grant calls me back. "Queen, someone waits for you at the ring. The male of the trinity."

"Hunter?"

"Yes Hunter. He asked to see you."

Realizing the quandary, I ask Grant to find Zekial and escort him to my study. Leaving the girls in their room, I wait at my desk.

The old fae enters and slides into the chair opposite me.

I lift my chin. "We should be quite frank with each other. I will no longer hide my true nature. I have been given gifts. Gifts that help secure our realm. I hid them because I feared what has already befallen me, to be deterred in my efforts to fulfill my purpose."

"You would be so brazen as to call yourself The One."

"Your words, not mine."

"They are repeated all over this castle."

"I believe we are all called to be one who helps defeat evil, each in our own way."

"But the prophecy is absolute."

"Believe what you may. I have not called you here to debate. Hunter Michaels waits for me at the ring. Do I have your permission to converse with him?"

"He should not enter this realm."

"May I cross to Upper Earth, then? Or should we shout across the portal? I just killed his half brother. I am sure he sensed it."

"I do not understand any of this." His wide eyes meet mine.

I lay my hand atop his, feeling the fine, soft skin of his aging fingers. "I will tell you all. But I need to go to Hunter."

"Go then. Cross into that realm. We shall speak tomorrow."

Thanking him, I jump to the windowsill and shoot to the ring. I request my guards wait in our realm and cross into Upper Earth.

His thoughts hit me the second I pass through the barrier. *Is Theron really dead? How do I tell Alena? She had so much hope for him.*

I land beside the leader of the witch lines. "There was no hope for Theron."

He jumps back. "A little warning would've been good."

"You came for me, and I am here. Forgive me, it has been a long day."

"I see." His surveys me from head to toe. "You lo—"

"I am covered in locust guts."

"And smell—"

"Of burned insects."

Insects?

"Theron took the form of a swarm of locusts. They have been plaguing our realm for months. He had no good in him, only hatred. He did say he loved her, but I cannot believe it to be true love, only lust for winning her from you, turning her against you, making her like him. If we did not stop him, he would have laid siege to you and all you loved. He told me himself."

So, all three of them are in Sheol then. This cannot be good.

My pulse quickens. "Sonia and Thanatos are dead as well?"

"I thought you knew all?"

"Your thoughts are very concentrated just now. No, this is not good. This is exactly what Lucifer wanted."

"Yes, I believe so."

"He means to make them original souls as he and Abaddon are." I pace away.

"I've come for you many times. Why didn't you answer me?"

Exhausted, I squat and sit on a patch of soft grass. "I have been charged with treason for aiding you in crossing to Lower Earth. They watch me night and day. I learned you were alive through our friend from Madagascar. I am happy to see you healthy."

She looks like she could keel over any time. I should not bother her now. Besides, I have to break the news to Alena.

I rise. "Go then, and we shall discuss this another time. I believe I convinced our elders to see my logic today."

His shoulders quiver. "I'll never get used to that."

"Again, apologies." I jump into the air and dive into Middle Earth, relieved as the silence quenches my mind. This lasts but a second as I process Hunter's fears.

"You look concerned." Grant greets me.

"It is for another day. Tonight, we celebrate our victory."

⸺◆⸺

SOAKING IN THE BATH, I FIND it hard to leave. I let the water cool, and body chilled, wrap in a huge throw. I look at Holden's tunic and sword, dreading the night ahead. *How quickly you lost your zing of adrenaline, needing no more than the love of your countrymen. You are tired, that is all. Tomorrow it will seem better.*

Dressing and rounding up the girls, we walk, arm in arm, to the grand ballroom. Tonight, the tables spread through the passageways and out into the courtyard as all the soldiers, workers, and as many others that want to join in our celebration. Seeing Foster with Grant and Adam, I lead us to the head table.

I recall Foster at my side earlier and how he had been there to help with the victory of my very first battle. *And he is here again, realized his error, and returned to you.* Perhaps Holden will as well, and maybe also Quinn. *You do not need them.* But large holes lay empty in their stead.

Standing in front of the middle seat, I direct my cousins to my right and Foster, Grant, and Adam to my left. Farther down, I wink to Father, Kane, and Alfreda.

Silence falls and I lift my chalice. "To Aubren! Long may we live in peace and prosperity."

Sipping the wine, I fold my skirt and sit down.

The others follow suit.

I lift my fork, and the hall chimes with music and voices again. I watch all: Zekial with his guards, the advisors, scientists, and soldiers, with some sadness that this is our lot, to be on constant watch for the evil below. Then I think of those above and of the privilege we bear. We have no significant illness, no worry for money, and seldom fret for food, except when kobold or locusts threaten our rings.

My thoughts turn to the evil lurking in Lower Earth, and I wonder if they wake because of the shift in power above. *Why does not matter. Sit and enjoy.* Next, my attention turns to Zekial and his threat. *Will they fear me? Seek to limit my power further? Will they suspect the girls' involvement? Can I protect my cousins, make the council see they need the information and power I have? Will enough testify on my behalf?* I would beg at Holden's feet if it comes to that.

"You are not enjoying your dinner." Foster's words float through my fog.

"You are right." I lift my goblet and force a smile.

This is what I wanted. A victory to prove to myself, and show my doubters, that I stand worthy, loved, and am lovable. *So why does it not feel such? Because of Hunter's fears? Because of Zekial? Savor your win. The locusts are gone. Theron lives no more. Perhaps even Lucifer will be expelled from your head.* I say a silent prayer to the goddesses it is so.

As plates clear, I motion to the fiddlers. All rise and move the tables to the wall. I round to the open space, wondering who to select to start the dancing. *Father? Kane? Foster?* I look at my cousins and wave them over. With curtsies to each other, we pose and begin the jig at the second bar. Although every muscle sears with wear, I dance with each who comes before me.

Foster and Grant hover steps away the whole evening, but I hold no disdain for their presence as my pride might have before. No, I have no need for airs of strength anymore. What I have in each moment is enough: breath, life, those I love… At least, most of them.

I last until midnight and round up the girls, dragging them to our rooms.

"You would think being heroes would get us an evening of no limits." Isla complains.

"When your mother hears of this tomorrow, she will descend with force. Be grateful you stayed till midnight."

"Alfreda made sure we wrote to her, to tell her of our safety." Gatuika informs me.

"Oh, thank goodness." I grasp her hand. "You are all so dear."

"Shall we sleep with you?" Isla asks.

My mind begs for solitude, but my heart cautions me. *What will you feel when they are gone?* I wave them into my room, and we shed our dresses and pile into my bed.

———

I WAKE FROM A DREAMLESS sleep with light blazing through my window. Light, pure sunlight. I stare at the brightness of it. No fae can ever take it for granted.

Seeing biscuits on the table, I rise in slow, sure movements, so as not to wake my cousins. Sitting on the windowsill looking over the meadow, I ponder my fears: Zekial and the evil that lurks underneath, growing more powerful every day. There shall always be some challenge, and we will be ready.

I flit to the door and slip out, closing it with a quiet click.

"There you are. It is almost noon. I have been waiting all morning." Zekial's hoarse voice startles me. Rising from a chair brought from my study, he shuffles towards me.

Ushering him into my work chamber, I lean on my desk. I look out over the meadow as I tell him I electrocuted the kobold who killed my brother, bested Ethan with a surge of power, drew power from the ring to escape Lower Earth, and shot a bolt of electricity through the metal web to end the locusts. Then, I reveal our fears that Sonia, Thanatos, and Theron will escape purgatory and join Lucifer and Abaddon.

He stares wide eyed as I finish. "I have never heard of such magick."

"And neither had I, but this is the truth. You may do with it what you will. You can allow me to be proactive, work with the trinity of witches to stop the growing evil waiting below us, or we can wait for it to come."

Clutching his cane, he rises. "I must take this to the council."

I stand upright. "I will not allow you to hold these debates in secret any longer. They should be free and open for all to hear. Ring Keepers have been endowed with magick through their lineages. This is no different."

"Their powers are defensive. They read minds. But this is an offensive magick. What if someone like Ethan or Gunther displayed such a power?"

My side ticks as I realize that divulging my secret could have been a grave error.

He shakes his head and retakes his seat. "This is why Keeper Aleem ceded his position? So that your secret would be safe? Why he allowed you to open the rings to let the trinity pass? He believes you are The One."

"We never spoke of it, but I believe so." I hold his gaze, daring to breathe, wondering what passes through his head. I await his next words, praying to be released from the council's confinement.

"This is dangerous information. It could plunge the realm into fear and hysteria. I assumed you a reckless teen who thought little of the consequences of your actions, but I have witnessed you using the utmost care. You exhibit knowledge and wisdom beyond your years. You worked tirelessly to solve the locust problem, sent your love away with such grace, allowed your much-loved cousin, the heir presumptive, to leave with the daughter of your enemy. You risked your own life for your kingdom. Foster is right. You are a true guardian of this realm."

Grateful for his words, I release my lungs, cross the space, and bow before him.

"What do you want, child?"

"Only for you to clear my name, my reputation. Tell the council, the whole realm, you find me trustworthy. Give me your blessings to work, however I may see fit, to ensure the evil below us never escapes its borders."

Leaning forwards, he rests a hand on my shoulder. "I will hold your secret and say prayers to the goddesses for your success. Go forth, and do great things, young guardian."

Chapter 20

Standing, he ambles to the door, leaving me in silence. *Guardian.* I favor the term. Although I would prefer not to just defend our realm but to end the evil that awaits below, to stop the cycle of violence that has plagued Middle Earth for centuries, nay, millennia. And Zekial just handed me permission to do so. My skin tingles with adrenaline.

But how to go about such a task? I lean on my desk. My thoughts jump to my cousins. I wonder if other family members share our gifts, and partnering with the trinity of witches and their heralds shall be vital. The girls will not balk at that, but they are so young. I cannot endanger them. They should not know the pain I experienced. And I guess their parents may want them home again soon. They must be protected above all. For we stand between our realm and the evil that awaits.

I will need more fae allies, should recruit more to my guard, believers like the round fae of Madagascar, Alemayehu. Pushing off the old wood of my bureau, my muscles ache, and I remember the prior day's drama. *Drama. You barely escaped with your life. You stand lucky to be walking.*

Exiting my chamber, I find Foster wide eyed. "What happened with Zekial? He told his guards they were leaving at once."

I smile. "Walk with me, Foster."

Winding through the garden, between the half-bare trees of the orchard, and into the meadow, I see him open and close his mouth several times, but I wait until we cross under the canopy of the forest to stop.

"Is it bad?" He clutches my arms.

I tug them from his grip. "No, quite the opposite. Zekial has given me leave of my punishment to pursue the evil spirits below."

"This is good. Why not just say that earlier? My stomach churns with anxiety."

"Sorry to worry you, but we cannot be overheard. I need to expand my guard, find ones who are willing to aid me in partnering with the trinity of witches to stop the growing evil."

"Does this need to happen today?"

"I guess not."

"Then, let us take time to enjoy our victory." He leaps into the air, motioning for me to follow him.

Flapping my wings, I find them sore but workable and follow at a slow pace. I catch up with him at the turn in the river. Jumping to the opposite bank, he slides a green velvet pouch from his pocket and holds it out.

"For safe keeping." He winks and ducks into a space between two large roots I would have thought too small to pass.

The crystals that ensure my ability to pass through the rings when desired remain safe. Part of me longs to hide them beneath the rock floor of my closet again, but that leaves them vulnerable to any would-be enemies. Seeing his orange head emerge from the brambles, I bite my lip. *Is it too much to ask any to join me in the fight to come?*

"Thank you for securing those. I know you risked much for me. It does not go unnoticed."

Shooting across the river, he lands in front of me. His lips form a thin smile, and one eyebrow pops up. "Yes, I am still waiting for my medal."

"I could give you the title of general. You deserve it."

He clasps my hands. "I desire something much different. You still have not answered my question of weeks ago."

"What? What question?"

Dropping to one knee, he raises my hand and kisses it. "Marry me."

I jerk my hand from his. "Surely you jest. Get up. I told you we should never speak of that again."

Standing, he runs his finger along my jaw to my chin. "I know that you have forgiven me, and you have seen that my heart is true. It tortures me to be with you day in and day out and not be able to profess my love for you."

My heart thuds in my chest. Studying his red, full lips and deep blue eyes, the cavern chiseled out by Holden cracks. "I do not feel that way for you anymore. That time passed long ago."

"Long ago? It has been but months."

"Months? I remember two months when I did not hear from you. Not one word."

"I was a scared boy then. I know my strength and my heart now. You are the woman I love, and I am worthy of you. No one could say less. Any would make me general if I asked."

How do I dissuade him, make him see that my heart will never be open for such? Yes, I may find one to marry, for the sake of my kingdom and alliances, but he shall be my husband in name only. The cave in my heart sears with the fear of losing another love.

"You are still hoping he will come back, cling to him as if you had long courtship. It was but weeks." He swoops his hand down for a rock and pitches it in the creek.

"He was my friend when I had few others. And he believed in me, stood by me. He loved me. And I loved him."

Turning to face me, his eyes hold mine. "He was there when I was not. And I shall forever regret that. Will you ever forgive me?"

"You know I have."

"Do I sense progress? Perhaps his wedding will help you get closure."

I ponder the thought but speak true from my heart. "All I know is that I never want to experience the pain of losing a piece of my heart again."

"It makes sense after losing your brothers."

"What do my brothers have to do with Holden?"

"You loved them all, and they all left you. Holden left just after the council's ruling. I wonder if it were easier to focus on the pain of losing him than the fear of losing your country."

"Why are we even speaking of this? We were to talk about my victory and your medal."

"I am not sure I will be able to speak with you in private before you send me away to spy again. You need to know my feelings. I am a patient man. I will wait for your heart to be ready again."

"Foster, you know my position. I may very well have to marry for alliance's sake."

"You do not need alliances, and you know that will not work. You need to marry a firstborn, but they are in line to lead their own kingdoms. And to marry a second born would be seen as below you. The only answer—"

"Let me guess. Is someone like you?"

"Very good, Queen. Now we are getting somewhere." He lifts a finger.

I place both my hands on his shoulders and look up into his eyes. "You said yourself I should take time to savor my victory. Do not remind me further of my broken heart today. I request that as your friend and queen."

"And I will oblige. As long as you promise to remember my question stands."

If there be one thing Foster is, it is persistent. "I promise."

A trumpet blares with the signal for a guest. I pop into the air and shoot above the canopy, wondering who would come. *Do not hope for him. Holden has other duties now.* Most likely it is my aunt Cassia, come to see her girls are safe.

Descending into the courtyard, I see a dark-headed fae with green wings encircled by my cousins.

"Quinn!" I throw my arms around him as I land. "Thank you for coming, cousin."

With a squeeze, he releases me and clasps my hands. "A million horses could not keep me from seeing my cousin alive and well this day."

Isla hooks her arm in mine, dragging me from Quinn's grasp. "Look at all these scrolls. They are each written to you with praise and thanks for defeating the locusts. One came from every kingdom."

Seeing the table piled high with scrolls assures me that perhaps I will be welcome and accepted among the other monarchs, but that does not hold what I want to focus on this day. For we should celebrate our victory and family, and I call for a picnic in the meadow and games on the lawn.

We spend the afternoon lounging on blankets, shooting arrows at targets, and racing to the stream and cooling our feet. In the evening, we dine with Mother, Father, and Alfreda. I look around the table and count myself the luckiest fae in the realm. *How could I not see the love I had right before me?* I focused so on what I lost that I forgot what I had.

After the meal, Quinn bids us farewell, and I pledge to write him each week, and he, I.

My cousins and I meander to my parents' study, each taking up our instruments for an evening of music around the fire. As the cool stone warms around us, my heart fills with joy to end the day in this way. My eyes travel often to Mother, who sits staring at the flames. I commit to re-starting our morning walks. I look at Father, thinking I should include him in the advisors' council, although he does seem to love his research projects. And then there sits Alfreda, with a wide smile and rose-colored cheeks, clapping to the tune. Her, I have ignored most of all.

As eyelids grow heavy, the girls and I stroll towards our quarters, hand in hand.

"You have not talked about what happened with Zekial this morning. He left in a hurry, and we are worried for you, cousin." Gatuika wraps an arm around my waist.

I stop mid-stride. "I cannot believe I forgot, but do not fret. All is well. He has released me to pursue the evil spirits of Lower Earth."

"Does this mean we get to meet the trinity of witches?" Makani blocks my path.

"And their heralds?" Isla flits into the air.

I gather them around the window, explaining my thoughts on recruiting more fae for my guard. They do not like that I have concerns about their ages. All three pledge to do all in their power to convince Cassia to let them stay here and continue schooling year-round.

"I imagine that you have all the best tutors. Probably better than those of Bedham." Gatuika insists.

"I will think about it. This should not be entered into lightly."

"But we can help," they chorus.

Smiling, I take each of their hands in turn, thanking them for their love and friendship.

"More importantly…" Makani's smile spreads on her face. "What were you talking to Foster about in the woods for so long?"

My face warms. I stand and wave them towards our rooms. "He is part of my guard. We had important matters to discuss."

"Alone? In the forest?" Isla bats her eyes and puckers her lips, making smooching sounds.

Cheeks flaming, I laugh. "It is not like that."

"But you are blushing, and you liked him before. Quinn told us so." Makani skips ahead.

I grab her hand. "Well, Quinn has divulged too many secrets."

"And look who is waiting now." Isla giggles and points ahead.

Foster stands opposite my doors, strawberry orange hair, broad shoulders, and perfect green uniform drenched in the moonlight.

"You all should get some rest. We have a banquet to plan for, and Alfreda will need much help." I plant kisses on their cheeks each in turn.

Approaching Foster, I take deep breaths, praying this will not be a repeat of the morning's conversation. Stopping in front of him, I smooth my skirt. "Foster, you are here late."

"I have reports on Quinn, Abeetha, Ethan, and Gunther." He motions to my study door.

Pulse racing, I lead him into the small room and light a candle. *Please, goddesses, do not make me regret welcoming Quinn into my court again.* Spinning to face Foster, I square my shoulders.

"Yes?"

"As soon as they saw Quinn approaching, two flew to Bedham to confirm Abeetha and her mother's location."

"And?" I wish he would just tell me the end result.

"They were there, at Quinn's family home. We followed Ethan and Gunther all day. No correspondence came or left, to Quinn, to Abeetha, her mother, Ethan, or Gunther."

"Good, so perhaps Quinn is right. We have nothing to fear from Gunther's family."

"It seems thus. And with such high praise from the other monarchs, I believe you to be in good standing."

Releasing my breath, I smile. "This is wonderful news. Finally, something good. I will rest easier with this information. Thank you for staying late to relay it."

"Will you attend Quinn's wedding? We need to plan security soon if so."

The weight of the topic and activities of the day catching up with me, I lean on my desk. "No. Quinn knows of my love for him, but I cannot support this marriage."

"And Holden's?"

I hold his gaze. *Does he remind me of this again on purpose?* I had just been happy moments ago. "It is late. I do not need to think about this now. I have plenty of other things to place priority on, like making sure there are enough crops for the winter, farmers are paid for their losses, soldiers to compensate for their additional hours of scouring the kingdom in search of locust beds, a festival weekend to plan, and family to take care of."

"It just over a month away. We need to secure quarters and plan for guards. I have put it off too long already. Unless you want to stay at their castle. Which I would guess not."

Wrapping my hand around the back of my neck, I peer out over the meadow. "I must attend. Father, as well as the girls, may accompany me. Perhaps we shall tour the kingdom as well. I will write to their mother tomorrow. Is that all?"

I look back at him, and his gaze focuses on mine.

"Yes, Queen." He dips his chin.

As he slips out the door, I wonder what he saw in my face. Frustration, anger, hurt, or betrayal, they lie just underneath my skin, waiting to engulf me. Spinning, I place my palms on the soft pine of the tabletop. Seeing the flame, I lift my hand and lower it to the fire. *No, Titania.* I fling out my hand and topple the candle. It rolls off the desk and onto the stone, flame dying with the impact. Wax lies splattered across the wood.

I hate this room. I remember once loving it. Holden told me he loved me here, but then he relinquished his tunic and sword to me in this very spot. Quinn admitted his feelings for Abeetha where I stand, and I asked him to marry me. Foster asked me to marry him. I should have this whole section torn down and construct a new suite for myself, complete with foyer, dining area, meeting room, private study, huge bath with inground pool, and bedroom. There would be windows from floor to ceiling so light shines into every chamber. And the girls' rooms could be next to mine. How happy they will be to knock down these old walls.

Was it not minutes ago when I took pleasure in my traditions? Sitting with Mother and Father and playing the harp? Pushing off the desk, I spin, exit the study, and traipse to my bedroom. I look up at the crystals overhead, swaying ever so little in the slight breeze. I let a few bad occurrences—yes, they were heartbreaking events—overtake my joy, strip my faith.

I must close the door on this chapter and start anew. It will not happen with me stuck in the same rut. Marching to the corner, I pick up Holden's tunic and sword. Flying over my bed, I land next to the chest. I open it and, folding his tunic in perfect thirds, place it atop my wool throw. I lay the sword on the bright green fabric, and the lance shines in the moonlight. With a sigh, I ease the lid in place.

Dressing in my nightclothes, I lie in bed. Movement catches my eye, and I gaze up to see faint dots of reflected light dancing on my ceiling. My crystals, my brothers. Yes, all will be well.

Green grass and flowers of purple, yellow, and blue grace the pasture. Blue sky shines bright above. In the distance, trees, stories high, carry ripe apples and pears. I swirl through the air, a trickle of sweet tunes dancing in my ears.

Three women appear below, and I alight in the grass before them. Their beauty is so ethereal, I place them with ease: Artemis, goddess of hunt; Athena, goddess of wisdom; and Bia, goddess of power.

Bia smiles and caresses my cheek with her hand. "Always choose love, child, and we will be with you."

~~THE END~~
UNTIL WE MEET AGAIN

A Note From the Author

I'm thrilled you embarked on this journey with Titania and her fae. *to be a Fae Guardian* is the second book of the *Realm Chronicles* series. If you haven't experienced the first book, download *to be a Fae Queen* to descend into the magical realm of the fae again.

Love the fae and fae lore? Join Tricia's fae lore newsletter to get more fae content. Also, stay connected with her in fantasy or general reader groups. Reader group members get advance content, ability to be an advance copy reader, coloring downloads, and more.

If you're a young adult fantasy fan, you may enjoy the crossover series, *Kingdom Journals*, a young adult urban fantasy series about a trinity of witches on a mission to save their people from eternal damnation.

Craving to know more about Sonia and Thanatos? Read the prequel to the *Kingdom Journals* series, *Kingdom of the Damned*.

Are you a vampires and witches fanatic? Love origin stories? Download the novella *Of Witches and Vampires* FREE to experience the true beginning of these races.

Visit www.triciacopeland.com today.

More about Tricia…

Tricia believes in magic. She thinks it infuses everything. Whether in nature, technology, art, or people, she sees everything as magical. Her characters embody what it looks like when one commits to discovering their own magic. She hopes you'll find that magic in her books and in yourself. Tricia's titles span from inspirational new adult to clean romance to fantasy and dystopian. You can find all her books at TRICIACOPELAND.COM If she's not out running or hiking with the family and pooch, you can find her on your favorite social media platform.

www.ingramcontent.com/pod-product-compliance
Lightning Source LLC
Chambersburg PA
CBHW010427120726
47992CB00010B/3343